Alexander Walker

The Life of Andrew Jackson

To which is added an authentic narrative of the memorable achievements of the

American Army at New Orleans, in the winter of 1814, '15

Alexander Walker

The Life of Andrew Jackson
To which is added an authentic narrative of the memorable achievements of the American Army at New Orleans, in the winter of 1814, '15

ISBN/EAN: 9783337253738

Printed in Europe, USA, Canada, Australia, Japan

Cover: Foto ©Raphael Reischuk / pixelio.de

More available books at **www.hansebooks.com**

THE

LIFE OF ANDREW JACKSON,

TO WHICH IS ADDED

AN AUTHENTIC NARRATIVE

OF THE

MEMORABLE ACHIEVEMENTS OF THE AMERICAN ARMY AT
NEW ORLEANS, IN THE WINTER OF 1814. '1!

BY ALEXANDER WALKER.

———◆———

PHILADELPHIA:
G. G. EVANS, PUBLISHER,
No. 439 CHESTNUT STREET,
1860.

INTRODUCTION.

THERE is no campaign in modern military history, which, for its extent, was more complete in all its parts, and more brilliant in its results, than that conducted by Andrew Jackson in 1814–15, in the defence of New Orleans. In the brief period of twenty-six days, a town of less than eighteen thousand inhabitants, including all sexes and ages, without forts—natural or artificial defences—exposed to approach and attack on all sides, by land and water—with an army of less than five thousand militia, hastily raised *en masse*, and illy armed and accoutred—was not only successfully defended against a veteran army of ten thousand of the best soldiers in the world, but was made forever glorious by the most brilliant victory, which has been achieved since the invention of gunpowder. The peculiarities of this victory are the astonishing and unprecedented disparity of loss between the combatants, and the marvellous proofs of steadiness, of skill and rapidity in the use of fire-arms, displayed by the American militia. The splendor of the closing victory has obscured many features of this campaign, which contributed largely to the final result, and, as valuable lessons and glorious illustrations of the valor of our citizen soldiers, and of the genius of the great Chief and Hero—whose lofty soul was the fountain of inspiration, from which all engaged in that defence, drew courage, confidence, and patriotic resolution—ought not to be forgotten or hastily glanced over. These sketches have been written with the hope of preventing such unpatriotic lapses of memory in the present generation.

It is believed that the campaign of 1814–15 has not received full justice, in the narratives, which have been published, the numerous merits of which have been marred by serious errors. By comparing these various versions and by constant consultations with those, who played prominent parts on both sides in this drama, it is believed that the following account, which does not aspire to the dignity of history, and is divested of cumbrous details and of military technicalities, is as faithful and exact as it is practicable to render a narrative of this description.

There are in most of the *histories* of this campaign, errors of a serious character, which ought to be corrected before the evidence thereof has perished or disappeared. Personal and political feeling and prejudice, which, in so many histories, have warped and tinged the facts of this epoch, have been studiously excluded from the mind of the writer of these sketches. His sole desire has been to do full justice to American valor and patriotism, and to present truthful and vivid pictures of that memorable defence, and of the conduct of the great Chief, who, springing from the people, a frontier warrior, without science, art or experience in military affairs, was enabled through the smiles of Providence, by his stout heart, his sagacious intellect, and ardent patriotism, to repel, punish, and nearly destroy one of the best appointed armies ever sent forth by the greatest Power of the earth. Ought such deeds to be permitted to fade from the memories of a patriotic people? Is it not a reproach to the present generation, that modern events of far less splendor and importance should occupy their minds, to the exclusion of memories like these we have invoked? It is demonstratable that in every aspect in which it may be viewed, the defence of Sevastopol in 1854–55 by the Russians, against the allied armies of Great Britain and France, is far less remarkable as a military exploit, than the defence of New Orleans in 1814–15 ; whilst the operations of the Allies have displayed less resolution and energy than were evinced by the veteran army of Packenham. The occurrence of the former operations presents a favorable occasion for the reproduction of the facts of the last-named campaign, in which will be found some remarkable coincidences, with the events of the Crimean Expedition. Thus, it will be perceived that the failure of the one, and the disastrous delays of the other expedition, may be traced to the same cause, namely the lack of promptitude and decision in the commander of the attacking party. It is conceded on all sides that if the Allied Army had advanced upon, and stormed Sevastopol immediately after the victory at Alma, it could have entered and captured the town. So, it is equally clear that General Keane could have marched into New Orleans after the battle of the 23rd December 1814. The strength of earth-works against the most powerful batteries, which was so strongly shown in Jackson's defence, was again illustrated on the southern side of Sevastopol, against the same British Engineering-officer who constructed the redoubts which Jackson's Artillery destroyed in three hours on the plains of Chalmette, on the first of January 1814; this unfortunate officer is Sir John Burgoyne, Inspector of Fortifications in the British army. The lesson at New Orleans should have taught another wholesome truth to the projectors of the Crimean Expedition—that of the great peril and difficulty of all attempts to capture a town, the communication of which, with the interior, is left open and unobstructed. In this respect the positions of New Orleans and Sevastopol were identical. Finally these two campaigns have demonstrated this other valuable and encouraging truth; that in the most remote and exposed points of a united Nation, we often find the most brilliant proofs of patriotism, courage, and devotion.

A. W

CONTENTS.

LIFE OF ANDREW JACKSON

PRELIMINARY CHAPTER.

Hugh Jackson, the grandfather of General Jackson, was a linen-draper, and resided near Carrickfergus, on the Lough of Belfast. He had four sons, who were plain respectable farmers, liberal and hospitable, of strict integrity, and, like their forefathers, firm in their adherence to the Church of Scotland. Andrew, the youngest, married Elizabeth Hutchinson, by whom he had two sons, Hugh and Robert, born in Ireland. Tired of the ceaseless turmoil and confusion that distracted the country, and despairing of the success of any attempt to relieve the Irish people from the grievances of which they complained, he sold his farm, and, in 1765, determined to seek a more tranquil and peaceful home in the western wilderness. Accompanied by three of his neighbors, James, Robert, and Joseph Crawford, the first of whom had married a sister of his wife, he embarked for America with his family, and landed in safety, at Charleston, South Carolina.

Dissatisfied with the low country bordering on the coast, the immigrants pushed into the interior of the colony. Lands were purchased, and they all settled near each other, on Waxhaw Creek, one of the branches of the Catawba, in Lancaster district, about forty-five miles from Camden, and near the boundary line of North Carolina. Here, in this fine and healthy region, agreeably diversified with hills and dales, and drained by the romantic Catawba, Andrew Jackson, the younger, was born, on the fifteenth day of March, 1767.

Not long after the birth of his third son, the elder Jackson died, leaving to his wife and children a limited property, yet with an honest and unsullied name. A double duty now devolved on the surviving parent. Faithfully and nobly was it discharged. To the resolute firmness and unflinching fortitude of the Spartan mother, she united the piety and resignation, the trustful faith and confidence, of the devoted Christian. Naturally gifted with a strong mind, early disciplined in the school of adversity, and strengthened by Him who is ever the stay and helper of the widow and orphan, no difficulties deterred her from the accomplishment of her high and holy task.

The property of which Mrs. Jackson was left in possession, consisted of a new farm, without slaves; and it required the constant practice of the most rigid economy and prudence, to enable her to provide for the maintenance and education of her three young sons. After her husband's death, she took charge of Mr. Crawford's family—her sister, Mrs. Crawford, being in feeble health. Her two younger sons, Robert and Andrew, remained with her, and the oldest went to reside with a neighbor. Hugh and Robert received only a common-school education; but Andrew was designed by the, perhaps, partial mother, for a more enlarged sphere of usefulness. She intended him for the church, and therefore sent him to the Waxhaw Academy, then under the charge of Mr. Humphries, where he acquired a knowledge of the various English branches taught at that time, and had made considerable progress in the Latin and Greek languages, when the ravages of the revolutionary war, approaching nearer to this remote settlement, put an end to his studies.

Boys though they were, the young Jacksons became deeply imbued with the prevailing spirit. This was especially the case with Andrew, who longed for the hour to arrive, when he would be able to shoulder a musket, and perform some doughty enterprise, in defence of the liberties of his country.

The officers charged with what proved to be the Sisyphian task of subjugating the colonial rebels, made their first principal efforts in the northern provinces. Foiled, or beaten here, they turned their attention to the South. Savannah was reduced in December, 1778, and South Carolina invaded in the spring of 1779. Among those who marched out to meet the enemy, was Hugh Jackson, the oldest of the three brothers; he belonged to the company commanded by Captain, afterwards Colonel Davie, and was present at the battle of Stono, on the twentieth of June, where he lost his life from the excessive heat of the day. Early in 1780, a more formidable effort was made by the enemy, in South Carolina. Charleston was invested by a strong force, under Sir Henry Clinton, on the thirtieth of March; General Lincoln, then at the head of the Southern army, stoutly defended the post, but was compelled to capitulate on the twelfth of May.

. Not long after, Lord Rawdon was dispatched by Cornwallis into the Waxhaw settlement, with a large body of troops, to practice the same sanguinary measures which had been adopted in other parts of the province. Upon the fall of Charleston, marauding parties of British dragoons were sent out to scour the country; the timid were conciliated, and the refractory punished; rapine, murder, and violence, were committed with impunity; members of the same family were arrayed against each other, and all were made to suffer the misery and wretchedness ever attendant on civil war. The loyalists, or Tories gladly hailed the appearance of the British troops; others consented to take protection, as it was called, in the hope, often a mistaken one of enjoying an immunity from attack; but there were many who refused to waver in their allegiance to the Confederation.

Mrs. Jackson and her two sons, with a number of the Waxhaw settlers, retired before Lord Rawdon, into North Carolina, where they remained for several days, and until he was recalled to Camden. Resistance had now nearly ceased; and the British officers began to flatter themselves with the belief that the province was completely subdued. But a few weeks elapsed, however, ere General Sumter, who resided near the Waxhaws, returned from North Carolina, where he had also been a voluntary exile, and raised the patriot standard, at the head of his small but gallant band. Other partisan corps, under Marion, Pickens, and Davie, were soon formed. Without pay; scantily supplied with clothing and subsistence; provided with guns of every form and calibre, and swords and lances fashioned out of the rude implements of husbandry; and mainly relying for ammunition on their captures from the enemy, —these brave yeomen rendezvoused in the swamps and forests of South Carolina, where the bivouacked, night after night, in the open air, and from which they darted forth on detached parties of British and Tories, like the eagle on its prey.

On the thirtieth of July, General Sumter, with about six hundred men, made an unsuccessful attack on the advanced post of the British, at Rocky Mount. Three desperate efforts demonstrated the impracticability of carrying the enemy's fortifications, and being entirely without cannon, he was obliged to draw off his command. He was now reinforced by a party of the Waxhaw settlers, under Colonal Davie, and, on the sixth of August, proceeded against the post at Hanging Rock, midway between Camden and the Waxhaws. The first onset was attended with complete success

The enemy were driven from their camp, and took shelter in the main work. Unfortunately, many of Sumter's men had fasted so long, that they preferred searching for something to eat and drink, rather than to advance and secure the victory, by carrying the post, which might then have been easily accomplished. A quantity of liquor was found in the camp, and they commenced drinking, in opposition to the urgent remonstrances of their commander. Apprehending the worst consequences if they remained, he resolved to retire to his encampment before they became wholly ungovernable.

The corps of Colonel Davie particularly distinguished itself on this occasion. Prominent among its members, were Lieutenant James Crawford, and Robert and Andrew Jackson — the latter a mere stripling, but thirteen years of age; yet, in heart and soul, he was a man. This was his first battle, and the accounts we have of it show that both he and his brother rendered good service.

Besides other affairs, of minor importance, but equally honorable to the American cause, the battle of the Cowpens, and the masterly retreat of General Greene, took place during the ensuing winter, while Mrs. Jackson and her sons, with other Waxhaw settlers, remained in North Carolina. Early in February, 1781, Cornwallis crossed the Yadkin, in pursuit of Greene; and she and her friends thereupon returned to their homes, although they were in the immediate vicinity of the British posts.

and the country around was full of armed parties of Tories, whose cruelties and enormities were every day becoming more barbarous and revolting.

The struggle now began to assume, especially in the Carolinas, a yet more direful aspect. A fierce war of extermination was waged between Whigs and Tories. The two parties, or factions—call them what we may— could not exist on the same soil. The former had imperilled everything in the effort to secure their independence, and they fought for the safety, not merely of themselves, but of their wives and children, their property, their all! Boys, as well as men, engaged in this bloody warfare, and it was amid its trying scenes, that the stern and inflexible daring and resolution were formed and manifested, which distinguished Andrew Jackson in after life.

After the departure of Cornwallis from South Carolina, Lord Rawdon, whose head-quarters were at Camden, was left in command. By this time, the stubborn patriotism of the Waxhaw settlers was well understood; and on being advised of their return, he dispatched Major Coffin, with a corps of light dragoons, a company of infantry, and a number of Tories, to capture them. On being informed of their danger, the settlers resolved that they would no longer fly, but maintain their ground at all hazards. A day was appointed for the male inhabitants in the settlement, capable of bearing arms, to assemble at the Waxhaw meeting-house, which was fixed upon as the place of rendezvous. Punctual, at the time and place, about forty of the settlers—Robert and Andrew Jackson being among the number—had collected, and were waiting for a friendly company, under Captain Nesbit, when they saw what they supposed to be the expected reinforcement—but which, in reality, was the detachment of Major Coffin, with the Tories, who wore the usual dress of the country, in front—approaching at a rapid rate. The deception was not discovered, till the British dashed in among them, cleaving down all who stood in their way. Eleven of the party were taken prisoners; the remainder sprang upon their horses, and most of them made their escape.

Andrew Jackson was accompanied in his flight by his cousin, Lieutenant Thomas Crawford; but, in passing over a piece of marshy ground, the horse of the latter mired and fell, and he was wounded and taken prisoner. Young Jackson, shortly after encountered his brother, who had also eluded pursuit. They remained together during the night, and, at dawn on the following morning, concealed themselves in a dense thicket, on the bank of Cain Creek, near the house of Lieutenant Crawford. During the day they became very hungry, and, deeming themselves secure, ventured out to the house. A boy was directed to watch the road; but while they were satisfying their hunger, a band of Tories and dragoons, who had discovered their retreat, and captured their horses and guns, which were left behind them, suddenly made their appearance, and surrounded the house. Resistance could be of no avail, and escape was impossible. They therefore surrendered themselves prisoners of war.

Not content with the capture of the two young men, the dragoons and Tories commenced abusing and mal treating Mrs. Crawford and her children. The crockery and furniture in the house were broken in pieces; and the beds and bedding, and all the clothing of the family including that of an infant at the breast, was torn into shreds. While the work of destruction was going on, the British officer, in command of the party, directed Andrew Jackson to clean the mud from his boots. As might be supposed, he indignantly refused to do the menial office. Enraged at this reply, the officer drew his sword, and aimed a dastard blow at the head of his unarmed prisoner. The latter parried it with his left hand, but, in so doing received a cut, the scar of which was carried to his grave. Disappointed in the spirit of the intrepid youth, the officer turned to his brother, and required him to perform the task. Robert likewise refused; a furious blow from the infuriated Briton was the consequence, and a wound was inflicted, from the effect of which his victim never recovered.

After this, the two Jacksons, with about twenty other prisoners, were mounted on captured horses, and the party set out on their return to Camden. Not a mouthful of food, or a drop of water, was given them on the road; and when they reached Camden, they were thrust into a redoubt surrounding the jail, in which some two hundred and fifty prisoners, besides those taken at the

2

Waxhaws, were confined. Here they were stripped of part of their clothing—Andrew losing his jacket and shoes; their wounds were undressed; no attention was paid to their wants; and when the relationship between the two Jacksons and Lieutenant Crawford was discovered, they were instantly separated, and kept in ignorance of each other's fate. The Provost was a Tory from New York, who, it was afterwards said, took the provisions intended for the prisoners, to feed a number of negroes whom he had collected from different Whig plantations, with the intention of disposing of them for his own benefit. Be that as it may, the prisoners were but sparingly supplied with bad bread; and to add to their wretchedness, the smallpox appeared among them, and made frightful ravages.

Amid the accumulated horrors of his prison-house with sickness and starvation staring him in the face, the groans of the dying constantly ringing in his ears, and hourly exposed to the ill-treatment of his captors, Andrew Jackson never lost the fearlessness of spirit which ever distinguished him. Availing himself of a favorably opportunity, he boldly remonstrated with the officer of the guard, in behalf of himself and his suffering companions. His remonstrances had the desired effect; meat was added to the rations, and, in other respects, the condition of the prisoners was decidedly improved.

Matters were in this situation, when General Greene returned from North Carolina, in April, 1781, and encamped, with his army, on Hobkirk's Hill, a little over a mile north of Camden, waiting only the arrival of his cannon, before making his dispositions to assault the post.

On the morning of the twenty-fourth of April, Andrew Jackson discovered indications of a design to attack General Greene. The jail and redoubt stood on the eminence upon which Camden is situated, and a fine view would have been afforded of the encampment on Hobkirk's Hill, had not the British taken the precaution to construct a high and tight plank fence on the redoubt, immediately after the arrival of the American army in the neighborhood. He was determined, nevertheless, to obtain a view of the anticipated conflict; and by working nearly all night with an old razor-blade, furnished the prisoners to cut their rations, he succeeded in digging out a knot in one of the planks. When Lord Rawdon led out his men, on the morning of the twenty-fifth, for a bold stroke at the American leader, Andrew mounted the breastwork, and placed himself at the look-out, while his fellow-prisoners gathered in groups below him, listening attentively, as he detailed the varied incidents of the day.

His voice was tremulous with apprehension, as he informed his companions, that the Americans had been taken unawares, and their pickets were driven in; it was pitched to a louder key, when the cannon of Greene opened their brazen throats, and vomited forth torrents of flame and iron, tearing and rending through the

British columns; again it sank, as the enemy rallied, and pushed boldly forward; it rose once more, when the regiments of Ford and Campbell pressed gallantly upon their flank—when Washington and his brave dragoons came thundering down in their rear—and he caught sight of the glistening bayonets of the 1st Maryland, and the Virginians, as they prepared to charge home upon their assailants; it fell again as the veteran regiment of Gunby recoiled before the British fire, and died away into a whisper, when all hope of deliverance vanished, as the beaten, but not routed Greene, retired slowly over the hill, and the pursuit was only checked by the timely charge of Washington's cavalry.

The Jacksons were not deserted by one friend, in their confinement—the mother who had reared them to serve their country, and who knew no prouder joy than to see them do their duty well. She followed them to Camden, to aid and succor them, and, soon after the battle of Hobkirk's Hill, procured their exchange, with five of their neighbors, for thirteen British soldiers, captured by a Whig partisan captain, by the name of Walker. Pale, emaciated, barefooted, almost naked, and infected with the smallpox, they presented themselves before their surviving parent. The wound in Robert's head had never been dressed; and this, in connection with hunger, and the disease that had fastened itself upon him, had reduced him so low, that he was unable even to ride, except as he was held on a horse.

There were but two horses for the whole party, consisting of Mrs. Jackson and her sons, and the other released prisoners, who accompanied them home. Mrs. Jackson rode one, and Robert was supported on the other by his companions. Thus wearily and sadly, did they perform their melancholy journey of more than forty miles, through a country blighted by the ravages of war, as if the lightnings of Heaven had scathed it. Within two hours' ride of the Waxhaws, they were overtaken by a shower of rain, by which the company were completely drenched. The smallpox was driven in on both the boys; Robert died in two days; and Andrew at once became delirious. The fever raged violently for several days, and his case was regarded nearly hopeless. The kind nursing of his patient and devoted mother, and the attentions of his physician, at length triumphed over the disease, and restored him to consciousness and health.

He had scarcely recovered his strength, when his mother, with characteristic energy and fortitude, in company with four or five other ladies, providing themselves with such necessaries as could be conveniently carried on horseback, set out to visit a number of the Waxhaw settlers, including some of the Crawfords, who had been taken by the enemy, and were confined on board the Charleston prison-ship—whose history, like that of the Old Jersey, at New York, is but a tale of unmitigated horror and suffering. These good Samaritan women reached Charleston, obtained permission to visit the vessel—a privilege that had always been refused to relatives and friends of the other sex—and delivered the supplies which they had brought. Mrs. Jackson, however, never returned from this errand of love and mercy. Enfeebled by constant care and privation, worn down by the numerous hardships and fatigues which she had endured, she was seized with the fever prevailing among the prisoners, which soon terminated her existence. She was buried near the enemy's lines, in the vicinity of Charleston, in an unknown grave; but her memory, in after times, was doubly honored, as that of the noble, self-sacrificing mother, of Andrew Jackson!

Solitary and alone, her orphan son, at the time when he most needed the care and advice of a parent, was cast upon the world, to buffet, as he might, the billows of adverse fortune. His home was, indeed, desolate. Like Logan, there ran not a drop of his blood in the veins of any living creature. Mother and brothers—all had perished—the victims of English cruelty!—Is it to be wondered, then, that he cherished such a feeling of animosity towards the British name; or that he hated everything akin to oppression, with a hatred so deep and fervent?

Andrew Jackson remained, for some time subsequent to the death of his mother, at the house of Major Thomas Crawford; but, in consequence of a difficulty with Captain Galbraith, an American commissary, whose quarters were at the same place, and who became offended with him for some trifling cause, he afterwards entered the family of Mr. Joseph White, an uncle of Mrs. Crawford. Mr. White's son was a saddler, and Andrew, though suffering all the while with the fever and ague, entered his shop, and assisted him as far as he was able.

Subsequently, young Jackson collected together the remains of his small property, and, bidding adieu to his friends, repaired to Salisbury, in North Carolina; where he commenced the study of the law, in the office of Spruce McCay, an eminent counsellor, and afterwards a distinguished judge of that State. His untiring industry and zeal, his talents, and his correct and manly deportment, soon won the favorable esteem of Judge McCay, and other prominent citizens of North Carolina, whose acquaintance he formed. His professional studies were completed under Colonel John Stokes, and, in 1786, he was admitted to the bar. · He remained in the State about two years subsequent to this, constantly gaining ground in the regard of his new friends and acquaintances; and in 1788, at the age of twenty-one, without solicitation on his part, he was appointed by the governor, solicitor for the western district, which afterwards became the State of Tennessee.

Near the close of the year 1788, in company with John McNairy, the newly appointed judge of the western district, he crossed the mountains, for the purpose of entering upon his official duties, and establishing himself in practice. Jonesborough was then the principal seat of justice, and they remained there for several months.

In 1789, Judge McNairy, and his friend, first visited the infant settlements on the Cumberland, including that at French Creek, near the present site of Nashville. Jackson was still undecided in regard to locating permanently in the district, when he arrived at the settlements on the Cumberland. He found, however, that the debtor class constituted a large proportion of the population, and that, having retained the only lawyer in West Tennessee in their interest, they were enabled to set their creditors at defiance. The latter flocked around him in crowds, and in a few days after his arrival he issued a great number of writs. Threats of personal violence were employed, in vain, to intimidate him; they had only the opposite effect, and induced him to remain, and establish himself in the neighborhood of Nashville. At that time there were no hotels, or regular boarding-houses, in the country, and none were needed, as travellers, men of business, and professional men, were cheerfully entertained by private families. Jackson, and the late Judge Overton, boarded together, with Mrs. Donelson, the widow of Colonel John Donelson, who had, some years previous, emigrated from Virginia to Kentucky, and thence to Tennessee.

When Andrew Jackson entered the family of Mrs. Donelson as a boarder, her daughter, Rachael, who had married a man by the name of Robards, in Kentucky, but had separated from him on account of his violent

temper and vicious habits, resided with her. Judge
Overton and himself occupied another cabin, a few
steps distant from that in which Mrs. Donelson lived,
but met with her family, at the same table. Mrs.
Robards was as distinguished for her beauty, her sweet-
ness of temper, and her winning deportment, as was her
husband for the possession of the opposite qualities.
Through the mediation of Judge Overton, Robards was
at one time reconciled to his wife, rejoined her at Mrs.
Donelson's, and commenced preparations for erecting a
cabin, on a tract of land that he had purchased, in
which he intended to reside.

Jackson was then a young man, frank and engaging
in his manners, and fond of female society. He
undoubtedly paid Mrs. Robards many flattering attentions, which—neither thinking aught of evil, or cherish-
ing an impure thought—were reciprocated as they
deserved, with kindness and friendly esteem, but nothing more. So far from rendering her husband more
morose and ill-tempered, this should only have led him
to appreciate better her charms and social virtues, and
encouraged him to become more pleasing and agreeable. But Iagos were not wanting to instill the doubts
and suspicions of jealousy, had not his gloomy and distrustful temperament predisposed him to such impressions. She was, in consequence, rendered very unhappy. On being made acquainted with this fact,
Jackson sought an interview with her husband, and
remonstrated with him, in a manly and honorable way.

This was of no avail, and he then left Mrs. Donelson's, and took board at Mansker's Station.

The excited jealousy of the husband could not be allayed, however; and, in a few months, he abandoned his wife a second time, and started for Kentucky—declaring to a companion on the road, that he designed never to return. Mrs. Robards now determined that the separation should be final; and on being afterwards informed that he intended to visit Tennessee and take her back with him to Kentucky, under the advice of her friends, she accompanied the family of Colonel Stark to Natchez, in the spring of 1791. Stark was an elderly man, and fearing that the Indians might attack him, he invited Jackson to make one of the party. The latter, perhaps unwisely—though he certainly never regretted it—accepted the invitation, and descended the rivers with them, to Natchez.

Robards had previously applied to the Legislature of Virginia for a divorce, and, soon after the return of Jackson to Nashville, the intelligence was received that his application had been granted. Desirous of testifying to the world, in the highest and most solemn man-ner, his confidence in her purity and innocence—pleased alike with the charms of her person and the graces of her mind, and deeming her at perfect liberty to form a new connection, Jackson forthwith repaired to Natchez, and tendered his hand to Mrs. Robards. She at first hesitated, but finally accepted him. They were married in the fall, and she returned with him to the Cumberland, where she was greeted with the warm and affectionate congratulations of her relatives and friends.

Two years after this marriage—in December, 1793, —Jackson was on his way to Jonesborough, with Judge Overton, when he learned, for the first time, equally to his chagrin and surprise, that the intelligence received in 1791, and upon which he had acted, was incorrect. Robards had, in 1791, procured the passage of an act in the Virginia Legislature, authorizing a suit to be brought for a divorce in a court in Kentucky, which suit had just been determined in his favor—no opposition, of course, being made to the proceedings. Communica-tions between the Atlantic country and the interior were then very irregular, and the exact particulars of the affair were not known, or inquired into, as it was uni-versally supposed in Tennessee, that the divorce had been actually granted. On his return home, in January, 1794, Jackson took out a license, and was now regu-larly married.

The circumstances of his acquaintance and marriage with Mrs. Robards were long after seized upon by his opponents, when he became connected with the political controversies of the day, as a candidate for the presi-dency, and were made the foundation of unmerited and groundless calumnies. There were features in the case, which, unexplained, might appear suspicious; but the evidence of all who were personally acquainted with them, whose assertions are worthy of a moment's con-sideration, acquit both parties of blame, and bear witness to the correct demeanor of Mrs. Robards, and the chivalric conduct of Andrew Jackson. "While he would have sacrificed his life," says his biographer, "to prevent Mrs. Robards' falling unwillingly into the hands of her cruel tormenter, her husband though he was, he never cast a look upon her, or indulged a thought, unworthy of the purest knight in the days of honorable chivalry. But, when no longer restrained by law, honor or religion, pity, admiration, and a species of regret, though free from guilt, yet akin to remorse, kindled into love as pure and as holy as ever glowed in the heart of man. Nor was the object unworthy of this exalted passion. The united testimony of all who had the pleasure of her acquaintance, the happiness which during life she shed over the domestic circle, radiating into the cabins of her servants and the houses of her neighbors, and, above all, the sacred fervor with which the bosom on which she rested in youth, cherishes her memory, bear unequivocal testimony, that she was one of the best of those beings whom God has given as the companion and solace of man."

After his marriage, Jackson devoted himself with more assiduity than ever to the practice of his profession. His firm and independent course in espousing the cause of the creditors, though it elevated him in the esteem of the better part of the community, rendered the debtors peculiarly inimical towards him.

In the course of his practice as a lawyer, Jackson discovered that extensive frauds had been committed in the North Carolina Land-office, which he deemed it his duty, as the former attorney of that State, to expose. Through his instrumentality, the perpetrators were in-dicted and punished. Some of the most prominent citi-zens of the western district were directly, or indirectly, concerned in these transactions, and had profited largely by them. Consequently, he incurred their hostility; and they sought by every means to injure him. In the state of society then existing, a man, like him, ex-posed to the hatred of powerful enemies, may be said to have constantly carried his life in his hand. Unawed by threats, he pursued his way steadily and unerringly —daily adding to the number of his friends, and gain-ing ground in the confidence and regard of the wise and good.

The necessary preliminary measures for the formation of a state government, were taken by the citizens of Tennessee, in 1795; and Andrew Jackson was chosen one of the delegates to the convention, without even offering himself as a candidate. The forest Solons and Numas composing that body, met at Knoxville, in the wilderness, on the eleventh of January, 1796, and ad-journed on the sixth day of February following; hav-ing in the short space of less than four weeks, framed and adopted a state constitution, which, for its republi-can simplicity, compared most favorably with those of other states.

On the first day of June, 1796, Tennessee was admit-ed into the Union as a State, and became entitled to one representative in Congress. Andrew Jackson was elected to the office, with great unanimity, and took his seat in the House of Representatives on the fifth of December, 1796. His reputation and popularity continuing to increase, he was chosen a senator in Congress the following year, when he had just reached the age prescribed by the Constitution. He appeared in the Senate of the United States on the twenty-second of November, 1797. At this session, the alien and sedition laws were passed. Jackson coincided and voted with the republican members, and was therefore in the minority. During the session, he became so much dissatisfied with the course of the administration, to which he was opposed in sentiment, that he returned home in April, 1798, and shortly after resigned his seat. He was succeeded by his friend and neighbor, Daniel Smith.

Upon his resignation of the office of senator, Jackson was appointed, by the Legislature of Tennessee, Judge of the Supreme Court of Law and Equity. The office was conferred on him unsolicited, and was accepted with reluctance.

His first court was held at Jonesborough, at which a man by the name of Russell Bean was indicted for cutting off the ears of his infant child, in a drunken frolic. The sheriff dared not arrest the offender, who was notorious for his strength and ferocity, though present in the courtyard, and returned to the court, that he would not be taken. Judge Jackson told the officer that such a return was an absurdity, and that the man must be taken, even though it became necessary to summon the *posse comitatus*. When the court adjourned for dinner, the sheriff summoned the judge and his colleagues, as part of the *posse*. Jackson saw that the officer desired to avoid performing his duty, and therefore accompanied him. Learning that Bean was armed, he provided himself with a loaded pistol. At sight of him, the former attempted to make his escape; but the judge directing him to stop and submit to the law, in a tone that showed he was not to be trifled with, his weapons were thrown down, and he quietly surrendered. This incident was not lost upon other turbulent spirits who had previously treated courts and officers with contempt, and nothing of the kind was afterwards attempted.

In 1801, an election was held by the brigadiers and field-officers of Major General Conway's division, to fill the vacancy occasioned by his death. Andrew Jackson, and John Sevier, formerly governor of the State, were competitors for the office; and the vote was equally divided between them. The appointment then devolved upon Governor Roane, who wisely conferred it on Andrew Jackson.

Governor Sevier was connected, to some extent, with a combination of land jobbers at Nashville, associated together for the purpose of manufacturing fraudulent grants of land, which Jackson had aided in breaking up. This circumstance, and the preference of Governor

Roane, rendered him a most implacable enemy and opponent. In 1803, he was a candidate for re-election as governor, and in the course of the canvass, his antipathy towards Judge Jackson was imbibed by his party friends. This was particularly the case in East Tennessee. In the fall, the judge proceeded to Jonesborough, to hold his court; and, having been taken seriously ill on the road, he retired to his room, immediately after his arrival, and lay down on the bed. In a few moments he was waited on by a friend, who begged him to lock his door—informing him that a large mob had collected, under a Colonel Harrison, and loudly threatened to tar and feather him. Jackson declined securing his door, but throwing it wide open, sent his friend to Colonel Harrison, with the message, that he was ready to receive him and his party, whenever they chose to wait on him, and that he hoped the colonel's chivalry would induce him to lead his men, and not follow them. This bold message operated like a charm; the mob dispersed; Colonel Harrison apologized for his conduct, and thereafter remained on good terms with Jackson.

The next court held by the latter, was at Knoxville, where the Legislature were then in session. They had just investigated the land frauds, of which mention has been made, and had found some evidence tending to implicate Governor Sevier. His excellency evinced a great deal of exasperation, and on leaving the courthouse, on the first day of the term, Judge Jackson found a large crowd gathered in front of the building, in the midst of which was Governor Sevier, with a sword in his hand, haranguing them in a violent manner. An altercation ensued between them, in which the governor was the aggressor, and the judge sent him a challenge. This was accepted, but the governor failed to give the promised meeting, and Jackson at once published him in the usual form. A second meeting was then appointed to take place, though without any formal arrangement.

Jackson repaired to the designated spot, but the governor failed to meet him. After waiting two days, he set out to return to Knoxville, but had proceeded only a short distance, when he encountered Governor Sevier, escorted by about twenty men, and armed with a brace of pistols and a sword. His friend instantly bore a challenge to the governor, who refused to receive it. Jackson was provided with a brace of pistols and a cane. On the return of his friend, with the insulting message of the governor, he levelled his cane, as the knight in olden times couched his spear in the rest, and dashed furiously upon his opponent. The latter hastily dismounted, in order to avoid the shock, but, in so doing, trod on the scabbard of his sword, and was thus rendered incapable of resistance. In the governor's escort there were mutual friends of both parties, who interfered to prevent any further collision, and Jackson accompanied them back to Knoxville.

Although Jackson was always prompt to defend him-

3

self from insult or injury, these altercations and disputes were by no means congenial to his spirit, and, anticipating their more frequent recurrence, for the reason that a number of cases, growing out of the fraudulent land sales, were about to be brought before him for decision, he concluded to retire from the bench; and his resignation was accepted by the Legislature, on the twenty-fourth of July, 1804, about six years after his original appointment.

Previous to his resignation of the judgeship, the services of General Jackson, in a military capacity, were invoked by the General Government, in consequence of the threatening aspect of its relations with Spain, which had taken umbrage at the purchase of Louisiana from France. Preparations were made to reinforce General Wilkinson, then at Natchez, at the head of a small force, with fifteen hundred men from the upper country, including five hundred cavalry from Tennessee. In October, 1803, General Jackson was requested to procure, without delay, a sufficient number of boats to transport the troops to New Orleans, and to keep them in readiness. The request was complied with; the boats were procured; and the general tendered his services to the government if they should be needed.

The firmness, caution, and prudence of Jefferson, rendered a resort to arms unnecessary; and in February, 1804, General Jackson sold the boats prepared for the expedition down the Mississippi. After resign

ing the office of judge, General Jackson retired to a
plantation on the Cumberland, which he had purchased,
to enjoy what he had long coveted, the quiet scenes of
domestic life, its gentleness and tranquillity, and the
society of his devoted wife. His fortune was not large,
but amply sufficient to satisfy his wants. He devoted
most of his time to superintending the labor on his
plantation, setting an example of methodical industry
and careful economy, worthy of general imitation, and
often wielding the axe or guiding the plough, with his
own hands. Fond of society, and frank and generous
by nature, he was distinguished far and wide for his
hospitality ; and it was remarked of him, that " though
he was a private citizen, he was the most public man
in Tennessee."

A match race was agreed upon by him, and a Mr.
Erwin and his son-in-law, Charles Dickinson, between
their two horses, for a wager of two thousand dollars,
with a forfeiture of eight hundred dollars, to be paid
in cash notes. Erwin and Dickinson subsequently chose
to pay the forfeit, and withdraw their horse. Some
difficulty arose in regard to the character of the notes
offered, but it was finally adjusted to the apparent
satisfaction of all parties. But the enemies of Jackson
were anxious that he should fight a duel with Dickinson, who was reputed to be the best shot in the country.
Through them, the dispute was revived. Several publications appeared in the newspapers, Dickinson grew
more and more insulting, and at length made a direct

imputation of cowardice. Jackson could endure his provocations no longer, and on the twenty-third of May, 1806, sent him a challenge. It was accepted by Dickinson, and the meeting was arranged to take place at Harrison's Mills, Kentucky, on the thirtieth instant.

Dickinson spent the intervening time in practising, frequently boasting how often he had hit his opponent chalked out on a tree, and offering to bet that he would kill him. This was reported to General Jackson, and the effect on his excitable temperament may be imagined. The parties met, as had been agreed on. At the word, Dickinson fired, and the dust was seen to fly from the clothes of his antagonist. Jackson fired the next instant, and the other fell mortally wounded.

Several years later—in the summer of 1813---General Jackson was concerned in an affray with Colonel Thomas H. Benton, so well and widely known, for many successive years, as a Senator in Congress, from the State of Missouri. The former had acted as the second of Governor Carroll, in a duel with a brother of Colonel Benton, which, the latter thought, was inconsistent with the friendly relations existing between himself and the general. An angry correspondence passed; bitter recriminations were made on both sides; and they afterwards encountered each other, and interchanged shots, at a public house in Nashville. In the affray, General Jackson's left arm was shattered by a pistol shot, and he was confined to his room for several weeks. The embittered feelings engendered during the progress of this controversy, were cherished for many years after the encounter, but they were subsequently entirely allayed, and when General Jackson became President of the United States, he had no firmer supporter or warmer friend than Colonel Benton.

Not long after General Jackson retired to private life, he entered into partnership with a merchant in Nashville. For a time their business appeared to be prosperous; Jackson took no active part in its management, but trusted everything to his associate. Some slight circumstances at length aroused his fears, and upon examination he found that the firm was not only insolvent, but that their liabilities exceeded their assets, by many thousand dollars. But one course—that dictated by honor and right—could be pursued. He instantly closed the business, sold his fine plantation where he lived, and paid off the debts of the firm, and removed to a log cabin on another plantation, to begin the world anew. By the exercise of strict economy and prudence, in a few years he once more gathered around him the fruits of prosperous industry.

The period now arrived which Jackson had long anticipated. War was declared against the enemy of his country and his race, on the eighteenth of June, 1812. It is easy to conceive the emotions which the intelligence must have awakened in his bosom. Recollections of the past came rushing and thronging into his mind. The cycles of Time rolled backward. Again he stood upon the threshold of his desolate home—on "the forest-clad banks of the Catawba"—orphaned by the cruelty of British officers and agents. Let him not be reproached, f motives of revenge quickened and sharpened his patri‧ otism. His desire for vengeance was almost holy in its character—it was based on fraternal affection, on filial love!

When the tocsin of war was sounded, the glad, prolonged echoes, came up from every valley and hamlet; but in no quarter of the country was the response more enthusiastic, than in the valley of the Mississippi. General Jackson immediately issued a stirring address to his division, twenty-five hundred men of which volunteered to follow wheresoever he saw fit to lead them. A tender of their services was made to the President, through Governor Blount, on the twenty-fifth of June, which was accepted on the eleventh of July.

On the first of November, Governor Blount issued an order, in conformity with a requisition from the War Department, directing him to organize and equip fifteen hundred infantry and riflemen, with whom he was instructed to descend the river to New Orleans, and reinforce General Wilkinson, then commanding that department. The necessary proclamation was issued, and, on the tenth of December, upwards of two thousand men rendezvoused at Nashville, many of whom had come miles upon miles, through cold, and sleet, and snow, undaunted by the rigors of the climate, and intent only on obeying the call of their country. On the thirteenth instant, the organization of the command, which consisted of one regiment of cavalry, not embraced in the requisition, but enrolled with the consent of Governor Blount, under Colonel Coffee, and two regiments of infantry, under Colonels Hall and T. H. Benton, was fully completed.

On the thirty-first of December, Colonel Coffee commenced his march with the mounted men, six hundred and seventy strong, by the overland route, to Natchez. On the seventh and eighth of January, 1813, General Jackson embarked on the Cumberland, in flat boats, with the two infantry regiments, numbering about four-teen hundred. Descending the river slowly—his progress being constantly impeded by large masses of floating ice—he reached Natchez on the fifteenth of February, near which he found the cavalry under Colonel Coffee.

At this point, General Jackson was met by a request from General Wilkinson, whose headquarters were at New Orleans, to halt his command, and report to him his force and instructions. Wilkinson held the rank of brigadier general in the regular army, with the brevet of major general; and it is not unlikely, that he suspected it was the intention of the government, that Jackson should supersede him. His request, doubtless, was prompted by this apprehension. As there was no indication of an attack on New Orleans, Jackson cheerfully complied with it. Natchez was a much more salubrious position for his troops, and having disembarked them, he marched to Washington, a few miles distant, where a cantonment had been previously established by a corps of regulars. The troops were placed in comfortable quarters, and a strong guard was detailed to protect the boats at Natchez.

Camp regulations were now adopted, and strict orders issued by the commanding general, to proceed with the discipline and instruction of the troops. Becoming impatient for active duty, he wrote to the Secretary of War on the first of March, suggesting the employment of his force on the northern frontier, if there was no prospect of invasion in the south, or if Congress did not authorize the taking possession of Florida. This suggestion was repeated in a second letter, written on the seventh of March. Before these letters reached Washington, an order had been issued from the War Department, directing him, on the receipt thereof, to consider his force dismissed from the service, and to take measures for the delivery of all articles of public property in his possession, to General Wilkinson. This unfeeling mandate concluded with a cold tender of thanks to himself and the corps under his command.

Deeply chagrined though he was, at the result of the expedition to Natchez, General Jackson was still anxious to take part in the active scenes of the war. The disasters on the northern frontier, in 1812, and the failure of the projected winter campaign under Harrison, in consequence of the incautious advance of General Winchester to Frenchtown, had produced a deep impression on his mind. His proud spirit smarted under the discredit of defeat; and, on the eighth of April, when on his way home, he wrote to the Secretary of War, informing him that he should be glad to execute any orders of the government in Canada, with his detachment, which could be augmented, if necessary. " I have a few standards," said he, " wearing the American eagle, that I should be happy to place upon the ramparts of Malden."

Within a few months after his return from Natchez, General Jackson was again called from his retirement, to lead a large body of troops into the Indian country on the southern borders of Tennessee.

On the thirtieth day of August, 1813, Fort Mims, about forty miles from Mobile, on the left bank of the Alabama river, and a short distance above its junction with the Tombigbee, was surprised by a party of Creeks, seven hundred strong, under their chief, Weatherford; the garrison consisting of one hundred and fifty of the 1st Mississippi volunteers, under Major Beasely, and twenty white families who had taken refuge in the fort, with their negroes, in all about three hundred and fifty persons, were cruelly massacred. But seventeen of the whites made their escape. The perpetration of this horrid tragedy excited the utmost consternation at the forts and stations on the Tombigbee, of which there were nearly twenty within a distance of seventy miles above Fort Stoddart. Most of the forts were abandoned, and the affrighted fugitives fled down the river to Mobile, which was itself extremely insecure.

General Claiborne, and Governor Holmes of the Mis-sissippi Territory, immediately called out a small militia force—all that it was in their power to bring into the field —for the protection of the Mobile country. In Tennessee the alarm was universal, and the whole population were aroused. But little aid could be expected from the General Government, all whose means and energies were employed in the prosecution of the northern cam-paign, and the defence of the Atlantic coast from the ravages of the more civilized, but not less brutal enemy. A public meeting of the citizens of Nashville was held on the eighteenth of September, at which resolutions were passed, urgently recommending the adoption, by the State Legislature, of prompt measures for the inva-sion of the Creek country. In accordance therewith, an act was passed on the twenty-fifth instant, authoriz-ing the governor to call out thirty-five hundred men, in addition to the fifteen hundred already required by the General Government, who were to be immediately put in service, and pledging the faith of the State to pay them, if Congress should refuse. A resolution was also adopted on the twenty-seventh instant, directing the governor to tender the services of the Tennessee troops to the United States.

The public sentiment, with one accord, fixed upon Andrew Jackson as the leader of this force. He was still confined to his room, on account of the arm frac-tured in the affray with Colonel Benton, which has been mentioned; but when his country called him to the field, he was ready to obey her behest. On the twenty-fourth of September, Governor Blount directed him to call out, without delay, two thousand men of his division, to rendezvous at Fayetteville—and to order Colonel Coffee into immediate service, with five hundred cavalry previously raised. The necessary instructions were issued, on the same day, to Colonel Coffee, who was further instructed, to incorporate with his regiment any companies of volunteer riflemen that might present themselves. He also ordered into service the volunteers who had accompanied him to Natchez, together with one thousand militia from his division.

On the twenty-fifth of September, General Jackson directed a part of the cavalry to repair to Huntsville, by forced marches. On the twenty-sixth, Colonel Coffee was ordered to move upon the same point and wait further orders, and on the twenty-eighth, he was instructed to proceed to Fort St. Stephen's, which was said to be threatened by the enemy. The state of his health did not permit the general to appear at Fayetteville on the fourth of October, the day appointed for the rendezvous; but he was represented on that occasion, by his aid, Major Reid, through whom he delivered to the assembled troops a most eloquent and spirited address. On the seventh instant he reached the place of rendezvous, with his arm in a sling, where he found a dispatch from Colonel Coffee, who had marched a short distance beyond Huntsville, with near thirteen hundred men, informing him that the Creeks had divided their forces—one portion moving towards the Georgia line, and the other advancing upon the frontiers of Tennessee—and that, in consequence of this, he had not proceeded to Fort St. Stephen's.

Had they not been grossly deceived and deluded by their prophets, the Creeks could never have hoped to accomplish anything against this formidable array. Indeed they seem to have been strangely infatuated throughout; for, instead of concentrating their whole force in an attack on Mobile, or the Mississippi or Georgia troops, neither of whom were yet fully prepared for the field, they advanced with their main body, weakened by a detachment sent towards the frontiers of Georgia, against the column under General Jackson, who was ready to meet them at any odds, and determined to defeat, when he did meet them. It is not probable that the British agents who instigated the Creeks to hostilities, anticipated that the latter would achieve any certain success. They only supposed that the savages would hold the Americans at bay, until a British army could be brought to succor them. The resistless energy and perseverance of General Jackson, defeated any such project. Long before England was able to dispatch a considerable force to the Gulf, he had fallen upon the Creeks like a thunderbolt, scattered their warriors, who escaped the deadly aim of his rifles like chaff before the wind, spread terror and devastation through their settlements, and forced them, as suppliants, humbly to beg for peace.

In two days, General Jackson reached Wills' Creek, a tributary of the Coosa, where he encamped till the morning of the twenty-ninth, to collect corn from the neighboring Indians—his army being entirely out of bread. On the twenty-eighth instant, Lieutenant Colonel Dyer was detached with two hundred cavalry, against the village of Littefutchee, which he attacked the following night; the village was burned, twenty-nine prisoners were taken; and considerable corn, and a number of beeves were collected from the vicinity. While at Wills' Creek, Jackson was again obliged to remove his contractors and employ others. On the thirtieth instant, he reorganized his troops. General Hall was placed in command of the first brigade, consisting of the first and second regiments of volunteer infantry, under Colonels Bradley and Pillow; and General Roberts in command of the second brigade, consisting of the first and second militia regiments, under Colonels Wynne and M'Crory. General Coffee, promoted from colonel, was placed in command of the cavalry brigade, which consisted of the volunteer regiment, Colonel Alcorn, and the mounted rifles, Colonel Cannon.

The march was then resumed for the Ten Islands. While General Jackson was cutting his way over the Coosa mountain, General Coffee was ordered to cross the river, at the fish-dams, with one thousand men of his brigade, to scour the country in the direction of the Ten Islands, and attack the Indian town of Talluschat·

chee, about thirteen miles distant in an easterly direc
tion, where a large force of the enemy had collected
The orders issued to General Coffee were gallantly
executed. On the morning of the third of November
he approached the town; the savages in vain attempted
to oppose his march; and they were driven rapidly
back upon their buildings, in and about which a fierce
and bloody contest took place, that terminated in their
complete rout and overthrow. Both men and women
fought with the utmost desperation. One hundred and
eighty-six of the enemy, including one of their prophets,
and a number of women and children were found dead
on the field of battle: and there were eighty-four taken
prisoners, all of whom were women and children. Gen.
eral Coffee had five men killed, and fourteen wounded.
Having destroyed the town and buried his dead, he
rejoined the main army, at the Ten Islands, in the evening of the same day, with his wounded and prisoners.

Harassed by constant care and anxiety—exposed,
at every turn to vexatious delays and hindrances, that
fretted and annoyed him—General Jackson never lost
that kindness and gentleness of spirit, which bloomed,
bright and pure, amid the intenser passions that burned
and blazed around it. Among the prisoners taken at
Talluschatchee, was an infant boy found clinging to
the breast of his dead mother. He was brought to
camp with the others, and General Jackson endeavored
to hire some of the captive women to take care of him.
They refused, saying, "All his relations are dead; kill

him too!"—Jackson then caused him to be fed with sweetened water, and afterwards sent him to Huntsville, where he was nursed at his expense. After the close of the campaign, he took the little orphan, who was named Lincoyer, home with him to the Hermitage, where he was reared and educated with parental care and kindness. At a proper age, he was apprenticed to a saddler in Nashville: but' he never lost his Indian tastes. His health began to fail before he reached the age of manhood, and he was removed to the Hermitage. He sunk rapidly into a consumption, and soon died, sincerely mourned and lamented by the general and his wife, who had watched over his sick bed with untiring assiduity.

At the Ten Islands, General Jackson established a post, called Fort Strother, on the right bank of the Coosa, opposite the mouth of Talluschatchee creek. The prisoners brought in by General Coffee were forthwith sent to Huntsville. No supplies had yet arrived; the army could not be furnished with regular rations; and it was hardly known one day what they were to subsist on the next. Once more the commanding general appealed to the contractors, by every consideration of humanity and patriotism, to forward the provisions, which could alone save his troops from starvation. He likewise again wrote to General White, who had arrived at Turkey Town, twenty-five miles above Fort Strother, to join him immediately. His dispatch was written on the seventh of November, and, late in the evening, before it was closed, a runner came in from Lashly's Fort, at Talladega, about thirty miles south of Fort Strother, and a short distance east of the Coosa, with the intelligence that a large body of Red Sticks had encamped near that place, which was occupied by friendly Indians, and were preparing to destroy it and the inmates. General Jackson could not hesitate to grant the desired succor. He determined to march forthwith; the urgent circumstances which induced him to advance, were mentioned in the dispatch to General White; and the latter was entreated to lose no time in reaching Fort Strother, to protect his depot and cover his rear.

Marching orders were issued in a few moments after the arrival of the runner, and at midnight General Jackson was on the march for Talladega, with his whole disposable force, consisting of twelve hundred infantry, and eight hundred cavalry and mounted rifles. His sick, wounded, and baggage, were left at Fort Strother. Crossing the Coosa in the night, he pressed forward with such celerity—officers and men vying with each other in zeal—that, on the evening of the eighth instant. he encamped within six miles of the Fort at Talladega which was occupied by one hundred and sixty friendly warriors, with their women and children. About mid night the chief Chennubby arrived from Turkey Town with a letter from General White, informing General Jackson that he had received an order from his division commander, General Cocke, to join him at Chattoog:

higher up the Coosa, and that he could not, therefore, advance to Fort Strother.

Jackson's cup of disappointment was almost full. Neither General Cocke nor General White wanted in patriotism; but they seem, more particularly the former, to have been impressed with the belief, that by remaining aloof from General Jackson, they would secure a larger share of the honors of the campaign. It seems almost painful to contemplate the struggles of the proud and ambitious spirit constantly thwarted by their unwise movements. Had they joined him at once, the war would have been brought to a close in a few weeks: but they preferred to linger behind, in safety and security, eating up the provisions better deserved by those who were enduring the severest fatigues and privations; and when they recovered from their inactivity, and advanced to strike a blow, it proved to be the only unfortunate one of the whole campaign.

The dispatch from General White made no change, however, in the determination of General Jackson. He resolved to dispose of the enemy in his front, and then fall back, with all possible speed, to Fort Strother, before the enemy would have time to profit by its defence-less condition. The prospect before his troops was disheartening in the extreme; if they conquered, there would be no food to refresh or reinvigorate them; yet his example inspired them with confidence, and they obeyed his commands without hesitation or reluct-ance.

5

Long before daylight on the morning of the ninth of November, the army was again in motion. Silently threading their way through the luxuriant forests, winding over the hills, and crossing the rich intervals, that separated them from the enemy, they approached their position. Within a mile, they were halted, and formed in order of battle. The infantry brigades were placed in the centre, General Hall's on the right, and General Roberts' on the left. They were flanked, on the right, by Colonel Alcorn's volunteer cavalry, and, on the left, by the mounted Rifles of Colonel Cannon. An advanced corps of riflemen, spies, and artillery, was formed under Colonel Carroll, the inspector-general, and a strong reserve of two hundred and fifty men, under Lieutenant Colonel Dyer.

At eight o'clock, the attack was ordered; and the whole column moved rapidly forward, all full of animation and enthusiasm. Colonel Carroll preceded the main body, with the advance, having received orders to rouse the enemy from the thicket on the banks of a small rivulet, in which they had concealed themselves, and then to retire towards the centre. The sharp quick report of his rifles, and the hideous yells and screams, soon apprised the remainder of the column that the savages had been started from their cover. Meantime, the infantry regiments, which had previously advanced by heads of companies, had deployed, in accordance with the orders of General Jackson, and the cavalry were extending themselves, to the right and left, so as to encircle the enemy. The orders issued by the commanding General required the cavalry to keep up their connection with the flanks of the infantry. This was neglected on the right, and the plan of attack, which was most skillfully formed, was partially defeated by this untoward circumstance. Colonel Bradley, the officer commanding the infantry regiment on the right, also halted his men on a rising ground, before he came in contact with the enemy, and the gap was thereby considerably widened.

When the fronts of the cavalry columns met on the further side of the enemy, they faced inwardly, and a general rush was made towards the centre. The Indians did not appear inclined to fly, at first, but made a bold onset upon the right wing of General Roberts' brigade. Three of the companies, after delivering their fire, began to stagger, and finally fell back in the rear. Colonel Bradley was then ordered to advance with his regiment, and fill up the vacancy. This he declined doing ; and General Jackson, much against his will, as he designed the reserve to pursue the enemy if they attempted to escape, was forced to direct Lieutenant-Colonel Dyer to dismount his men, and engage them. Observing this movement, the retiring militia rallied and did good service.

The action was not of long continuance. The savages could not withstand the destructive fire poured in upon them from every side, and in fifteen minutes they commenced flying hither and thither, within the circle, seeking some avenue of escape. Whichsoever way they turned, they encountered the rifle and the bayonet. At length, they discovered the opening between Colonel Alcorn's regiment of cavalry, on the right, and the volunteers of Colonel Bradley. Through this numbers of them dashed, hotly pursued by both cavalry and infantry, who followed them for nearly three miles, strewing the ground throughout the whole distance with their dead bodies. The Indian force numbered one thousand and eighty warriors, of whom two hundred and ninety-nine were found killed on the field of battle, and many more must have perished in the woods. The Americans lost but fifteen killed, and eighty-five wounded, some of the latter mortally.

General Jackson complimented his troops, in the highest terms, for their gallantry in this action. All the officers, with the exception of Colonel Bradley, who was placed under arrest, but afterwards released, were mentioned in his dispatches in terms of marked approbation.

An instant retreat to Fort Strother was now necessary. The horses were suffering for the want of forage, and the men were half-famished, when they turned their backs on the field of victory, and commenced their retrograde march. Jackson was with the van of the army, and on the way discovered a quantity of acorns lying on the ground. Dismounting from his horse, he threw the bridle over his arm, and, having gathered a few of the nuts, sat down on the roots of a tree to eat them. He was thus engaged in satisfying his hunger, when a soldier approached him, and demanded something to eat. "I never turn away the hungry," said the general, "while I have anything to give them." He then offered the soldier a few acorns, adding "I will most cheerfully divide with you such food as I have." Mortified and surprised, the man shrunk back among his companions, who thereafter repressed every disposition to murmur or complain.

The army reached Fort Strother on the evening of the eleventh of November, but it was only to be once more disappointed. No provisions, except the limited quantities forwarded by the contractors, had yet arrived; and the private stores of the general had been almost exhausted, in order to supply the wants of the sick and wounded. Still he assumed a cheerful and confident tone, though sad enough at heart, and resorting to the slaughter-pens, provided himself with tripes with which he made what he termed a comfortable repast. His example was imitated by the soldiers, who seemed inclined willingly to endure the hardships of the campaign.

But matters could not long continue in this situation. The battles of Talluschatchee and Talladega had satisfied, to a considerable degree, the desire for adventure which had previously animated the troops in the midst of the most embarrassing difficulties, and they soon began to pine for the comforts of home. Starvation was far more terrible to them than "an army with banners." They were brave—this could not be doubted—and they would have gladly followed their general into the very heart of the Creek country, if they could only have been assured that a reasonable supply of food would be provided; of the two enemies whom they met in the wilderness, they feared the savage least; and was it not asking too much that they should encounter both?

On the sixteenth, General Jackson commenced his preparations for the abandonment of Fort Strother; but, on reflecting how much this movement would reinspirit the savages, he declared that he would not leave the post, if only two men would remain with him. Captain Gordon, of the spies, instantly volunteered to be one of his companions, and through his exertions, and those of some of the members of the general staff, one hundred and nine men were found who agreed to stay.

Feeling confident, however, that supplies were close at hand, General Jackson marched with the militia, apprising them, in advance, that they would be ordered back if his expectations should be realized. Within ten or twelve miles of the fort, they met one hundred and fifty beeves. The column at once halted; the cattle were knocked down, and eagerly cooked and eaten by the half-starved troops. But when the order to return was issued, none obeyed it. One company, indeed, had resumed the march, before the general discovered the mutinous disposition which prevailed among the troops. He immediately dashed ahead of the men who were moving off, and with General Coffee, a part of the staff, and a few soldiers, formed a line across the road, and declared that he would fire on them if they endeavored to pass. Well knowing that he was not the man to forfeit his word, they fell back to the main body, who were soon discovered to be likewise infected with the spirit of mutiny. Arguments and entreaties proved of no avail—the troops all formed, and were on the point of continuing their march to Fort Deposit. As a last resort, the general snatched a musket, threw it across the neck of his horse, and placing himself in front of the column, declared that he would shoot down the first man who moved a single step in advance.

The piece which General Jackson had seized was too much out of order to be fired, and his arm was so weak that he could not aim it with any precision ; but the men before him knew nothing of this, or, if they did, thought not of it. They only saw his flashing eye, and his determined look. General Coffee and some of the staff took their places in silence beside him. Two faithful companies also formed in his rear. All were ready to fire when he gave the signal. For several moments not a word was uttered. At length the power of numbers quailed before the iron will, the moral greatness of that one man. The mutineers signified their willingness to return, and in a short time they were retracing their steps to Fort Strother.

While General Jackson was engaged in quelling the disturbances in his camp, the East Tennesseans, under General White, were proceeding against the Hillabee towns, the warriors from which had been present at the battle of Talladega. Intimidated by the result of this action, they had applied to General Jackson, on the thirteenth of November, for terms of peace. On the seventeenth he replied, making known to them the conditions upon which their request would be granted. On the same night, General White, who had been detached for this service by General Cocke, on the eleventh of November, with all his cavalry and mounted infantry, approached the principal Hillabee village, having previously destroyed Little Oakfuskie, Genalga, and Netta Chaptoa. At daylight the town was surprised, sixty warriors were killed, and two hundred and fifty taken prisoners, without the loss of a drop of blood on the part of General White's command.

This unfortunate movement—unfortunate, inasmuch as the blow fell with crushing weight upon a people already subdued, and anxious to make peace on any terms—confirmed General Cocke in the opinion which he had previously formed and communicated to General Jackson on the fourteenth of November, that it was far better to unite his forces with those of the latter, and act in concert with him, than, by remaining separate, to paralyze his efforts, and defeat his plans. Thereafter he made no attempt to operate independently of General Jackson, and on the twelfth of December joined him at Fort Strother, with fourteen hundred and fifty men.

After allaying the mutiny in his camp in November,

General Jackson visited Fort Deposit and Ditto's Landing, to make arrangements for supplying his army, preparatory to another forward movement which he had in contemplation. Requisitions were issued for furnishing a suitable number of rations at Fort Strother, Talladega, and the junction of the Coosa and Tallapoosa, together with wagons and pack-horses for their transportation. He then returned to Fort Strother with the first regiment of volunteers. Shortly after his return a new cause of disturbance arose. The volunteers had originally engaged to serve for twelve months, and they claimed that their term of service would expire on the tenth of December. General Jackson, however, contended that the period which elapsed between the time of their dismissal, after their return from Natchez, and that of their subsequent re-muster, at Fayetteville, must be deducted. Each party insisted on its particular view of the case; and in the evening of the ninth of December, General Jackson was informed by General Hall, that his brigade were preparing to move off, with, or without permission, on the following morning.

General Jackson had become familiar with scenes of this character, and he immediately issued an order, stating that an actual mutiny existed in the camp, and commanding all officers and soldiers to unite in putting it down. He further directed the volunteer brigade to parade on the west side of the fort; the company of artillerists were ordered to take post, with one piece in front, and one in rear, of their line; and the militia under Colonel Wynne, were instructed to occupy the eminences in advance. These dispositions being made, the general rode in front of the volunteers, and addressed each company separately, in eloquent and animated terms, informing them that he had submitted the question in dispute to the governor, and that, until his decision was known, or reinforcements joined him, he could not dispense with their services. He appealed to every noble and worthy motive to induce them to remain; but declared, that he should do his duty, regardless of consequences; and that they could not leave him, without passing over his dead body. "Now," said he, in conclusion, "argument is at an end; and you must choose, and that at once, whether you will go or stay!"

Not a word was uttered in reply by the volunteers. He then demanded a prompt answer. Still there was no response. He now ordered the artillerists to prepare their matches. Ere the order was obeyed, the obstinacy of the men gave way before his unyielding firmness. "Let us return," was whispered from one to another, with trembling lips; and the officers soon came forward, and pledged themselves and their men, to remain until the general should hear from the governor, or the expected reinforcements arrive.

On the twelfth of December, General Cocke reached the camp from Fort Armstrong, with the East Tennesseans. General Jackson then issued an address to the volunteer brigade, offering to permit those who desired to leave him, to return at once to Nashville, and those who chose to remain, to organize themselves into a separate corps, with officers of their own selection. But one man in the whole brigade, Captain Williamson, consented to stay; the remainder were marched back to Nashville, by General Hall, and soon after discharged from the service.

The regiment of volunteer cavalry belonging to General Coffee's brigade, claimed the same indulgence with the volunteer infantry, and the mounted rifles insisted that they were only bound for a three months' tour of duty. About one-half the brigade abandoned the service, at Huntsville, and the other half returned to Fort Deposit, but they also subsequently deserted their commander—General Coffee exerting himself, in vain, to induce them to remain—and returned home. These defections, and the expiration of the terms of service of a portion of General Cocke's division, reduced the force under General Jackson, at Fort Strother, to six hundred militia, two companies of spies, under Captains Gordon and Russell, one of artillery, under Captain Deadrick, and a few volunteers from the various corps, who had been, "faithful among the faithless found." The militia demanded their discharge at the expiration of three months, although it had been supposed they were enlisted for six, and it was not thought advisable to compel them to remain.

All these difficulties in keeping the troops in the field arose from the want of sufficient supplies. Had General

Jackson been properly supported in this respect, it is probable there would not have been a single case of defection, and the first of January, 1814, would have witnessed the complete subjection of the Creeks. Still he was determined to prosecute the campaign, as soon as he should be in a condition to move forward. After the return of the militia, he was left with only about one hundred men, and was, in consequence, obliged to employ the friendly Cherokees in garrisoning Fort Armstrong, and protecting the stores at Camp Ross. Generals Cocke and Roberts, Colonel Carroll, and Major Searcy, the aid of the commanding general, were at this time absent in Tennessee, exerting themselves to raise additional troops.

On being informed of the situation of General Jackson, Governor Blount advised him to fall back from his advanced posts, and content himself with defending the frontiers of the State, until he was placed in sufficient force to carry on the war. On the twenty-ninth of December, 1813, the general unburdened his whole soul to the governor,

> "In thoughts that breathe, and words that burn."

"What!" said he, in his letter, "retrograde under . such circumstances! I will perish first. What! a governor of a patriotic State, whose citizens pressed for war, who bawled for permission to exterminate the Creeks, to pause or hesitate at such a crisis as this? Such conduct cannot be justified, cannot be excused. Hear the voice of a friend: If you compel me to retro grade, the awful responsibility must and will be ascribed to you. * * * I shall do my duty. I will retain the post, or die in the struggle, unless ordered to retreat by my commanding general!"

The earnest appeals of General Jackson, whose intrepidity of spirit and resoluteness of purpose appeared only the more conspicuous, when fortune smiled the most unkindly on him, were not without effect. On the thirteenth of January, 1814, he was joined at Fort Strother, by two regiments of mounted men, eight hundred and fifty strong, under Colonels Perkins and Higgins, who had volunteered for sixty days. Previous to this time, he had ascertained that the hostile Indians from several towns on the Tallapoosa, had concentrated in a bend of the river, thirty-five miles south east of Talladega, near the mouth of the Emuckfaw Creek, and were either preparing to attack Fort Armstrong, or the Georgia troops.

The volunteer cavalry having been enlisted for so short a period, it was necessary to act speedily if he desired to avail himself of their services. On the day of their arrival at Fort Strother, he issued orders directing them to hold themselves in readiness for the march, and, on the fifteenth and sixteenth of January, crossed the Coosa with his whole force, numbering seven hundred and sixty-seven men, though the official reports, which were not corrected lest the army should be intimidated by the knowledge of its weakness, showed a total of nine hundred and thirty.

At Talladega, General Jackson was joined by two hundred friendly Creeks and Cherokees. The march was continued without intermission, and on the night of the twentieth instant, he encamped at Enotochopco, one of the Hillabee villages, within twelve miles of Emuckfaw. In the morning of the twenty-first, the army proceeded direct towards the bend of the river where the enemy were said to be fortified. About the middle of the afternoon, the spies discovered two Indians, who were pursued, but made their escape. Advancing a short distance further, they came upon the main trail of the savages. The general then determined to encamp and reconnoitre the surrounding country. A proper position having been selected, the army encamped in a hollow square. Pickets and spies were thrown out on every side; the sentinels were doubled; fires were built in a circle around the encampment; and every precaution taken to guard against a surprise.

Moments and hours of the night passed by in anxious suspense. From time to time the orders enjoining strict caution and vigilance were repeated. The darkest hour of the morning—the time usually selected by the Indians for their attacks—approached; and when everything was the most quiet and undisturbed, all at once there rose a loud pealing yell on the left of the encampment, and with it came a hurtling volley of rifle-balls. A deafening responsive shout went up, within that fiery circle, like the wild pibroch of some Gaelic clan, rousing the martial spirit of all who heard it. The enemy kept up a rapid and unintermitting fire; but they could not approach near enough to effect any execution, without entering the line of light which the timely precaution of Jackson had thrown around his men; and whenever a single swart form, or painted visage, was disclosed, the American bullet sped away on its sure errand of death.

When the alarm was first given, General Coffee, Colonel Carroll, and Colonel Sitler, the adjutant-general—who, with a number of other officers previously belonging to different detachments, had remained with the commander to whom they were devotedly attached, and formed themselves into a corps, without privates— mounted their horses and rode to the left. Their presence inspirited and encouraged the troops, and the savages were held firmly at bay till the dawning light enabled objects to be distinguished with precision. A company of infantry were then ordered to that flank, and thus strengthened, General Coffee, supported by Colonels Higgins and Carroll, led the whole line to the charge. The red warriors were driven from their coverts at the point of the bayonet, and pursued for more than two miles; the friendly Indians joining in the chase, and marking their pathway with the blood of the slain.

Victorious as he was, General Jackson was still in a precarious position. His men had few rations left, and the horses had not had corn or cane, for two days. The main object of the expedition—a diversion in favor of the Georgia troops—had been accomplished, yet his small force was seriously crippled, and it was to be feared, if he remained at Emuckfaw, that the Red Sticks would rally in greater numbers, and attack him once more, under all his disadvantages. He therefore decided to fall back to Fort Strother as soon as practicable. The remainder of the day was spent in burying the dead, in taking care of the wounded and preparing litters for their transportation, and in fortifying the camp. The militia sentinels were repeatedly alarmed during the night, probably by their own fancies, as no enemy was discovered; and on the morning of the twenty-third without having been again molested, the army commenced the return march.

Not a solitary Indian was seen through the day, except those attached to the command. They defiled without interruption, through a hurricane, covered with the huge bolls of prostrate oaks and pines, with straggling branches of trees flung in every direction, and closely-matted weeds and brambles, in which there were numerous hiding-places that might have afforded shelter to an enemy; and just before sunset, they arrived at Enotochopco, where they halted for the night, selecting a strong position, which they fortified, within a quarter of a mile of the creek.

In the evening, small parties of the hostile savages were seen prowling about the encampment, although no attack was made. This circumstance, in connection with the fact that he had not been molested during the day, convinced General Jackson that the enemy had go in the advance, and were lying in wait for him at a dangerous defile where he had forded the creek on his outward march. He therefore sent out his pioneers, who discovered another crossing, about six hundred yards lower down, which was approached through open woodlands; and, unlike the other, its banks sloped gently down, and were tolerably free from reeds and underbrush. The lower ford was, of course selected, in preference to the one above.

Presuming that the Indians would rush upon his men, when they were engaged in passing the stream, the general made his preparations with great care, and issued his orders with unusual precision. Colonel Carroll was ordered to take command of the centre of the rear-guard; Colonel Perkins of the right column; and Colonel Stump of the left. Captain Russell was directed to bring up the rear with his company of spies. If attacked, Colonel Carroll was instructed to face about, display, and maintain his ground; while the right and left columns were to face outward, wheel back on their pivots, and then attack the Indians on both flanks.

In this order the crossing proceeded on the morning of the twenty-fourth. The front-guard, the wounded, and a part of the flank columns, had passed over; and the artillery were in the act of entering the creek—General Jackson being on the bank superintending the movement—when an alarm gun was fired in the rear. The instant after the whole troop of Indians, who had discovered the effort to turn their position, came plung-

4

ing down upon the rear-guard. Captain Russell received
them gallantly, and fell back in good order. Colonel
Carroll had scarcely given the order to halt and form,
when the right and left columns, headed by their offi
cers, broke and fled down the bank. Colonel Stump
was among the foremost, and as he approached General
Jackson's position, the latter attempted to cut him down
with his sword.

All was now confusion and disorder. The panic was
communicated to the rear-guard, most of whom followed
the example of their companions. Colonel Carroll and
Captain Quarles were left with only twenty-five men,
yet they sustained the unequal contest with unflinching
bravery. The savages were checked in their advance,
but the men were rapidly falling, and the iron hail
came thicker and faster. General Jackson fairly boiled
over with rage and indignation; yet, smothering his
passion, he gave his orders coolly and calmly, but in a
tone that rang like the blast of a trumpet. Words of
encouragement were not wanting; and when the fearless and intrepid Coffee sprang from his litter into the
saddle, he cried, "We shall whip them yet, my men !—
the dead have risen and come to aid us !"

The company of artillery, who were armed with muskets, now rushed up the acclivity, and ranged themselves by the side of Colonel Carroll and his little band,
while their commander, Lieutenant Armstrong—Captain Deadrick being absent—and a few of his men,
dragged up their six-pounder. The gun had been un

limbered at the foot of the height, and when they prepared to load it, the rammer and picker were missing.
No time was to be lost, as the savages were fast closing
upon them. One of the men instantly wrested off his
bayonet, and rammed the cartridge home with his
musket; another used his ramrod as a picker, and
primed with a musket cartridge. Twice was the gun
loaded and fired with grapeshot. At the second discharge, the enemy were thrown into confusion, when
Colonel Carroll pressed upon them with the bayonet,
and forced them to retire a short distance, though they
still persisted in the attack.

Meanwhile, Captain Gordon, whose company had
been in the advance, had moved round and thrown himself upon the left flank of the Indians; and a few moments later, General Jackson brought up a considerable
number of the rear-guard and flankers, whom he had
rallied and reformed, with the assistance of General
Coffee, Colonel Higgins, and other officers. Finding
themselves baffled at every point, the enemy gave up
the contest and made a hasty retreat, throwing away
their packs as they fled, and leaving twenty-six of their
warriors dead on the field.

In this series of engagements, at Emuckfaw and
Enotochopco, General Jackson lost twenty men killed,
and seventy-five wounded, four of them mortally. One
hundred and eighty-nine dead bodies of the enemy were
counted; but they removed all their wounded, and, pro
bably, many who were killed outright.

The brilliant successes of General Jackson in the Creek country now began to attract unusual attention. The commander of the military district, General Pinckney, referred to his conduct in terms of strong approbation, and suggested his name to the Secretary of War, for an appointment in the regular army. He had fought himself into the confidence and affections of the public, and he had no further need to depend on the reluctant services of a disorderly and half-mutinous soldiery.

So far from being offended at the tone and language of General Jackson's letter, Governor Blount properly appreciated the feelings of the writer, and made every possible exertion to send him both troops and supplies. Men were not wanting to enroll their names; for there were hundreds and thousands who longed to fight beneath the standard, and under the eye, of Andrew Jackson. On the third of February, General Doherty arrived at Camp Ross with two thousand men from East Tennessee; and, shortly after, General Johnston reported himself at Huntsville, with over seventeen hundred men, from West Tennessee. Two regiments of cavalry, one from each section of the state, under Colonels Dyer and Brown, also appeared, and were organized into a brigade, under General Coffee. On the sixth of February, the 39th infantry, under Colonel Williams, about six hundred strong, joined General Jackson at Fort Strother, and about the same time, the Choctaws took up the hatchet against the Red Sticks, and offered him their services.

While the general was making his preparations at Fort Strother, most of the detachments composing the force under his command remained in the rear, that the supplies thrown forward to that post might not be too quickly consumed. During this period of inaction, the spirit of mutiny again made its appearance among the West Tennessee troops. He felt that he had so far dealt too leniently with this offence, and determined to visit it with summary punishment. A private belonging to General Johnston's command was convicted of open mutiny, and sentenced to death. This was his second offence, and the general firmly refused to pardon him. The sentence was carried into effect, and the example thus presented exerted a most salutary influence on the whole army.

Early in March, General Jackson had finally completed his arrangements. Colonel Dyer was ordered to scour the country between the Coosa, Blackwarrior, and Cahawba, as low down as the old Coosa towns; the Choctaws and Chickasaws were directed to watch the country west of the Tombigbee, and prevent the escape of any of the Red Sticks beyond the Mississippi; and the Cherokees received instructions to range about the headwaters of the Tallapoosa. At the same time, there was a large force of North Carolina and South Carolina militia, under Colonel Pearson, who had relieved the Georgia troops under General Floyd, on the eastern borders of the Creek country, in readiness to coöperate in any simultaneous movement upon the fastnesses of the hostile Indians.

Leaving a garrison of four hundred and fifty men at Fort Strother, under Colonel Steel, General Jackson commenced descending the Coosa, having embarked his stores in boats, with the remainder of his force, on the sixteenth day of March. Arrived at the mouth of Cedar Creek, he established a dépôt at this point, and commenced the construction of a fort, which he named Fort Williams. The work on the fort being in a suffi· cient state of forwardness, he took up the line of march across the country to Emuckfaw, on the morning of the twenty-fourth instant, with about two thousand men. A strong detachment was left at Fort Williams, to pro· tect the supplies, and continue the labor on the fortifications.

Not far from five miles below the battle-ground of the twenty-second of January, at Emuckfaw, is the great bend of the Tallapoosa, called by the Indians Tohopeca, or Horse Shoe. At this place, the warriors from the hostile towns of Oakfuskie, Oakchoya, Eufau· lee, New Youca, the Hillabees and Fish Ponds, had concentrated their forces, near one thousand strong, for a last desperate struggle. Across the narrow neck of land, or isthmus, by which the peninsula formed by the crooked river was entered, they had erected a breast-work of logs, from five to eight feet high, with double portholes, arranged with no little skill and ingenuity.

Within the inclosure, there were about one hundred acres of land; the centre was high ground, covered with brush and fallen timber; and on the river bottom, at the lower extremity of the peninsula, was the Indian village.

On the night of the twenty-sixth of March, General Jackson encamped within six miles of the Horse Shoe, and early on the following morning, General Coffee was detached, with the mounted men and most of the friendly Indians, under instructions to cross the river at a ford two miles below Tohopeca, and take possession of the high grounds on the opposite bank, so as to cut off all chance of escape in that quarter. General Jackson then marched the remainder of his force to a position in front of the enemy's breastworks, where he halted his men, until the pre-arranged signal announced that General Coffee had drawn a cordon of soldiers around the elevated ground overlooking the river and the hostile town and fortification. The main column immediately moved forward; the two pieces of artillery, a six and a three pounder, were planted on a hill eighty yards distant from the left of the enemy's line; and at half past ten o'clock in the forenoon, the action was opened by a brisk fire, which was warmly returned by the Red Sticks.

The firing on the American side was mainly confined to the artillery, though a rifle or musket was occasionally discharged, whenever the dark warriors incautiously exposed their persons. For nearly two hours, the

cannonade was kept up, with spirit and activity, though
without producing any sensible impression. Meantime,
the friendly Indians had advanced to the left bank of
the river, while General Coffee remained on the high
ground with the rest of his troops. Some of the Cherokees now discovered that the enemy's canoes, which
were drawn up on the shore, near their village, had been
left unguarded. They instantly plunged into the stream,
swam across, and, in a few moments, returned with a
number of the canoes. Means being thus provided for
passing over, the Cherokees, headed by their chief,
Richard Brown, and Colonel Morgan, and Captain Russell's company of spies, crossed to the village, set it on
fire, and attacked the enemy in the rear.

Surrounded though they were, the hostile Indians
fought with the utmost bravery and desperation. Every
avenue by which they might have fled was occupied by
the American troops, and their habitations were in
flames; still they refused to surrender, and successfully
resisted every attempt of the spies and Cherokees to
dislodge them. The soldiers with General Jackson
clamored loudly to be led to the assault, but he hesitated·
to give the order, till he became convinced that the
party in the rear were not strong enough to overcome
the opposition they encountered. The command to
storm the works was then received with shouts and
acclamations. General Doherty's brigade, and the 39th
infantry, under Colonel Williams, promptly advanced
to the attack. The result of the contest did not long re-

main in doubt. A fierce struggle was maintained for a
short time, through the portholes, muzzle to muzzle; the
action being so close, as remarked in the dispatch of the
commanding general, " that many of the enemy's balls
were welded to the American bayonets." Major Mont-
gomery, of the 39th infantry, was the first to spring
upon the breastwork, but was shot dead among his comrades, who were rushing forward to sustain him. A
smothered cry for vengeance rolled along the line—and
the whole column dashed over the feeble barrier, like
the avalanche, crushing and bearing down everything
before it.

The Indians, fighting with the fury of despair, met the
shock with clubbed muskets and rifles, with the gleaming knife and tomahawk. Some few attempted to
escape by swimming the river, but were shot down in
their flight, by the spies and mounted men under General Coffee. Most of them, however, fought and died,
where they stood—behind the ramparts which they
were unable to defend. The conflict—nay, we may call
it without reproach to the victors, the butchery—was
continued for hours. None asked for quarter. The
Tallapoosa ran red with the blood of the savages,
and the dead were piled in mangled heaps upon its
banks.

Driven from the breastwork, a considerable number
of the enemy took refuge among the brush and fallen
timber on the high ground in the centre of the peninsula. General Jackson sent them an interpreter, to offer

terms of capitulation, but they fired on and wounded him. The cannon were brought to bear on their position, and a partially successful charge was made, yet they were not dislodged. Finally, the brush was set on fire. The flames spread with rapidity, snapping and crackling as they caught the dry bark and leaves, and licking up everything in their way, like some huge, greedy monster. The Indians were now forced from their concealment; and all who attempted to fly, or offered resistance, were shot down. Night at length put an end to the carnage, and, under cover of the darkness, a few of the survivors of that fatal field escaped into the adjoining forests.

Five hundred and fifty-seven dead bodies of the enemy were found within the peninsula; and there were over three hundred taken prisoners, nearly all women and children. The total loss of the Red Sticks, in killed alone, must have been near eight hundred; as a number of the dead were thrown into the river previous to the final rout, by their surviving friends, or shot by General Coffee's men while attempting to make their escape. Among the slain were three prophets, one of whom, by the name of Monohoe, was struck by a grape-shot in his mouth, out of which had issued the lies which had lured his nation to their ruin.

General Jackson lost fifty-five men killed, and one hundred and forty-six wounded. Twenty-three of the killed, and forty-seven of the wounded, were friendly Creeks and Cherokees.

The campaign was now drawing to a close, but its hardships were not quite ended. The roads were flooded by the heavy rains, and the streams scarcely fordable; and, consequently, the march was tedious and difficult. General Jackson was much worn by the fatigues and privations which he had encountered, but his capability of endurance was not yet exhausted; and the strength of constitution he manifested, though belied by the apparent weakness of his frame, gave rise to the *sobriquet* of " Old Hickory," which was applied to him by his soldiers, and adhered to him through life.

The terrible vengeance taken at Tohopeka, for the massacre at Fort Mims, and the other monstrous cruelties perpetrated by the Red Sticks, put an end to the war. The great body of the hostile savages fled in dismay before the advancing columns of General Jackson. Many of the fugitives were killed by a detachment of the 3rd infantry, under Colonel Russell, but numbers effected their escape into Florida, on account of the remissness of Colonel Milton, the officer in command of the South Carolinians, who were then on the left bank of the Tallapoosa, not far above its junction with the Coosa. McQueen, one of the most prominent chiefs among the Red Sticks, was captured, but afterwards escaped to the Escambia river, with five hundred adherents.

Arrived at Hoithlewalee, General Jackson found the town abandoned. On the fourteenth of April it was destroyed, with several other villages in the vicinity.

The general then divided his command into two columns; one scouring the country on the left bank, and the other, with which he remained in person, advancing down the right bank of the Tallapoosa, to the confluence, where a fort was constructed, called by General Pinckney, in honor of the gallant Tennessee commander, Fort Jackson. At this point most of the Hickory Ground chiefs came in and submitted to the conqueror. Weatherford also voluntarily surrendered, and the great prophet of the Creeks, Hillinghagee, was taken prisoner. The only terms prescribed by the victorious general were, that all who surrendered themselves should retire to the country north of Fort Williams, where, if their conduct was good, they would be permitted to remain unmolested. In a few days after his humane and generous proposition was made known, numbers of the fugitives were on their way to the neutral territory.

On the twentieth of April, General Pinckney arrived at Fort Jackson, and on the following day assumed the command. General Jackson shortly after repaired to his home in Tennessee, to recruit his health and strength, which had suffered materially during his long and arduous campaign. The thanks of the government and the applause of the nation followed him in his retirement. An opportunity was soon afforded for rewarding his services by an appointment in the regular army. On the resignation of General Harrison, President Madison nominated him as a brigadier general, and major general by brevet; and, a short time afterwards, he was appointed a full major general, to fill the vacancy occasioned by the retirement of General Hampton. Both commissions were received at the same time, and the latter was accepted.

In the summer of 1814, General Jackson was ordered to take command of the seventh military district, and established his headquarters at Mobile. Associated with Colonel Hawkins, he concluded a favorable treaty with the Creek nation, by which, with the exception of a small portion of the tribe who chose to remain in Florida, they were prevented from again taking up arms during the continuance of the war with England.

In the month of August, Captain Gordon, of the spies, visited Pensacola, and ascertained that a large body of savages had been organized there by Colonel Nicholls, of the British army, and were then being instructed and drilled by British officers, in the presence, and with the knowledge, of the Spanish governor; that Fort Barrancas was occupied by between two and three hundred British troops; and that there were three armed vessels belonging to the same nation, in the bay, from which a considerable quantity of arms and provisions had been disembarked. Another reconnoissance was subsequently made by Lieutenant Murray, of the Mississippi militia, which fully confirmed the report made by Captain Gordon. On the twenty-ninth of August, also, Colonel Nicholls issued a proclamation, dated at his "headquarters, Pensacola," addressed to the inhabitants of the southern and southwestern states, and inviting them to join his standard, in which he informed them that he was "at the head of a large body of Indians, well armed, disciplined, and commanded by British officers; a good train of artillery, with every requisite; seconded by the powerful aid of a numerous British and Spanish squadron of ships and vessels of war."

General Jackson was not disposed to stand idly by, and see the rights of his country violated, and her interests jeoparded. He forthwith dispatched an express to the governor of Tennessee, requesting the whole quota of the militia of that State to be brought into the field without delay, and commenced his preparations for a march on Pensacola. On the fifteenth of September, Colonel Nicholls appeared before Fort Bowyer, thirty miles below Mobile, at the entrance of the Bay, with four vessels containing a number of siege pieces, and several hundred sailors, marines, and savages. The heavy guns were landed, the fort invested, and a lively cannonade opened upon it. Major Lawrence, of the 2nd infantry, the commander of the post, with its garrison of one hundred and twenty men, made a brave defence, and finally forced the enemy to retire, with the loss of one of their ships, and over two hundred killed and wounded.

Having been joined by about two thousand men from Tennessee, General Jackson took up the line of march for Pensacola, with all his disposable troops. His whole force consisted of upwards of three thousand men, but a small part being regulars, and the remainder militia from Mississippi and Tennessee, with a few Choctow warriors. On the sixth of November, he arrived near Pensacola, and sent a flag to the Spanish governor, to communicate the purpose of his visit. The bearer of the flag was fired on from the batteries in the town, and forced to return. Dispositions were then made for carrying the fort by assault, which was discovered to be defended by both British and Spanish troops, on the following day. On the morning of the seventh, the general entered the town with his troops, under a heavy fire from the fort, and the British flotilla in the harbor, and carried one of the advanced batteries at the point of the bayonet. The governor now supplicated for mercy, and surrendered the town and fort unconditionally; the British troops retiring to Fort Barrancas, and their savage allies seeking shelter in the everglades of Florida, whither they were driven by a detachment from the American army under Major Blue.

L

IN the rear of the city of New Orleans, and about a mile from its centre, there is a small, narrow, winding, and still stream, called, in the South, a Bayou, which communicates with Lake Pontchartrain. This bayou, no doubt, once flowed from the Mississippi, but in the progress of time and in the process of accretion, its source has been thrown some distance from the river, and now starting in the swamp above the city, it steals through an indentation of the delta, winds along the base of the Metairie Ridge (a curious protrusion from the level plain in which New Orleans is built), and, approaching the suburbs of the city, turns abruptly to the east, and then, with sluggish current, meanders towards the lake. A canal, commenced by that great benefactor of New Orleans, Baron Carondelet, the labor of which was performed by slaves belonging to the citizens, who were levied upon for that purpose, which was completed in 1796, connects the bayou with

6

the city, and thus supplies the latter with an excellent
water communication with the lake, through which, in
the early days of its history, much of the commerce of
New Orleans was conducted. Biloxi, the Bay of Saint
Louis and Pass Christian were then flourishing settlements, where the French established their first colonies,
before the mouth of the Mississippi had been discovered, and where most of the shipping engaged in the
foreign and coastwise trade came to anchor, and trans-
shipping their cargoes into smaller crafts, sent them to
New Orleans through the Bayou Saint John (the name
of the stream we have described), and the canal
Carondelet. There, at the head of navigation on the
bayou, and about half a mile from the mouth of the
canal, is the old settlement of Saint John, which existed
when the present site of New Orleans was an unbroken
swamp, the favorite retreat of alligators and other reptiles. But time has wrought a striking change in the
character and aspect of these localities. The seashore
settlements no longer resorted to for purposes of trade,
are now only known as places of summer sojourn and
recreation. Thither flock the jaded denizens of the city,
to refresh their wearied frames, to invigorate broken
constitutions, to relieve their minds of the oppression
of all business cares, and to inhale an atmosphere of
luxurious and exhilarating salubrity.

Alas! this ancient canal and bayou followed the fortunes of the ancient population of New Orleans, and,
in the march of Anglo-American enterprise, lost its
value and importance as a vehicle of commerce, when a
new canal of larger dimensions was constructed in
another part of the city, where the all-conquering invaders from Northern climes had "pitched their tents."

The fame and history of this old bayou and canal had become classical, as relics of a past age and generation. They were intimately associated with the early glories of New Orleans, and were, therefore, held in warm veneration by the old inhabitants. Several attempts have been made to restore the fortunes of the old bayou, and render it what it appears to be so admirably designed for, an additional means of transit for the great and rapidly increasing commerce between New Orleans and the growing towns and settlements on the Lake and Gulf shore; but thus far they have not proved successful.

The Bayou St. John empties into Lake Pontchartrain at a distance of seven miles from the city. Here, at its mouth, may be seen the remains, in an excellent state of preservation, of an old Spanish fort, which was built many years ago by one of the Spanish Governors, as a protection of this important point; for, by glancing at the map of New Orleans and its vicinity, it will be seen that a maritime power could find no easier approach to the city than through the Bayou St. John. This fort was built, as the Spaniards built all their fortifications in this State, where stone could not be procured, of small brick, imported from Europe, cemented with a much more adhesive and permanent material than is now used for building, and with walls of great thickness and solidity. The foundation and walls of the fort still remain, interesting vestiges of the old Spanish dominion. On the mound and within the walls, stands a comfortable hotel, where, in the summer season, may be obtained healthful cheer, generous liquors, and a pleasant view of the placid and beautiful lake, over whose gentle bosom the sweet south wind comes with just power enough to raise a gentle ripple on its mirror-like surface, bringing joy and relief to the wearied townsman, and debilitated invalid. What a different scene did this fort present forty years ago! Then there were large cannon looking frowningly through those embrasures, which are now filled up with dirt and rubbish, and around them clustered glittering bayonets and fierce-looking men, full of military ardor and determination. There, too, was much of the reality, if not of "the pomp and circumstance" of war. High above the fort, from the summit of a lofty staff, floated not the showy banner of Old Spain, with its glittering and mysterious emblazonry, but that simplest and most beautiful of all national standards, the Stars and Stripes of the Republic of the United States.

From the Fort St. John to the city, the distance is six or seven miles. Along the bayou, which twists its sinuous course like a huge dark green serpent, through the swamp, lies a good road, hardened by a pavement of shells, taken from the bottom of the lake. Hereon, city Jehus now exercise their fast nags, and lovely ladies take their evening airings. But at the time our narrative commences, it was a very bad road, being low, muddy, and broken. The ride, which now occupies some twenty minutes very delightfully, was then a wearisome two hours' journey.

It was along this road, early on the morning of the 2d December, 1814, that a party of gentlemen rode at a brisk trot, from the lake towards the city. The mist, which during the night broods over the swamp, had not cleared off. The air was chilly, damp and uncomfortable. The travellers, however, were evidently hardy men, accustomed to exposure, and intent upon purposes too absorbing to leave any consciousness of external discomforts. Though devoid of all military, display and even of the ordinary equipments of soldiers, the bearing and appearance of these men betokened their connection with the profession of arms. The chief of the party, which was composed of five or six persons, was a tall, gaunt man, of very erect carriage, with a countenance full of stern decision and fearless energy, but furrowed with care and anxiety. His complexion was sallow and unhealthy; his hair was iron grey, and his body thin and emaciated, like that of one who had just recovered from a lingering and painful sickness. But the fierce glare of his bright and hawk-like grey eye, betrayed a soul and spirit which triumphed over all the infirmities of the body. His dress was simple, and nearly threadbare. A small leather cap protected his head, and a short Spanish blue cloak his body, whilst his feet and legs were encased in high dragoon boots, long igorant of polish or blacking, which reached to the knees. In age, he appeared to have passed about forty-five winters,—the season for which his stern and hardy nature seemed peculiarly adapted.

The others of the party were younger men, whose spirits and movements were more elastic and careless, and who relieved the weariness of the journey with many a jovial story.

Arriving at the high ground near the junction of the Canal Carondelet with the Bayou St. John, where a bridge spanned the bayou, and quite a village had grown up, the travellers halted before an old Spanish villa, and, throwing their bridles to some grinning negro boys at the gates, dismounted and walked into the house. On entering the gallery, they were received

in a very cordial and courteous manner, by J. Kilty
Smith, Esq., then a leading New-Orleans merchant of
enterprise and public spirit, and who, a few months ago,
still survived, one of the most venerable of that small
band of the early American settlers, in the great commercial emporium of the South, who, out-living several
generations, still linger in green old age, amid the scenes
of their youthful struggles, and survey, with proud satisfaction, the greatness to which that city has grown,
whose tender infancy they witnessed and helped to
nurse and rear into a sturdy and robust maturity. On
the bayou, in an agreeable suburban retreat, Mr. Smith
had established himself. Here he dispensed a liberal
hospitality, and lived in such a style as was regarded in
those economical days, and by the more frugal Spanish
and French populations, as quite extravagant and
luxurious.

Ushering them into the marble-paved hall of his old
Spanish villa, Mr. Smith soon made his guests comfortable. It was evident that they were not unexpected.
Soon the company were all seated at the breakfast
table, which fairly groaned with the abundance of generous viands, prepared in that style of incomparable
cookery, for which the Creoles of Louisiana are so
renowned. Of this rich and savory food, the younger
guests partook quite heartily; but the elder and leader
of the party was more careful and abstemious, confin-
ing himself to some boiled hominy, whose whiteness
rivaled that of the damask table-cloth. In the midst of
the breakfast, and whilst the company were engaged in
discussing the news of the day, a servant whispered to
the host, that he was wanted in the ante-room. Excus-
ing himself to his guests, Mr. Smith retired to the ante-

room, and there found himself in the presence of an indignant and excited creole lady, a neighbor, who had kindly consented to superintend the preparations in Mr. Smith's bachelor-establishment, for the reception of some distinguished strangers, and who, in that behalf, had imposed upon herself a severe responsibility and labor.

"Ah! Mr. Smith," exclaimed the deceived lady, in a half-reproachful, half-indignant style, "how could you play such a trick upon me? You asked me to get your house in order to receive a great General. I did so. I worked myself almost to death to make your house *comme il faut*, and prepared a splendid *déjeûner*, and now I find that all my labor is thrown away upon an ugly, old Kaintuck-flat-boatman, instead of your grand General, with plumes, epaulettes, long sword, and moustache."

It was in vain that Mr. Smith strove to remove the delusion from the mind of the irate lady, and convince her that that plainly-dressed, jaundiced, hard-featured, unshorn man, in the old blue coat, and bullet buttons, was that famous warrior, Andrew Jackson.

It was, indeed, Andrew Jackson, who had come, fresh from the glories and fatigues of his brilliant Indian campaigns, in this unostentatious manner, to the city which he had been sent to protect from one of the most formidable perils that ever threatened a community. Cheerfully and happily had he embraced this awful responsibility. He had come to defend a defenceless city, situated in the most remote section of the Union, —a city which had neither fleets nor forts, means nor men—a city, whose population were comparative strangers to that of the other States, who sprung from

a different national stock, and spoke a different language from that of the overwhelming majority of their
countrymen—a language entirely unknown to the
General—to defend it, too, against a power then victorious over the conqueror of the world, at whose feet the
mighty Napoleon lay a prostrate victim and chained
captive.

After partaking of their breakfast, the General, taking out his watch, reminded his companions of the
necessity of their early entrance into the city. In a
few minutes, carriages were procured, and the whole
party rode towards the city, by the old bayou road.
The General was accompanied by Major Hughes, commander of the Fort St. John, by Major Butler, and
Captain Reid, his Secretary, who afterwards became
one of his biographers, Major Chotard, and other
officers of the staff. The cavalcade proceeded to the
elegant residence of Daniel Clark, the first representative of Louisiana, in the Congress of the United States,
a gentleman of Irish extraction, who had acquired
great influence, popularity, and wealth, in the city, and
died shortly after the commencement of the war of
1812. Here Jackson and his aids were met by a committee of the State and city authorities, and of the
people, at the head of whom was the Governor of the
State, who, in earnest but rather rhetorical terms, wel-
comed the General to the city, and proffered him every
aid of the authorities and the people, to enable him to
justify the title which they were already conferring
upon him of "Savior of New Orleans." His Excellency, W. C. C. Claiborne, the first American Governor of Louisiana, a Virginian, of good address, and
fluent elocution, then in the bloom of life, was sup-

ported by the leading civil and military characters of the city. There, in the group was that redoubtable naval hero, Commodore Patterson, a stout, compact, gallant-bearing man, in the neat undress naval uniform. His manner was slightly marked by *hauteur*, but his movement and expression indicated the energy and boldness of a man of decided action, as well as confident bearing.

Here, too, was the then Mayor of New Orleans, Nicholas Girod, a rotund, affable, pleasant old French gentleman, of easy, polite manners. There, too, was Edward Livingston, then the leading civil character in the city,— a tall, high-shouldered man, of ungraceful figure and homely countenance, but whose high brow, and large, thoughtful eyes, indicated a profound and powerful intellect. By his side stood his youthful rival at the the bar—an elegant, graceful, and showily-dressed gentleman, whose figure combined the compact dignity and solidity of the soldier, with the ease and grace of the man of fashion and taste, and who, as the sole survivor of those named, retained, in a remarkable degree, the elegance and grace, which characterized his bearing forty years ago, to the day of his very recent and lamented decease. We refer to John R. Grymes, so long the veteran and chief ornament of the New Orleans bar.

Such were the leading personages in the assembly which greeted Jackson's entrance into New Orleans.

The General replied briefly to the welcome of the Governor. He declared that he had come to protect the city, and he would drive their enemies into the sea, or perish in the effort. He called on all good citizens to rally around him in this emergency, and, ceasing all differences and divisions, to unite with him in the patriotic resolve to save their city from the dishonor and disaster, which a presumptuous enemy threatened to inflict upon it.   This address was rendered into French by Mr. Livingston.   It produced an electric effect upon all present.   Their countenances cleared up.   Bright and hopeful were the words and looks of all, who heard the thrilling tones, and caught the heroic glance of the hawk-eyed General.   The General and staff then re-entered their carriages.   A cavalcade was formed, and proceeded to the building, 106 Royal street—one of the few brick buildings then existing in New Orleans, which now stands but little changed or affected by the lapse of so many years.   A flag unfurled from the third story, soon indicated to the population the headquarters of the General who had come so suddenly and quietly to their rescue.

It was true he had come almost alone, without troops, without arms, without money.   Nor did he seek to supply these deficiencies with big words, large promises, and loud vauntings.   He had a more efficient means of influencing men, a more powerful wand to wield over the minds and hearts of the people.   His army and his armor, his strength and means, consisted in the prestige of a name and history, which were then as familiar as household words to all the people of the Valley of the Mississippi, a recurrence to which never failed to enkindle the enthusiasm and excite the pride of the emporium of that valley.

What were these glorious antecedents, that drew so much of popular admiration and confidence to Andrew Jackson, and constitute some of his titles to the renown, which history and all nations assign to him?   Let us briefly sketch them.

A wild and desolate place called the Waxhaw Settlement, in a remote district of South Carolina, was the scene of Jackson's birth and boyhood. Throughout the wide Union it would be difficult to find two more dreary and desert-looking localities, than those, which have been consecrated by the birth of the two most eminent men in the history of America—George Washington and Andrew Jackson.

Jackson was born on the 15th March, 1767. His parents were emigrants from the north of Ireland, but of Scotch descent. They had fled from the persecutions and dissensions of the Old World, in pursuit of peace and happiness in the New. They had been two years in the country when Andrew was born. Like most great men, he was blessed with a mother of uncommon intelligence and vigor of mind. With such an instructress and guardian, his intellect early developed, and his spirit expanded into premature manliness. He needed only the occasion to cast his thoughts and feelings in that heroic mould, which constitutes true greatness. Such opportunity was presented, when in beardless boyhood, he found himself in the very midst of some of the most gloomy scenes of the Revolution of 1776.

In old age, when time and infirmity pressed heavily upon that sanguine and dauntless spirit, and the impressions of youth came out upon the memory with more distinctness, that tottering old man of the Hermitage, with his shrivelled visage and snowy locks, but with eye still undimmed and piercing as ever, would recall, with frightful accuracy, the horrible scenes of carnage, rapine, and desolation which had made that boyhood, to which most men recur as the bright period of their lives, the gloomiest and saddest epoch in his career.

When a stripling of thirteen, with scarcely the strength to raise a musket, he joined a party of patriots, under the heroic Sumpter, and in the action at Hanging Rock, and in various skirmishes, showed himself to be a boy only in years. His biographers relate several instances in which his ready courage and self-possession saved himself and his companions from death and capture. Even then he was a chief among men, and often assumed the leadership of those who were old enough to be his father.

Captured, at last, by the British, with his brother, he was subjected to the most cruel treatment. When, with characteristic spirit, he refused to perform some menial office for a British officer, he was dastardly cut down by the blow of a sabre, the mark of which was visible ever afterwards. A similar cruelty to his elder brother eventually produced his death. Closely confined in a British prison, Andrew contracted a disease from which he barely escaped with his life, and the effects of which were felt by him for many years after. It was whilst suffering with this disease, and nearly mad with fever and pain, that the young soldier, hearing that a battle was to be fought within view of the prison windows, contrived, by the exertion of all his strength, to climb up the wall to a small port-hole, which commanded a view of the field of strife. It was thus the boy warrior witnessed the first and only pitched battle that ever oc curred under his observation previous to the events we are about to relate.

This was the severely-contested battle of Camden, of which Jackson never failed to retain a clear, distinct, and vivid recollection.

Such were the scenes and sufferings amid which the

boyhood of Jackson was passed. It was a severe school, and its effects were quite perceptible in that staunch, unyielding spirit, heroic fortitude, and dauntless resolution, which distinguished him through life.

At the close of the Revolution, Jackson found himself alone in the world, the solitary survivor of a family, which, twenty years before, had left Ireland, with bright hopes of finding in the forests of America, a peaceful, happy home. These circumstances were well calculated to impart to the character of Jackson, that tinge of melancholy which it wore through life. This feeling oᶠ loneliness and keen sense of wrong, in the high-day of youth, broke out into reckless dissipation, which, however, was always redeemed and qualified by a spirit of generosity and chivalry. Conquering this tendency, after expending his patrimony, Jackson, with dauntless heart and iron will, threw himself among the hardy and reckless frontiersmen of Tennessee, and engaged in the perilous practice of law, at a time, and in a country, when and where a good eye, steady nerve, and prowess and courage in personal combat, were more essential to the success of a lawyer, than a knowledge of Coke and Blackstone. Jackson possessed these qualifications of "sharp practice" in an eminent degree. His professional career was a perilous and contentious one. It was better adapted to train and form the warrior than the jurisconsult. The courage, which had been so severely tested in the Revolution, was frequently required to repel the aggressions of those pestilent bullies, who always abound in frontier settlements. Through many dangerous conflicts, the impetuous young Carolinian had to fight his way to a position, which secured him the fear and awe of the disorderly, and the respect and con fidence of the hardy settlers. Chivalrous and generous, as determined and ferocious, he was the leader in all enterprises to protect the weak and defenceless. Patriotic and high-toned, he was ever ready to risk his life, to maintain the laws of his country, and enforce justice and lawful authority. Thus the "Sharp Knife" and "Pointed Arrow" of the Indians, was not only a terror to the prowling aborigines, who hung around the settlements, but to the even more ferocious frontiersmen, who straggled from more populous and better organized districts, in the hope of getting beyond the reach of the law and justice, and finding larger and safer fields for their deeds of violence and crime.

Called by the people successively to the civil offices of member of the State Convention, Representative and Senator in Congress, and lastly Supreme Judge of the State, Jackson displayed in all these positions, the same firm spirit and fearless courage, united with great sagacity, and that remarkable courtesy and impressiveness of manner, which excited so much surprise in all persons, who never having before seen him, but familiar with his character and acts, were suddenly brought into his presence.

The life and character, we have thus imperfectly described, clearly indicate the man who would be selected from a million for high military command. And yet, when the war of 1812 broke out, Jackson sought a command in vain. His friends and neighbors understood and appreciated his merits; but those charged with the administration of the Federal Government did not. He only asked for a commission, offering to raise the command himself in thirty days. But he was no intriguer, and his pretensions were ignored. Others were appointed. Disaster after disaster followed. The tragedy of the River Raisin, and the disgraceful failure of the Northern Campaign, filled the whole country, and especially the gallant West, with grief and humiliation. Thousands panted to wipe out these blots from the escutcheon of the Union, with their heart's blood. But alas! the Government at Washington was in the hands of "closet warriors," and political abstractionists,— "ideologists," in the sense of Napoleon's characterization of the Republicans of the Abbé Sièyes school. Slighted and rejected by the government, Jackson's ardor and ambition to serve his country were not extinguished in the chagrin of personal disappointment. He determined to force himself into the service, by raising a large volunteer corps, and so organizing it, that the government would be compelled to recognize its value and muster it into service. The gallant youth of Tennessee quickly rallied to his call. Having soon collected, and organized the requisite force, he at once tendered his services, was accepted by the government, and ordered to proceed to Natchez, a distance of a thousand miles. This march was performed in the depth of winter, through a wild and difficult country, with new and young soldiers.

On his arrival at Natchez, he was destined to receive new mortifications. Suddenly there came an order to disband his troops, and deliver over the public stores, arms, and munitions to an agent of the government. It was a cruel and incomprehensible order. The soldiers were youths, the sons of his neighbors and friends He was bound to them by stronger and dearer ties, than even those of the chief to his followers. He had pledged his honor to venerable fathers and mothers, to loving wives and sisters, to protect their sons, husbands, and brothers, and lead them back to their homes. Could he obey this revolting command, and then go home and face his old friends and neighbors, who had been thus shamefully deceived? To the soldier and citizen it was a severe alternative, but Jackson did not hesitate. He disregarded the order, and marched his whole command back to Tennessee, through incredible toils and sufferings. He had encountered no enemy, and yet, in that brief campaign, he had displayed higher and nobler traits, than those which shine through the smoke and carnage of battle. He had shown that iron firmness and fortitude, that heroic devotion to his companions, which secured him their lasting gratitude, affection, and confidence, to a degree that rendered his control and influence over them unlimited. When the war-blast sounded, the youth of Tennessee knew in whom to find a chief worthy to lead them.

It was not long before the tocsin rang throughout the West.

Tecumseh, the great Indian Chief, aided by the intrigues of the Spaniards in Florida, and the British, had succeeded in uniting the formidable tribes of Indians in the Mississippi Territory, the Chickasaws, Cherokees, and Creeks, into a powerful league and conspiracy to attack and destroy the most exposed white settlements. The fearful massacre at Fort Mimms was the first demonstration of this design. It fell like a thunder clap from a cloudless sky, on the southwest. A public meeting was held at Nashville, to devise means of arresting and punishing these depredations. With one voice Jackson was designated by the people as the chief in such enterprise. He accepted the responsible duty, and

issued a thrilling appeal to the young men of Tennessee
to assemble around his standard. Twenty-five hundred
gallant and patriotic men promptly responded to this
call.

At the head of this force, though still suffering from a
severe wound received in a personal rencontre with the
Bentons, Jackson marched rapidly to the southward to
the scene of the Indian cruelties. After many delays
and difficulties, which would have crushed the energies
of almost any other man, Jackson found his blood-thirsty
enemy strongly posted at Tallahatchie. His "right
arm," the intrepid Coffee, was thrown forward with a
portion of his force, with orders to dislodge the savages.
The order was obeyed by Coffee with characteristic
energy and promptitude, and after an obstinate conflict,
the Indians were entirely routed, with a loss of two
hundred killed and eighty-four prisoners. Thence, after
issuing requisitions for reinforcements from Tennessee,
and after establishing Fort Stockton, Jackson advanced
rapidly to the relief of Fort Talladega, where a small
force of Americans was surrounded and threatened with
instant destruction by more than a thousand fierce war
riors. Without resting his men, Jackson pushed forward
and fell, with the fury of a tempest, on the surprised
savages. The field for some distance around was strewn
with the gory bodies of painted warriors. Those who
survived the attack and escaped the vengeance of
"Sharp Knife," fled with terror into the deepest recesses
of the forest. But these victories, prompt, brilliant, and
decisive as they were, did not afford the best tests of
Jackson's military genius. His real trial was yet to
come. He did not have to wait long for it.

7

Jackson had moved so rapidly, and penetrated so far from the base of his operations, that he soon found himself in great stress for provisions and munitions. The promised supplies had failed. There was no evidence in the Southwest, of the existence of a central Government, to aid and further military operations. Thus far, he had maintained himself by his own credit. This resource was exhausted, and now Jackson found himself in the severest strait of the military commander. He had to keep up the spirits and discipline of raw volunteer troops, under the pressure of hunger, want, and sickness. Never did his heroic soul shine out with greater splendor than in this emergency. Cheerfully he shared the bitterest trials and sufferings of his men, selecting the offal of the few cattle left to them for his rations, and allowing his sick men the wholesome meat, dividing his acorns with a fellow-soldier, and giving his blankets, so much needed for his own wasted frame, to some wounded companion. But even this example of heroic fortitude could not prevail over the gnawings of hunger. His men grew clamorous and mutinous. What he would not concede to violence, he cheerfully yielded to reason. He consented to return, until they could meet some supplies. The troops had not proceeded far before they met a large drove of cattle, which had been dispatched to them by some of Jackson's agents. Oh, with what zest and eagerness did those famished men devour the fresh meat, which the foresight and energy of their General had thus procured for them! But safety did not restore their spirits, nor invigorate their sense of duty. They still longed for their homes, and persisted in returning. Jackson, ordered them to retrace their steps, and pursue the enemy. They sullenly refused to obey, and, forming the column, were about to resume their march homeward.

Now was the time for action, for resolution, for heroic, sublime courage. Mounting his charger, Jackson rode to the front, and seizing a musket from one of the men, levelled it at the head of the column, and swore, " by the Eternal," he would shoot the first man who advanced a step. The men were astounded by his audacity and resolution. They knew he was a man of his word. Two thousand impatient, fiery, self-willed frontiersmen, who were little accustomed to restraint or control, thus awed, by one emaciate, weak, broken-armed man! Presently, some of the men, ashamed of their conduct, went over to him and pledged their lives to sustain him. Finally, they yielded to Jackson's resolution, and agreed to resume their march forward.

New difficulties and sufferings again aroused the spirit of mutiny, and another attempt to depart homeward was made and resisted in the same prompt and decisive manner. At last, Jackson having carried his point, and entirely suppressed the rebellious tendencies of his men, deemed it best to send home the greater part of his troops, and defer further operations for some months. With a few faithful officers and soldiers, he established himself at Fort Stockton.

In January, 1814, having been joined by a force of raw troops, Jackson pushed forward to Emuckfaw, on the Tallapoosa. Near this place he was suddenly attacked with great fury, by a powerful force of Indians, whom he defeated in a close hand-to-hand fight. But his force was too weak to follow up this advantage, so he determined to return to Fort Stockton. It was on his return march, that the enemy surprised Jackson's rear guard, at Enotchhopo. A momentary panic was created, and the Indians were rapidly breaking into the very centre of the column, when the gallant Armstrong (the late General Robert Armstrong, of the Washington Union), arrested their advance by the effective discharge of a small piece of ordnance, of which he had charge, and by the side of which he fell, desperately wounded. As he lay bleeding on the ground, with crowds of savage enemies pressing around him impatient for his scalp, Armstrong called out, "Some of us must fall, but save the gun!" Carroll, too, a young and intrepid officer, rushed to the relief of Armstrong. He was followed by the famous spy-captain of Duck River, Gordon, who, pressing closely on the left of the enemy, held them in check until Jackson could bring up the main body, which he rapidly effected, and falling upon them, soon put them to flight with great loss, causing their precipitate dispersion through the country in the most destitute and panic-stricken condition.

This affair concluded Jackson's second campaign. He returned to Fort Stockton, and discharged his men with high testimonials to their good conduct. Soon after, he was joined by a fresh army of nearly three thousand men, with which he determined to advance, and annihilate, at one blow, the hostile tribes. Learning that the Indians had collected in large force, in a spot regarded by them as holy ground, situated in the bend of the Tallapoosa River, called from its shape Tohopeka, or the Horse-shoe, he marched thither.

The Indians were stationed behind a well-constructed breastwork thrown across the neck. Sending Coffee to surround the bend, Jackson opened a cannonade upon their defences in front. This plan not succeeding against so agile and wary a foe, Jackson resolved to storm their works. This was done with the greatest ardor and heroism by the intrepid Tennesseans. It was a close and bloody fight, of man to man. The Indians, instigated by superstition, as well as by their natural blood-thirstiness, fought with more than usual desperation. They bared their breasts to the gleaming knives, and with their small tomahawks fearlessly threw themselves on the bayonets of their pale-face enemies. It was as terrible, and for the numbers engaged, as destructive a conflict as ever occurred. The breastwork was stormed by the Tennesseans; the charm of invincibility was broken, and the " sacred ground " of the Red Sticks was strewn with eight hundred dead warriors. There were no wounded in those battles. The Red Stick was only conquered in battle when life was extinct.

Thus Jackson redeemed his pledge. The Red Sticks, as a tribe, were annihilated. The few survivors fled to the Spanish settlements in Florida. Some humbly sought for peace and pardon, which Jackson, as generous as brave, cheerfully granted.

This victory for ever destroyed the power of the warlike tribes of the Southwest, and made them ever afterwards, either friends or very timid foes of the whites. It was a brilliant conclusion of Jackson's Indian campaign. He began now to be known abroad. The people all over the country applauded his heroic bearing, under all circumstances, against starvation, mutiny, desertion and disaffection, as well as against the rifles and tomahawks of his savage enemies. Even the torpid Government at Washington, which had failed to recognize his rights before, now hastened to redeem its error, by appointing him to the Major-Generalship, made vacant by the resignation of William Henry Harrison. Jackson's first duty, in his new command was, to nego- tiate a treaty of peace with the Indians, and to guard generally the Southwestern frontier.

It was in the discharge of this duty he approached the Gulf shore, to observe the intrigues of the Span- iards, who were charged with giving aid and comfort to the Indians in their inroads on the white settlements. A much more formidable and important enemy, was also implicated in that infamous alliance with barbarians. The British were virtually in possession of Pensacola. The soul of Jackson fired with the recollection of the cruelties his family had suffered at the hands of his hereditary enemy, in the Revolution of 1776. He longed to avenge those wrongs, not by like cruelties, but by legitimate victories obtained in manly warfare. We shall soon see, whether he was disappointed in this hon- orable revenge ; whether the military genius, which had been nursed amid the fearful struggles of the War of Independence, which had been trained and disciplined by the trying scenes and perils of frontier life, and in warfare against brave and desperate savages, will not shine even more brilliantly and gloriously in a higher sphere, and on a grander scale of warlike achievement.

II.

LAFITTE, "THE PIRATE."

About one mile above New Orleans, opposite the flourishing City of Jefferson, and on the right bank of the Mississippi, there is a small canal, now used by fishermen and hunters, which approaches within a few hundred yards of the river's bank.

The small craft that ply on this canal are taken up on cars, which run into the water by an inclined plane, and are then hauled by mules to the river. Launched upon the rapid current of the Mississippi, these boats are soon borne into the Crescent port of New Orleans. Following this canal, which runs nearly due west for five or six miles, we reach a deep, narrow, and tortuous bayou. Descending this bayou, which for forty miles threads its sluggish course through an impenetrable swamp, we pass into a large lake, girt with sombre forests and gloomy swamps, and resonant with the hoarse croakings of alligators, and the screams of swamp fowls.

From this lake, by a still larger bayou, we pass into another lake, and from that to another, until we reach an island, on which are discernible, at a considerable distance, several elevated knolls, and where a scant vegetation and a few trees maintain a feeble existence. At the lower end of this island, there are some curious aboriginal vestiges, in the shape of high mounds of shells, which are thought to mark the burial of some extinct tribes. This surmise has been confirmed by the discovery of human bones below the surface of these mounds. The elevation formed by the series of mounds, is known as the Temple, from a tradition that the Natchez Indians used to assemble there to offer sacrifices to their chief deity, the " Great Sun." This lake or bayou finally disembogues into the Gulf of Mexico by two outlets, between which lies the beautiful island of Grand Terre.

This island is a pleasant sea-side resort, having a length of six miles, and an average breadth of a mile and a-half. Towards the sea it presents a fine beach, where those who love " the rapture of the lonely shore," who delight in the roar and dash of the foaming billows, and in the ecstasy of a bath in the pure, bracing surge, may find abundant means of pleasure and enjoyment.

Grand Terre is now occupied and cultivated by a creole family, as a sugar plantation, producing annually four or five hundred hogsheads of sugar. At the western extremity of the island stands a large and powerful fortification, which has been quite recently erected by the United States, and named after one of the most distinguished benefactors of Louisiana, Edward Livingston. This fort commands the western entrance or strait leading from the Gulf into the lake or bay of Barataria. Here, safely sheltered, some two or three miles from the gulf, is a snug little harbor, where vessels drawing from seven to eight feet water, may ride in safety, out of the reach of the fierce storms that so often sweep the Gulf of Mexico.

Here may be found, even now, the foundations of

houses, the brickwork of a rude fort, and other evidences of an ancient settlement. This is the spot which
has become so famous in the history and romances of the
Southwest, as the " Pirate's Home," the retreat of the
dread Corsair of the Gulf, whom the genius of Byron,
and of many succeeding poets and novelists, has consecrated as one who

> " Left a corsair's name to other times,
> Linked with one virtue and a thousand crimes."

Such is poetry—such is romance. But authentic history, by which alone these sketches are guided, dissipates all these fine flights of the poet and romancer.

Jean Lafitte, the so-called Pirate and Corsair, was a
blacksmith from Bordeaux, France, who, within the
recollection of several old citizens now living in New
Orleans, kept his forge at the corner of Bourbon and St.
Phillip streets. He had an older brother, Pierre, who
was a seafaring character, and had served in the French
Navy. Neither were pirates, and Jean knew not
enough of the art of navigation to manage a jolly boat.
But he was a man of good address and appearance, of
considerable shrewdness, of generous and liberal heart,
and adventurous spirit.

Shortly after the cession of Louisiana to the United
States, a series of events occurred which made the Gulf
of Mexico the arena of the most extensive and profitable privateering. First came the war between France
and Spain, which afforded the inhabitants of the French
islands a good pretence to depredate upon the rich commerce of the Spanish possessions—the most valuable
and productive in the New World. The Gulf of Mexico and Caribbean Sea swarmed with privateers, owned

and employed by men of all nations, who obtained their
commissions (by purchase) from the French authorities
at Martinique and Guadalupe. Among these were not
a few neat and trim crafts belonging to the staid citizens
of New England, who, under the tri-color of France,
experienced no scruples in perpetrating acts which,
though not condemned by the laws of nations, in their
spirit as well as in their practical results, bear a strong
resemblance to piracy. The British capture and occupation of Guadalupe and Martinique, in 1806, in which
expeditions Col. Ed. Packenham, who will figure conspicuously in these sketches, distinguished himself, and
received a severe wound, broke up a favorite retreat of
these privateers. Shortly after this, Columbia declared
her independence of Spain, and invited to her port of
Carthagena, the patriots and adventurers of all nations,
to aid her struggle against the mother country. Thither
flocked all the privateers and buccaneers of the Gulf.
Commissions were promptly given or sold to them, to
sail under the Columbian flag, and to prey upon the
commerce of poor old Spain, who, invaded and despoiled
at home, had neither means nor spirit to defend her distant possessions.

The success of the privateers was brilliant. It is a
narrow line, at the best, which divides piracy from privateering, and it is not at all wonderful that the reckless sailors of the Gulf sometimes lost sight of it. The
shipping of other countries was, no doubt, frequently
mistaken for that of Spain. Rapid fortunes were made
in this business. Capitalists embarked their means in
equipping vessels for privateering. Of course they
were not responsible for the excesses which were com
mitted by those in their employ, nor did they trouble

themselves to inquire into all the acts of their agents, Finally, however, some attention was excited by this wholesale system of legalized pillage. The privateers found it necessary to secure some safe harbor, into which they could escape from the ships of war, where they could be sheltered from the northers, and where, too, they could establish a depot for the sale and smuggling of their spoils. It was a sagacious thought which selected the little bay or cove of Grand Terre for this purpose. It was called Barataria, and several huts and store-houses were built there, and cannon planted on the beach. Here rallied the privateers of the Gulf, with their fast-sailing schooners, armed to the teeth and manned by fierce-looking men, who wore sharp cutlasses, and might be taken anywhere for pirates, without offence. They were the desperate men of all nations, embracing as well those who had occupied respectable positions in the naval or merchant service, who were instigated to their present pursuit by the love of gain, as those who had figured in the bloody scenes of the buccaneers of the Spanish Main. Besides its inaccessibility to vessels of war, the Bay of Barataria recommended itself by another important consideration : it was near to the city of New Orleans, the mart of the growing valley of the Mississippi, and from it the lakes and bayous afforded an easy water communication, nearly to the banks of the Mississippi, within a short distance of the city. A regular organization of the privateers was established, officers were chosen, and agents appointed in New Orleans to enlist men, and negotiate the sale of goods.

Among the most active and sagacious of these town agents, was the blacksmith of St. Phillip street, who,

following the example of much greater and more pretentious men, abandoned his sledge and anvil, and
embarked in the lawless and more adventurous career of
smuggling and privateering. Gradually by his success,
enterprise, and address, Jean Lafitte obtained such
ascendancy over the lawless congregation at Barataria, that they elected him their Captain or Commander.

There is a tradition that this choice gave great dissatisfaction to some of the more warlike of the privateers,
and particularly to Gambio, a savage, grim Italian, who
did not scruple to prefer the title and character of
"Pirate," to the puling, hypocritical one of "Privateer."
But it is said, and the story is verified by an aged Italian, one of the only two survivors of the Baratarians,
now resident in Grand Terre, who rejoices in the
"*nom de guerre*," indicative of a ghastly sabre cut
across the face, of "*Nez Coupé*," that Lafitte found it
necessary to sustain his authority by some terrible example, and when one of Gambio's followers resisted his
orders, he shot him through the heart before the whole
band. Whether this story be true or not, there can be
no doubt that in the year 1813, when the association
had attained its greatest prosperity, Lafitte held undis-
puted authority and control over it. He certainly conducted his administration with energy and ability. A
large fleet of small vessels rode in the harbor, besides
others that were cruising. Their store-houses were filled
with valuable goods. Hither resorted merchants and
traders from all parts of the country, to purchase goods,
which, being cheaply obtained, could be retailed at a
large profit. A number of small vessels were employed
in transporting goods to New Orleans, through the

bayou we have described, just as oysters, fish and game are now brought.

On reaching the head of the bayou, these goods would be taken out of the boats and placed on the backs of mules—to be carried to the river banks—whence they would be ferried across into the city, at night. In the city they had many agents, who disposed of these goods. By this profitable trade, several citizens of New Orleans laid the foundations of their fortunes. But though profitable to individuals, this trade was evidently detrimental to regular and legitimate commerce, as well as to the revenue of the Federal Government. Accordingly, several efforts were made to break up the association, but the activity and influence of their city friends generally enabled them to hush up such designs.

Legal prosecutions were commenced on 7th April, 1813, against Jean and Pierre Lafitte, in the United States District Court for Louisiana, charging them with violating the Revenue and Neutrality Laws of the United States. Nothing is said about piracy—the gravest offence charged, being simply a misdemeanor. Even these charges were not sustained, for, although both the Lafittes, and many others of the Baratarians, were captured by Captain Andrew Holmes, in an expedition down the bayou, about the time of the filing of these informations against them, yet it appears they were released, and the prosecutions never came to trial, the warrants for their arrest being returned " not found." These abortive proceedings appear to have given encouragement and vigor to the operations of the Baratarians. Accordingly, we find on the 28th July, 1814, the Grand Jury of New Orleans making the following terrible exposure of the audacity and extent of these unlawful transactions :

"The Grand Jury feel it a duty they owe to society to state that piracy and smuggling, so long established and so systematically pursued by many of the inhabitants of this State, and particularly in this city and vicinity, that the Grand Jury find it difficult legally to establish facts, even where the strongest presumptions are offered.

"The Grand Jury, impressed with a belief that the evils complained of have impaired public confidence and individual credit, injured the honest fair trader, and contributed to drain our country of its specie, corrupted the morals of many poor citizens, and finally stamped disgrace on our State, deem it a duty incumbent on them, by this public presentation, again to direct the attention of the public to this serious subject, calling upon all good citizens for their most active exertions to suppress the evil, and by their pointed disapprobation of every individual who may be concerned, directly or indirectly in such practices, in some measure to remove the stain that has fallen on all classes of society in the minds of the good people of our sister States."

The Report concludes with a severe reproof of the Executive of the State, and of the United States, for neglecting the proper measures to suppress these evil practices.

The tenor of this presentment leads to the belief that the word "piracy," as used by the Grand Jury, was intended to include the more common offences of fitting out privateers within the United States, to operate against the ships of nations with which they were at peace, and that of smuggling. Certainly the grave fathers of the city would not speak of a crime, involving murder and robbery, in such mild and measured terms, as one "calculated to impair public confidence, and injure public credit, to defraud the fair dealer, to drain the country of specie, and to corrupt the morals of the people." Such language, applied to the enormous crime of piracy, would appear quite inappropriate, not to say ridiculous. It is evident from this, as well as other proofs, that the respectable citizens, several of whom now survive, who made this report, had in view the denunciation of the offence of smuggling into New Orleans, goods captured on the high seas, by privateers, which, no doubt, seriously interfered with legitimate trade, and drew off a large amount of specie.

However, indictments for piracy were found against several of the Baratarians. One against Johnness, for piracy on the Santa, a Spanish vessel, which was captured nine miles from Grand Isle, and nine thousand dollars taken from her ; also, against another, who went by the name of Johannot, for capturing another Spanish vessel with her cargo, worth thirty thousand dollars, off Trinidad. Pierre Lafitte was charged as aider and abettor in these crimes before and after the fact, as one who did, " upon land, to wit: in the city of New Orleans, within the District of Louisiana, knowingly and willingly aid, assist, procure, counsel and advise the said piracies and robberies." It is quite evident from the character of the ships captured, that had the indictments been prosecuted to a trial, they would have resulted in modifying the crime of piracy into the offence of privateering, or that of violating the Neutrality Laws of the United States, by bringing prizes taken from Spain into its territory and selling the same.

Pierre Lafitte was arrested on these indictments. An application for bail was refused, and he was incarcerated in the Calaboose, or city prison, now occupied by the Sixth District Court of New Orleans.

These transactions, betokening a vigorous determination on the part of the authorities, to break up the establishment at Barataria, Jean Lafitte proceeded to that
place and was engaged in collecting the vessels and
property of the association, with a view of departing to
some more secure retreat, when an event occurred, which
he thought would afford him an opportunity of propiti-
ating the favor of the government, and securing for
himself and his companions a pardon for their offences.

It was on the morning of the second of September,
1814, that the settlement of Barataria was aroused by
the report of cannon in the direction of the gulf. Lafitte
immediately ordered out a small boat, in which, rowed
by four of his men, he proceeded toward the mouth of
the strait. Here he perceived a brig of war, lying just
outside of the inlet, with the British colors flying at the
mast-head. As soon as Lafitte's boat was perceived,
the gig of the brig shot off from her side and approached
him.

In this gig were three officers, clad in naval uniform,
and one in the scarlet of the British army. They bore
a white signal in the bows, and a British flag in the
stern of their boat. The officers proved to be Captain
Lockyer, of his Majesty's navy, with a Lieutenant of the
same service, and Captain McWilliams, of the army.
On approaching the boat of the Baratarians, Captain
Lockyer called out his name and style, and inquired if
Mr. Lafitte was at home in the bay, as he had an important communication for him. Lafitte replied, that
the person they desired could be seen ashore, and invited
the officers to accompany him to their settlement. They
accepted the invitation, and the boats were rowed
through the strait into the Bay of Barataria. On their

way Lafitte confessed his true name and character; whereupon Captain Lockyer delivered to him a paper package. Lafitte enjoined upon the British officers to conceal the true object of their visit from his men, who might, if they suspected their design, attempt some violence against them. Despite these cautions, the Baratarians, on recognizing the uniform of the strangers, collected on the shore in a tumultuous and threatening manner, and clamored loudly for their arrest. It required all Lafitte's art, address, and influence to calm them. Finally, however, he succeeded in conducting the British to his apartments, where they were entertained in a style of elegant hospitality, which greatly surprised them.

The best wines of old Spain, the richest fruits of the West Indies, and every variety of fish and game were spread out before them, and served on the richest carved silver plate. The affable manner of Lafitte gave great zest to the enjoyment of his guests. After the repast, and when they had all smoked cigars of the finest Cuban flavor, Lafitte requested his guests to proceed to business. The package directed to " Mr. Lafitte," was then opened and the contents read. They consisted of a proclamation, addressed by Colonel Edward Nichols, in the service of his Britannic Majesty, and commander of the land forces on the coast of Florida, to the inhabitants of Louisiana, dated, Headquarters, Pensacola, 29th August, 1814; also a letter from the same, directed to Mr. Lafitte, as the commander at Barataria; also a letter from the Hon. Sir W. H. Percy, captain of the sloop of war Hermes, and commander of the Naval Forces in the Gulf of Mexico, dated September 1, 1814, to Lafitte; and one from the same captain Percy, written on 30th

8

August, on the Hermes, in the Bay of Pensacola, to Captain Lockyer of the Sophia, directing him to pro- ceed to Barataria, and attend to certain affairs there, which are fully explained.

The originals of these letters may now be seen in the records of the United States District Court in New Orleans, where they were filed by Lafitte. They con- tain the most flattering offers to Lafitte, on the part of the British officials, if he would aid them, with his vessels and men, in their contemplated invasion of the State of Louisiana. Captain Lockyer proceeded to enforce the offers by many plausible and cogent argu- ments. He stated that Lafitte, his vessels and men would be enlisted in the honorable service of the British Navy, that he would receive the rank of Captain (an offer which must have brought a smile to the face of the unnautical blacksmith of St. Philip street), and the sum of thirty thousand dollars : that being a Frenchman, proscribed and persecuted by the United States, with a brother then in prison, he should unite with the English, as the English and French were now fast friends; that a splendid prospect was now opened to him in the British navy, as from his knowledge of the Gulf Coast, he could guide them in their expedition to New Orleans, which had already started; that it was the purpose of the English Government to penetrate the upper country and act in concert with the forces in Canada; that everything was prepared to carry on the war with unusual vigor; that they were sure of success, expecting to find little or no opposition from the French and Span- ish population of Louisiana, whose interests and manners were opposed and hostile to those of the Americans; and, finally, it was declared by Captain Lockyer to be the purpose of the British to free the slaves, and arm them against the white people, who resisted their authority and progress.

Lafitte, affecting an acquiescence in these propositions, begged to be permitted to go to one of the vessels lying out in the bay to consult an old friend and associate, in whose judgment he had great confidence. Whilst he was absent, the men who had watched suspiciously the conference, many of whom were Americans, and not the less patriotic because they had a taste for privateering, proceeded to arrest the British officers, threatening to kill or deliver them up to the Americans. In the midst of this clamor and violence, Lafitte returned and immediately quieted his men, by reminding them of the laws of honor and humanity, which forbade any violence to persons who come among them with a flag of truce. He assured them that their honor and rights would be safe and sacred in his charge. He then escorted the British to their boats, and after declaring to Captain Lockyer, that he only required a few days to consider the flattering proposals, and would be ready at a certain time to deliver his final reply, took a respectful leave of his guests, and escorting them to their boat, kept them in view until they were out of reach of the men on shore.

Immediately after the departure of the British, Lafitte sat down and addressed a long letter to Mr. Blanque, a member of the House of Representatives of Louisiana, which he commenced by declaring that "though proscribed in my adopted country, I will never miss an occasion of serving her, or of proving that she has never ceased to be dear to me." He then details the circumstances of Captain Lockyer's arrival in his camp, and encloses the letters to him. He then proceeds to say: "I may have evaded the payment of duties to the Customhouse, but I have never ceased to be a good citizen, and all the offences I have committed have been forced upon me by certain vices in the laws." He then expresses the hope that the service he is enabled to render the authorities, by delivering the enclosed letters, "may obtain some amelioration of the situation of an unhappy brother," adding with considerable force and feeling, "our enemies have endeavored to work upon me, by a motive which few men would have resisted. They represented to me a brother in irons, a brother who is to me very dear, whose deliverer I might become, and I declined the proposal, well persuaded of his innocence. I am free from apprehension as to the issue of a trial, but he is sick, and not in a place where he can receive the assistance he requires." Through Mr. Blanque, Lafitte addressed a letter to Governor Claiborne, in which he stated very distinctly his position and desires. He says:

"I offer to you to restore to this State several citizens, who, perhaps, in your eyes, have lost that sacred title; I offer you them, however, such as you could wish to find them, ready to exert their utmost efforts in defence of the country. This point of Louisiana which I occupy is of great importance in the present crisis. I tender my services to defend it, and the only reward I ask is, that a stop be put to the prosecutions against me and my adherents, by an act of oblivion for all that has been done hitherto. I am the stray sheep wishing to return to the sheepfold. If you are thoroughly acquainted with the nature of my offences, I should appear to you much less guilty, and still worthy to discharge the duties of a good citizen. I have never sailed under any flag but that of the Republic of Carthagena, and my vessels are perfectly regular in that respect. If I could have brought my lawful prizes into the ports of this State, I should not have employed the illicit means that have caused me to be proscribed. Should your answer not be favorable to my ardent desires, I declare to you that I will instantly leave the country to avoid the imputation of having co-operated towards an invasion on that point, which cannot fail to take place, and to rest secure in the acquittal of my own conscience."

Upon the receipt of these letters, Governor Claiborne convoked a council of the principal officers of the army, navy and militia, then in New Orleans, to whom he submitted the letters, asking their decision on these two questions : 1st. Whether the letters were genuine ? 2d. Whether it was proper that the Governor should hold intercourse or enter into any correspondence with Mr. Lafitte and his associates ? To each of these questions a negative answer was given, Major General Villéré alone dissenting—this officer being (as well as the Governor, who, presiding in the council, could not give his opinion), not only satisfied as to the authenticity of the letters of the British officers, but believing that the Baratarians might be employed in a very effective manner in case of an invasion.

The only result of this council was to hasten the steps which had been previously commenced, to fit out an expedition to Barataria to break up Lafitte's establishment. In the meantime, the two weeks asked for by Lafitte to consider the British proposal, having expired, Captain Lockyer appeared off Grand Terre, and hovered around the inlet several days, anxiously awaiting the approach of Lafitte. At last, his patience being exhausted, and mistrusting the intentions of the Baratarians, he retired. It was about this time that the spirit of Lafitte was sorely tried by the intelligence, that the constituted authorities, whom he had supplied with such

valuable information, instead of appreciating his generous exertions in behalf of his country, were actually
equipping an expedition to destroy his establishment.
This was truly an ungrateful return for services, which
may now be justly estimated. Nor is it satisfactorily
shown that mercenary motives did not mingle with those
which prompted some of the parties engaged in this
expedition.

The rich plunder of the " Pirate's Retreat," the valuable fleet of small coasting vessels that rode in the Bay
of Barataria, the exaggerated stories of a vast amount
of treasure, heaped up in glittering piles, in dark, mysterious caves, of chests of Spanish doubloons, buried in
the sand, contributed to inflame the imagination and
avarice of some of the individuals who were active in
getting up this expedition.

A naval and land force was organized under Commodore Patterson and Colonel Ross, which proceeded to
Barataria, and with a pompous display of military
power, entered the Bay. The Baratarians at first thought
of resisting with all their means, which were considerable. They collected on the beach armed, their cannon
were placed in position, and matches were lighted, when
lo! to their amazement and dismay, the stars and stripes
became visible through the mist.

Against the power which that banner proclaimed,
they were unwilling to lift their hands. They then surrendered, a few escaping up the Bayou in small boats.
Lafitte, conformably to his pledge, on hearing of the
expedition, had gone to the German coast—as it is called
—above New Orleans. Commodore Patterson seized
all the vessels of the Baratarians, and, filling them and
his own with the rich goods found on the island, returned

to New Orleans loaded with spoils. The Baratarians, who were captured, were ironed and committed to the Calaboose. The vessels, money and stores taken in this expedition were claimed as lawful prizes by Commodore Patterson and Colonel Ross. Out of this claim grew a protracted suit, which elicited the foregoing facts, and resulted in establishing the innocence of Lafitte of all other offences but those of privateering, or employing persons to privateer against the commerce of Spain under commissions from the Republic of Columbia, and bringing his prizes to the United States, to be disposed of, contrary to the provisions of the Neutrality Act.

The charge of piracy against Lafitte, or even against the men of the association, of which he was the chief, remains to this day unsupported by a single particle of direct and positive testimony. All that was ever adduced against them, of a circumstantial or inferential character, was the discovery among the goods taken at Barataria, of some jewelry, which was identified as that of a Creole lady, who had sailed from New Orleans seven years before, and was never heard of afterwards.

Considering the many ways in which such property might have fallen into the hands of the Baratarians, it would not be just to rest so serious a charge against them on this single fact. It is not at all improbable-- though no facts of that character ever came to light-- that among so many desperate characters attached to the Baratarian organization, there were not a few who would, if the temptation were presented, " scuttle ship, or cut a throat" to advance their ends, increase their gains, or gratify a natural bloodthirstiness.

But such deeds cannot be associated with the name of Jean Lafitte, save in the idle fictions by which the taste of the youth of the country is vitiated, and history outraged and perverted. That he was more of a patriot than a pirate, that he rendered services of immense benefit to his adopted country, and should be held in respect and honor, rather than defamed and calumniated, will, we think, abundantly appear in the chapter which follows.

III.

LAFITTE, THE PATRIOT.

Though repudiated and persecuted by the authorities of the State and Federal Government, Jean Lafitte did not cease to perform his duties as a citizen, and to warn the people of the approaching invasion. The people, as is often the case, were more sagacious on this occasion than their chief officials. They confided in the representations of Lafitte, and in the authenticity of the documents forwarded by him to Gov. Claiborne. One of the first manifestations of these feelings was the convocation of an assembly of the people at the City Exchange, on St. Louis street. This was after the tenor of Lafitte's documents and the character of his developments had become known, to wit: on the 16th of December, 1814. This assembly was numerous and enthusiastic. It was eloquently addressed by Edward Livingston, who, in manly and earnest tones, and with telling appeals, urged the citizens to organize for the defence of their city, and thus, in a conspicuous manner, refute the calumnies which had been circulated against their fidelity to the new Republic, of which they had so recently become "part and parcel."

These appeals met a warm response from the people.

Nor did the enthusiasm which they excited vent itself in mere applause and noisy demonstrations. They produced practical results. A Committee of Public Safety was formed, to aid the authorities in the defence of the city and supply those deficiencies which the exigency should develop, in the organization of the Government, as well as in the characters of those charged with its administration. This committee was composed of the following citizens: Edward Livingston, Pierre Foucher, Dussau de la Croix, Benjamin Morgan, George Ogden, Dominique Bouligny, J. A. Destrehan, John Blanque, and Augustin Macarté. They were all men of note and influence.

The leading spirit of the committee was Edward Livingston, a native of New York, and once Mayor of that great city. He had emigrated to New Orleans shortly after the cession and organization of the territory. Of profound learning, various attainments, great sagacity and industry, possessing a style of earnest eloquence and admirable force, which even now render the productions of his pen the most readable of the effusions of any of the public men, who have figured largely in political or professional spheres in the United States, Edward Livingston could not but be a leading man in any community.

The talents which many years afterwards adorned some of the highest offices under the Federal Government, and reflected so much distinction on Louisiana in the United States Senate, were eminently conspicuous and serviceable in rallying the spirits, and giving confidence and harmony of action to the people of New Orleans, during the eventful epoch to which these sketches relate. He was ably supported by his associates. Destrehan was a native of France, a man of science, resolution and intelligence, though somewhat eccentric. Benjamin Morgan was one of the first and most popular of the class of American merchants, then composing a rising party in New Orleans. P. Foucher was a creole of Louisiana, of great ardor and activity in the defence of his natal soil. Dussau de la Croix, was a Frenchman of the *ancien régime*, an exile, who found in Louisiana the only sovereignty and the only soil which he deemed worth fighting for. A. Macarté was a planter of spirit, patriotism and energy. George M. Ogden was a leader of the Young America of that day, and possessed great zeal, activity, and influence among the new population. John Blanque was an intelligent, industrious and prominent member of the State Legislature. Dominique Bouligny represented the old Spanish and French colonists, who in turn had possessed Louisiana, his family being one of the oldest in the State. He was a staid, solid and true man, who afterwards filled a seat in the United States Senate, and held other offices of dignity and trust in the State.

Such was the composition of the Committee of Public Safety in New Orleans. The first act of the commitee was to send forth an address to the people. This document bears unmistakably the imprint of Edward Livingston's genius. It is a fervid and thrilling appeal, which produced, wherever it was read among the excitable population of Louisiana, the effect of a trumpet blast, rallying the people to the defence " of their sovereignty, their property, their lives, and the dearer existence of their wives and children."

There can be little doubt that this highly important movement and effective address were induced by the information supplied by Lafitte. Edward Livingston, the chief in the movement, had been the confidential adviser and counsellor of Lafitte since 1811. His intercourse with that much maligned individual had dispelled all doubts as to his honorable purposes. The date of the address, being about the time of Lafitte's retirement from Barataria, and the absence of other information of the designs of the British, whose army had not then left the Chesapeake and England, all tend to the conclusion that Lafitte's representations aroused the people to take the defence of the city into their own hands. But the value of Lafitte's intelligence did not end here. Claiborne, persevering in his reliance in the verity of the documents dispatched to him by Lafitte, sent copies of them to General Jackson, who was then stationed at Mobile, watching the movements of the Spanish and British at Pensacola.

The perusal of these letters, under the popular impression as to the character of the parties from which they were obtained, drew from the stern and ardent Jackson a fiery proclamation, in which he indignantly denounced the British, for their perfidy and baseness, and appealed in fervid language to all Louisianians, to repel "the calumnies which that vain-glorious boaster, Colonel Nichols, had proclaimed in his insiduous address." The calumnies referred to were the assertions that the creoles were crushed and oppressed by the Yankees and that they would be restored to their rightful dominion by the British. Herein we may observe the germ of that feeling which led even Jackson into some errors, and the British into the most ridiculous delusions. It was the apprehension or doubt as to the fidelity and ardor of the French settlers and creoles of Louisiana, in the defence of the State. Subsequent events will show, despite the grossest misrepresentations of ignorant or designing persons, that in no part of the United States did there exist greater hostility to the British, or a more earnest determination to resist their approach to the city, than among the descendants of that race, which had been from time immemorial England's national, if not natural enemy.

It is remarkable, that whilst making use of the information furnished by Lafitte, General Jackson indulges in the strongest language of denunciation of the " Pirates of Barataria," styling them " a hellish banditti." It would not be consistent with the acknowledged generosity and manly frankness of Jackson, as well as with subsequent events, to suppose that he knew at the time this language was used, how great a debt was due to the chief of that " hellish banditti," for the very information upon which his energetic measures were based. Though severe and violent against evil doers, and especially against those who were implicated in transactions having the aspect of cruelty, of lawless violence and oppression, Jackson was at the same time remarkable for that prompt magnanimity which would extend justice, protection and even generous forbearance to all brave and sincere, but guilty and erring men.

A striking example of these qualities of Jackson, which was given but a few months before the occurrences we are describing, and is connected with events that belong to this history, may not be inappropriately introduced in this place.

After the disastrous battle of the Horse-Shoe, the broken-spirited chiefs of the Red Sticks, who had been dispersed over the country, crept singly, or in small squads, into Jackson's headquarters, at Fort Jackson, humbly suing for his pardon and protection. The last to stoop to this degradation, was the famous half-breed chief, William Weatherford, familiarly known as "Bloody Bill." This chief was truely one of Nature's noblemen. Though uneducated, he possessed an excellent native intellect, great magnanimity of soul, clouded but not obscured by his savage education and habits. He moved with a dignified, graceful, and courtly bearing, not only in his favorite home, the forest, but even among the haunts and in the circles of the white man. His eyes were large, dark, and piercing. His proportions were symmetrical yet powerful, sinewy, and agile. He possessed those virtues which would have adorned a knight in the days of chivalry, bravery, generosity, truth and honor. His vices were those of his race, vindictive ferocity, unsparing and undying hate of the whites.

Weatherford led a thousand warriors against Fort Mimms in the summer of 1813. Falling upon the garrison, he took it by surprise, and after a gallant resistance slew the whole party, consisting of several families and a military force. It was this event which had drawn Jackson from his civil pursuits, into his first Indian campaign. The descriptions of that bloody massacre greatly excited his ardent and sympathetic nature, and no doubt gave vigor and determination to the measures employed by him to punish such atrocities.

After several fights, in which he displayed his usual courage and address, Weatherford encountered a strong force under General Claiborne, at another "Holy Ground" of the Indians, on the Alabama River, where a fierce and protracted conflict ensued. Fighting to the last, Weatherford discovered that his men had deserted him, and were passing over in the boats to the other side of the river, leaving him alone amid his enemies. As soon as he perceived his situation, he put spurs to a splendid grey charger of unsurpassed activity and fleetness, which he always rode in battle, and coursing along the bank of the Alabama, came to a ravine, where there was a perpendicular bluff, ten or fifteen feet above the surface of the river. Over this, with a mighty bound, leaped the dauntless chief, and both rider and charger sunk out of sight beneath the waves. Soon, however, they rose again, the chief grasping the mane of his horse with his left hand and firmly holding his rifle in his right. Swimming boldly forward, he gained the opposite bank of the river, and shouting a loud defiance at his foes, plunged into the forest and disappeared. This feat has given name to the bluff where it was performed, and ever since it has been known throughout Alabama, as Weatherford's Leap."

Deserted by his men, alone, amid the solitudes of nature, Weatherford roamed the forest unsubdued and undaunted. Hearing that General Jackson had offered a large reward for his capture, and that many, even of his old followers, were on his track, he resolved to go in person and surrender himself to Jackson, and thus thwart the treacherous designs of the recreant of his own race. Mounting the noble charger that had borne him over the bluff at the Holy Ground, he rode within a few miles of Fort Jackson, when, a fine deer crossing his path, and stopping within rifle distance, he fired at and killed it. Reloading his rifle with two balls, for the purpose of shooting " Big Warrior," a renegade of his own tribe, then in Jackson's camp, should he offer him any insult, he threw the deer across his horse's shoulders, and advanced to the American outposts. Some soldiers, of whom he politely inquired for Jackson's whereabouts, gave him unsatisfactory and rude replies, which sorely tried the temper of the fiery chief, when a grey-headed man, pointing him to the General's marquée, Weatherford contemptuously turned his back upon his revilers, and rode up to the tent, where, suddenly checking his horse, he discovered the treacherous Big Warrior standing before him. "Ah! Bill Weatherford," exclaimed Big Warrior, "have we got you at last." The fearless chief cast a glance of ineffable scorn at the renegade, who shrank under his keen glance, and exclaimed in a determined voice, "You base traitor, if you give me any impudence I will blow a bullet through your cowardly heart."

General Jackson, hearing the altercation and the name of Weatherford, rushed out of his tent, and in a furious and threatening manner cried out, "How dare you, sir, ride up to my tent after having murdered the women and children at Fort Mimms?" Assuming an attitude of fearless defiance, folding his arms with the resignation of a hero, Weatherford replied, "General Jackson, I am not afraid of you. I fear no man, for I am a Creek warrior. I have nothing to ask for myself. You can kill me if you desire. But I came to beg you to send for the women and children of the war party, who are starving in the woods. Their fields and cribs have been destroyed by your people, who have driven them to the woods without an ear of corn. I hope you will send parties to relieve them. I tried in vain to prevent the massacre of the women and children at Fort Mimms; I am now done fighting. The Red Sticks are nearly all killed. If I could fight you any longer, I would most heartily do so. Send for the women and children; they never did you any harm; but kill me, if the white people want it."

At the conclusion of these, words, several persons of the crowd that had gathered around the chief exclaimed, "Kill him, kill him!" Gen. Jackson commanded silence, and in an emphatic manner said, "Any one who would kill as brave a man as this in cold blood, would rob the dead!" He then invited Weatherford to alight, drank with him a glass of brandy, and entered into cheerful conversation with him under the General's marquée. Weatherford gave the General the deer, and they were ever afterwards good friends.

The magnanimity thus displayed to the chief, in one of the bloodiest Indian massacres recorded in our annals, would have revolted at the application of terms, "hellish banditti," to men, whose leader had, at such great sacrifices of personal advancement and interest supplied the information of the designs of the British against New Orleans, furnishing the key by which Jackson was enabled to arrange and prepare his unparalleled and glorious defence. Much more satisfactory is the conclusion, that Jackson was kept in ignorance of the means by which this intelligence was obtained, and knew only the fact, that propositions had been made by the British to the Baratarians, whom vulgar and prevalent report characterized as savage and blood-thirsty pirates.

Thus conspicuous and valuable were the services which Jean Lafitte rendered to the State of Louisiana.

The long agony was now over. The suspense and doubt which had agitated the whole country, were, for he first time, dissipated. The designs of the British

9

were laid bare. Their vast preparations were now understood. The point upon which they were to throw themselves with the powerful force which was now hurrying towards the West Indies, was clearly perceived. The deeply-laid scheme of the British Cabinet, by which all the disasters of the war were to be redeemed in a blaze of glory, was exposed to the world. In the confidence that secresy had been preserved, the politicians of Great Britain, at home and on the Continent, boldly proclaimed the conquest and occupation of New Orleans as *fait accompli*. " I expect at this moment," remarked Lord Castlereagh, at Paris, about the middle of December, 1814, "that most of the large seaport towns of America are by this time laid in ashes; that we are in possession of New Orleans, and have command of all the rivers of the Mississippi valley and the Lakes, and that the Americans are now little better than prisoners in their own country."

It has been asserted by British writers that the secret of the expedition transpired through the carelessness and blundering of one of their own naval officers, who communicated the tenor of his instructions to a Jew trader, whilst a portion of the fleet lay off the West Indies. This is the English story—but it is an error. Before the fleet arrived near Jamaica, Lafitte had transmitted the documents already referred to, which developed the design of the British on New Orleans, and led to the measures which were set on foot for its defence. Had Lafitte assented to the proposals of the British authorities, and permitted them to occupy his port at Barataria, giving them the use of his fleet of small vessels, they would have been able to transport their army with rapidity and ease to the Mississippi River, at a point above New Orleans. Thus having the means of cutting off reinforcements and supplies from the West, the capture of the city would have been inevitable. By examining the map of Louisiana, it will be seen that there is no easier access to the city from the Gulf, than through the Bay and Bayou of Barataria, a circumstance which has induced the General Government to expend so large a sum on the fortifications at Grand Terre, that command the entrance of the Bay.

Let the truth then be now told! Time scatters the mist of prejudice and passion, and patient inquiry dissipates the gaudy and ingenious web of poetry and romance. In truthful history Jean Lafitte must ever occupy a conspicuous position among the gallant spirits of 1814 and 1815, for the brilliancy and efficiency of the services which he rendered his adopted country, whose authorities destroyed his fortune, blasted his prospects, and handed his name down to posterity as that of a blood-thirsty corsair and outlaw, the hero of numerous fictions, written to inflame youthful imaginations and satisfy a morbid appetite for scenes of blood, of murder, of reckless daring, and lawless outrage. A name which he had, by such honorable self abnegation, hoped to redeem from all dishonor, and connect with conspicuous and patriotic services, became the favorite *nom de guerre* of every desperate adventurer and roving corsair of the Gulf.

Less cruel was that terrific Norther which, a few years after the events we have described, when misfortune had crushed his spirit, bowed his manly form, dimmed the lustre of that eye, that once possessed such power "to threaten or command," and sprinkled with premature snows those raven locks that once gave so

much effect to his handsome face—more merciful,
indeed, was that resistless hurricane which, sweeping
over the Gulf in the fall of 1817, struck the little
schooner, laden with all that remained of the once
princely fortune of Jean Lafitte, which he was bearing
to some distant land, where the odious epithet of pirate
would not follow him—where he might end his days in
peace and contentment. Amid the shrieks of the storm-
bird, the roar of the elements, the crash of thunder, and
the screams for mercy of erring men, Jean Lafitte, with
all his worldly goods, found in a watery tomb, that
oblivion and rest which were denied to him in this life.
Peace to his soul! Justice to his memory!

Barataria, once so busy a scene, where roystering
freebooters held their noisy wassail, where sharp-eyed
peddlers were wont to gather as to a fair, to purchase
great bargains from traders more skillful in handling a
pike and cutlass than in higgling over silks and jewelry;
and where, not unfrequently, might be seen some of the
chief men of New Orleans, who, from the profits of their
transactions with the unsophisticated but very successful
privateers, became millionaires in full time to repent of
their early irregularities, and establish for themselves
high reputations, as punctilious merchants and law-
abiding citizens; where floated a gallant little fleet of
fast sailers, trim, arrow-like craft, armed to the teeth,
and ready for any emergency; where, on the low coast,
quite a formidable battery of cannon stood ready to
defend the valuable stores, and to dispute the passage
through the narrow strait by which New Orleans could
be reached in the shortest distance from the Gulf of
Mexico, the scene of all this life, jollity, and lawless
adventure, is now one of the most solitary, dreary, and

desolate along the whole low, flat coast of the Gulf of Mexico. Barataria, no longer a doubtful or disputed territory, has long since passed from the possession of the freebooter into that of the republic of the United States, which now proclaims and enforces its title by a powerful fortification, that completely commands the entrance of the bay, from whose ramparts the eye, following the winding strait, can discern the quiet little cove, now restored to its original desolation and solitude, and the dreary, storm-beaten shore, where a few dark mounds and crumbling heaps afford the only vestiges of the brief but brilliant reign of Jean Lafitte, the blacksmith of St. Philip street, New Orleans, miscalled the Pirate of the Gulf of Mexico.

IV.

It was in the middle of September, 1814, when Jackson learned definitely the design of the British against New Orleans. Before he could leave for that scene of operations, it was necessary to ascertain what was the object of the several British ships that were hovering about the Gulf coast, as well as of the preparations that were going on at Pensacola, with the connivance of the Spanish authorities. It was quite evident that the British had selected this important post as the base of their operations. In the summer of 1814, the brig Orpheus, under the command of the Hon. Sir W. H. Percy, a youthful officer, who inherited the courage and enterprise of his ancestors—immortalized in the fine old ballad of "Chevy Chase"—landed at Apalachicola, and dispatched several officers to intrigue with the neighboring Choctaws, with a view of obtaining their aid in operations against Fort Bowyer. As far as promises and assurances would go, these intrigues were quite successful. The Choctaws are a cunning tribe, who prefer the money, the blankets, the gew-gaws and whisky of the whites, to all the scalps, trophies and glories of war.

Shortly after the arrival of the Hermes, two British sloops of war appeared in the same waters. These sloops had on board a small land force, intended as the nucleus of an army, to be augmented by additions from the Spanish and Indian populations of the country. These were under the command of Col. Nichols, an Irishman by birth, and an officer of much daring, activity and energy, but of blustering manners, of quick and violent temper, and unscrupulous character.

On his way to the Florida coast, Nichols stopped at Havana and endeavored to persuade the Captain-General to coöperate with the means and force of that colony, in the enterprise against Louisiana and Florida. But the cautious Spaniard was not to be enticed into such a perilous adventure. Nichols then proceeded to Pensacola, landed his force without asking leave of the authorities, and commenced organizing an expedition to march into the interior. The Indians were invited to come in and join the party. Runners were sent in every direction to collect and conduct them to Pensacola. There, they were supplied with arms and uniforms, and drilled according to the civilized mode of warfare. Grotesque and ludicrous in the extreme, was the appearance of these untutored savages, as they paraded the streets of the quaint old town of Pensacola, arrayed in the gaudy scarlet uniforms of the British army.

Almost the first act of Nichols, after arriving at Pensacola, was to dispatch Captain Lochkyer to Barataria, for the purpose of obtaining the aid of Lafitte and his men, and particularly of his invaluable small craft, so necessary in coast operations. The result of that mission has already been related. Meantime

Nichols continued to organize and strengthen his motley command at Pensacola.

The conduct of the Spanish authorities, in conniving at and permitting such an organization within their territory and against the United States, naturally excited much indignation throughout the Union. General Jackson had been sent specially to prevent and punish such violations of neutrality and good faith. He had full authority to call upon the neighboring States for troops. His call upon Louisiana was promptly responded to, and Governor Claiborne held all the available force of the State ready to march to Jackson's aid. But the timely approach of the indefatigable and unfailing Coffee with his mounted gunmen, together with several detachments of regular troops then in the territory, supplied Jackson with a force sufficient to check any movements of the British from that quarter, and to put a stop to the proceedings at Pensacola. His keen eye, in surveying the coast, quickly discovered that a great error had been committed in the evacuation of Fort Bowyer, a point, from which the British would be exposed to much annoyance in any operations in the Lakes and along the Gulf coast. This fort not only commanded the entrance into Mobile Bay and the navigation of the rivers which empty into it, but also the passes of the Lakes on the west side. The fort stood at the extremity of the tongue or isthmus extending between Lake Borgne and Bon Secour, or mouth of the Mobile Bay. To this fort, Jackson sent Major Lawrence, of the regular army, with one hundred and thirty men, including officers and twenty pieces of cannon. By great exertions, the fort was placed in a situation to make a vigorous defence, in time for the arrival of the British fleet, whose commander, seeing the importance of the point, hastened to attack it.

On the evening of the 12th September, 1814, the outpost sentinel of the fort descried a dark, confused mass of men coming over the low beach from the Lake Borgne side of the isthmus. It was nightfall, and the party having halted, bivouacked on the beach. The next day, as soon as it was light, they advanced in battle array against the fort. It was quite a formidable force. There were about two hundred Indian warriors, who had acquired some experience and familiarity with warlike operations, in the recently concluded campaigns of Jackson; most of them disguised in British jackets, bearing awkwardly heavy muskets, and wearing swords that dangled between their naked legs, and tripped them up on the sand. They came towards the fort in one long, straggling line—their flanks being supported by compact lines of British marines. Permitting them to approach within good range, Major Lawrence suddenly opened upon them with a few well-directed discharges of grape, which soon drove them howling and screaming, like wild beasts, foiled of their prey, beyond the reach of his guns.

In the meantime the British squadron approached the fort in front. This was a more serious affair. Major Lawrence assembled his men, and called on them to join in a solemn oath, not to surrender the fort. The spirit of his gallant namesake prevailed in that heroic band—"Don't give up the fort," was the oath and motto of the garrison.

The British ships were four in number. The Hermes, 28; the Charon, 28; Sophia, 18; Anaconda, 16; all thirty-twos, making an effective battery of ninety guns, manned by six hundred sailors and marines. These ships approached within musket range of the fort, and casting anchor, opened a tremendous fire upon it. At the same time, their land forces having thrown up a battery within seven hundred yards of the fort, commenced firing from that direction. Major Lawrence returned both fires with great vigor. For some time the cannonade was maintained on both sides with the greatest fury, the fort and ships being completely enveloped in smoke. The American batteries, though managed by infantry, were more effective than the British. Soon the flag of the Hermes was shot away. Major Lawrence, with the chivalric consideration of a true soldier, suspended his firing. The Hermes having restored her flag again poured her broadsides into the little fort with redoubled fury. The reply of the fort was equally earnest. At last the cable of the Hermes was cut, and her situation became very critical. Struck by the current, she was borne towards the fort, and her bows presented to its cannon, which raked her decks fore and aft. Soon she drifted ashore, when her commander, Captain Percy, setting fire to her, abandoned the wreck and escaped aboard the Charon. About this time the flag of the fort was shot away, and whilst Major Lawrence was fastening it to a sponge-rod to elevate it again, the British force on land rushed towards the fort, thinking it had surrendered. A few discharges of grape, however, from the fort, soon sent them back again in double-quick time. The other vessels were then, with difficulty, hauled off, and finally, the enterprise was abandoned by the British.

with a loss of one hundred and sixty-two killed and seventy-two wounded. Major Lawrence lost four killed and four wounded.

Never was there a more poignant disappointment than that which prevailed at Pensacola among the Spaniards and British, when the result of this expedition was known. The Spaniards had been excited by the hope of reclaiming the valuable territory which the Americans had snatched from them four years before. The Indians had been enticed, by the prospect of revenge, of bloodshed and rapine. The British confidently hoped to secure the key to their future grand designs against the Southwest. But in place of these splendid results, behold their fleet, creeping in such crippled state slowly into Pensacola, with signs of defeat and disaster, that might move the pity of their enemies. Their noble commander's laurels have shrivelled, and the lofty pride of the Percys suffered an abasement, which must indeed have sent a bitter pang to the heart of the aristocratic young sailor, whose once gallant ship now lay a smouldering wreck on the dreary coast of Bon Secour.

The feelings of the impetuous Irishman, who was the soul and author of this enterprise, may be better imagined than described. To the mental chagrin of defeat in a cherished undertaking, Colonel Nichols had the misfortune, on this occasion, to add the agony of a severe and painful wound received in the action.

Major Lawrence and his gallant associates well deserved the thanks which Jackson, in his own, and in the name of the Republic, conveyed to them as the heroes of one of the most gallant but least noticed affairs of the war of 1812.

Jackson now began to chafe with impatience at the long delays in the approach of the troops, for which he had for some months before issued his requisitions. He perceived very clearly the plan of the British. The "Pirate's" information was now confirmed. It was quite evident that the attack on Fort Bowyer was a feeler, a preliminary step to the occupation of a more important place, the only considerable town in the Southwest. New Orleans was the game for which they were "beating the bush." Jackson soon disseminated this conviction. The news flew through the country, not with electric fleetness, but as rapidly as the imperfect communications of that period would permit, that New Orleans was to be attacked—*that* New Orleans, for the possession of which, the population in the Mississippi valley had struggled so long, even to the point of threatening to dissolve the Union and involving the nation in war, rather than permit so important a depot of their trade to remain in the hands of another Power. The city, which was destined to become the second in commerce in the Union, the metropolis and capital of the great empire of the Mississippi valley, whither the vast and various population of this great region would resort for trade, pleasure, information—was not to be yielded up on any consideration or at any sacrifice.

All depended on the West. The South was too weak in resources and population, to offer a prompt and effective resistance to the invader. The Government at Washington, so incapable in its own immediate neighborhood, had neither the energy, nor the means to afford any prompt aid in defence of so remote a settlement. President Madison's "inability to view scenes of carnage with composure," to which Jackson ascribed that sad disgrace at Bladensburg and Washington, had quite unnerved him ever since the destruction of the Capitol by a British force one-fourth as large as that which was reported to be on its way towards New Orleans. In place of men and munitions, the Government sent Jackson to create both. Thus it redeemed the most criminal neglect.

The occasion had brought forward the man. Undaunted, whilst the whole country was filled with the gloomiest forebodings, Jackson commenced his preparations to receive the enemy. He sent forth proclamations, full of ardent patriotism and inspiring energy, to the people of the South and West, entreating them to leave their peaceful homes, their families, and their civil duties, and hasten to the point where the honor of the Republic was threatened. No class of citizens was omitted in these rallying appeals. Even the colored freemen of Louisiana, so generally excluded from political rights and duties, were invited to co-operate with their white brethren in the defence of a common country.

Before leaving Mobile to commence his personal superintendence of the defence of New Orleans, Jackson determined to rid that quarter of an annoyance from which he might experience some embarrassment in his future operations. We refer to the proceedings at Pensacola, where the hostile British and Indians found constant aid and encouragement from the faithless Spaniards. The opportune arrival of some new levies from Tennessee, together with detachments of regular troops, a troop of Mississippi dragoons, amounting in all to four thousand effective men, supplied him with an efficient force, which he immediately set in motion, and after a long and wearisome march, appeared suddenly before Pensacola.

After some negotiations conducted through Major Peire—a gallant and high-toned young officer—a native of New Orleans, the Spaniards refusing to accede to demands which were equally just, and necessary to their own security and the preservation of their neutrality, Jackson pushed his column into the town, carrying a Spanish fort which opened upon him, at the point of the bayonet, with the loss of eleven killed and wounded. The Governor then sent a flag of truce and hostilities ceased. But the commander of Fort St. Michael, refusing to surrender that post, Major Peire was directed with eight hundred men to take it, Jackson, at the same time, withdrawing the greater part of his force from the town, under the fire of the English ships anchored in the harbor. The commandant of the fort, after much equivocation and delay, at last surrendered to Major Peire just as that officer was forming his storming party.

The moderation and good conduct of the Americans soon reconciled the Spaniards to the vigorous measures which Jackson had employed against them. Jackson next advanced against Fort Barancas, on the other side of the bay, but seeing his approach, the Spaniards blew it up, and retreated to the British ships, which shortly after weighed anchor, and dropped over the bar.

It was in this attack on Pensacola, that two of the most gallant of Jackson's young officers were grievously wounded. The forlorn hope in this attack was composed of the company of Captain Laval, of the Third Regiment. Laval was a South Carolinian. His father had been an officer in the French service, who came over to

America in the legion of the Duke of Lauzun in the war of independence.

Calling upon his men to follow, Capt. Laval rushed forward at the head of his company, through a tempest of grape and round shot, until he reached the foot of the Spanish battery, when a large grape shot tore his .eg to pieces, and he fell apparently lifeless to the ground At the same moment Lieutenant Flournoy lost his leg, and fell by the side of Captain Laval. Both these gallant men survived their injuries, and are now living in robust health and vigor.

Captain Laval, who resides in Charleston, after filling the offices of Secretary of State of South Carolina, Controller General, Assistant Treasurer of the United States, is now the Treasurer of his native State, universally respected for his many virtues, and admired for his manly bearing and striking military appearance.

Lieutenant Flournoy, now Dr. Flournoy, is a highly respectable citizen of Louisiana, residing in the parish of Caddo.

By these vigorous measures, Jackson relieved himself of all trouble and annoyance in this quarter. Establishing garrisons in Pensacola, he marched the greater part of his force back to Mobile. From this point he dispatched all his disposable troops to New Orleans, and then left for this scene of his more trying and important duties.

The State authorities of Louisiana had not been idle. Governor Claiborne, having convened the Legislature on the 5th October, 1814, called their attention to the impending invasion, and to the duty and necessity of meeting it in a vigorous and effective manner. The Legislature proceeded to business, but under most dis-

couraging auspices. The members were divided into
several factions. The most trivial disputes engrossed
their minds. By one party the Governor was so cor-
dially hated, that the members, in the manifestation of
their hostility, did not perceive, or did not care, that
their conduct was communicating discouragement and
discord to the people. There was no union or harmony
of action; no confidence in one another, or between
officials, under the same Government. Besides, there
was the prejudice and jealousy of races. The Americans distrusted the loyalty of the Creoles, and the Creoles
could not believe that the new settlers would risk their
lives for the defence of the soil whereon they had so
recently "pitched their tents."

Both distrusted the foreign population, though it contributed some of the boldest and most efficient of the
city's defenders. Prominent in this class were the Irish
and French emigrants, all of whom, then residing in
the city, and capable of bearing arms, came forward
promptly and determinedly to fight for their adopted
country, and for freedom, against their hereditary
oppressor and enemy.

Seeing their chiefs and leaders thus divided, the people
grew alarmed, distrustful, and despairing. They complained of the Legislature; the Legislature complained
of the Governor; the Governor complained of both the
Legislature and the people. Time and money were
consumed in these idle disputations, and in the discussion of various schemes of defence, concocted by " rising
politicians," smart lawyers, enterprising merchants, and
pretentious planters. There was neither money nor
credit in the city. The country had been drained of
its specie. New Orleans being exclusively an exporting

city, ceased to possess any resources when its foreign commerce was cut off. The banks had suspended payment; small notes were put in circulation; and dollars cut in pieces to make small change. Capitalists and merchants hoarded their means. All kinds of arms and munitions of war were scarce.

Indeed, never was a city so defenceless, so exposed, so weak, so prostrate, as New Orleans in the fall of 1814. There was not sufficient time to obtain aid from the West. There was no naval force in the port or the adjacent waters; not a regiment of armed men in the city. The resources of the whole State were scarcely adequate to the production and organization of two militia regiments. The population of the city was a new and mixed one, composed of people of all nations and races, who had been too recently admitted into the Union to feel that strong attachment for the government and flag, which characterizes an old and homogeneous community. Besides, there was a vast amount of valuable property, merchandise and produce accumulated in the storehouses, which would be in danger of destruction in case of an attempt to repel the invader. To save his property, would be a strong inducement to a surrender and capitulation of the city. Few, indeed, were here who could look these perils and difficulties in the face, and entertain the idea of a serious defence of the city against any well-organized and well-conducted expedition.

It was at this gloomy moment Jackson arrived. He was worn down by fatigue, anxiety and sickness. That most distressing and enervating of all the diseases of the soldier, the dysentery, had left him scarcely the strength to stand erect or sit upon his horse. He came

10

to the city with no display of power; with no loud pro-
testations, brilliant promises or extravagant boasts. And
yet his presence in New Orleans was like that of " an
army with banners ;" his name was " a host;" his words
communicated confidence and hope to all. The stories
of his gallantry, his invincibility, his heroic resolution
and Spartan fortitude, were familiar as household ditties
to the people of New Orleans. No wonder, then, their
spirits rallied and their courage grew strong, when the
electric words flew through the city and its faubourgs—
" Jackson has come !" The people were now thoroughly aroused to a sense of their duty. A resolute
determination to defend the city to the last pervaded all
classes. Jackson did not permit their ardor to cool.
He proceeded to organize the military force of the
city, which at that time consisted of two small militia
regiments, and a weak but gallant battalion of
uniformed volunteers, commanded by Major Planché, a
firm, sedate, gallant creole, who now lives in New
Orleans, respected and honored by all his fellow citizens.
This corps was composed chiefly of young creoles, who
were full of military ardor and courage. The companies were variously uniformed, and highly disciplined
and trained. They marched with the port and precision
of regular soldiers to the music of a fine band.

    This battalion had been formed about a month before
the arrival of Jackson. It originated with the company
of " *Carabiniers d'Orleans*," the first independent volunteer corps organized in New Orleans after the cession
of Louisiana to the United States, which had already
been in existence, under the command of Captain
Planché, for two years, when it was proposed, in view
of the threatening aspect of affairs, to form other com

panies, in numbers sufficient to make a battalion. Accordingly, four other companies were organized, under the respective names of "Hulans," or Foot Dragoons, under captain St. Geme; "Francs," Captain Hudry; "Louisiana Blues," Captain Maunsel White; "Chasseurs," Captain Guibert. The rank and file of the battalion amounted to three hundred and eighty-five men. Captain Planché was elected Major on the 15th December, and Captain Roche succeeded him in the command of the Carabiniers.

Forty years and more have now elapsed since this gallant *corps d'élite* of citizen soldiers was formed. Death has not spared its ranks; still there linger in our midst, not a few of these veterans, who were the first to illustrate and stimulate that military ardor, which has ever distinguished New Orleans above all other communities; and which, thirty-four years after, enabled a city of one hundred thousand inhabitants to contribute in a few weeks, six fine regiments of volunteers, who abandoned homes and families, to march to a distant and foreign land, to defend the flag and sustain the arms of the Republic.

The names of the men of the bataillon d'Orleans who still survive, deserve to be mentioned in sketches, that aim to revive and invigorate the gratitude and veneration, in which the present generation should hold those whose gallant bearing gave so much courage and confidence to the population of New Orleans in its day of trial and peril. Those names are as follows: J. B. Planché, major; Maunsel White, captain of the Louisiana Blues; E. J. Forstall, corporal; Tricou, Borcas, Pelerin, Pedesclaux, P. Lanaux, P. DeBuys, W. DeBuys, Garidel, H. McCall, Vincent Nolte, Carabiniers. A. Fernandez, Fauchet, musicians. Of the Hulans there

are but three survivors—Correjoles, Duplantier, and
Barnet.   Of the Francs there are also three living,
C. Toledano, R. Toledano, P. D. Henry.   Of the Louisiana Blues, besides their captain, Messrs. John Hagan
and H. W. Palfrey survive.   The latter is now the Brigadier General commanding the Louisiana Legion, a large
military force composed of several battalions, of which
the Carabiniers of 1814 was the origin.   Of the Chasseurs the survivors are J. R. Lepretre, Lamothe fils,
S. Cyr, G. Montamat, C. W. Duhy, S. M. Lapice, S. Pey-
rouse, L. Ferranderie, Meunier, M. Melleur and Bournos,
making in all thirty-six.

Jackson called together all the engineers in New
Orleans, to obtain the necessary information in regard
to the topography of the city, and consult about the
defences.   He saw at a glance, that the city could be
approached by various large bayous, which, starting
near the Mississippi, flow into the gulf or the numerous
bays that indent the Gulf shore.   By his order, Governor
Claiborne caused the mouths of the principal of these
bayous to be filled up with earth and trees.   Next,
Jackson visited all the forts in the neighborhood of the
city, ordered them to be strengthened, and new forts
and fortifications to be established at various points.
He gave special attention to strengthening and rendering impregnable Fort St. Philip, below the city, and
occupying a most favorable position to prevent the
passage up the river of ships of war.

And now the people of New Orleans breathed freely
and slept soundly.   They had neither armies nor navies,
but they had the bold heart, the strong mind, and the
unconquerable spirit of a Jackson—to defend their
firesides, and they felt secure, confident and courageous.

V.

THE BRITISH REVIEW AND EMBARKATION.

ABOUT the first of September, 1814, there was a great stir and commotion in the good old seaport town of Plymouth, England. Everybody was on the *qui vive*. The streets thronged with people, elate with the excitement of some public festivity, and dressed for some gala occasion. All was life, happiness and enjoyment. All the clouds that had lowered upon the island were now dissipated by the treaty of Paris. The dread Napoleon was playing Emperor on the island of Elba. The Continental war had ceased to be the "thought by day and dream by night" of the pacific and commercial classes, who composed the majority of the population of Great Britain. There was only one speck on the horizon of England's happiness, and that was too distant to excite any serious apprehensions, or interrupt the general contentment.

The enthusiasm and excitement, which had aroused the usually staid and lethargic population of Plymouth, on the present occasion, were due to the expected review of one of the finest regiments in the British service,—a regiment which did not return, as so many others had straggled into Plymouth, shattered and démoralized, broken in body, spirit, and soul—ghastly remnants of

the fierce struggles that had destroyed the constitutions
and moral control of so many men, who might otherwise have proved useful members of society, but by the
ambition of monarchs or ministers, were converted either
into crippled invalids or reckless vagabonds.

Not in this condition did the Ninety-third Highlanders return to Plymouth, from their long and peaceful
sojourn at the Cape of Good Hope. Their history, their
long absence—the reputation of the regiment for moral-
ity and even piety, had surrounded the Ninety-third
with more than usual interest and *éclat*, in the view of
the Plymouth people. This regiment was the junior
Highland corps of the service, having been organized
by General Wemyss, in 1803. The men were chiefly
enlisted in Ross and Sutherland counties of Scotland.
Hence they were usually styled the Sutherland Highlanders. In 1811 the numerical strength of the regiment, including non-commissioned officers, was one
thousand and fifty men, of whom one thousand were
Scotch, seventeen were Irish, and eighteen English.
The uniform of the regiment was very rich and showy,
being of a bright tartan with kilts, high caps trimmed
with yellow and red. The men were of the most stalwart proportions, having been recruited with particular
reference to size, height and youth. On account of the
admirable discipline and moral character of this regiment, it was kept on home service until 1805, when, for
the first time, the pibroch was played at its head, and
the Ninety-third was mustered into the Expedition
against the Cape of Good Hope, under Major General
Sir David Baird. In this enterprise the Ninety-third
was greatly distinguished. After the capture and occupation of the Cape, the regiment remained there in

garrison until 1814, when it embarked for England. During its long sojourn at this remote station, the Ninety-third continued in excellent condition, its discipline and moral tone being admirably preserved. As an evidence of this, we may cite the remarkable fact, that in the Light Infantry company, which is composed usually of the youngest, most reckless and volatile of the regiment, no man was punished for eighteen years. A strong feeling of piety pervaded the regiment; the charity and thrift of the men were strikingly illustrated by the fact that during their sojourn at the Cape they were in the habit of sending considerable sums of money home for charitable and religious purposes.

The review of such a regiment could not but be interesting to a people not much accustomed to military display. The Prince of Orange, with a splendid staff, had come down from London to attend this review. The parade was brilliant and impressive. The Ninety-third was out in all its strength, over a thousand rank and file. The men, habited in bran new tartans, with bright muskets, waving banners, and the pipers sending forth their wildest and most warlike strains, presented a most exciting martial spectacle. When formed in line to receive the Prince of Orange and staff, the broad breasts, wide shoulders, and stalwart figures of the Highlanders gave their front a more extended and formidable aspect, than even the strength and number of the regiment appeared to justify.

Never did a commander regard his men with more pride than the gallant Colonel Dale did his splendid corps, nor were a people ever more pleased and delighted with a military display than were the good citizens of Plymouth with this parade of soldiers, who were

no less remarkable for their orderly habits than for their
fine military condition and appearance, who presented
to them the novel anomaly in the British army, of
peaceable and sober soldiers. The review passed off
very pleasantly, and a ball and other festivities concluded the gaieties of the day. The report to the Horse
Guards of the review and inspection of the Ninety-
third, represented that there was no regiment in his
Majesty's service in such effective and complete condition.

But was this a mere holiday display and parade? So
the people thought, so they desired, for the English were
heartily sick of war and military glory. So, too, thought
the Highlanders, though they had long panted for an
opportunity of showing that they were as brave in action
and efficient in war, as they were sober and orderly in
peace. But no opportunity seemed open to them.
England was at peace with all the world, except the
United States, and the hostilities with the latter power
were believed to be hastening to a close. Commissioners
of the two nations were then engaged in discussing and
arranging the terms of a peace and settlement.

It was not many days after the review we have
described, that a large fleet of ships-of-war and transports sailed into the port of Plymouth. Soon the news
flew through the town that these vessels were to be
employed in some highly important secret expedition.
Various were the surmises and conjectures as to the
object of such expedition, few of which, we imagine,
approached the truth. That it was a serious affair, was
soon confirmed by the fact of the Ninety-third receiving
marching orders, and proceeding on board the transports. Here they were joined by fragments of other

corps, by six companies of the 95th Rifles, of the famous Rifle brigade, which, under Crauford and Barnard had participated so largely in the glories of the Peninsular war, with detachments of artillery, sappers and rocketers, and a squadron of dragoons of the 14th. This force, it was soon known was placed under the command of Major General John Keane, a young, gallant and ambitious officer, of approved courage and experience.

Keane was a native of the North of Ireland, and entered the army very young. Of an active temperament, full of enterprise and devotion to his profession, he rose rapidly in rank. In the expedition to Egypt, under Sir Ralph Abercrombie, Keane, who was then a subaltern, obtained the high praise of his superior officer. He was next attached to the Sicilian army, under Sir William Bentinck and Sir John Murray, and in the expedition to Catalonia against Suchet. He soon rose to the command of a brigade, to which was attached that celebrated fighting regiment, the 27th, or Enniskillins. Though the conclusion of the operations in this quarter was disastrous, it was from no want of gallantry or hard fighting on the part of the troops engaged. The chief brunt of the fighting fell on the 27th. Nobly did that gallant corps bear up against the splendidly-disciplined and admirably-managed columns of that accomplished soldier, Marshall Suchet, the most successful of Napoleon's Lieutenants in the Peninsular war. To show the spirit and ardent gallantry of the Enniskillins, the following incidents may not be uninteresting.

Previous to this first encounter with the Enniskillins, it happened that a wag of an Irishman, who had been taken prisoner by the French, enjoyed some free conversations with the Marshal, in the course of which he intimated that the Irish were strongly hostile to the British, and only awaited a good excuse and a fair opportunity to go over to the French. Suchet bit at the bait. Accordingly, on the first occasion of meeting the Enniskillins in battle, he directed several officers to advance in front, and cry out at the top of their voices, " Vive Irelandois !" at the same time, extending the hand of friendship and fraternity. Keane, discovering at a glance the purpose of the French, formed the regiment into a hollow, and ordered it to assume a resting position. The French, deceived by the attitude of the Enniskillins, pushed forward enthusiastically to the very centre of the line, giving the wildest demonstrations of joy and delight over the fraternization with such formidable foes. Suddenly Keane roared the order, " Charge them Enniskillins, charge ! charge !" when the whole line dashed forward like a drove of famished wolves, and firing one volley into the thick columns of the French, sprung at them with their bayonets and made fearful havoc in their ranks.

It was the same regiment which, on another occasion, was drawn up to receive the charge of the enemy, when a tall grenadier officer stepped out of the French ranks, and challenged to mortal combat any officer of the 27th. The challenge was eagerly accepted by Captain Waldron, who advanced half-way to the front, and meeting the boastful Frenchman, crossed swords, and, after a few passes, clove his head in twain. Then the Enniskillins raised a loud, wild shout of exultation, and rushed upon the French with irresistible fury. Such were some of the antecedents of the associates and companions in arms of an officer who is destined to figure conspicuously in these sketches, to whom was entrusted the command of the expedition which was organized at Plymouth in the fall of 1814.

When the fleet weighed anchor, and set sail from Plymouth on the 18th September, 1814, there were not three in the hundreds composing the expedition, who were cognizant of its object and design. The prevalent idea was, that they were proceeding to join Gen. Ross in America, Keane having been designated as the second in command to that gallant and enterprising officer.

About this time, the little army of Gen. Ross, which had executed one of the most daring expeditions of modern times, found itself under the necessity of with-drawing from the further prosecution of its designs against Baltimore. The wanton excesses, and barbarous outrages, the vandalic destruction of unoffending buildings devoted to scientific and civil uses, and even of monuments erected to commemorate the triumph of American valor over the native tribes of Barbary, have so sullied and disgraced the character of this expedition, that its merits, in a military point of view, have never been appreciated. The death of Ross, and the subsequent disasters of his army, have prevented even English writers from doing justice to the daring, bold-ness, and effectiveness of that gallant dash of four thousand men into the very heart of a nation of eight or ten millions—capturing and destroying their Capitol, and slowly retiring, bearing away a large quantity of spoils, and encamping in the midst of a country which swarmed with partisan soldiery, composed of men who were personally as brave as any in the world, but whose leaders and chiefs were mainly of that class which is so justly the subject of burlesque, ridicule and distrust— militia officers—a class made up chiefly of saddlebag

lawyers—the keepers of cross-roads groceries, and ex-
pectant members of Congress, who are elected in time
of peace pretty much on the principle embodied in the
celebrated sarcasm of Pitt, in his amendment to the
proposition that the militia of Great Britain should never
be ordered out of the country, "except," Pitt added,
"in case of invasion." It was by the gross and palpable inefficiency of the superior officers, and of the Government, and the absence of a leader, that those stains
were inflicted upon our national escutcheon, which
could only be obliterated by the heroic valor of a Jackson, and expiated by the bloody sacrifice on the Plains
of Chalmette!

The merit, and but little of the infamy of the expedition to Washington, were due to General Ross. He
was a very gallant and successful officer, who possessed,
to a remarkable degree, the confidence of his superiors
and inferiors in the army. In the Peninsular war, he
was distinguished for his activity, daring and steadiness.
No man could hold a column of men better in hand,
and manœuvre them with more coolness under fire.
Besides his military qualities, Ross was a generous,
high-toned and kind-hearted gentleman. His soul revolted at the outrages which his Government had
commanded him to inflict on the Americans, and he
cheerfully transferred to that willing and fit instrument,
in deeds of barbarism and atrocity, Admiral Cockburn,
the direction of that desolation, by which the British
Ministry had commanded him to mark his course, along
the sparsely settled and undefended shores of Virginia
and Maryland.

The circumstances of Ross' death were very impressive, and to the British disheartening. He was advanc-

ing upon Baltimore, along the banks of the Petapsco, with the same army, somewhat augmented in strength and numbers, with which he had fought at Bladensburg and captured Washington, when his advance and flanking companies became engaged with some of the light infantry of the brigade of the American General Stryker. Capt. Aisquith, of the Baltimore Sharp-Shooters, a corps which still exists in that city, so famous for the efficiency and brilliancy of its volunteer military, had been thrown forward by Stryker to reconnoitre on the very road which Ross was pursuing. The Sharp-Shooters having scattered in small squads on either side of the road, became engaged with the British flank patrols, and quite a brisk firing ensued.

Ross immediately rode to the front to observe the character of the attack, and had reached the most advanced party of his skirmishers, accompanied by his aid, Major McDougal, when suddenly, as they reached the top of a slight hill in the road, two of Aisquith's Sharp-Shooters, H. G. McComas and Daniel Wells, appeared before them, and coolly levelling their rifles, fired at the British, Ross was struck in the side and fell into the arms of his aid, who lifted the wounded General from his horse and laid him under a tree by the side of the road. The General's horse, released from restraint, galloped wildly to the rear, carrying in his terrified aspect and blood-stained saddle the sad tidings to the British troops, who pressed forward in quick time, full of apprehension and grief. As soon as they perceived their General fall, the British skirmishers rushed to the front and avenged his death by killing the two Sharp Shooters,—who met their fate like men, and were over-whelmed by superior numbers whilst gallantly fighting.

They were honest, patriotic mechanics of Baltimore,— a class of men who give such efficiency to the Volunteer corps of the United States. The grateful citizens of the "monumental city" have erected a handsome monument commemorative of the defence of the city, on which are inscribed the names of the two heroic volunteers, who thus fell, after avenging upon the British leader, the indignities and barbarous outrage committed by the army under his command. Their exploit was a gallant and daring one. Subsequent events will show how important it was in its consequences.

There on the same road, separated by a distance of two hundred yards, lay the bodies of the British General who had fallen in an expedition to lay waste the country and destroy the lives of a free people, who had done him or his nation no wrong,—and those of his destroyers who had risked and lost their lives in defence of their honor and the honor of their country. The British soldiers, as they passed the corpse of their dead General, uttered many a deep groan of real sorrow; whilst the bodies of the gallant American mechanics were spurned and cursed, as if they had not, but a few moments before, been the tenements of nobler souls and higher virtues, than even those which were embodied in their gallant young chief, now a gory corpse, a sad sacrifice to Moloch.

The British were greatly disheartened by the loss of their chief. He left no officer who could fill his place in the hearts and confidence of the army. Colonel Brook, of the Fourth, a gallant man and good commander of a battalion, but unused to the direction and control of a large force, succeeded to the command. After a pretty severe action with a detachment of the

Americans, and some slight successes, the British Commander discovered that the further advance of his army was rendered impracticable, and having consulted with Sir Alexander Cochrane, Commander of the Squadron, he determined to withdraw the army to the fleet. This was done in such good order and with so much secrecy, that before the Americans could learn anything of their movements, they had gained their fleet and disappeared from the coast, which they had kept for several weeks in a state of continual terror and distress. Whither had they gone? For what purpose had they come? It appeared, certainly, to be a wild, reckless, thoughtless enterprise, thus to penetrate the very centre of a nation of nine millions of people, with four thousand troops, who, during the greater part of their operations, were cut off from communication with their squadron. What glory, what advantages, what political objects could be gained by such an enterprise?

The idea that it was prompted by a mere spirit of revenge, by a reckless purpose of inflicting an indignity upon a hostile nation, would not comport with the practical judgment and good sense, which, more than passion or a love of military glory, usually characterize the plans and orders of the British Government. Subsequent events will afford the key of this expedition, and show that the attacks upon Washington and Baltimore were mere diversions—blinds for a more important and apparently more practicable design.

James, in his naval history of Great Britain, says: "In our account of the unfortunate demonstration before the city of Baltimore, we mentioned as one cause of the abandonment of the enterprise and the tepidness with which it had been conducted, an ulterior object in the view of the Naval Commander-in-Chief. That ulterior object was the city of New Orleans, the capital of the State of Louisiana."* Confirmatory of this view, we may mention the fact, that the force which left Plymouth on the 18th of September, under General Keane, em‑barked about the same time the British were retiring to the fleet from before Baltimore, for the same rendez‑vous for which the squadron, having Brook's command on board, shaped its sails.

The attack on Baltimore was no doubt prompted by the hope of capturing, in that port, a large number of small vessels, for which Sir Alexander Cochrane had great need in the execution of his "ulterior design." This effort was gallantly and effectively thwarted by the vigorous defence of North Point and Fort McHenry.

The fleet with Brooks' army sailed out of the Chesa‑peake on the 4th of October, 1814. Giving out that he was bound for Halifax, Sir Alexander Cochrane in the Tonnant, and with the greater part of the squadron, set sail in a northern direction. His real purpose was to effect a junction with the squadron, which was bearing Keane's command from England. Meantime, the ships having on board the army of the Chesapeake, proceeded in a Southern course towards Jamaica.

This army was composed of very choice troops. There was the Fourth, or "King's Own," a very gal‑lant and distinguished regiment; the Forty-fourth, which had borne itself with great steadiness in Egypt, and in some of the most trying scenes of the Peninsular War; the Eighty-fifth, a light-infantry regiment, com‑manded by one of the most distinguished light-infantry

---

* James' Naval History of Great Britain, vol. 7, page 355.

officers in the British service, Col. Wm. Thornton, who won more laurels and received more wounds, in the British operations in the South than any other officer in the army, and who, at the time the army sailed out of the Chesapeake, was suffering from a severe wound received at the battle of Bladensburg.

The Fourth, Forty-fourth, and Eighty-fifth, having passed through the Peninsular campaign, embarked at Bordeaux on the 2d of June, 1814, for America, and touching at Bermuda, were joined by the Twenty-first, the North British Fusileers. These, with a battalion of marines and a strong body of artillerists and sappers and miners constituted the army, which Ross led against Washington and Baltimore, the remains of which sailed for the West Indies in the beginning of October, 1814.

The squadron arrived safely at Jamaica, and not many days after, the troops were joined by those which had been sent from Plymouth.

The tropical sun shone upon a brilliant and animated scene in the bay of Negril, in the island of Jamaica, on 24th November, 1814. That was the day appointed for a general review of the troops and ships, which Great Britain had so mysteriously assembled in this remote quarter of the globe. It was a grand display of naval and military power. Two large squadrons had been combined—those of Cochrane and Malcolm. The bay was crowded with every description of sailing craft, from huge three-deckers to little pinnaces. Rarely, if ever, has Great Britain collected a braver or more powerful fleet. It was commanded, too, by chiefs, whose valor had built up for England those impregnable wooden walls which enabled her to defy the conqueror of Europe. An enumeration of this fleet will confirm

11

our estimate of its strength, and serve to rescue from oblivion, one of the series of proofs of the great importance attached to the expedition, in which it was employed, and of the gigantic preparations by which the British Ministry had nearly justified the confident boast of Castelreagh.

The following are the names of the ships, the number of their guns, and their commanders, which rendezvoused at Negril bay, under Sir Alexander Cochrane, on the 24th November, 1814.

Tonnant, 80 guns, Vice-Admiral Sir Alexander Cochrane, Rear-Admiral Sir Edward Codrington, Captain Kerr; Royal Oak, 74 guns, Rear-Admiral Malcolm, Captain Wroot; Norge, 74 guns, Captain Dashford; Bedford, 74 guns, Captain Walker; Ramilies, 74 guns, Sir Thomas Hardy; Asia, 74 guns, Captain Skeens; Dictator, 56 guns, Captain Crofton; Diomede, 50 guns, Captain Kippen; Gorgon (s. s.), 44 guns, Captain R. B. Bowden; Annide, 33 guns, Sir Thomas Trowbridge; Seahorse, 35 guns, Captain James Alexander Gordon; Belle Poule, 38 guns, Captain Baker; Traave, 38 guns, Captain Money; Wever, 38 guns, Captain Sullivan; Alceste, 38 guns, Captain Lawrence; Hydra, 38 guns, Captain Dezey; Fox, 36 guns, Captain Willock; Cadmus, 36 guns, Captain Langford; Thames, 32 guns, Captain Hon. C. L. Irby; Dover, 32 guns, Captain Rogers; Bucephalus, 32 guns, Captain D'Aith; Calliope, 16 guns, Captain Codd; Anaconda, 16 guns, Westphall; Borer, 14 guns, Raulins; Manly, 14 guns, Loche; Meteor (bomb), 6 guns, Roberts; Volcano (bomb), 6 guns, Price; Ætna (bomb), 16 guns, Gardner; Pigmy, schooner, 6 guns, Jackson; Jane (cutter), Speedwell, schooner.

There were also the following transports : Norfolk, Golden Fleece, Thames, Diana, Woodman, Active, Cyrus, Elizabeth, Kah, Daniel Woodruffe, and George. Such was the squadron which, by great diligence, Sir Alexander Cochrane had collected to desolate the shores of America. It consisted of at least fifty sail, carrying more than a thousand guns. The officers of the squadrons were the very *élite* of the British navy. Associated with the silver-haired veterans, Vice-Admiral Cochrane, and Rear-Admiral Malcolm, were several officers who had achieved world-wide reputations. Among these was Sir Thomas Hardy, in whose arms Nelson died at Trafalgar, and to whom he addressed those remarkable words— " Kiss me, Hardy ; I die content ;" Sir Thomas Trowbridge, an officer who had displayed great ability and gallantry in many brilliant actions ; Captain (afterwards Sir) James Alexander Gordon, a cork-leg, sturdy sailor, who, with his famous frigate, the Sea-horse, is even now remembered with awe and terror on the banks of the Potomac, for his daring and skill. Rear-Admiral Codrington, then regarded as the most promising officer in the British navy, who, though in the meridian of life, had reached the high post of Rear-Admiral, and afterwards became famous as the commander of the allied fleet at Navarino—an affair too inglorious in its aims and motives to reflect any distinction upon those engaged in it.

But as, after all, the chief duty and responsibility of the expedition devolved upon the army, we must endeavor to be as exact as possible in the enumeration of its force.

The following returns, as published in the English and Jamaica journals of the day, and, in some cases, obtained from the muster-rolls, exhibit in round numbers the strength of the British army in this enterprise.

The army of the Chesapeake counted as follows:

4th Regiment Foot, Colonel Brook,	600
21st Royal North British Fusiliers, Lieut. Colonel Patterson,	800
85th Buck Volunteers, Light Infantry, Col. Wm. Thornton,	600
44th East Essex Foot, Lieut. Colonel Hon. Thos. Mullens,	600
Artillery, Sappers and Miners, &c.	500
Total,	3,100

The reinforcements brought by Gen. Keane were as follows:

93d Highlanders, Lieut. Colonel Dale,	1,000
6 Companies of 95th Rifles, Major Mitchell,	600
1st West India Regiment, Lieut. Colonel Whitby,	800
5th West India Regiment, Lieut. Colonel Hamilton,	800
14th Duchess of York's Light Dragoons, Colonel Baker,	390
Artillery, Rocket Brigade, Sappers, Engineers, &c.	800
Total,	4,350
Grand total of Keane's army,	7,450

To this considerable force the squadron were able to contribute at least fifteen hundred marines and sailors, who could do good service on land.

On the 26th of November, 1814, the squadron, having on board this large and well-appointed army, sailed out of Negril Bay, and directed its course towards the Gulf of Mexico.

The news of the gathering of ships and troops at Negril Bay had reached the United States shortly after the departure of the fleet. Its destination was generally believed to be the Gulf of Mexico. The intelligence furnished by Lafitte was the chief reliance for this belief. That the design had been kept very quiet and secret is satisfactorily shown by the brief period of time elapsing between the departure of Cochrane's squadron and the commencement of Gen. Jackson's defensive preparations. When Jackson reached New Orleans, the British fleet had completed half of the voyage to the Gulf coast, and only four days thereafter the Tonnant, the Vice Admiral's flag-ship, was reported off the coast of Florida.

Never did a fleet and army proceed towards their destination with higher hopes and in better spirits than the British expedition for New Orleans. So confident were they of success that a full set of civil officers to conduct the government of the Territory accompanied the army. There was also a government editor and printing press, to expound the policy and publish the orders and proceedings of the new government. There were many merchant ships in the squadron, which had been chartered expressly to bear away the rich spoil that was expected to reward their capture and occupation of the city. It was indeed regarded an expedition to occupy, rather than invade a defenceless country, as a pleasure party and speculative adventure more than a serious warlike enterprise. Hence the festivity and high-hearted jollity which enlivened the crowded decks of the British war vessels and transports, as they moved majestically over the calm water of the Gulf.

Music, dancing, and even dramatic entertainments, aided by the wives of the officers, who in considerable numbers accompanied the expedition, varied the monotony of the voyage, whose termination was looked forward to as an appropriate conclusion of the prevail-

ing gaiety, as a grand national jubilee when the banner
of old England would be planted on the soil which
France, Spain, and the United States had been unable
to hold and defend, and when her gallant soldiers, the
hardy and scarred veterans of the Peninsula, might rest
from their long fatigues and perils, and revel in the
wealth, luxury, and abundance of the Queen City of
" the sunny South."

Among the fair participants in these festivities and
hopes was the noble and accomplished lady of an officer
commanding a veteran and distinguished regiment in
the expedition, the Hon. Mrs. Mullens, who abandoned
the luxuries and comforts of an aristocratic home to
share the glory and trials of her husband. The object
of such devotion will surely prove worthy of it, and
bear his part nobly in the coming struggle. There, too,
in that gay and hopeful crowd were the buxom daughters, five in number, of one of the civil officials of the
conquered colony, who had vacated a profitable office in
Bermuda to try his fortunes in a new country, where
his daughters might display their charms in a new
sphere, in which females of the Saxon style of beauty
and accomplishments were too rare not to be highly
admired and appreciated.

Such were some of the hopes of that gay and sanguine
expedition.

VI.

BATTLE OF LAKE BORGNE.

A FIERCE storm on the 9th of December, 1814, greeted the first appearance of the British fleet off the coast of the Gulf of Mexico. To minds less buoyant and confident, than those of the sanguine and hitherto irresistible veterans of that gallant array of naval and military power, this occurrence might have appeared as an evil augury. Soon, however, the storm lulled, the clouds passed quickly away, and the bright sun came forth to cheer the hearts of the crowded crews. A favorable wind bears the squadron rapidly onward, in the direction of the entrance of Lake Borgne. The huge Tonnant, the same which was captured at Abouquir in Nelson's great fight, after the gallant Dupetit Thouars had flooded her decks with his noble blood, flowing from a dozen wounds,* now commanded by the white-haired British Vice-Admiral, and the gallant Sea-horse, with her cork-legged Captain, lead the van. Behind follow the long train of every variety of sailing craft, from the

---

* Lamartine has an appalling description of this tragedy, he says; "Captain Dupetit Thouars commanding the Tonnant never slackened his fire for a moment at sight of this disaster (the burning of L'Orient.) He no longer fought for glory or life, but for immortality. One arm carried off by a cannon shot, both legs broken by grape, he called upon his crew to swear never to strike his flags and to throw his body overboard, that even his remains might not become captive to the British."

great ships of war, with their frowning batteries, to the little trim sloops and schooners of fifteen or twenty tons, designed to penetrate the bays and inlets of the coast. The pilots, who have accompanied the fleets from the West Indies, have announced that land is not far off, and all parties are on deck, eagerly straining their eyes for a view of the desired shore. There, in the distance, they soon discover a long, shining, white line, which sparkles in the sun like an island of fire. Presently it becomes more distinct and substantial, and the man at the look-out proclaims "land ahead." The leading ships approach as near as is prudent, and their crews, especially the land troops, experience no little disappointment at the bleak and forbidding aspect of Dauphine island, with its long, sandy beach, its dreary, stunted pines, and the entire absence of any vestige of settlement or cultivation. Turning to the west, the fleet avoids the island, and proceeds towards a favorable anchorage in the direction of the Chandeleur islands, the wind in the meantime having chopped around, and blowing too strong from the shore to justify an attempt to enter the lake at night.

As the Tonnant and Sea-horse pass near to Dauphine Island, the attention of the Vice-Admiral is called to two small vessels, lying within the island, near the shore. They are neat little craft, sloop-rigged, and evidently armed. They appear to be watching the movements of the British ships, and when the latter take a western course, they weigh anchor and follow in the same direction. At night-fall the signal "to anchor" is made from the Tonnant, and the order is quickly obeyed by all the vessels in the squadron.

The suspicious little sloops, as if in apprehension of a

night attack of boats, then press all sail and proceed in the direction of Biloxi Bay. They prove to be the United States gun-boats No. 23, Lieutenant McKeever, (now Commodore McKeever), No. 163, Sailing-Master Ulrick, which had been detached from the squadron of Lieutenant T. Ap Catesby Jones (now Commodore Jones), who had been sent by Commodore Patterson, with six gun-boats, one tender, and a dispatch-boat, to watch and report the approach of the British. In case their fleet succeeded in entering the lake, he was to be prepared to cut off their barges and prevent the landing of troops. If hard pressed by a superior force, his orders were to fall back upon a mud fort, the Petites Coquilles, near the mouth of the Rigolets, and shelter his vessels under its guns.

The two boats which had attracted the notice of the British Vice-Admiral, joined the others of the squadron that night near Biloxi. The next day, the 10th of December, at dawn, as soon as the fog cleared off, Jones was amazed to observe the deep water between Ship and Cat Islands, where the current flows, crowded with ships and vessels of every calibre and description. The Tonnant having anchored off the Chandeleurs, the Sea-horse was now the foremost ship. Jones immediately made for Pass Christian with his little fleet, where he anchored, and quietly awaited the approach of the British vessels.

In compact and regular order, the fleet moved slowly through the passage between Cat and Ship Islands, and along the east coast of the former island, presenting, under a bright sun and cloudless sky, a most impressive marine panorama. Soon, however, the soundings warned the British that they were getting into shallow water,

and the line-of-battle ships came to anchor. They were
now, however, safe within American waters, in Lake
Borgne; and preparations were actively commenced to
relieve the ships of the impatient and restless mass of
belligerent mortality with which they were crowded.
The troops were therefore embarked on the transports
and smaller vessels. Before, however, the landing could
be attempted, it was necessary to clear the lake of the
agile and well-managed little boats, which hovered in
their front, and appeared ready to pounce down on any
smaller craft that might trust themselves too far from
the shelter of the batteries of the ships of the line.

Vice-Admiral Cochrane, who directed all the movements relating to the landing of the troops, proceeded
to organize an expedition of barges to attack and destroy
the gun-boats. The command of this enterprise was
confided to Capt. Lockyer, who was presumed to be
better acquainted with the coast than any other officer,
and is the same person, with whom Lafitte had an interview on the second of September, 1814. Captain Lockyer had also commanded one of the sloops in the attack
of Fort Bowyer, and, no doubt, panted for an opportunity of wiping from the escutcheon of the British Navy
the disgrace of that defeat. All the launches, barges
and pinnaces of the fleet were collected together. The
barges had been made expressly for this expedition, and
were nearly as large as Jones' gun-boats, each carrying
eighty men. To these were added the gigs of the Tonnant and Sea-horse. There were forty launches, mounting each one carronade 12, 18 or 24 calibre; one launch,
with one long brass pounder; another with a brass nine-
pounder; and three gigs, with small arms. There were,
therefore, in all, forty-five boats and forty-two cannon,

manned by a thousand sailors and marines, picked from the crews of the ships.

Captain Lockyer was ably seconded in the organiza· tion and direction of this formidable fleet by his subor· dinates, Montressor, of the Manly, and Roberts, of the Meteor, both veteran and experienced officers.

On the evening of the 12th the flotilla moved in beautiful order, from the anchorage of the squadron near Ship Island, in the direction of Pass Christian. It consisted of three divisions under the three officers named. Gallantly, and in perfect line, these divisions advanced along the white shores of the Mississippi territory for a distance of thirty-six miles, the boats being rowed by the hardy sailors, without resting.

When morning broke on the 13th, the flotilla had arrived near the Bay of St. Louis, whither three of the barges were detached, to capture the small schooner Sea-horse, which Jones had sent into the bay, for the purpose of removing some stores deposited there.

As soon as the barges came within range of her guns, the Sea-horse opened upon them a well-directed and effective fire. At the same time two six pounders, placed in battery on the shore, followed up the discharge of the Sea-horse, and striking the barges, wounded several of the men. The barges then drew off towards the main body of the flotilla, when, thinking they had retired for reinforcements, and apprehending a renewal of the attack by the whole force of Lockyer, the captain of the Sea-horse blew her up, and set fire to the stores on shore, which were entirely destroyed.

But the British commander had no idea of diverting his energies from the serious task before him. The staunch little gun-boats lay just ahead in battle array, as if inviting rather than avoiding the combat.

It is due, however, to Jones' reputation as a good officer, to add, that he had attempted to obey Patterson's order, and fall back to the fort at Petit Coquilles. In vain he tried to beat into the Rigolets, against the strong current of that strait. Finally, his vessels were carried into the narrow channel between Malheureux Island and Point Clear on the main land.

There they became unmanageable, several of the vessels sticking fast in the mud. Then Jones resolved to bide the issue of a fight.

At daylight on the 14th, the flotilla could be seen at anchor nine miles off. The men were refreshing themselves after their severe rowing. Jones called aboard of his flag-ship, a little sloop of eighty tons, all the officers of his Lilliputian squadron, and addressing them in the style of a blunt, sturdy sailor, gave them their several commands, and prepared for a vigorous resistance. His officers were all young men, full of courage, vigor, and activity. His orders were to form with their boats a close line abreast across the channel, anchored by the stern, with springs on their cables. At a given signal they were to open upon the enemy with their long guns, and when the barges closed upon them, they were to ply their musketry with all their activity.

The squadron consisted of the following gun-boats: No. 5, with five guns and thirty-six men, commanded by sailing-master, John D. Ferris; gun-boat No. 23, with five guns and thirty-nine men, under Lieutenant (now commodore) Isaac McKeever; gun-boat, No. 156, with five guns and forty-one men, under Lieutenant commanding T. Ap Catesby Jones; gun-boat No. 162, with five guns and thirty-five men, under Lieutenant Robert Spedden; gun-boat No. 163, with three guns and thirty-one men, under Sailing-Master Ulrick—total, five gun-boats, twenty-three guns, and one hundred and eighty-two men. This was certainly a small force to repel the powerful flotilla which was bearing down upon them.

The morning was bright, cool and bracing. There was not a breath of air to stir the surface of the placid lake. The men in the British flotilla took their breakfast as gaily and pleasantly as if it were a sportive occasion, and then stood to their arms. The flotilla approached with all the precision of soldiers in line; Jones' gunners fixed their eyes steadily upon the imposing array of bristling barges, measuring coolly the distance, in order to ascertain when they might come in range of their long guns. Just as the Americans are about to level their pieces, the flotilla comes to a grapnel, and appears to be deliberating on the expediency of attacking so determined a little squadron. A division of the barges is now detached from the main line of the flotilla, and bears towards the west. The object of this movement is understood in Jones' fleet, when a little white speck is discerned in the distance, which soon assumes the shape of a small fishing-smack. This proves to be the Alligator, a little tender, armed with a four-pounder and eight men, under sailing-master, Richard S. Sheppard.

The Alligator was making every effort to join Jones' squadron, to take part in the approaching combat, but the wind had lulled and she could make no progress.

Lockyer detached four boats, with nearly two hundred men, under Captain Roberts, to capture this formidable *ship-of-war*, with her eight sailors and toy-gun. It is due to the British Navy to state that they succeeded in effecting this object without much loss. Roberts returned to the flotilla in triumph with his *splendid prize*, and was received with three loud cheers. The stout sailor could not, however, suppress a smile when he boarded his capture, and ascertained her force and metal. Perhaps, under all the circumstances, Captain Lockyer may be excused for the slight exaggeration, in his description of this little cockle-shell "as an armed sloop." But it is due to history to state, that this high-sounding designation has been conferred on Commodore Porter's old gig !

Somewhat animated by this little achievement, Lockyer ordered his men to refresh themselves with a hearty meal, adding an extra allowance of Jamaica rum, to increase their appetite for the feast and the fray which was to follow. At half-past ten the flotilla weighed anchor, and bore down upon Jones' squadron in open order, forming a line abreast, extending nearly from the main land to the Malheureux Island. The appearance of the flotilla, as the barges with unbroken front swept rapidly and boldly forward—the six oars on each side dipping in the water with the regularity of clock-work, and glittering in the sunbeams as they rose and fell—the red shirts of the sailors, the shining muskets of the marines, and the formidable carronades which protruded so threateningly from the bows of the barges, constituted an impressive spectacle, one well calculated to try the nerves of that heroic band which stood on the decks of those little sloops, with lighted matches and muskets cocked, ready to meet quadruple their numbers in deadly combat.

So calm and quiet was the aspect of Jones' fleet, that the British believed they were about to surrender without essaying so vain a resistance against an overpowering force. But they were soon aroused from this delusion by the booming of McKeever's thirty-two pounder, and a shower of grape-shot that carried destruction among the flotilla, and seriously disturbed their line. With amazing rapidity this gun continued her fire, and presently the other guns of Jones' fleet joined in. The barges, though evidently crippled and damaged by this heavy fire, pushed steadily forward, and began a lively response with their carronades. A brisk firing was continued for some time ; but Lockyer soon perceived that in such a contest the gun-boats had the advantage, and, accordingly, he ordered the barges to close in and board.

Owing to the force of the current and the unmanageable state of the boats, Jones' and Ulrick's vessels (156 and 163) had been borne out of line one hundred yards in advance of the others—Jones' boat was a little ahead. Captain Lockyer seeing this, determined to attack the boats in detail. Breaking his flotilla into three divisions, he pressed forward with the advance, composed of four barges and two gigs, against the flag-boat. He was met by a most destructive volley of grape and musketry. Every shot appeared to take effect. Two of the barges were capsized, and the men were barely saved from drowning by clinging to their sides until others could come up and rescue them. Nearly all the men on board these barges were killed or wounded. Undismayed by this awful scene of destruction, four other barges pushed forward and renewed the attack, and getting near Jones' boat, poured upon her decks an incessant fire of musketry.

Jones, standing on the deck exposed to this fire, determined to sell his life as dearly as possible, and singling out the officer who in the captain's gig appeared to be the most active in inciting the British sailors and marines discharged his pistol at him, and the Briton fell mortally wounded in the arms of the sailors. This officer was Lieutenant Pratt, the first of the Sea-horse, the same who under the orders of Admiral Cockburn, burnt the Capitol and other buildings, at Washington, in the summer of 1814.

The British sought immediate revenge for the fall of their gallant young officer, and a dozen muskets were brought to bear upon Jones at once, several balls passed through his clothes and cap,—but one struck him in the shoulder, where it has remained ever since.

The wound was so painful that he could not stand up under it, and he was dragged below by his men, crying out, however, to Parker, his second in command, "Keep up the fight, keep up the fight, keep up the fight." Parker shouted, "Aye! aye!" but the words had hardly escaped his lips, when he was shot down, and the British now closing upon the little boat, clambered up her sides, and appeared on her deck in such overwhelming force as to render further resistance vain. In accomplishing this feat, however, they had suffered most grievously. Lockyer had received three wounds, all severe ; and poor Lieutenant George Pratt, was fairly riddled with balls, yet he continued to fight to the last. The fighting on No. 156 was now over ; but, strange to say, the stars and stripes still continued to wave at her mast-head, and so remained until the fighting was over in the other boats. Perhaps, considering the heavy loss they had sustained for so small a capture, the British did not think they were entitled to lower the American flag. Indeed, their commander was too sorely wounded, and in too great pain, to think of any further action after he had gained the decks of the flag-boat, upon reaching which he fainted from loss of blood, and was taken below and laid by the side of his gallant antagonist.

Meantime, the guns of Jones' boats were turned upon the others, under the direction of Lieutenant Tatnall, a gallant and enterprising officer—the same who had been captured by the French in a bloody naval contest a few years before—who, escaping from a French prison in the guise of a monk, reached the sea-shore of France, and, in a small open boat, joined the English fleet in the channel.

At the same time, Captain Montressor, with his division of barges, closed upon Ulrick's boat. They were held at bay for some time, but being reinforced by the other division under Roberts, soon succeeded in overpowering the little vessel. The guns of these two boats were then concentrated upon the other gun-boats, and particularly upon the nearest one, under Lieutenant Robert Spedden; but that gallant young officer undaunted by the disasters, which had overtaken his companions, returned this fire with an alacrity and vigor, which drove the barges to take shelter behind the two boats that had been captured. Here, combining and arranging their forces into one powerful division, Montressor and Roberts again threw themselves upon Spedden's little craft, with more than a dozen barges, filled with several hundred sailors and marines. Though sur-

12

rounded, the little gun-boat did not yield, but showered her iron hail upon the crowded barges with most destructive vigor. A grape-shot had shattered Spedden's left arm at the elbow. Regardless of his wounds, the brave young sailor held his post, giving orders to his men, and cheering them with his words, and with a countenance in which gallantry and heroism conquered the agony of a painful wound. Occupying an exposed and conspicuous position on the deck of the boat, Spedden became the target of the British marines for their musket exercise. He noted particularly one fellow in the bow of the nearest barge, aiming at him with the coolness and precision of a sportsman shooting a pigeon. He was a good marksman, and lodged a musket-ball in Spedden's shoulder which deprived him of the use of his right arm.

He was thus left without the use of either arm. Mutilated and covered with blood,—his men rapidly falling around him (the other boats being in the hands of the enemy), this gallant young man did not yield until, overpowered by numbers, he was forced below by the. British, who rushed upon deck and took possession of the boat. The guns of the captured boats were next turned upon Ferris's boat, No. 5, with such effect as to dismount her most effective weapon, a twenty-four pounder; and, after this, the barges encountered but little difficulty in boarding and capturing her. Meantime, McKeever, on No. 23, kept up a brisk fire on the barges with his thirty-two pounders. But the guns of the other boats were all turned upon him, and further resistance became vain—so he surrendered at half-past twelve P.M.

Thus closed this very remarkable and gallant action.

It was maintained by both parties for three hours, with great courage and activity. Both did their duty faithfully. The British, though numerically and in metal vastly superior to the Americans, were in open boats, exposed to a heavy fire for some time, without the ability to return it with effect. They certainly displayed great gallantry and determination in advancing against such a fire as Jones opened upon them. But the Americans, too, labored under great disadvantages. Owing to the state of the tide and wind, Jones's boat having become detached from the others, the British were able to concentrate upon it a powerful force, and its capture rendered that of the others inevitable. The gun-boats could thus be attacked in detail. It was, therefore, really, when the close fighting commenced, a combat between one or two gun-boats of ten guns and less than a hundred men, and some twenty-five or thirty barges, with more than six hundred men. The other boats, in the meantime, could not take part in the fight when the barges closed upon their companions, as they could not use their guns. Having captured two of the gun-boats, the British could turn their own guns on the remaining ones, which lay entirely at their mercy.

The results will show how severe and gallant an action it was. The Americans lost, in killed and wounded, about one-third their number. Among the wounded were Jones, Spedden, McKeever and Parker. The British loss was much more severe. Thirteen British ships of war were represented in the ghastly heap of killed and wounded that were strewn upon the decks of the gun-boats, after this severe action. Of these, three midshipmen, thirteen seamen, and one marine were reported dead; and one captain, four lieutenants, one lieutenant of marines, three master-mates, seven mid-shipmen, fifty seamen, and eleven marines were wounded. Many of the wounded died before they got to the squadron, and not a few were killed and wounded who did not figure in the returns.

It would not be extravagant to estimate the number of those in the British flotilla, placed *hors de combat* in this action, as fully equal to the whole number of Americans engaged. Of the officers, Captain Lockyer was very badly wounded in several places—not, as has been frequently stated, in a hand-to-hand fight, on the deck of Jones' flag-boat, but in attempting to bring his barge alongside. Lieutenant George Pratt, second of the frigate Sea-horse, who was in the same boat with Lockyer, was shot down by his side several times, in attempting to board the gun-boat. Lieutenant Tatnall, of the Tonnant, had his boat sunk, and, rescuing himself and his men, succeeded in getting into another barge. Lieutenant Roberts, also of the Tonnant, was wounded in closing with the gun-boats. Besides these, there were ten midshipmen killed and wounded. These results show that the victory of the British was a costly one. There was not much rejoicing and exultation over it. The groans and cries of the wounded were the prevalent notes in that melancholy squadron, as it returned to the anchorage of the British fleet.

And yet their victory was one of great value and importance. It not only cleared the Lake of all enemies, but supplied Sir Alexander Cochrane, with a very important addition to his fleet of smaller vessels, so much needed in effecting a landing of the army. It was late in the afternoon when the barges and gun-boats returned to Ship Island. On their appearance they were loudly

cheered by the sailors and soldiers on the ships; but
they were too much wearied and oppressed by the severity of their loss, to give more than a feeble and faint
response. It was more like a wail than a cheer. The
wounded were removed to a large store-ship, the Gorgon, where the Americans were attended by the same
surgeons who ministered to the British. Jones and Spedden being very severely wounded, were confined in the
cabin for many weary days. Though all that skill and
kindness could accomplish was done for them, their condition was one of nervous anxiety and painful apprehension for the fate of the city, for whose defence they had
so gallantly fought. From the port-holes of the hospital
ship they could perceive the movements going on in the
fleet around them, the arrival and dispatch of troops,
the hum and buzz of preparations for the disembark-
ation. The agony of their wounds was dreadfully increased by the reflection that the city had no means of
defence—-that it must inevitably fall into the hands of
their powerful foe. They had not heard of the arrival
of any troops there. Jackson had not reached the city
when their little fleet left the port to watch the entrance
of the Lake. Nothing, it seemed to them, but a miracle
could save New Orleans.

The officers of the British fleet were kind and con-
siderate to their unfortunate and gallant foes, but even
they could not conceal their exultation, their confidence
in the complete success of the expedition, and of the
measures referring to their comfort and enjoyment,
which were to follow that event.

Among other incidents, illustrative of the confidence
of the British, and full of painful interest to the wounded
prisoners, was the introduction to them of the future

collector of the revenue of his Britannic Majesty in the
Port of New Orleans, in the person of a tall and gentle-
manly individual, who conversed freely with the Americans respecting his future arrangements for the discharge of his duties.   How these painful feelings of the
young American sailors fluctuated and varied with
every indication of the occurrences, which, unknown to
them, were transpiring on the main land—how eagerly
they hearkened to the distant roar of artillery, kept up
continuously for fourteen days—with what agonizing
suspense they observed boats returning to the fleet with
wounded men, and reloading with fresh recruits from
the ships, including the greater part even of the common sailors, and with large cannon taken from the decks
of the ships of war—how they were struck with the
silent and changed expression of the British officers,
who gave their orders in sharp, angry, anxious tones;
and how, at last, their pains grew lighter, their wounds
were forgotten, the groans and dying sighs of those
around them were unheeded, when the gloomy portents
and signs in the English fleet began to proclaim more
emphatically than words could, the astounding and glorious result; and how, despite wounds, debility, and the
presence of their enemies, these gallant sailors could
not, even in that awful place, surrounded by the dead
and dying, suppress the involuntary cheer of joyful
exultation over these proofs of the triumph of American
valor; and how, then, with a smile on his face, the gallant Spedden submitted cheerfully to the terrible operation of amputation of his arm; and the heroic Jones
could regard with pride, rather than sorrow, the mutila-
tion of the same member, are transitions, whose intensity
can be better imagined than described, which have been

rarely equalled in dramatic effect, by any of the realities of history, or the creations of poetry.

As soon as intelligence of the capture of the gallant tars was received in New Orleans, Mr. Shields, a purser in the Navy, and Dr. Morrell, were dispatched by Commodore Patterson, with a flag of truce to the British fleet at Cat Island, for the purpose of affording to the wounded prisoners such comforts and necessaries as their situation might demand. On their arrival off Cat Island, they were received by Vice-Admiral Cochrane, and were told that their visit was a very inopportune one, and he should be compelled to detain them. They protested against such conduct, as contrary to the laws of nations; as they came under a flag of truce, and merely to relieve the sufferings of their unfortunate fellow-citizens, who had been wounded. Their protest was disregarded, and they were assigned a room in the cabin of the flag-ship, where they were closely guarded. Suspecting from the interrogatories of the British Commander, that every word which fell from them would be eagerly caught up and reported to the Vice-Admiral, Shields and Morrell in their conversations never failed to dwell on the powerful force which Jackson had collected to defend the city, or the myriads of Western riflemen that were flocking to his standard, and the severe chastisement which awaited the British, if they dared to advance upon the city. These artful statements produced the desired effect on the minds of the British commanders, and contributed to that deliberation and slowness of movement which marked their subsequent course.

The capture of the gun-boats gave the British command of the lake, and enabled them to land at any point they desired, without the fear of disturbance, or even detection.

The troops were now all moved forward through Pass Christian, in the smaller transports and vessels until they arrived at that bleak and desolate Island, one of the Malheureux, called Ile des Poix, lying at the mouth of Pearl River. Save a very scant vegetation, which grows around the lake or pond in the centre of this island, it consists of little more than a circle of white sand. Here the British succeeded in effecting a landing on the 16th of December. Without tents or any shelter, the condition of the troops was exceedingly uncomfortable, especially when a heavy rain came on and threatened the submersion of the whole island. Then a severe frost followed, freezing the wet clothes on the bodies of the men and causing many deaths, especially among the black troops, brought from the West Indies. From the 16th to the 20th the boats were actively employed in landing the troops. On the 20th, General Keane reviewed his army. It was a bright, frosty morning, and though the men were greatly fatigued by their incessant labors, exposure and deprivations, their appearance, drawn up on that lonely and desolate beach, was quite formidable and impressive. Despite their trials, the soldiers preserved their health and vigor to a remarkable degree. Their gallant young General, with his handsome, genial countenance, and noble bearing, inspired all around him with hope, confidence and energy.

He immediately entered upon the formation of his army. The Light Brigade, which had been so effective in the operations on the Chesapeake coast, was broken up, and in its place three battalions were formed into an advanced guard. These battalions were the 4th, the

85th, and 95th, all tried Peninsular troops, the two first of which had been engaged in the attacks on Washington and Baltimore. Attached to this corps were a party of rocket men, two light three-pounders, with a few light artillerists. The advance was placed under the command of Colonel Thornton of the 85th, the most active and enterprising officer in the division, who was presumed to be familiar with the habits and modes of fighting of the Americans, having scarcely yet recovered from a bad wound received at the battle of Bladensburg. The rest of the troops were arranged into two brigades. The first, composed of the 21st Fusileers and one black regiment, was entrusted to Colonel Brook of the 4th, who had succeeded General Ross, in the operations against Baltimore, in the command of the army of the Chesapeake, and the second under Colonel Hamilton, of the 7th West India regiment, consisted of the 93d Highlanders and the other black corps. The 14th Dragoons, about 300 in number, were attached to the general, as an escort, for special duty. Having thus disposed of his army, Keane hastened his preparations to effect a landing.

In a consultation with certain Spaniards, formerly residents of New Orleans, and with some fishermen, who were familiar with the coast, Sir Alexander Cochrane had ascertained that about fifty miles due west from Pea Island there was a bayou, which approached within a few miles of New Orleans, and was navigable for barges of a large size. This was the Bayou Bienvenu. It was formerly called the St. Francis River, and is an important stream, being the principal drain of the basin below the Bayou St. John. Commencing behind the Faubourg Marigny, it flows southeasterly, receiving the waters of several other bayous and of numerous canals. It is navigable for vessels of one hundred tons, as far as Pienas Canal, twelve miles from its mouth. Its width is one hundred and ten yards. Its principal branch is Bayou Mazent, which receives the waters from the plantations below the city. This bayou, like all the scenery of the events which we narrate, remains now but little changed since 1814. Though presenting great advantages for commerce, it has not been much used for this purpose, and is chiefly resorted to by fishermen and hunters.

To satisfy himself of the feasibility of approaching the city, through this stream, Sir Alexander Cochrane dispatched a boat, in the charge of the Hon. Captain Spencer of the Carron, son of the Earl of Spencer, and Lieutenant Peddie of the Quartermaster's Department. They arrived safely at the Fishermen's Village, a collection of miserable huts on the left bank of the bayou, inhabited by certain Spaniards and Portuguese, who supported themselves by sending fish through the canal to the city for sale. These men had been bought over by the British, and were engaged in bringing them information of the state of affairs in the city.

On the 20th of December, Spencer and Peddie arrived at the village, and, procuring a pirogue, employed two of the fishermen to row them up the bayou. Disguised in the blue shirts and old tarpaulins of the fishermen, these officers succeeded in passing up the bayou and through Villere's Canal, from the head of which, they walked to the banks of the Mississippi, and after slaking their thirst with draughts of the cool and sweet water of "the Big Drink," they proceeded to survey the country around, and to gather such information as was

obtainable from the negro slaves, whom they encountered. They were not entirely unobserved, and indeed
narrowly escaped detection and arrest. Having accomplished their object, these officers returned to Ile des
Poix, and reported that the proposed route was quite
practicable.

VII

THE BRITISH LANDING AND BIVOUAC.

WHILST encamped on Pea Island, Gen. Keane was persuaded to send an embassy to the formidable tribe of Choctaws, who hovered around Apalachicola, Florida, where they were supported and protected by the Spaniards, with a view of rendering them hostile and annoying to the United States. Nichols, whose intrigues with the Indians have already been referred to, was placed at the head of this embassy. To give the mission *éclat*, and produce a favorable impression on the untutored savages, some of the most stalwart and commanding looking officers of the army were selected to accompany Nichols. Dressed in full uniform, and preceded by a trumpeter, who made the forests ring with his blasts, frightening the poor savages in their lairs, the embassy made its appearance in the Choctaw village, bearing a friendly flag, with outstretched hands, and every demonstration of cordial amity. A talk was held. The wary Choctaw was more than a match for the enlightened Briton. The chiefs greatly admired the gay uniforms, the large cocked hats and nodding plumes, the golden epaulets and highly-finished swords and scabbards of their new friends. They examined with curiosity, and with frequent grunts, the symbols and quarterings on a stand of colors.

But amid all their admiration and awe for their friends from across the "Big Lake," they did not forget the remorseless energy and ferocity of "Sharp Knife," which were written in such bloody characters on the memories of the aboriginal tribes at Emuckfaw and Tehopeka. Their respect for and confidence in the British had been somewhat weakened by the inglorious defeat before Fort Bowyer. Hence they were timid, cautious, and wily. The British plied them with rum. They got drunk, as Choctaws always have done since their knowledge of alcohol, and as they ever will do, until the last of the tribe, now nearly extinct, shall disappear before the greatest of the foes of the poor Indian, and of too many of his pale-faced enemies. All that the British could obtain from the Choctaws was a pledge to aid their army, which pledge would be kept as long as the supply of rum was continued. As hostages of their good faith, two of the chiefs consented to accompany the mission back to the camp.

This was certainly a small result of so imposing an embassy, though it must be confessed that the warriors in their scarlet jackets and old-fashioned steel-clasped cocked hats, with heavy shoes and no other covering for their legs than a girdle, tied around their loins, with their tomahawks and scalping knives stuck in their embroidered and bead-figured buckskin belts, their long hair braided and bound up with pieces of burnished metal, and decorated with plumes, purchased from the Spaniards, presented quite a novel and startling appearance among the neat and trim soldiers in the camp on Pea Island. Their candor was quite as novel and

refreshing as the simplicity of their taste and attire.
They assured the British that they would join them,
because they believed that they were stronger than the
Americans, and they expected to get "rum plenty"
when New Orleans was taken.

Such confessions might have provoked in the minds
of the more conscientious of the British army, the inquiry whether their motives were a whit more honorable, whilst their candor was not so open and explicit
as that of these simple children of the forest. Certainly
the conduct of these poor Indians will be viewed with
indulgence and forgiveness, when contrasted with that
of other parties who visited the British camp. These
were deserters, traitors and refugees from New Orleans,
who left the city in full confidence that it would not and
could not be defended. They represented that Jackson
was an ignorant militia general, a tyrant, who was
detested by the inhabitants, and who had no means of
defending the city. In justice to Louisiana, be it said
that these individuals were ex-officials of the old Spanish
Government in Louisiana and Florida, who had never
acquiesced in the transfer of the country to the United
States, and were deluded with the hope of regaining the
lost provinces, and by the interposition of their powerful allies, the British, restoring Spanish rule in this fine
country. No American name can be found in the list
of these refugees, nor despite the gross errors and false-
hoods which have crept into the histories of these transactions, can any such base conduct be traced to a single
citizen of New Orleans, or French creole of Louisiana.

The representations of these persons produced the
most joyful enthusiasm and confidence in Keane's army.
Officers and men were all impatient to land and hurry

up to the city, where they would terminate their troubles and fatigues, and console themselves with untold wealth and unrestrained enjoyment. With cheerful alacrity they entered upon the preparations for the landing. All the launches and boats in the squadron were collected in front of the island. All the tenders and small craft, many of which had done good service in the Chesapeake, under that ruthless and indefatigable Vandal, Rear-Admiral Cockburn, were also held in requisition. A few of the launches were armed with carronades in the bows. The gun-boats taken from the Americans were also pressed into service. After all these exertions and preparations, it was discovered that there were only boats enough to transport one-third of the army. Keane's impatience would brook no further delay. He knew that every hour would add to the strength of his antagonist; so he determined to push forward with one-third of the army, and take a position on the main land.

Accordingly, at nine o'clock on the 22d of December, the advance of the army, under Lieutenant Colonel William Thornton, entered the boats. The advance consisted of eighteen hundred men. It was accompanied by General Keane and staff, by the Chiefs of the Engineers and of the Commissariat Department, and by the Choctaw Chiefs, and two of the "Traitors," of the Fisherman's Village. The morning was dark, chilly, and cloudy. But no "skyey influence" could damp the ardor of the excited and enthusiastic Britons, intent on so grand a design, the conquest of so rich a city.

At a signal from the indefatigable and almost omnipresent Sir Alexander Cochrane, the boats pushed boldly off, the sturdy sailors pulled vigorously at the oars, and the flotilla glided rapidly over the smooth surface of the lake. It was soon discovered by the soldiers that their voyage was not to be a pleasant one. They were crowded together so closely that they could not change their positions or stretch their limbs. To add to their discomfort, the clouds blackened and soon burst into a terrific rain, which drenched the men to the skin. But there was no pause. The flotilla pushed on in perfect order, as gallantly as if all around were bright and comfortable. Not a sound was heard during the whole voyage, save the splash of the oars and a few half-whispered orders of the naval officers who were conducting the flotilla. The boats moved in sections ten abreast. Two light cutters led the van, a little ahead of the first section. A like number protected the flanks, and three others covered the rear of the flotilla. All the precision and regularity of an advance in presence of an enemy, were observed by the cautious veteran, who directed the whole movement. Each division of boats had its appointed commander, who in a light gig flew backward and forward, as occasion required, whilst the veteran Vice-Admiral, in a small schooner, kept just far enough off to see at a glance everything that transpired in the flotilla, and prevent any confusion or disarrangement of his plan of debarkation. The flotilla, moving with such mechanical precision and order, was a striking illustration of the efficiency of the British navy. Though exposed to so many discomforts, the soldiers could not but regard the spectacle with elation and pride.

Finally, towards the afternoon, the rain ceased, the clouds cleared off, and a cold, biting wind blew up. The men in their wet clothes, with their feet resting in the pools of water in the bottoms of the boats, required all their fortitude and philosophy to preserve their mannood under the discomforts of their positions. To afford some relief and rest, the order at last passed along the lines to cease rowing and come to a grapnel. It was cheerfully obeyed by the nearly exhausted sailors. Fires of charcoal in tin pans were then kindled, with which the soldiers sought to warm their benumbed limbs. The shades of evening were gathering around them, when an hour having been allowed for rest, the boats were ordered to get under way.

The flotilla was again in motion. The sailors were kept steadily at their oars all night. Just as the coming day, destined to be a memorable one in the history of Louisiana, began to prelude its march with a few dim streaks on the distant Mississippi shore, the low, dark, flat coast of Louisiana loomed up before the advanced boats. As they approached nearer, the repulsive features of the coast became manifest. There was nothing to be seen but a wide, flat expanse of swamp, covered with reeds. Not a vestige of human settlement or cultivation was perceptible. Save a few melancholy cranes and frightened gulls, no living object could be discerned in the whole landscape. And this was Louisiana—El Dorado of the Peninsular warriors !

Wheeling down the coast in a southern direction, the flotilla proceeded in search of the mouth of the bayou through which the boats were to pass. They reached it in safety about daybreak, without encountering a single enemy. Never was an invading army more favored by secrecy. Keane was now within twelve miles of Jackson's headquarters, and no one in New Orleans had the slightest suspicion of his approach. It was a complete surprise, which only required rapidity, boldness, and energy, to be converted into an overwhelming victory.

13

Let it not be imagined that this success of the British was due to any want of vigilance or care on the part of Jackson. The bayou Bienvenu had early attracted Jackson's attention, and Major Villeré, whose father's plantation was situated at the head of the bayou, had been ordered to send a picket to the Fisherman's Village, to watch the entrance of this inlet.

The picket consisted of a sergeant, eight white men, and three mulattoes. Closely following the tracks of Spencer and Peddie on their return to the British camp, they arrived at the village on the night of the 21st, and found there but one man, who pretended to be sick; the other inhabitants, under pretence of fishing, had gone to the British camp to hire their boats and their labor to the British, to aid the debarkation.

The detachment occupied the huts of the fishermen. Sentinels were posted, and boats sent out to reconnoitre in various directions. There is too much reason, however, to apprehend that the vigilance of these sentinels, and their dispositions, were not such as might have been expected from regular soldiers. Instead of housing themselves in the village, which was a quarter of a mile from the mouth of the bayou, they should have been stationed on the lake-shore to watch out for the enemy. Nothing occurred to attract the notice of this picket, until about midnight on the 22d, when the sentinel on duty in the village called his comrade, and informed him that some boats were coming up the bayou. It was no false alarm. These boats composed the advanced party of the British, which had been sent forward from the main body of the flotilla, under Captain Spencer, to reconnoitre and secure the village.

The Americans, perceiving the hopelessness of defending themselves against so superior a force, retired for concealment behind the cabin, where they remained until the barges had passed them. They then ran out and endeavored to reach a boat by which they might escape. But they were observed by the British, who advanced towards them, seized the boat before it could be dragged into the water, and captured four of the picket. Four others were afterwards taken on land. Of the four remaining, three ran into the cane-brake, thence into the prairie, where they wandered about all day until worn down with fatigue and suffering, they returned to the village, happy to surrender themselves prisoners. One only escaped, and after three days of terrible hardships and constant perils, wandering over trembling prairies, through almost impervious cane-brakes, swimming bayous and lagoons, and living on reptiles and roots, got safely into the American camp.

The prisoners were shut up in one of the huts and closely guarded. One of them, a native Louisianian (Mr. Ducros), was separated from his companions and placed in a boat, in which were Captain Spencer and other British officers. The boat returned to the lake and near the mouth of the bayou was met by the main body of the British flotilla, when Captain Spencer introduced his prisoner to a tall, black-whiskered, youthful man in military undress, as General Keane, and to another rough and stern-looking, white-haired old gentleman, in plain and much worn clothes, as Sir Alexander Cochrane. These two distinguished officers then proceeded to interrogate Mr. Ducros very closely. But with the prompt Irish wit of the one, and the deep Scotch calculation of the other, they did not succeed in extracting any very valuable or pleasing intelligence from the shrewd Creole.

Valuable the information was not to the British, but as the sequel will show, invaluable to the Americans, was one item of news which Mr. Ducros succeeded in passing off upon the inquisitive British. It was the statement that Jackson had from twelve to fifteen thous· and armed men to defend the city, and four thousand at the English Turn. By a preconcert the other prisoners confirmed this estimate. It greatly surprised the General and Admiral, and led them to doubt the character and veracity of the fishermen, who had made so light of the defences of the city, and rendered it necessary that the greatest caution and prudence should be observed in their movements. Thus it is that traitors and renegades are distrusted, even when they have truth on their side. The timely fiction of the prisoners proved a shield for the city. So deeply was it impressed on the minds of the British that it has been embodied in all their histories. That prejudiced, though graphic writer, Alison, has eagerly adopted for the protection of British fame, an invention which served as a protection of an American city. He estimates Jackson's force at twelve thousand, when the British landed, which was more than the whole male population of New Orleans at that time.

Cochrane went ashore at the village to remain and hurry up the other divisions. The boats which had entered the bayou were ordered to push forward with all speed. The sailors stood to their oars, and the boats swept rapidly up the stream, the banks on either hand closing in upon them as they advanced, and gradually contract· ing their front, until at last there was only space suffi·

cient for one boat at a time. Passing into Bayou Mazent, the southern branch of the Bienvenu, the stream
became so narrow that oars could not be used, and the
boats had to be propelled by punting. Finally the front
boats took the ground. The sailors were then ordered
to jump out, and see if a road could be found on the
banks of the bayou, which was practicable for the
troops. They reported that there was a narrow slip of
solid land along the bank of the stream, where a path
was discernible. The troops were then marched ashore
in single file, and the whole brigade stood at rest for
half an hour until General Keane and Rear-Admiral
Malcolm (who had remained in the rear to see that there
were no stragglers), could come up. On their arrival
at the head of the column, a brief consultation was held,
the men were hurriedly inspected, the column was
formed with the deserters and guides in front, and the
engineers sent ahead to cut away the trees and other
obstacles, and bridge the numerous narrow and deep
streams that run into the bayou.

The order to march was then given, and the active
Thornton led his column briskly forward in the narrow
path along the bayou, from which it would be dangerous to stray on account of the quagmire. Some delay
was occasioned by the severe labors imposed upon the
engineers in clearing the rank vegetation, which frequently obstructed the path, and in constructing rude
bridges across the ditches. The scenery for some distance continued to present the same dreary monotony.
Soon, however, the ground began to grow firmer and
the path more distinct. The files were now widened,
and the men were ordered to quicken their steps. With
the greatest alacrity they obeyed their orders, and pushed

rapidly through the low, stunted cypress woods which had succeeded to the cane-brake. Suddenly the leading files found themselves emerging into open and cultivated fields. Extending their front, they advanced rapidly and joyfully in the direction of an orange grove, through which several houses could be discerned. Forming his front into companies, so as to make as wide a sweep as possible, Thornton, with one company, stole rapidly along Villeré's Canal, and succeeded, under cover of the grove, in surrounding the principal house.

Major Gabriel Villeré, son of the General, had been directed to guard the approach from the Bienvenu, and in the execution of his orders, had dispatched the picket which fared so badly at the Fisherman's Village. Secure in his outposts, the Major was sitting on the front gallery of the house, looking towards the river, and quietly enjoying his cigar, whilst his brother Celestin was engaged in cleaning a fowling-piece. Suddenly the Major observed some men in red coats running towards the river. Immediately he leaped from his chair and rushed into the hall, with a view of escaping by the rear of the house. What were his horror and dismay to encounter at the back door several armed men. One of these was Colonel Thornton, who with drawn sword, called to the Major to surrender. There were no braver men than the Villerés; their heritage was one of dauntless courage and chivalry—but resistance under such circumstances would have been madness. With infinite mortification the young creole surrendered. Celestin had already been arrested in the yard. The two young men were then confined in one of the rooms, closely guarded, until General Keane could come up. These events occurred at half-past ten o'clock, on the morning of the 23d of December. Surrounded and vigilantly guarded by his captors, Major Villeré watched eagerly for an opportunity to escape. He felt that if he should remain imprisoned, the calumniators of his race would find, in the circumstance, some color for the aspersions of the patriotism and fidelity of the creoles of Louisiana. To repel so base an inference, he determined to incur every peril. Springing suddenly from the group of soldiers, he leaped through the window of the room in which he was confined, and throwing down several of the British, who stood in his way, ran towards a high picket fence which enclosed the yard; clearing this at a bound, in the presence of some fifty British soldiers, several of whom discharged their arms at him, he made for the woods with that celerity and agility for which the young creole hunter is so distinguished. The British immediately started in hot pursuit, scattering themselves over the field so as to surround the fugitive. "Catch or kill him," was Thornton's order.

Traversing the field behind the house, Villeré plunged into the cypress forest which girts the swamp, and ran until the boggy nature of the soil began to impede his progress. He could distinctly hear the voices of his pursuers rallying one another and pointing out the course which he had taken. His re-capture now seemed inevitable, when it occurred to him to climb a large live-oak and conceal himself in its thick evergreen branches. As he was about to execute this design, his attention was attracted by a low whine or cry at his feet. He looked down and beheld his favorite setter crouched piteously on the ground, by her mournful look and action, expressing more strongly than could the human face or form, her sympathy for the perils of her

master, and her desire to share his fate. The faithful
creature had followed her master in his flight. What
could Villeré do with the poor animal? Her presence
near the tree would inevitably betray him. There was
no other hope of escape. His own life might not be of
so much value, but then the honor of his family, of a
proud lineage, the safety of the city of his birth, with
whose fortunes those of his family had been so conspicuously associated, the imminent peril in which Jackson
and his soldiers would be placed by the surprise of the
city,—these, and other considerations, such as should influence and control a gallant and honorable man, suppressed and overwhelmed all tender emotions of pity
and affection. The sacrifice had to be made. With a
deep sigh and eyes full of tears, the young creole seized
a large stick and striking the poor, fawning, faithful
dog, as she cowered at his feet, soon dispatched her.
Concealing the dead body, he ascended the tree, where
he remained until the British had returned to their
camp, and the pursuit was relinquished. He then slip-
ped stealthily down, and stealing along the edge of the
woods, hurried to a plantation below, where he found
his neighbor, Colonel de la Ronde, who hearing of the
approach of the British, was hurrying up from Terre
aux Bœufs to join Jackson. Obtaining a boat, Villeré
and De la Ronde rowed across the river and reached
in safety the plantation, on the right bank of the Mississippi, of P. S. Dussau de la Croix, one of the Committee of Public Safety of New Orleans. Horses were
quickly saddled, and Villeré, De la Ronde, and De la
Croix, leaping upon them, put spurs to their animals
and rode towards the city as rapidly as the swift little
creole ponies could bear them.

Thirty-seven years had passed, and the gallant young creole hero of this adventure, emaciated by long sickness, and prematurely old, surrounded by a family of gallant sons and lovely daughters, sat in that very gallery, and on the very spot on which he was surprised by the British, and related with graphic distinctness, with kindling eye and voice, hoarse with emotion, the painful sensation, the agonizing remorse which agitated his soul, when compelled to sacrifice his faithful dog to prevent the surprise of his native city and save his own honor. A few weeks after, his worn frame was consigned to the mausoleum, which encloses the mortal remains of many other members of a family, whose name is so highly honored in the annals of Louisiana.

Finding all his precautions thwarted—having, in fact, observed the fugitives galloping towards the city on the opposite bank of the river, General Keane, who had now reached the head of the column, ordered the troops to be formed in battalion. He then marched them by Villeré's house, and right-wheeled into the road, which, at a distance of about a hundred yards from the river, proceeds directly to the city. Having arrived at the upper line of Villeré's plantation, at a point where the levee suddenly diverges almost at a right angle to the road, he ordered the three regiments, composing the advance, to take position. They were accordingly formed in three close columns in the field, within musket shot of the river. In front, where the advanced posts were stationed, were a fence and ditch. The Rocket company was stationed on the bank of the river to defend the rear of the camp. Outposts and pickets were posted far out in the field, and a strong advance was thrown forward up the river towards the city. Keane and

Thornton established their headquarters at Villeré's house. The three small cannon brought up with the advance, were placed in battery in the yard.

It was afternoon before these dispositions were completed. Strong parties had been, in the meantime, sent in every direction to see if any enemy was near. They all reported that there was no sign of a foe. The farmhouses had been abandoned by the whites, and the negroes were unable to give any information of what was going on. Under these circumstances, Colonel Thornton warmly urged General Keane to advance and march into the city, which lay in a defenceless state, about eight miles off, without an obstacle between it and the British army. The troops, this sagacious and enterprising officer declared, were fresh and in excellent spirits, and full of confidence and ardor. But General Keane had been seriously impressed by the representations of the prisoners taken at the Fisherman's Village, as to Jackson's force. He was apprehensive that his communications with the fleet might be cut off, and his little army be surrounded by overwhelming numbers. He did not perceive that he was already separated by a wide chasm from his supplies, and the main body of his command, which lay at a distance of forty or fifty miles off.

He, therefore, concluded to delay his advance until the other divisions came up. Fatal error for the British! Thornton was vastly Keane's superior in sagacity and military skill.

Arriving at Villeré's at eleven o'clock, if Keane had pushed forward, he might have been the first to announce his arrival to the surprised garrison and people of New Orleans. It would be rash to conclude that the bold genius, the inexhaustible resources and dauntless energy of Jackson, would not have supplied some defence, against even a column of regular soldiers, of experienced warriors, equal in number to his own command of raw militia, separated in detached parties, occupying an area of seven or eight miles; but there can be no doubt in the mind of any person, who views the condition of affairs in the city at this juncture, that it would have required a miraculous intervention to have saved it from capture or destruction, if Colonel Thornton's counsel had prevailed. Without walls or available forts, scattered over so wide a space, the city could only have been defended by a system of street guerrillaism, the consequences of which would have been deplorable and heart-sickening.

It is essential to a clear and correct comprehension of subsequent events, that we should describe the character and situation of the country in which General Keane now found himself established. The position occupied by his army was eight miles below the city, following the road near the levee. The Mississippi River at this period of the year is higher than the plains on either side, which gently decline from its banks. To prevent its overflow, levees are constructed, usually about seven or eight feet high, varying with the elevation of the plain, which is greater in some places than in others. The land on both sides of the river is of alluvial formation, and runs off into low swamps, which are covered with cypress and other trees. The swamps are relieved by numerous bayous, which find their way to the lake. The lake being lower than the river, the plantations are drained into it through the swamp. The culture of sugar, the only extensive product of South

Louisiana, demands a very thorough drainage, and the alluvion is subject to a constant infusion from seepage or transpiration water. To draw off this, and prevent the injurious effects of moisture on the cane, the planters cut numerous ditches in every direction, so as to enclose spaces of one or two acres, it being an established fact in cane culture, that the labor and expense of ditching and drainage are the best investments of the planter.

The plantation establishment, at the time of which we are now writing, was simple and cheap, compared with the present grand and expensive arrangements and constructions. Instead of large brick sugar-houses, with powerful machinery, propelled by steam, at a cost of many thousand dollars for fuel, with a complete and intricate apparatus, embracing many ingenious inventions of modern science, with long brick wings extended on each side of the sugar-house, forming a huge T, called the purgeries, in which the hogsheads of green sugar are deposited on rafters over a large cement cistern, so that the syrup (*sirop*) may drain from the sugar, and leaving the crystallized particles and solid matter dry, form in the cistern that article so much desiderated by juveniles, called molasses. These, with many other expensive improvements, which it would not be appropriate to describe in this place, render the sugar plantations of Louisiana, objects of great interest to strangers and others, who are curious about the application of science and art to the production of one of the great comforts of life.

How different were the arrangements of the sugar planters thirty-nine years ago! Then an ordinary mill of circular shape, made of cypress plank, set in motion by the labor of mules, served by a very simple, though awkward and uncertain mechanism, to press the juice from the cane. This was collected in kettles and boiled in the open air over rude fires, until crystallization was obtained, when the kettles would be emptied into troughs and put out to cool. In this process, the laborers employed were exclusively African slaves, the only species of labor adapted to the cultivation of sugar in Louisiana, which requires that the planter should have absolute control over the labor thus employed. A delay or interruption of taking off his crop, such as would frequently occur under any system of free labor, would be fatal to the prospects and interests of the planter. These negroes were then, as they are now, treated with great kindness and indulgence, though of late years great improvements have been made in their condition and comforts. It is always the interest of the planter to promote the comfort, health and vigor of those upon whose labor he is dependent.

This motive, aside from the ordinary feelings of humanity, which prompt all civilized beings to desire to see their fellows happy, contented and comfortable, will always secure kind treatment for the negroes employed on the plantations of the South. There are, no doubt, exceptions to the remark, but they are not more numerous than the exceptions to the proposition, that parents desire the happiness of their children, or husbands that of their wives. Wife-killing, and the cruel treatment of children by their parents, in some of the very central districts of civilization and Christianity, are more common than the instances of brutality and cruelty to slaves in the Southern States.

At the period to which our sketches refer, the negroes on the plantations lived in small huts, constructed of light wooden frames, filled in with adhesive mud, taken from the batture of the Mississippi. Now, however, their dwellings consist of neat cottages of wood or brick, built some feet from the ground, with windows, chimneys, doors, and all the essentials for comfortable lodging, with a small patch of ground in the rear of each cabin, for a garden. The cabins are usually built in two rows, with the main road of the plantation passing between the rows. We are thus minute, because a very common error prevails, and has been repeated by many writers and speakers in England and the United States, that the negroes employed in the sugar culture of Louisiana are subjected to very severe toils and hard treatment. It is susceptible of satisfactory demonstration, that the condition of these negroes is greatly superior to that of any of the agricultural laborers, white or black, of other countries. The happiness, health, and especially the great fecundity of the negroes in Louisiana, as well as their own enthusiastic testimony, will establish this fact.

The planters' dwelling-houses in 1814 were usually neat wooden edifices, either in the cottage style, like General Villeré's, the first headquarters of the British army, the whole building being on one floor, with wide galleries in front and rear ; or in the château style, like Bienvenu's and Macarté's, in front of the British camp, which consisted of two stories and an attic, the ground-floor being usually paved with brick or marble, and the galleries supported by brick pillars, circling the whole building. These houses were surrounded by trees and shrubbery, so that, at a short distance, they could scarcely be seen. They looked to the river, and were built usually at a distance of a few hundred yards from its bank, with cultivated gardens, or neatly trimmed lawns, shaded by spreading live oaks and pecan trees, and hedged around with a thick growth of orange and lemon trees, extending in front to the road, which follows the levee. The plantations were divided by slight but durable fences of cypress pickets, with ditches on both sides. Their fronts usually averaged a mile or three-quarters on the river, with about the same depth, terminating in the cypress swamp, which extends the whole distance from the mouth of the Mississippi to the highlands, a distance of over two hundred miles, leaving between it and the river, a narrow neck of solid and cultivable land.

It was this neck which General Keane now occupied. His camp was entirely within Villeré's plantation, and stretched from the head of the canal, near the mansion, to the upper line of the plantation. There were some twelve or fifteen plantations, large and small, over which he must pass to reach the city. A two hours' march would have accomplished the task. After leaving Villeré's, he would have passed into Lacoste's, from Lacoste's to De la Ronde's, from De la Ronde's to Bienvenu's, from Bienvenu's to Chalmette's. We need not go further, as these five plantations embrace the full extent of the British advance, and of the operations which we are about to describe. The upper line of Chalmette's is marked by a small canal or ditch, called Rodriguez' Canal, which was dry the greater part of the year, and only contained a small quantity of water when the river was high. This canal was never passed by a hostile Englishman who did not perish in the act.

The plantations between the Canal Rodriguez and the British camp were under good culture. The crops had

just been gathered, and the families had been residing
on them a few days before the British arrived. The
rolling season, as it is called, was just over, and the sugar
safely stored in the barns and warehouses on the plantations. That portion of the cane, which is retained to
be planted for the next crop, was left in the fields,
having been cut and piled into mattresses, covered with
a slight layer of fodder and dirt, to protect it from the
frost—a process called by the planters matlaying. It is
a notable coincidence, that the three plantations first
named in the preceding enumeration, where most of
the events to be described occurred, were owned by
gentlemen, who, at the time of the arrival of the British,
were actively and efficiently engaged in aiding Jackson
to defend the city.

General Villeré was in command of the first division
of Louisiana militia, employing his influence and talents
in rallying the people of the rural districts to the defence
of the city, and in organizing various bodies of troops.
The services of Colonel De la Ronde were similarly
employed, and Major Lacoste, aided by his son (now
General Lacoste, Paymaster-General of the State, and
long a member of the State Senate), was engaged in
forming and disciplining that efficient battalion of free
men of color, to which frequent allusion will be made
hereafter.

The front view from the British camp was interrupted
by the turn in the river, which, at Lacoste's, declines to
the west. The position of Keane was well adapted for
defensive, but too narrow and circumscribed for offensive operations. The swamp afforded a secure protection
for his right, and for his line of communications with
the squadron in the lake. The river protected his left

flank from attack by land troops, but not against any armed vessel that might drop down the stream, nor from batteries on the opposite bank. There was the weakness of his position. Had the vessels of war succeeded in coming up the river, and anchored in rear of the camp, this deficiency would have been remedied. But as it was, having determined not to advance until he was joined by the remainder of his troops, it is quite evident, to even an unmilitary eye, that General Keane had placed his army in a position of great peril and embarrassment.

14

VIII.

THE ALARM—THE RALLY—THE MARCH.

THE first intelligence which greeted Jackson on his return from his tour below the city and in the neighborhood, was of the disastrous and alarming capture of the gun-boats. By and by the details of the combat—of the heroic defence—the bloody and destructive resistance against an overwhelming force, reached headquarters, and produced the most lively emotions of pride and courage in the breast of Jackson.* This result, the

---

* General Plauche, in a brief review written by him, relates the following facts:

On reaching the position which he had been ordered by Jackson to occupy with his battalion at the Bayou Bridge after the review of the 18th, Major Plauche proceeded to make a survey and reconnoissance of the adjacent country, and particularly of the bayous by which the rear of the city could be approached. In the discharge of this duty he proceeded to Fort St. John at the mouth of the bayou, where he held a conference with Major Hughes, who commanded this post. Shortly after his arrival at the fort, two small schooners arrived from the direction of the Rigolets, having on board a white man of the name of Brown, and a passenger named Michaud, who were strongly suspected of being spies. Brown, when closely interrogated by Major Hughes, said that he had seen and counted three hundred and forty-eight barges, carrying each forty or fifty men, infantry, cavalry, and two regiments of negroes, that had disembarked at Ile-aux-Poix; and that they were accompanied by twenty or twenty-five armed ships. The negro Michaud, when questioned by Major Plauche, said that he had served as pilot for Brown, by whom he was paid. He confirmed his statement as to the number of British barges, and said that they had endeavored to secure his services and those of Brown to pilot them. These men were immediately sent to Headquarters at New Orleans to be examined by the General. It was from them the first positive intelligence was received of the landing of the British at Ile-aux-Poix. On the person of Michaud a billet was found, signed "Labat," dated Pass Christian, 10

near approach of that powerful army, instead of shocking or astounding the soul, gave more fire and vigor to
the energies of this heroic chief. In calm and resolute
terms he communicated the intelligence to the Legislature, eulogizing "the valor and firmness with which our
gallant tars maintained the unequal combat, leaving no
doubt that, although compelled ultimately to strike,
their conduct had been such as to reflect honor upon
the American name and navy." He added, "the
ascendency which the enemy had now acquired on the
coast of the lake, increases the necessity for enlarging
our measures for defence."

Look at the map of New Orleans, and you will observe a small bayou, called the Chef Menteur, which
approaches very near the rear of the city, and from the
head of which starts a fine road on high land, running
into the city, called the Gentilly road. The bayou communicates with Lake Borgne, and the road commands
the bayou. Nothing was easier than for the British to
reach the city through the Chef Menteur, as they had
entire command of the lake, provided the road was not
defended by strong works and a large force. Jackson's
first act was to protect this point. Lacoste's free men
of color, with two pieces of cannon, were stationed
here; these were afterwards reinforced by the dragoons

Decembre, 1814, addressed to his sister in New Orleans. From this letter we translate
the following extract :

"I write you these few lines to give you the news. At the same time I wish you to
learn that on this side of Pass Christian some sixty English barges are visible; that
they have attacked the gun-boats and captured them, with forty barges containing
thirty men each. They give no quarter, but in four days will enter the city. Hasten
to leave, for they will burn everything that comes in their way. They have burnt the
seahouse and a storehouse at Chopitoula, belonging to us; they hold no parleys, but
proceed steadily forward to their object. Of the sixty sails visible, forty are brigs and
corvettes. I beg of you in any event to retire to the swamp, for there are too many
risks to run. It is the city they are aiming for."

of Feliciana, a volunteer corps, one of the first from the country to reach Jackson's camp. Many other precautions were taken, which it would be tedious and uninteresting to describe in full. Dispatches were sent to Coffee, Carroll and Thomas, informing them of the destruction of the gun-boats, and urging them to use all dispatch in hastening to the city.

The Government at Washington was also informed of the condition of affairs, of the great need of all the munitions of war, of the non-arrival of arms, for which a requisition had been made as far back as the summer months, but which did not reach New Orleans until the middle of January, 1815. By special agreement the contractor who brought these arms in flat-boats, was allowed the privilege of trading, as he descended the river, a privilege which he largely used. There was certainly no Carnot at Washington to support and aid the Militia General, who had been sent to cope with the conquerors of Napoleon.

All classes of a population, which but a few days before was sunk in despondency and gloom, now became inspired with the heroism and valor of the intrepid chief. The free men of color formed a second battalion, which was drilled and organized by Savary, a veteran of the St. Domingo revolution, and commanded by Major Daquin. This battalion was composed almost entirely of fugitives from St. Domingo. Sailors were scarce, and, on the recommendation of Governor Claiborne, bounties were offered by the Legislature for their enlistment. Thus Patterson was enabled to augment his forces, and to equip and man the schooner Carolina and the ship Louisiana, a merchant vessel, which had been purchased and fitted up for warlike uses. These

would be eminently useful in case of the advance of the
enemy along the river banks. Among other judicious
acts adapted to the emergency, the Legislature passed a
bill suspending the collection of debts for three months.

The eighteenth of December, eighteen hundred and
fourteen, was a stirring and glorious day in New
Orleans. It was the day fixed by Jackson for the
review of the militia of the city. At an early hour the
citizens were aroused by the roll of drums, and the
clangor of trumpets, calling the people from their peaceful pursuits to the Place d'Armes. Promptly they assembled with arms, accoutrements, and that invariable
badge of the creole soldier, the *bouquet* of mother, sister, or lady-love. They gathered on classic ground, too,
when they stood on the greensward, and beneath the
venerable trees of that honored spot, where all the great
events in the history of the city had been duly celebrated. In front, the old Cathedral of St. Louis reared its
quaint and time-stained towers, an object well calculated
to kindle the love of country of the creoles, and incite
them to deeds of noble daring and patriotic sacrifices.
It was in that sacred edifice, beneath that vaulted roof,
they had received, by Christian baptism, the names
which they were pledged to preserve unsullied—it was
there they had so long performed those religious duties
and devotions which the faith of their fathers taught
and enjoined—it was through those large doors, open
alike to all, as the house of God should be, they had led
their blushing brides—it was within those massive walls,
and under that solemn dome, that the delicate charms
of creole beauty produced their deepest and warmest
influence, and where many a tender passion had its
birth ripened into lasting affection, and conducted to

connubial bliss. Alas! that rude, dingy, and venerable
relic of Spanish power and piety, around which clustered so many dear associations and fond remembrances
has disappeared before the remorseless spirit of modern
innovation (miscalled improvement), to make way for a
far less impressive, though, perhaps, more architectural
edifice.

And, beside that venerable Cathedral, the Principal
and the Calaboose, the old Square, too, had its proud
associations. We have said it was a classical, we might
add, a sacred spot, to all Louisianians. It was the stage,
on which had been enacted, all the prominent events
in the stirring drama of the city of Bienville.

Here all public transactions were authenticated.
Here Ulloa had received the surrender of the colony of
Louisiana from the hands of the French officials, amid
the universal grief of the colonists. Here had been
exhibited that exciting spectacle of the second surrender of the city to that fierce Irish adventurer, whom the
Spanish Government sent over to reclaim the almost
revolutionized colony, Don Alexander O'Reilly, whose
grim battalions of twenty-five hundred men, drawn up
in perfect military order, glared fiercely upon the small
command of French troops in front under Aubry, who
bore the keys of the city and of the ports,—and at the
waving of whose hand the artillery sent forth its thunder, the shouts of the multitude arose to heaven, and
the white banner of France, sinking from the head of
the staff where it had long waved in pride and glory,
was quickly succeeded by the gorgeous standard of
proud old Spain. Here, too, Spain had redelivered the
colony to its ancient founder, with equal pomp and display ; and here, last and happiest cession of all, the French

tri-color, after a brief triumph, had descended amid loud huzzas and with other manifestations less gorgeous and showy, but more real and sincere than those which had attended the previous ceremonies of cession,—and in its place slowly and grandly arose that starry banner of the great Republic, which has ever since waved over that historic spot. Here all distinguished characters have received the salutations and hospitalities of the city; and here all notable events and anniversaries have been celebrated by the customary tokens of popular feeling. Though time and events have produced great changes in the aspect of the place,—so that now it could scarcely be recognized by those of the ancient population whom fortune has long detained from their native city, —and though the name of "Jackson" has appropriately and justly supplanted its ancient designation, still its historical associations are warmly cherished by all the natives and old residents of New Orleans.

Here assembled the scant force which New Orleans could contribute for its defence out of its small and mixed population. This force consisted of two weak and badly equipped regiments of militia; of Planché's fine battalion of uniformed volunteers; and of one battalion of free men of color. These troops were poorly armed—many of them having only ordinary fowling-pieces, and many being without flints. They were, however, animated by the greatest ardor and impatience to meet the foe. Jackson's eye brightened, the care-worn expression of his face cleared up, before that proud smile of confidence, a smile once seen and never forgotten, as his Aid, Edward Livingston, read, in the centre of the square, that impassioned address, whose sentences even now, when pronounced aloud, stir the heart and excite the senses like strains of martial music, reminding those gallant young warriors "that though the sails of the enemy covered the Lake, to the brave, united in patriotism, and in a noble enthusiasm to protect their homes, their altars, their firesides, the honor of their wives, sisters, daughters, and mothers,—there was naught that was terrible in their aspect, and that the only rivalry among Americans, resisting a brutal and insolent invader, should be for the prize of valor and of fame."

This address was received with loud acclaims, and the flashing eyes and resolute expression, the erect and manly bearing of the young soldiers, assured Jackson that he was surrounded by troops who would brave every peril to save their city and the honor of their flag; who would follow whithersoever he might lead. After allowing them a short time to visit their families, Jackson directed the various corps of this small force to take positions at various points in the suburbs of the city, which were assailable.

Jackson next proceeded to relieve himself of the embarrassments of the divided and contentious, though probably well-disposed State officials, by declaring martial law, and suspending the writ of *habeas corpus.* Though no doubt there was much calumny and exaggeration in the reports, diligently circulated by scandal-mongering and mischief-making persons, respecting the fidelity of certain public officials and citizens—and perhaps among no other people, situated as they were, would there have been more union and patriotism;—yet from the insidious nature of the printed and circulated appeals of the British to the French and Spanish races, and from the fact that several former citizens of New Orleans, connected with families resident in the city, were reported to be in the British camp,—but, more than all, from a consideration of the injurious and indecent partisan contests that were going on in the Legislature and among the State officials, Jackson deemed it prudent, and he was so advised by the highest judicial and other authority, to assume the entire police of the city in order to produce that unity of action, which was so necessary in this emergency.

The wisdom and necessity of this act have been so ably vindicated by the first intellects of the country, that it would be quite inappropriate and supererogatory to discuss it in this place. The results of this measure were conspicuously beneficial. Thenceforward every thing proceeded with the utmost order and regularity. Every individual had his particular duty and post. The prisons were opened, and those of the occupants who could be trusted, were allowed an opportunity of redeeming their characters and expiating their offences against society, by serving their country on the battle-field. All able-bodied men, of every age, color, and nationality, except the British, were pressed into service. Suspicious strangers and neutral foreigners were ordered out of the city. All persons entering the city were required immediately to report themselves to the Adjutant General, and on failing to do so were to be arrested and detained for examination. No one could depart from the city or beyond the chains of sentinels, but by permission from the commander, nor any vessel or craft sail on the lake or river. The lamps were to be extinguished at nine o'clock, and all persons found in the streets after that hour were to be arrested and detained for examination. The aged and infirm constituted themselves into a veteran guard to maintain the police of the city and occupy the forts. One of this band was the Historian of Louisiana, and late its Chief Justice for thirty years, whose deficiency of sight rendered him incompetent for military duty. We refer to the venerable Francis Xavier Martin.

At this juncture Jean Lafitte, true to his pledges, came forward and offered to organize his late associates into efficient corps to aid in the defence of the city. There were still a number of the Baratarians in prison, others were lurking in the swamps. Jackson was solicited by a committee of the Legislature, at the head of which was Mr. Bernard Marigny, who still survives a remarkable representative of the three nationalities, which in turn have possessed Louisiana, under all of which he has held offices of honor and trust, to enroll the Baratarians under the American flag. At first the General was not favorable to the proposition, but at the suggestion of Judge Hall, before whom the Baratarians had been arraigned,—and by a unanimous recommendation of the Legislature, the District-Attorney acquiesced in the release of these men from prison, and Jackson consenting, these experienced sailors and mariners, who had seen much service in various parts of the world, were released and organized into two artillery detachments under Dominique You and Bluche. The first was a Frenchman, a very wiry, agile, bright-eyed man, of indomitable will and great skill in the use of all weapons of warfare. The epitaph, on a tomb of showy and quaint form and structure now to be seen in the cemetery of St. Louis, describes Dominique You as a warrior who had signalized his valor in a hundred combats on sea and land, who was a modern Bayard *sans peur et sans reproche*, who could calmly face the destruction of the world, was not more hyperbolical than epitaphs usually are.* You was a warrior by nature, by taste, and habit. He was no more a pirate than Paul Jones. He abhorred cruelty, meanness and cowardice. Long after the events we are now describing, he continued to reside in the city—which he had aided to save, respected by all who knew him, and when he died, his remains were followed to the grave by one of the largest and most impressive funeral processions ever witnessed in New Orleans. If we needed further testimonials of his merit, of the grossness of the calumny, which seeks to identify him with deeds of piracy, robbery and cruelty, it may be found in the fact that when, some years after the war, the illustrious Jackson visited this scene of his glory, almost his first inquiry was for his " old friend Dominique." And that on no occasion did that great and good man seem better pleased than when sitting at the hospitable breakfast table of his famous artillerist, misnamed the " Pirate Dominique."

Bluche, the other commander of the Baratarians, was a creole by birth. He is now a commodore in the Venezuelian Navy. Bluche was a tall, imposing look-ing man, full of valor, enterprise and fond of adventure. Such men could not have been pirates in the ordinary and proper sense of the word.

They organized out of the Baratarians two excellent artillery companies, whose services will appear here-after. Other Baratarians enlisted in other corps, or were stationed in the various forts guarding the ap-proaches of the city.

* " Intrépide guerrier sur la terre et sur l'onde,
Il sut dans cents combats signaler sa valeur.
Et ce nouveau Bayard, sans reproche et sans peur,
Aurait pu sans trembler voir s'écouler le monde."

New Orleans was now a camp. All day and night the streets resounded with martial airs—with the war-songs of the young creole soldiers—many of them sons of the old Republicans of '89 and '93—with all the notes of warlike preparation, indicating the thoroughly aroused spirit and enthusiasm of the people, and their firm determination to resist to the last the invader who was advancing so rapidly and resolutely upon the city. Instead of gloom, anxiety and fear, no other expression could be observed in the countenances of all classes of citizens, but that of confidence, courage, and heroic resolve. The old and young, male and female, bond and free, all shared the universal enthusiasm and warlike spirit. The bright smiles of beauty fell in rosy showers upon the gallant volunteers, as with measured tread they paraded the streets. Mothers regarded with proud joy their beardless sons, who, with scarce the strength to bear up under the weight of fowling-pieces, were sturdily and bravely fulfilling the duties of regular soldiers and of full-grown men. Wives hugged closer their little ones to their throbbing bosoms, as peeping forth with mingled pride and anxiety from half-closed windows, they beheld their husbands—not so intent on their military duties that they could not cast fond glances at those dear pledges of affection, of devotion, and patriotism.

The venerable priests and ministers of God stretched forth their hands and blessed the servants in a good cause, imploring for them the aid and protection of the Almighty in maintaining the honor, the rights and liberties of a free people. Little boys, catching the prevailing enthusiasm, formed themselves into companies, mimicking their fathers and grown brothers, and marched the streets in military array, to the music of toy drums, and charging numerous imaginary bands of *capotes rouges*, performed prodigies of valor to the great delight of admiring fathers and the discomfort of anxious mothers. With equal ardor the African slaves, appreciating the kind and paternal authority under which they lived, in so much comfort and happiness, entered into the spirit of the occasion and labored incessantly on the various works ordered by Jackson, and in burnishing the arms, and preparing the munitions of their masters.

Such was the frame of mind into which one man, and he a stranger, could in a few days mould a large and discordant population. Such are the electric effects of true genius and heroism! Such results alone would proclaim Jackson a chief and leader among men. The blaze of a victory, won by a powerful effort of courage, skill and prowess must pale before the greater splendor of such achievements as these, by which weakness is converted into strength, harmony is educed from discord, order from chaos, and even the errors and weaknesses of men are made subservient to a great and glorious end. It was for such deeds the sagacious Romans assigned a crown of far more lustre and value than the laurel chaplet of the triumphant warrior. And yet during all these exciting events, Jackson had barely the strength to stand erect without support; his body was sustained alone by the spirit within. Ordinary men would have shrunk into feeble imbeciles, or useless invalids under such a pressure. The disease contracted in the swamps of Alabama still clung to him. Reduced to a mere skeleton, unable to digest his food, and unrefreshed by sleep, his life seemed to be preserved by some miracu lous agency. There, in the parlor of his headquarters on Royal street, surrounded by his faithful and efficient aids, he worked day and night, organizing his forces, dispatching orders, receiving reports, and making all the necessary arrangements for the defence of the city.

Jackson was thus engaged at half-past one o'clock P.M. on the 23d of December, 1814, when his attention was drawn from certain documents he was carefully reading, by the sound of horses galloping down the streets with more rapidity than comported with the order of a city under martial law. The sounds ceased at the door of his headquarters and the sentinel on duty announced the arrival of three gentlemen who desired to see the General immediately, having important intelligence to communicate. "Show them in," ordered the General. The visitors proved to be Mr. Dussau De la Croix, Major Gabriel Villeré and Colonel de la Ronde. They were stained with mud and nearly breathless with the rapidity of their ride.

"What news do you bring, gentlemen?" eagerly asked the General.

"Important! highly important!" responded Mr. De la Croix. "The British have arrived at Villeré's plantation, nine miles below the city, and are there encamped. Here is Major Villeré, who was captured by them, has escaped, and will now relate his story." The Major accordingly detailed in a clear and perspicuous manner the occurrences we have related in the preceding chapter, employing his mother tongue, the French language. which De la Croix translated to the General. At the close of Major Villeré's narrative, the General drew up his figure, bowed with disease and weakness, to its full

height, and with an eye of fire and an emphatic blow
upon the table with his clenched fist, exclaimed,
" By the Eternal, they shall not sleep on our soil !"
Then courteously inviting his visitors to refresh themselves, and sipping a glass of wine in compliment to
them, he turned to his Secretary and aids and remarked : " Gentlemen, the British are below, we must fight
them to-night."*

* A controversy arose some three or four years ago, at the time of General Gabriel
Villeré's death, as to the correctness of the general belief that the first announcement
of the arrival of the British was made by Major (afterwards) General Villeré. The
following card, which was published in one of the city papers, sets up a new claim to
this merit.

[*Communicated.*]

To the Editor :—Having seen an error committed by Mr. Marigny, the author of the
obituary notice of William G. Villeré, I request you to insert in the Louisiana Courier
the following details touching the arrival of the English at New Orleans.

The English came to Mr. Villeré's plantation on the 23d December, 1814, between
twelve and one o'clock. As well as I can recollect, some officers who preceded the
army, took Major Villeré prisoner. As I was passing along at the time, I made all haste
to give information to Mr. Ducros, who was posted on Mr. Jumonville's plantation.
Captain Ducros said to me. " As you are on horseback, go to the city and let General
Jackson know that the English are on Villeré's plantation." I set out immediately,
and passed, in spite of the efforts of the English to stop me. I reached Mr. Bienvenu's plantation ; my horse being unable to go any further, Mr. Bienvenu,
sen., procured for me the horse of a dragoon who was sick in bed at his house, and I
went to General Jackson's quarters in the city and gave him the news. A few minutes
afterwards, three discharges of cannon gave the alarm, and drums beat to arms
through the streets. I remained in the city one or two hours, hunting for a musket, so
that I might join one or other of the companies ; but no gun could be had. Then, believing that my company had crossed the river in a flat belonging to Mr. Danois, I resolved to descend along the right bank of the river. While on my way, I met Major
Villeré about two miles below, opposite the widow Bienvenu's plantation. Mr. Villeré
related in what way he had escaped from the English, and said he had left my company on Mr. Caselard's plantation. We then parted ; he pursued his way to town,
and I went on to Mr. Caselard's plantation, where I found my company. Mr. Caselard
crossed us over in a flat-boat, and we arrived at the left bank as the army was marching along to attack the English.

This does not in the least take from the hardihood and heroism of Major Villeré's
escape from a band of armed men.

Any one doubting the truth of this satement, may call upon Messrs. Casimir, Lacosta,
Marcel, Tiervile, Bienvenu, and Mr. Jules Villeré, who all were members of Captain
Ducros' company.   AUGUSTIN ROUSSEAU.

P. S.—In 1840, in presence of Mr. James W. Breedlove, General Jackson recognised
me as the volunteer who first brought to him information that the English were on Mr
Villeré's plantation.   AUGUSTIN ROUSSEAU.

. Never was there a bolder conception! Never was there one which indicated greater courage and resolution. Here was the practised, professional, and experienced soldier, who had fought under Abercrombie, Moore and Wellington, against the renowned veterans of Napoleon, receiving a reproof and lesson of inestimable value from a farmer—lawyer—General, who had never commanded a regiment of regular soldiers in his life. Here was the master stroke of a native military genius. Had Keane been a Jackson, he would not have waited for the attack, which the latter now prepared to make upon his camp. Had Jackson been a Keane, or almost any other man, he would as soon have thought of attempting to scale the heavens, as of instantaneously marching with his raw and weak levies against the heroes of Vittoria, of Badajoz, and Salamanca.

What were his resources for so daring an enterprise? On the 18th we have seen that he had in the city only the Louisiana militia and the regulars, the latter numbering eight hundred and eighty-four men, including Col. McRea's artillery. The regulars were the 44th, under Col. Ross, and the 7th, under Major Peire.

From the 18th he had received daily accessions. First came a fine troop of horse from Mississippi, organized in the southern part of the Territory, including many

<hr>

The truth of the latter part of this statement, is supported by Colonel James W. Breedlove, formerly collector for the port of New Orleans, who declares that he was present in 1840, when Mr. Rousseau was recognized by General Jackson, as the person who brought him the first information that a portion of the British army had landed and was then at Villeré's plantation. General Casimir Lacosta, Paymaster General of the State, also certifies to the truth of Mr. Rousseau's statement.

On the other hand, Mr. Jules Villeré and Mr. Dassau De la Croix published counter-statements, declaring their non-recollection of the facts stated by Mr. Rousseau, and vouching for the truth of the statement which we have adopted, without, however, assuming to determine which of the two parties gave the first information of the arrival of the British.

Louisianians as well as Mississippians. It was commanded by that impetuous and gallant officer, Major Hinds. This reinforcement was closely followed by the greater part of Coffee's brigade, which had performed the remarkable and tedious march from Fort Jackson, on the Alabama, around the lake, to the Mississippi river, which they reached by the old Spanish road, at Sandy creek, a few miles above Baton Rouge. Hastening to this town, Coffee found there a messenger from Jackson, acquainting him with the capture of the gunboats, and directing him to push forward with all rapidity, leaving his sick and baggage at Baton Rouge. Coffee immediately selected all his strong men and horses, and with them started for New Orleans in a brisk trot. In two days he reached the suburbs of the city, having, in that time, marched one hundred and fifty miles, with men and animals who had just performed a wearisome journey of eight hundred miles through a wilderness. There is no march to equal this in the history of modern warfare. Encamping on the Avart plantation, just above the city, Coffee rode to town to report to Jackson.

It was a warm meeting between these two gallant soldiers, who had shared so many perils and hardships, and passed through so many eventful scenes together. Coffee was in the meridian of life, not having reached his fortieth year. A native of North Carolina, he had settled, in early youth, in Tennessee, where he formed a friendship for Jackson, which lasted during their lives, and may now be read in a beautiful epitaph, written by Jackson on the tomb in which the remains of his gallant associate, the "right arm" of his army, were deposited

15

in the year 1836, in a family burying-ground near the pretty village of Florence, Alabama.*

Coffee was a man of noble aspect, tall and herculean in frame, yet not destitute of a certain natural dignity and ease of manner. Though of great height and weight, his appearance on horseback, mounted on a fine Tennessee thorough-bred, was striking and impressive. Coffee brought with him less than eight hundred men. They were, however, admirable soldiers, who had been hardened by long service, possessed remarkable endurance, and that useful quality of soldiers, of taking care of themselves in any emergency. They were all practiced marksmen, who thought nothing of bringing down a squirrel from the top of the loftiest tree with their rifles. Their appearance, however, was not very military. In their woollen hunting-shirts, of dark or dingy color, and copperas-dyed pantaloons, made, both cloth and garments, at home, by their wives, mothers and sisters, with slouching wool hats, some composed of the skins of raccoons and foxes, the spoils of the chase, to which they were addicted almost from infancy—with belts of untanned deer-skin, in which were stuck hunting-knives and tomahawks—with their long unkempt hair and unshorn faces, Coffee's men were not calculated

---

* The epitaph on the tomb of the late General John Coffee, written by Gen. Andrew Jackson :

Sacred to the memory of Gen. John Coffee, who departed this life on the 7th day of July, A. D. 1833, aged 61 years. As a husband, parent and friend, he was affectionate, tender and sincere. He was a brave, prompt and skillful general, a disinterested and sagacious patriot, an unpretending, just and honest man. To complete his character, religion mingled with these virtues her serene and holy influence, and gave him that solid distinction among his fellow-men, which detraction cannot sully, nor the grave conceal. Death could do no more than remove so excellent a being from the theatre he so much adorned, in this world, to the bosom of the God who created him, and who alone has the power to reward the immortal spirit with exhaustless bliss.

to please the eyes of the martinet, of one accustomed to regard neatness and primness, as essential virtues of the good soldier. The British were not far wrong when they spoke of them as "a *posse comitatus*, wearing broad beavers, armed with long duck guns." But the sagacious judge of human nature could not fail to perceive beneath their rude exterior those qualities, which, in defensive warfare at least, are far more formidable than the practised skill and discipline of regulars.

Coffee's men were hardly established in camp, before Carroll, another of Jackson's favorite officers, arrived at the levee before the city, with a number of barges and flat-boats full of men. These were the Tennessee militia, for whom Jackson had made requisition in September preceding. Carroll had used the greatest activity and diligence, but was unable to procure a sufficient number of boats to transport his troops, who assembled in a few days after the call was published to march fifteen hundred miles from their homes to defend a distant point of the Republic. He was, therefore, subjected to the most vexatious delays. Even when he had succeeded in collecting a goodly number of rude barges, flats and rafts, many of his men were without arms and equipments. Carroll's Division left Nashville on the 19th of November. It appears like an interposition of Divine Providence, that just before Carroll embarked on the Cumberland, that river, which is seldom boatable at that season of the year, was suddenly swelled by unexpected rains and torrents. Another fortunate event happened to the great relief of the gallant Tennesseeans. On their passage down the Mississippi, they intercepted certain boats having on board arms and munitions, which were leisurely proceeding down the Mississippi from Pittsburg, in charge of Government employés, of which the Tennesseeans took possession. But for this accident, Carroll would have reached the city with an unarmed crowd of men, brave and devoted, but utterly inefficient and useless for the want of the most ordinary weapons of war. As it was, however, he brought into camp on the evening of the 22d of December, a regiment of young and inexperienced soldiers, but skillful marksmen, who were eager for any service however trying and perilous. They were fortunate in their commander.

Carroll, though quite a young man, had, by the force of his character, his decided military qualities, and many popular traits, attained high distinction and influence at Nashville, to which place he had emigrated some years before, an industrious and skillful artisan from Pittsburg, Pennsylvania. He was in the prime of manhood, and had seen much hard service under his devoted friend and companion in arms, Andrew Jackson. In person, Carroll was of the ordinary height, of stout, compact, muscular form, upright and soldierly in his bearing and carriage. The same inflexible devotion and friendship continued through life to mark the relations of Jackson and Carroll. More than once did they risk their lives for one another. Even at the time of which we write, Jackson was suffering from a cruel wound received in a personal rencontre which grew out of a quarrel in which Carroll was one of the principals.

This was Jackson's whole force when it was announced to him that the British were but nine miles off. At the very moment when Villeré communicated the startling intelligence, to wit, at half-past one o'clock, P. M., on the twenty-third of December, this small force was scattered as follows : Planché's battalion was at the Bayou St. John, two miles from the headquarters; Coffee was at Avart, five miles off; the Louisiana militia and half of the free colored battalion were on Gentilly road, three miles off, the Regulars were at Fort St. Charles and in the barracks in the city. These various posts embraced remote points in an area of eight or nine miles. Apprehending that the British might creep up through the upper branch of the Bienvenu, Jackson's first act was to dispatch Carroll to that point, to command the head of the stream. Further up on the Gentilly road, Governor Claiborne was stationed with the State militia. He next ordered Coffee's brigade, Planché's and Daquin's battalions, Hind's dragoons, and the Orleans rifles to break up their camps and proceed to Montreuil's plantation below the city, where they would be joined by the regulars, and march against the enemy. Commodore Patterson, who was at Fort St. John, was ordered to hurry up to the city and get the Caroline under weigh, with a view of co-operating in the attack.

In issuing these orders, the General used no unnecessary words, even of incitement or encouragement; the time was past for such stimulants; they were not now necessary. The promptitude and daring of his conduct, the unbounded confidence which he manifested in their valor and devotion, were eloquent enough to strengthen the hearts and nerve the courage of his men.

Completing these arrangements, and resolving upon his plan of attack, Jackson took a hasty repast, and then reclining his exhausted frame upon a sofa, sought a few moments' rest.

The Cathedral clock had struck three o'clock, P. M., when, from every quarter of the city and suburbs, troops were seen hurrying to the Fort St. Charles—the lower fort of the city, now the site of the United States Branch Mint. This was the general rendezvous, or point of departure for all the troops. Jackson was early on the ground to observe and animate the various corps. His position was in front of the gates of the fort. Near him, drawn up with admirable precision, were the compact lines of the 44th Regulars, a fine regiment of newly raised but highly-disciplined men, commanded by Capt. Baker, a young but efficient officer, and numbering 331 muskets. Peire, with the 7th infantry (465 muskets), a detachment of marines, 60 strong, two six-pounders, and twenty-two artillerists, under Col. McRea and Lieut. Spotts of the artillery, had already been sent forward to occupy the road below the city. They were preceded in their march by a company of sharpshooters, with long rifles, blue hunting-shirts, and citizen's hats, who advanced with unusual vivacity and rapidity, eager to be the first on the field to meet the foe.

This was the famous corps of Beale's Rifles. It was composed of picked men, leading merchants and professional characters of the city, who had formed themselves into a volunteer corps, and solicited the post of danger in the coming contest. One of the officers of this corps was Judge Joshua Lewis, of the First District Court of New Orleans, who laid aside the judicial robes to fulfill the duties of the patriot and soldier. The members of this gallant corps were in the flower of youth. The neatness of their equipments, the intelligence of their countenances, and the ready promptitude of their movements, showed that they were no ordinary soldiers. They were all expert in the use of the rifle.

Between the Rifles and the Tennessee mounted men

of Coffee's command, there grew up quite a warm
rivalry, relative to their comparative skill in the use of
that fatal and favorite weapon of the American citizen
soldier, the rifle. It is due to history to say, that when
the war was over, and there were no other contests to
engage in but those of honorable rivalry among friends
and brothers, this controversy was brought to a satisfactory test and conclusion by a trial of skill, which resulted
in favor of "the crack shot" of Beale's Rifles.

Presently, a heavy cloud of dust on the levee, and
the rumbling sound of many feet striking the earth,
announced the approach of a considerable cavalry force
from the upper limit of the city. Emerging from this
dust, and dashing up at a hand gallop, Hind's dragoons
announced their presence, and delighted the eye of the
General by their gallant, dare-devil bearing.

Then followed, moving in a rapid trot, the long line
of Coffee's mounted gunmen, who, from their careless
carriage, *outré* dress, and singular equipments, presented
more the aspect of backwoodsmen, going out on a "deer
drive" or bear hunt, than of soldiers marching against
the veteran warriors of Wellington. At their head rode
their gallant leader, who, halting his column when it
arrived in front of Jackson's position, advanced to the
general-in-chief and held a brief conversation with him.
Then quickly resuming his position in front of the column, in a loud voice he gave the order to "forward at a
gallop;" and, setting the example himself, started off at
a brisk pace, which, being followed by his command,
soon carried them out of sight.

These corps had hardly disappeared, before a dark
and varie-colored mass of men was seen moving rapidly
down one of the cross-streets, towards the left of the

44th. "Ah! there come the brave creoles," exclaimed Jackson to one of his Aids, whose handsome countenance lit up with a proud and joyful expression at this compliment to his own race, of whose noble traits the gallant and enthusiastic Devézac was a fine embodiment. This was Planché's battalion, which had run the whole distance from the Bayou St. John to join the column of attack. Many of the battalion were delicate young creoles, mere boys in age and strength; and yet they bore their heavy muskets and knapsacks with as much alacrity as practiced veterans. With their gay and various uniforms, characterized by that good taste and regard for proportion and effect, which distinguish the French race—with their bold, handsome countenances, and uniform size, the Orleans Battalion was certainly a corps of which any commander might be justly proud.

In the rear of this battalion was the corps of freemen of color, under the command of Major Daquin, a gallant and effective force, well officered, and capable of any service.

Jackson had now seen his whole disposable force march by. We must not forget, however, to add that there was a small band of Choctaw Indians, under Captain Jugeat, attached to the column.

The simple order to the troops was to hurry as rapidly as possible to Canal Rodriguez, six miles below the city, and there take up position and prepare to advance upon the enemy. With vivacity, but without noise or parade, the troops moved forward. As they advanced along the levee hundreds of snowy handkerchiefs were waved towards them, and bright eyes from every window and balcony cheered their hearts and warmed their courage. Unlike the females in most beleaguered cities, the

women of New Orleans, instead of flying into the
country for protection and safety against an approaching
army of invaders, whose shameful excesses on the Peninsula, and the shores of the Chesapeake, gave but little
hope that they would be restrained within any bounds
of decency and humanity, remained at home to share
the perils and sufferings of their husbands, sons and
brothers, and to give their aid, their cheering presence,
and their gentle consolations in the great emergency.

On that very day, a number of the ladies of the city
met at the residence of Mrs. Cenas, at present the con-
sort of Colonel William Christy, himself a veteran of
1814–'15, for the purpose of plying their needles in the
noble task of preparing clothing for the soldiers of Jackson's army, many of whom arrived on the levee in a
very ragged and destitute condition. Whilst they were
thus busily engaged, the news was brought into the
room that the enemy had just landed, and were marching on the city. Of course the ladies were a little nervous at first, when the alarming intelligence was communicated, but Mrs. Cenas remarked that they need be
under no fear as long as they had Jackson to defend
them. At the suggestion, however, of one of the party,
a message was dispatched by the ladies to the General,
inquiring " what they were to do, in case the city was
attacked ?" " Say to the ladies," Jackson promptly replied, " not to be uneasy. No British soldier shall enter
the city as an enemy, unless over my dead body."
Never was pledge more faithfully or literally kept.
British soldiers did enter the city, but it was in such a
plight as gave full employment for the noble charity of
these ladies, who nursed and comforted them, with the

same care and kindness which they extended to their own wounded countrymen.

We should not forget to add, that many of these ladies, on hearing of the approach of the British, provided themselves with daggers, which they wore in the same belt to which their needle cases were attached. The rumored war-cry of the British—"Beauty and Booty"—had nerved their hearts to a desperate resolve, which, in case the brutal threat had been attempted, would have rendered this city as illustrious for female devotion and heroism, as Saragossa, or old Rome in her palmy days.

The soldiers had all moved out of sight, still Jackson maintained his position on the levee. It was evident that his programme was not complete. The anxious glances which he threw across the river betrayed some solicitude. At last, however, the frown faded from his brow, as he observed a small, dark schooner cast off from the opposite bank of the river, and begin to float slowly down with the current. This was the Carolina, with Commodore Patterson, Captain Henly, and a gallant band of seamen on board. Then Jackson put spurs to his charger, and, accompanied by his aids, Captains Butler, Reid, Chotard, and Messrs. Livingston, Duplessis and Davezac, galloped rapidly down the road which had been followed by his little army.

Jackson's plan of attack was simple, judicious and practical. The Carolina was ordered to drop down in front of the British camp, and, anchoring at musket-shot, to open her batteries upon them at half-past seven o'clock. At this signal, the right, under Jackson, consisting of the regulars, Planché and Daquin's battalions, McRea's artillery and the Marines, was to push forward, being guided by Major Villeré, who volunteered for the occasion, and attack the enemy's camp near the river. Whilst they were thus engaged, Coffee, under the guidance of Colonel De la Ronde, was ordered with his Brigade, with Hind's Dragoons and Beale's Rifles, to scout the edge of the swamp, and advancing as far as was safe, to endeavor to cut off the communications of the enemy with the Lake, and thus hem in, and, if possible, capture or destroy them.

Such was the simple plan of the battle of the 23d of December, 1814.

IX.

BATTLE OF THE TWENTY-THIRD OF DECEMBER, 1814.

For some hours after the British were encamped on
the levee, all was well with them. Scouting parties,
which had been sent in every direction, reported that no
enemy could be seen or heard of. After posting a strong
advance of the 95th Rifles far up the road, and pickets
at every approach to the camp, Keane felt tolerably
comfortable, and determined to wait patiently for the
arrival of the other two brigades, for which the boats
had hurried back immediately after the advance had
stepped ashore. Thornton did not feel so confident.
He feared greatly that before morning broke they
should have serious cause to lament the folly of the
General in halting. In earnest discussion the two officers walked the gallery of General Villeré's house, ever
and anon casting anxious looks in the direction of the
swamp and of the road to the city. Meantime the men
proceeded to make themselves comfortable for the night.
Bivouacked in the open field, about two hundred yards
from the river, and extended for a half a mile along its
banks, they began to light their fires and cook their
suppers. The cypress pickets made good firewood, and
camp-kettles were soon brought into requisition. Not

content with the salt meat and rum allotted to them
by the Commissary, small parties were permitted to go
out in pursuit of more desirable delicacies. Spreading
themselves over the country, as far as was prudent, they
penetrated every house, every dairy and negro cabin,
pig-sty and poultry-yard, seized everything that was
eatable or drinkable and bore it into camp. The officers
were allotted the first choice of these luxuries, which
consisted of ham, cheese, poultry, wine, brandy, and
other delicacies with which the houses of the planters
are always abundantly supplied. It may be imagined
with what zest these wearied soldiers, who had been for
weeks crowded in ships on a long voyage, and whose
appetites had been greatly sharpened by the fatigues of
the march, partook of these rare comestibles.

After satisfying their appetites, the soldiers generally
lay on the ground to snatch a few moments of sleep.
It was now about half-past four in the afternoon, and
the most profound quiet and security reigned in the
British camp, when suddenly some excitement was perceived in front, at the furthest outpost on the road. This
was produced by the alarm of a sentinel, who observed
some suspicious horsemen approaching the post by the
main road. The guard immediately mustered, and concealing themselves behind the levee, waited until the
horsemen had approached within musket range, when
they delivered a well-directed volley, which killed one
of the horses and wounded two of the men of the party.
They then wheeled and retired down the road. This
detachment proved to be a scouting party, composed of
the Feliciana Dragoons, who had been sent forward to
reconnoitre; and one of the wounded men was the late

Thomas Scott, of East Feliciana, long a highly esteemed citizen of that parish, who had the misfortune to be the first man of Jackson's army, who received a wound at the hands of the British.

An hour more passed, and no other event had occurred to disturb the British, who were now wide awake, on the look-out for their foes. Just as the sun was sinking behind the dark forests on the opposite bank of the river, the outposts were again aroused by a still more formidable demonstration in front. A squadron of horse, at least one hundred in number, were seen trotting boldly down the road. On reaching a certain point they suddenly widened their front, and scattering over the field, charged boldly and fearlessly towards the outposts. The daring and impetuosity of these horsemen excited the astonishment of the British. They said to one another, that they would no longer have to complain that they had to hunt up the Americans to beat them. They had found an enemy who knew what the offensive in warfare meant. Their new foes charged their pickets as boldly as if they had been on the Peninsula, and had crossed swords with Napoleon's Cuirassiers. Driving in the sentinels, they came down in a brisk trot to a ditch, in which a number of the Rifles had been posted, and halting at a distance of one hundred yards, the officer in command coolly surveyed the British position ; and then wheeling his squadron, galloped back towards the city, not heeding a heavy volley which the Rifles sent after them. This was Hind's troop of Horse which had been sent as a reconnoitering escort to Colonel Hayne, the Inspector-General of Jackson's army, for the purpose of ascertaining the force and position of the enemy.

These intruders disappeared from view, and solitude again resumed its sway over the broad fields in which the British were bivouacked. The soldiers repaired to their agreeable repasts and slumbers. Darkness began to gather over their camp. The sentinels were doubled, and the officers walked the rounds with restless anxiety. But the thoughtless and careless men, intent only on present comfort and enjoyment, trimmed their fires, so as to give cheerfulness to the scene, and reproducing the remnants of their midday feast, began to make good use of their kettles and pans in preparation for a comfortable supper. Many, too exhausted to eat, lay down to sleep. They were not, however, entirely without anxiety, and for better security their arms were kept within reach, ready for instant use. About seven o'clock, the attention of several officers was drawn to a vessel which was stealing slowly down the river. From the bold and careless manner in which she approached their camp, many of the British thought that she was one of their own cruisers, which had passed the Fort, and after proceeding a short distance up stream to observe the enemy; had now arrived most opportunely to cover their left flank in their advance upon the city. They hailed her—no answer was returned. Several muskets were fired, of which she took not the slightest heed. With amazing audacity the men on board were seen quietly fastening the sails, and the vessel continued to sheer in close ashore, swinging her starboard broadside right abreast of the camp. Then her anchor was let loose—a slight movement was observed on board—lighted matches were discerned through the darkness, and in the stillness of the night, and of a spectacle, which by its mysterious character had made the British

speechless with astonishment, a loud voice was heard
from the ship, exclaiming, " Give this for the honor of
America." The words were followed by a simultaneous
flash from a score of cannon and firearms, and a perfect
tornado of grape-shot and musket-balls, which swept
the levee and the camps in the field, killing and wounding many men, some of whom were asleep when struck,
and scattering their fires and camp utensils in every
direction. The havoc was the more terrible from its
suddenness. For some minutes the British were struck
with consternation. Disorder prevailed through the
camp. One of the officers says, " they were driven into
the most dire confusion, which caused a tenfold panic.
The scene beggared all description. No mob could be
in a more utter state of disorganization." They were
mowed down by the fire of an unseen and unknown
enemy. Nor did the Carolina—for it was that vessel,
with Commodore Patterson, Captain Henley, and an
efficient crew, which had dropped down so inoppor-
tunely on the British camp—give them much time to
collect their senses. She continued her fire with amazing rapidity and accuracy, embracing in its range the
whole area of the field, in which the British soldiers ran
wildly to and fro, in pursuit of shelter. The rocketers
on the levee made a feeble effort to bring their weapons
to bear upon the schooner, but they produced no effect,
and only elicited the jeering laughter of the sailors of
the Carolina. Finally, the intrepid Thornton came to
the rescue of his affrighted men, and ordered them to
leave the open fields, and shelter themselves under the
levee. Never was an order more quickly obeyed.
Reaching the levee, the men lay down at full length,
listening in painful silence to the pattering of grape-shot

in their camp, and the shrieks of the wounded in the field, who, unable to gain the cover, were knocked and tossed about like logs of wood, by the remorseless shot of the schooner.

It was now so dark that the men could not discover an object of any size, more than a few feet off. The Carolina slackened her fire, and the prostrate British began to breathe freer, when a new cause of alarm arose. It was a firing at their outposts. First, there were a few isolated reports, evidently of the sentinels. Then came volleys of the pickets. These increased every second, and came from every part of the field. Finally, a blaze of fire seemed to encircle the camp. It was evident they were surrounded. Here was apparent confirmation of the wisdom of Keane's conduct. There must be at least twelve thousand men to justify such an attack on a camp of Peninsular veterans, and to cover and out-flank so large a front. But there was no time for reflection or speculation. They were surrounded, and must fight or yield. The latter was never thought of.

With his usual boldness, Thornton ordered the 85th and 95th to rush from under the levee, and fly to the support of the pickets, whilst the 4th, stealing under cover of the levee, formed on the right bank of Villeré's Canal, in front of the headquarters, so as to act as a reserve and protect their communications with the Lake. Major Gubbins led the 85th on the right, and Major Mitchell the 95th on the left, whilst Colonel Thornton directed the movements of the whole force. They were soon engaged in one of the fiercest, most severely, and evenly-contested night combats that ever occurred. To

16

comprehend the order of the battle, we must follow the movements of the attacking party.

Marching his men to Rodriguez Canal, about two miles from the British camp, Jackson made this ditch, running perpendicularly from the river to the swamp, the base of his operations. Coffee with eight hundred men, including his mounted gunmen, Hind's Dragoons, and Beale's rifles, was dispatched towards the left, with orders to advance along the edge of the swamp, until he reached the boundary line between Lacoste's and Laronde's; and dismounting his men there to leave his horses, and push boldly forward, so as to gain the enemy's right, turn his position, break up his communications, and destroy him. Waiting for a few minutes, until he could hear the broadside of the Carolina, which was to be the signal for the commencement of the battle, and when those joyful notes, a little before the appointed hour, fell upon his ear, delaying for a few minutes longer, until they could produce their full effect upon the enemy, Jackson gave the order to advance.

The right division, consisting of the regulars, the two battalions of volunteers, the artillery and the marines—in all 1,147 muskets—and two six pounders, and led by Jackson himself, advanced by heads of companies as near the river as possible. The battle was opened by a company of the 7th, under Lieutenant McClelland, which, however, was led by that gallant staff officer, Colonel Piatt. This company, being on the extreme right, filing through the gate of Laronde's plantation, advanced as far as the boundary of Lacoste's, when it was received with a brisk discharge from one of the out posts of the enemy, established near the road, and lying under cover of a fence. This outpost consisted of eighty men of the 95th, commanded by Captain Hallem. Their resistance to a single company of the 7th Infantry, has been exaggerated by one of the British historians, into "an achievement to which neither ancient or modern history can produce a parallel, as Captain Hallem," says this veracious writer, "was opposed to Jackson's whole army, three thousand strong." The truth is, the *gallant* Captain Hallem and his eighty men were posted in a ditch and behind a fence, when he was attacked by the right company of the 7th.

Calling to them to come out and fight like men in open ground, Piatt attacked them with great vigor, and forced them to retire, occupying the ground they had abandoned. The British, however, being reinforced, returned to regain their lost position, and opened a heavy fire upon Piatt's detachment, who as briskly replied. For some minutes the firing was very severe and destructive, the combatants being but a few yards apart. Piatt received a ball in the leg, McClelland and a sergeant were killed, and several of the men were wounded. Meantime, the artillery advanced up the road, covered by the marines under Lieutenant Bellevue, and began to blaze away at the enemy's outposts with great vigor. Collecting a strong force, the British made a bold push for the guns. Their heavy fire caused a recoil of the marines, and some of the horses being wounded, one of the pieces was upset in the ditch. Jackson and his staff being near, rode swiftly to the point of danger, and, indifferent to the shower of bullets which whistled around him, Jackson called out— "Save the guns, my boys, at every sacrifice!" Aided by Captain Butler and Captain Chotard, of his staff he succeeded in repairing the momentary disorder, and rallying the marines and a company of the 7th, soon had the guns safely protected.*

These events all transpired in a few minutes. Meantime the other companies of the 7th advanced briskly, and forming in battalion *appuyé* on the river, opened a brisk fire on the British, who in a like manner had strengthened their lines. The 44th, forming on the left of the 7th, soon joined in the fire. The engagement now became general, and the fire was kept up on both sides with great steadiness. Both lines extended perpendicular from the river some distance out, being embraced within an old levee and the new levee. In such a state of affairs both became liable to be outflanked, and turned, the British on the right and the Americans on the left. The British line was rapidly extending beyond that of the Americans, and a strong force had began to file off behind the old levee, towards the rear of the left of the 44th, and that regiment was compelled to oblique to the left, being forced back, when Planché and D'Aquin fortunately came into line, and forming under a severe fire at pistol shot, advanced in close column.

Just as Planché's battalion was wheeling into line on the left of the 44th, some of his platoons on the right, lapping those of the 44th, mistook them for the enemy and fired a volley at them, which wounded several men. Planché quickly repaired the unfortunate error, and led his battalion into the very face of the enemy, who gave

---

* Jackson used to say, familiarly, when complimented on the gracefulness of his bow, that he learned the art on the night of the twenty-third, when though the British thought differently, he never wasted so much politeness in his life in bowing to their bullets as they whistle] around his head.

way rapidly. D'Aquin's battalions followed Plauché, and the two very soon reinstated the 44th in its recti linear position, and then opened a heavy fire upon the enemy, which caused them to give way still more. Seeing the effect of his fire, the men called out to charge bayonets, and Plauché was about to give the order for the charge, when Colonel Ross, who had command of the volunteer battalions, countermanded the order, and directed him to hold his position. This was for the Americans the most unfortunate event of the affair, as was shown afterwards when the situation of the British became known. If the charge had been made, a large portion of the British army, including a whole regiment, would have been cut off from the rest, and compelled to surrender. Finally, however, the British being so vigorously pressed, deemed it prudent to retire and resume their original position on the boundary line of Lacoste and Villeré's. In this movement they were favored by a heavy fog, which arose about half-past eight o'clock.

So much for the operation on the right. Meantime Coffee was not idle. Dismounting his men at the ditch, which forms the boundary line of Laronde and Lacoste, and leaving one hundred men in charge of the horses, he advanced rapidly with Beale's rifles on his left in extended order, skirting the swamp. When he had reached the boundary line of Villeré's, and believed that he had gained the enemy's right, he wheeled his column to the right, and advanced with front face to the river. The Rifles on his left spread themselves over Villeré's, and penetrated the very centre of the British camp, killing many of the enemy and taking several prisoners.

Whilst advancing, Coffee ordered his men to be sure of their mark in firing, not to lose a shot, and to fire at short distance. They were soon engaged with the outposts, and the quick-sighted Tennesseeans had picked off several sentinels before their approach was known, so noiseless and wily did they move. Soon, however, the British 85th rushed forward to meet them, and the two lines became warmly engaged. Both sides were remarkable for their sharp-shooting. The 85th were light infantry, and had long enjoyed a high reputation for the efficient manner in which they handled their guns. But the Tennesseeans were more than a match for them. They fired faster and with greater accuracy. The British suffered severely, losing several officers, among others Major Harris, the Brigade Major.

For some time the battle raged fiercely in this part of the field, but without much order or system. It was a war of detachments and duels. The officers would hastily collect small bodies of men, as they could find them, and starting out in pursuit of a hostile detachment, would rush at them, and soon be mingled in a hand-to-hand fight. Owing to the darkness, friends could not be distinguished from foes, and not a few fell by the bullets of their companions and fellow-soldiers. Approaching within a few yards of one another, they would shout some vague name or call, beating, as it were, around the bush, to ascertain who their neighbors were before delivering their fire. In these manœuvres, as each party could disguise his character to get nearer his enemy, many lamentable mistakes were made on both sides, by which several brave men lost their lives.

Among Lacoste's negro cabins several parties of the British Rifles were posted, who kept up a running fire

on Coffee's right companies. The Tennesseeans, how
ever, recognizing the sharp crack of the rifle, gave these
parties the preference, and directed their particular
attention to them. It required severe fighting to dislodge the Rifles ; but they were soon beaten with their
own weapons. The short rifle of the English service
was not equal to the long and deadly instrument of the
western hunter and Indian fighter. For many years
after, the huts of Lacoste bore striking proofs of the
accuracy of the aim of the Tennesseeans, and of the
severity of the combat in this part of the field. Concealing themselves behind the huts, the British waited
until the Tennesseeans got into the midst of them. Then
they rushed forward and engaged with them hand to
hand. Neither party having bayonets they were forced
to club their guns, and thus many fine rifles were ruined.
But the more cautious of the Tennesseeans preferred their
long knives and tomahawks to thus endangering that
arm which is their chief reliance in war, their inseparable companion in peace and war. Many a British soldier who was found dead on the field, with heavy gashes
on his forehead, or deep stabs in his bosom, and who
was buried under the conviction that he came to his
death by that military and chivalric weapon, the sword,
fell, in fact, beneath those more barbarous instruments
which the Tennesseeans had learned from the savages to
wield with deadly skill—the tomahawk and hunting-
knife. After being driven from the grove at Lacoste's,
the Rifles fell back before Coffee's steady advance, rallying, however, as they were joined by fresh reinforcements, and keeping up a continuous fire on the Tennesseeans. At last they gained the old levee, not far from
the road, and preferring for the time the peril of the

Carolina's broadsides to the unerring rifles of the Tennesseeans, they took post behind the levee on the river side. This position was deemed too strong by Coffee to be carried. Besides he did not wish to expose his men to the unceasing fire of the Carolina. Accordingly, he sent a dispatch to Jackson acquainting him with his position, and received in return an order to join the right division.

If the design of Planché of charging the already retiring line of the British had not been prevented by Colonel Ross, the two divisions would have united, and thus the British left would have been inevitably cut off. But in the meantime the right column of Jackson, finding the fog too thick, had fallen back to its original position, and Coffee following it, at last took up position near the old levee, where the battle had commenced, from which he kept up an irregular fire on the British stragglers and outposts. It was while moving in this direction, that Major Mitchell, commanding the British 95th (an officer who had won great distinction in leading the storming party at Ciendad Rodrigo, and in other actions in the Peninsular war), advanced towards the British right for the purpose of ascertaining the character of the men who were approaching. As the 93d Highlanders were expected every moment to reach the camp, Major Mitchell was strongly impressed with the belief that Coffee's men, who wore hunting-shirts, which, in the dark, were not unlike the Highland frock, were the men of the 93d, and greatly needing their aid, he eagerly advanced, calling out, " Are those the 93d ?" " Of course," shouted the Tennesseeans, who had no particular number. Mitchell thereupon pushed boldly forward within a few feet of the men, when Captain Donaldson stepped in front, and slapping the astounded Briton on the shoulder, called out, "You are my prisoner," and requested the Major's sword. This request was enforced by half a dozen long rifles which covered his body at every assailable point.*

With infinite mortification the gallant Major surrendered, and with several other prisoners was borne off by the Tennesseeans. Though at the moment of his capture, and subsequently, Major Mitchell was treated with the kindness and generosity due to a gallant foe, he never recovered his good humor, and embraced every opportunity of exhibiting his spleen and disgust. The oblique movement of Coffee's brigade to the right produced some disasters which were sorely lamented by the Americans.

In the last charge of Coffee, just before he received the order to retire, the left of his line, including two hundred Tennesseeans and Beale's Rifles, under Colonels Dyer and Gibson, got separated from that portion which moved under Coffee's immediate command. The British perceived the gap, and immediately rushed into it, forming a strong line of troops between Coffee and Dyer. To this line Dyer hastened, trusting it was Coffee's. On approaching, they were hailed by the British, ordered to stop and report who they were. Dyer and Gibson advanced and called out that they were the Second Division of Tennesseeans. Observing that his answer was not understood, he ordered his men to wheel and retire towards the swamp. As they were retiring, the

---

* It was rather an apochryphal additon to this story which was no doubt provoked by the haughty demeanor of Mitchell, that when captured, seeing a tomahawk in the hands of one of his swarthy foes, he cried out with an expression of great terror, "Oh! Mr. Indian don't scalp me!—don't scalp me!"

British opened a heavy fire upon them, and then charged. In the retreat Gibson stumbled and fell, and a British soldier, more active than his companions, reached him before he could rise and pinned him to the ground with his bayonet. Fortunately the bayonet only pierced his flesh, and Gibson, who was an active and powerful man, seized the musket, and forcing it from his assailant, knocked him down and then escaped to his companions. Col. Dyer had retreated but fifty yards when his horse was shot, himself wounded, and entangled with the dying animal, which lay upon his legs. At this moment, when his capture or death seemed inevitable, he had the presence of mind to order his men to halt and return the enemy's fire; they did so, and the British were checked, and the Colonel was enabled, with the aid of some of his men, to release himself. Finally, the whole party of Tennesseeans succeeded in reaching Coffee. There was a portion of Dyer's command which was not so fortunate.

On the extreme left of the Tennesseeans were Beale's Rifles, extended in open order for some distance across Lacoste's and into Villeré's field. Fighting singly, or in small squads, they had penetrated the very centre of the British camp, and gave such annoyance to the enemy as to lead to the belief that they composed a whole regiment. Whilst pressing forward the Rifles became separated into two parties, by the fence and ditch of Lacoste's; and when Coffee moved towards the right, the party of the Rifles on the extreme left did not observe the movement and follow it. The consequence was, that they were cut off by the British closing in between them and the first division of the company. Finding themselves thus cut off, the Rifles separated and endeavored to escape by starting in different directions. One party of them retreated in the direction of the swamp, and had nearly reached it, when they observed a line of men advancing from the swamp towards them. Deceived in the same manner, in which Mitchell had been, they concluded from the dress of the men that they were Coffee's "Hunters," and eagerly pressed forward calling out :—

"Where is the first division ?"

"Here they are," was the reply, with a broad Scotch accent, and the line closed in upon them at a charge, and the gleaming bayonets produced the sad conviction on the minds of the Rifles that they had been entrapped and must surrender. They were immediately taken in charge by a detachment of the British, and hurried towards the canal, where they arrived just in time to be placed in the boats which had brought their captors, who proved to be the Grenadier company of the 93d Highlanders. These prisoners were taken down the bayou to the fleet.

Those who were thus captured embraced several of the most respectable citizens of New Orleans. Among them were Benjamin Story, Esq., long one of the most respected, wealthy and prosperous merchants and bankers of the city, and for many years President of the Bank of Louisiana ; William Flower, one of the oldest merchants of the city, who now survives at a very advanced age. These two gentlemen had been badly wounded. There was also among the prisoners the late John Lynd, and that wild rollicking citizen, of Irish birth, famous for his wit and valor, Kenny Laverty. Others of the Rifles endeavored to escape by the river, and a few succeeded. Two of them, however, were not so fortu-

nate. They were Denis Prieur, late Collector of the
Port of New Orleans, several times Mayor of the city,
and one of the most sagacious, enlightened and intelligent public officers whom the city and State have ever
employed, and a Scotchman by the name of McGillvray.

After remaining together for some time, these two
gentlemen agreed to separate. McGillvray was to endeavor to escape by the river, and Prieur through Lacoste's field. Accordingly they parted. Prieur advanced
towards the right, keeping under cover of a fence until
he thought he was beyond reach, and then started in
full run across the field. He had not gone far before
coming to a ditch; he leaped it, and suddenly found
himself surrounded by twenty British soldiers, to whom
he surrendered. McGillvray was captured after being
wounded. These were the last captures of the British.
Prieur, who was a creole, was taken to General Keane's
headquarters, where the General held a long conversation with him, and endeavored to impress upon his
mind the idea that the British did not come to Louisiana
to wage war against the ancient population, but to oust
the Yankees, who had no right to the country, and
ought not to be tolerated by the Creoles. The General,
however, had more than his match in Prieur, than whom
there are few more sagacious and astute men. He parried the General's interrogatories very adroitly, except
the one relative to Jackson's force, which, of course, he
was too shrewd not to exaggerate. Satisfied that he
had made a very deep impression upon the unsophisticated young creole, Keane ordered him to be released
on his parole. Accordingly, early next morning, Prieur
had the pleasure to rejoin Jackson's army at Rodriguez
Canal.

Keane subsequently complained very savagely of the bad faith of the creoles, who, not appreciating his kindness to them, had been the most active and ferocious enemies of the British, from the commencement to the close of the campaign. He should have remembered that he who endeavors to tamper with the loyalty and patriotism of a free people offers the most serious provocation and insult, and justifies a greater bitterness of hostility and severer punishments than were dealt out to the British on the plains of Villeré.

The other captive "Rifles," did not fare so well. They were taken to the British fleet then lying off Ship Island, and subjected for some time, as prisoners of war, to many hardships. We have mentioned among the names of those prisoners those of John Lynd and Kenny Laverty. Lynd was a notary public, a quaint, sedate and solemn-visaged, but very shrewd and sagacious person. Upon the strength of his profession, having been connected with the administration of law, the British founded the humorous conceit, which has been recorded in several publications, that in the capture of the twenty-two members of Beale's rifles, they had actually taken prisoners all the lawyers and notaries of New Orleans. Such a capture would have deprived Jackson of no less than five aids who were really the leading members of the Bar of the city, to wit: Edward Livingston, John R. Grymes, Abner L. Duncan, Devezac and P. L. B. Duplessis. Lynd and Laverty, the latter on account of a most alarmingly treacherous brogue, and the former for his sanctimonious gravity, became frequent butts for the gibes of the British officers. Unfortunately, however, for their reputation as wits, they obtained but few victories in their encounters with the dry, solemn and quaint notary and the quick witted Irishman. Many instances of their discomfiture are related by the old people, who cherish with much devotion the stories and the witticisms, however simple, of the times in which they played their parts. On one occasion the prisoners, being taunted with a want of hospitality and generosity towards their visitors, who had been led to believe that they would be received with much pomp, and entertained with dinners and balls," the ready Irishman replied, " and faith we did receive you with balls—and as for the dinners, from what we had heard of ye, we thought you could provide for yourselves." This was a delicate allusion to the hen-roost-robbing reputation, which the British brought from the Chesapeake, and probably to the threat of Sir Alexander Cochrane, to eat his Christmas dinner at New Orleans.

During their detention in the fleet, the prisoners, as well as the sailors, were placed on half rations. This was a sore trial to Americans, Orleanians, who were accustomed to an abundance of the luxuries and comforts of life. One day, as some of the officers of the fleet were amusing themselves by catching sharks near Cat Island, where they abound, Sir Alexander Cochrane, who was looking on, remarked that he never saw fish bite so greedily.

" Probably yer honor, they are like meself, prisoners on half rations," respectfully suggested Laverty, with a face an ell long. When it was suggested, in allusion to his " rich Irish brogue," that the British Government might treat him as a deserter, whose allegiance had never been surrendered, Laverty, with an air of great gravity, asseverated that he had " drawn his first breath

in a pretty little village, in the good old State of Philadelphia," which declaration he subsequently justified
by the ingenious explanation that no man breathed at
all before he breathed the air of liberty.   Strongly contrasted with Laverty's light-hearted jollity was the ora-
cular solemnity of his sedate companion, who never
omitted an opportunity of warning the British of the
gloomy fate which awaited them when General Jackson
should get fairly aroused.   When the British would
boast of their achievements on the 23d December,—
they would be awe-stricken by the mysterious and dole-
ful expression, the ominous shaking of the head and
rolling of the eye-balls, with which the American seer
would accompany his invariable and prophetic reply—
" Oh, the end has not come yet! the end has not come
yet!"   The ship in which the prisoners were detained
was the Royal Oak.   At the time they were taken
aboard the captain was absent.   On his return to his
ship, what was the captain's surprise to recognize, in
Mr. Pollock, one of the prisoners, a bosom friend who
had officiated as groomsman for him at his marriage,
which event had occurred in New York, previous to the
war.   Of course, the friends forgot they were nationally
enemies, and soon became as cordial and happy as if
the two nations which they were respectively serving
were living on the very best terms.   In consequence of
this recognition, the captain of the Royal Oak caused
a very elegant dinner to be prepared for the prisoners,
which was attended by all the officers of the Royal
Oak and several of the other ships.   The dinner was
quite a jovial and protracted one.   There was an abundance of good old wine, of which the Americans partook with such gusto as might be expected in men who

had been on "short commons" for several days. This
indulgence came near destroying the harmony of the
occasion, as some political allusions having been dropped by some of the British officers, several of the
Americans fired up and declared that they could whip
the British, man to man,—Kenny Laverty offering to
take for "his share two of the brawniest chaps in the
fleet." But the ill-feeling and exaltation passed with
the fumes of the liquor, and thenceforward the relations
of the parties were pleasant and amicable.

Much less sensible, though perhaps more dignified,
was the conduct of the principal British officer, who
was captured by the Americans on the night of the 23d,
Major Samuel Mitchell, of the 95th Rifles, whose misfortune has been related above. The Major's disgust and
chagrin were visibly increased when he learned the
character of his captors. It was while suffering under
these feelings, after he had arrived in the rear of the
American camp, in charge of a guard of Coffee's men,
that Mr. Harrod, of the Quartermaster's Department,
(and now a respected merchant of New Orleans) waited
upon him at the order of General Jackson, with the
compliments of the General, and a request that he would
inform Mr. Harrod what he needed in the way of clothing and other comforts, and his wants would be immediately attended to. The Major, swelling with pride
and chagrin, replied, "Return my compliments to General Jackson and say, that as my baggage will reach me
in a few days, I shall be able to dispense with his polite
attentions." Had the Major persisted in this rash determination, he would never have been in a condition to
partake of the hospitalities which were lavished upon
him, during his necessarily disagreeable detention in

New Orleans, and in Natchez, to which place the prisoners were sent by Jackson.

It was whilst on the journey to Natchez, that the Major stopped at night at the hospitable mansion of Mr. Sauvé, a sugar planter, residing some twelve or fifteen miles above New Orleans, by whom he was invited to take a seat at the family supper table. One of Mr. Sauvé's daughters, now the estimable Mrs. Trudeau, was then in the bloom of her beauty, and the admiration of the country around for her many charms and accomplishments. The Major being a gallant and refined gentleman, who spoke French fluently, soon became engaged in a lively conversation with the beautiful Creole. Allusion having been made, in the course of this conversation, to Jackson's army, Miss Sauvé spoke with great enthusiasm of a party of Tennesseeans, whom her father had entertained a few days before. The circumstances of his capture still preying upon the mind of the haughty Briton, he could not refrain from observing to her—"Miss, it astonishes me that one so refined can find pleasure in the society of such rude barbarians."

"Major," replied the high-spirited Creole belle, "I had rather be the wife of one of those hardy and coarsely-clad, but brave and honest men, who have marched through a wilderness of two thousand miles to fight for the honor of their country, than to wear an English coronet."

Let us return to our narrative of the events of the 23d. Jackson, seeing it impossible to effect anything further, owing to the heavy fog which now enveloped the field, had drawn off the men of his division and posted them among Laronde's buildings. Coffee, following this

17

movement, had inclined the same direction, and taken up position nearly on Jackson's left. Before, however, all the men of the two divisions could be assembled together at these points many detachments and small parties had wandered off from the main lines and continued the combat in various parts of the field, to the great annoyance of the British, who, with such enemies, never knew when the battle ended. In these detached operations many deeds of personal daring were performed, which have no place in history. Swords were crossed and bayonets locked; pistols were used at a few paces. It was a night of duels. Many men, who had never been engaged in personal combats before, were that night transformed into heroes, and fought like practiced veterans. Many whose whole careers since have been characterized by the greatest gentleness and peacefulness, were that night as ferocious as tigers and brave as lions. The present generation can scarcely realize the truth of history, when they see in those mild, gentle and amiable old men, who on public anniversaries assemble around the tattered and time-worn banner of the "Veterans of 1814 and '15," the survivors of the terrible scenes of that memorable night-battle. A British officer, who participated in this bloody action, bears the following graphic testimony to its severity and sanguinary character:

"In wandering over the field, the most shocking and disgusting sights everywhere presented themselves. I have frequently beheld a greater number of dead bodies in as small a compass, though these, indeed, were numerous enough; but wounds more disfiguring or more horrible I certainly never witnessed. A man shot through the head or heart, lies as if he were in deep slumber, insomuch that when you gaze upon him, you experience little less than pity. But of these, many had met their death from bayonet wounds, sabre cuts, or heavy blows from the butt-ends of muskets, and the consequence was, that not only were the wounds themselves exceedingly frightful, but the very countenances of the dead exhibited the most savage and ghastly expressions. Friends and foes lay together in small groups of five or six—nor was it difficult to tell the very hand by which some of them had fallen. Nay, such had been the deadly closeness of the strife, that, in one or two places, an English and American soldier might be seen with the bayonet of each fastened in the other's body."

Jackson had accomplished more than he expected by this attack. He had not destroyed the British, but he had impressed them with a proper awe and respect for him. He had given them the first of a series of blows, which he felt satisfied would eventuate in their rout. He had in a few hours made his raw levies veterans. They were now ready and eager for service. They had been under fire. All that indecision and nervousness of fresh troops, when first subjected to this test, had been supplanted by cool courage, confidence and self-reliance. A few hours of real service had supplied months, nay years, of theoretical training. Besides, the enemy were astounded by the vigor of the attack, and erroneously ascribed it to the overwhelming force of Jackson. Keane, in his dispatch, magnifies Jackson's army into five thousand men. Whatever might be its number, it was evident that it was quite a different army—so Thornton and the men of the 85th and 4th thought— from that which they encountered at Bladensburg. "This boldly attacking us in our camp is a new feature in American warfare," was the general observation of the British officers. Such an attack was well calculated to make the British General pause and determine to delay his advance until his whole force had come up from the

Lake. He never imagined that with the troops which had reached him before the battle was over, he could have outnumbered and overwhelmed Jackson, and marched into the city. Hence the great importance of the battle of the 23d. It was the master-stroke of Jackson's genius. It was entirely his own idea and plan. Many of his officers deemed it the height of rashness. But all were willing to follow him, and when his spirit animated them fears and doubts disappeared.

In the execution of his plan, he was ably seconded by his officers. No men could have behaved better than Coffee, Piatt, Planché, Peire, D'Aquin, McRea, and others. Coffee appeared to be in every part of his extended line at the same time. Cool and self-possessed, he kept his men well together, and restrained, within the bounds of prudence, the natural impetuosity of the frontier-fighter, which is continually pushing him forward to fight "on his own hook." The Tennesseeans fought with great steadiness and gallantry. No body of men could have behaved better than the 7th Infantry, under the gallant creole officer Major Peire, a native of New Orleans. The 44th, a younger and newer regiment, under Captain Baker, had a very severe service and exposed situation, being compelled continually to oblique to the left to prevent the British from outflanking them. This duty they performed with great valor and steadiness. Planché's Battalion bore itself with the most brilliant courage, and moved with the precision of regulars, forming into battalion under a heavy fire, and charging the enemy until he was forced back. D'Aquin supported Planché promptly and efficiently with his Battalion of Free colored men The marines on the river were very efficient in protecting the artillery, which, during the whole action, played with great effect upon the enemy's camp. Owing to the numerous ditches and fences, Hinds' Dragoons were not brought into action, but maintained their position in the centre of Laronde's plantation. Nor did the British bear themselves with less than their usual valor on this occasion. Though surprised and taken at great disadvantage, the veterans of the Peninsular campaigns sustained the reputation which they had won in a hundred combats with Napoleon's renowned armies. From the nature of the combat, the officers had to take the lead in fighting, and they were always in their places. Their heavy loss proves the severity of the conflict and the ardor of both officers and men. The British had at least four hundred officers and men placed *hors du combat* in this affair. Their reported loss was three hundred and five killed, wounded and missing.* The number of the latter was eighty-five. The American loss was twenty-four killed, and one hundred and fifteen wounded and seventy-four prisoners—in all two hundred and thirteen.

Among the Americans no loss was more deeply lamented than that of Lieutenant Colonel Lauderdale, of Coffee's Brigade, who fell in the charge on Lacoste's huts, by the ball of one of the 95th Rifles. Lauderdale was an officer of high promise, of undaunted courage, great address, and decided military capacity. He had served with distinction under Coffee in the Indian wars, and enjoyed the warm admiration and confidence of Jackson. Lieutenant McClelland, who, at the head of the 7th, fell whilst leading the charge and opening the action, was esteemed one of the most energetic and

---

* The author of the " Campaigns, etc.," states the British loss at five hundred.

promising officers of that gallant regiment, which, from its origin to the present day, has maintained its reputation unsullied.

The British, too, lost some of their best officers. In addition to Major Harris, of the 85th, acting as Major of the Brigade, Captain Grey, another excellent officer of the same corps, was also killed by a rifle ball, described as so small that it scarcely left a mark on the forehead which it had penetrated. The 21st lost an excellent officer, a Captain Corsan, and the 4th a distinguished Peninsular hero in Captain Johnstone. Lieutenant John Souther, of the same regiment, was also killed. Of the severely wounded, there were Lieutenant Colonel Stoven, since Sir Frederick Stoven, Assistant Adjutant-General; Major Hooper, also Assistant Adjutant-General, who lost a leg, and Lieutenant Delacy Evans, of the 3d Dragoons, Deputy Assistant Quarter-Master General, an officer who has since acquired distinction as Sir Delacy Evans, a prominent member of the House of Commons of Great Britain, as General of a Spanish Legion in the Carlist revolution, and late commander of one of the divisions in the British army in the expedition to the Crimea, Lieutenant J. Christie, of the Royal artillery; Moody, of the 4th; Captain Knox, Lieutenants Willings, Maunsell and Hickson, of the 85th, Captain William, Lieutenants Forbes and Farmer, of the 95th, were all severely wounded, several losing limbs and being incapacitated for further service. Major Mitchell, of the 95th, Lieutenant W. Walker, and ensign Ashlier, of the 85th, were taken prisoners.

The author of the narrative of British Campaigns at Washington and New Orleans, presents the following harrowing picture of the spectacle, which was exhibited by the British Hospital, after the battle of the 23d. We should remark that General Keane had vacated Villeré's house, and the hospital had been established there :—

"Every room in the house was crowded with wretches, mangled, and apparently in the most excruciating agonies. Prayers, groans, and, I grieve to add, the most horrid imprecations smote upon the ear, wherever I turned. Some lay at length upon the straw, with eyes half closed and limbs motionless; some endeavored to start up, shrieking with pain, while the wandering eye and incoherent speech of others, indicated the loss of reason, and usually foretold the approach of death. But there was one among the rest, whose appearance was too terrible ever to be forgotten. He had been shot through the windpipe, and the breath making its way between the skin and the flesh, had dilated him to a size absolutely terrific. His head and face were particularly shocking. Every feature was enlarged beyond what can well be imagined, while his eyes were completely hidden by the cheeks and the forehead, as to destroy all resemblance to an human countenance. Passing through the apartments where the private soldiers lay, I next came to those occupied by officers. Of these there were five or six in one small room, to whom little better accommodations could be provided than to their inferiors. It was a sight peculiarly distressing, because all of them chanced to be personal acquaintances of my own. One had been shot in the head and lay gasping and insensible. Another had recived a musket ball in the belly, which had passed through and lodged in the backbone. The former appeared to suffer but little, giving no signs of life, except what a heavy breathing produced; the latter was in the most dreadful agony, screaming out and gnawing the covering under which he lay. There were many others there, some severely and others slightly hurt."

As to the forces engaged on the 23d, the usual estimates are very erroneous. Jackson marched from the city in the afternoon of the 23d with 2132 men and two cannons. Deducting the men left in charge of Coffee's horses and Hinds' Dragoons, there were not 1800 men engaged. This was very near the number of the British advance which had reached the river at noon. When it is considered that the troops on the one side were entirely new levies, few of the regulars having been in action, the disparity will be very glaring. But during the action the British were reinforced. After the departure of Thornton with the advance from Pea Island, a large portion of the remainder of Keane's army were placed in the small schooners and gun-boats, which followed the flotilla and arrived near the mouth of the Bienvenu about four o'clock in the afternoon. There they were met by the returning boats and barges, and were speedily disembarked.

Proceeding up the bayou, these troops, comprising a part of Brook's Brigade, could distinctly hear the firing of the Carolina, which announced the commencement of the battle. Pressing forward with all haste, they reached the field in time to take part in the action. The 93d Highlanders were the first to gain the camp, and a detachment of them was met by orders from Keane, to push forward with bayonets against Coffee's line, which was hastening to join the American right. They did not succeed, however, in reaching Coffee, who, after delivering a heavy fire, continued to oblique towards the position which he afterwards maintained. Four companies of the 21st also arrived in time to protect the British right. From these facts, which are admitted in Keane's report of the action of the 23d, it will be seen that besides Thornton's advance of 1800 men, there were four companies of the 21st and several of the 93d, actually engaged, making the whole number of the British army on the night of the 23d, about twenty-five hundred men. This estimate is confirmed by the dispatch of Sir Alexander Cochrane. This inequality, however, was more than compensated by the efficiency of the batteries of the Carolina, which, during the whole ac·tion, kept up its fire on the British camp, and continued it long after the battle was over.

. The newly arrived troops encamped as they came upon the field, extending from the woods as far towards the river, that the advance, by wheeling up, might complete the line from the river to the swamp. But the advance was still fastened to the levee by that unsparing schooner, whose batteries seemed in one continual blaze, and whose grape-shot rained on the field like hail. It was only when all the fires were extinguished and perfect darkness shrouded the field, that the Caro-:ina weighed anchor and moved to the other side of the river, keeping, however, a close eye on the British all the while.

Keane's army passed a miserable night. The men lay on the damp ground without any covering, exposed to a thick fog, which appeared to combine all the discomforts of rain and frost. Few were allowed to sleep even under these uncomfortable circumstances, a large number being required for outpost duty, and attendance on the wounded. Comfortless as the night was, the British had but little satisfaction in anticipating the break of day, as it would only expose their position to the fire of the schooner, which had already so grievously distressed them.

And so it proved, though even worse than was apprehended. On the morning of the 24th, the Louisiana, a merchant ship, fitted up as a war vessel, joined the Carolina, and as soon as light exposed the British camp, both vessels opened their batteries with most destruc-

tive effect. All that day was the British advance compelled to cling to the protection of the levee, so that
even parties that were sent out to collect the wounded
and bury the dead, were frequently compelled to abandon these duties.

Such was the pitiable condition of the British army
from its arrival until the night of the 24th, when the
men were ordered to withdraw from the levee and encamp behind the sugar-house and outbuildings of Lacoste. Acccordingly they filed off to the right, company by company, and passing through the village of
negro huts, established themselves in the field beyond,
interposing the chateau, the out-buildings, sugar-house
and negro huts between them and their untiring perse-
cutors. A small picket was left to occupy the levee
and river bank. This movement secured the British
some comfort and peace, of which they immediately
commenced to avail themselves by lighting fires and
cooking their suppers. Many of them had become so
cramped with cold and inaction, during their supine
position under the levee, that they found it necessary to
rub their limbs with spirits before the circulation of
blood could be restored.

What in the meantime had Jackson done with his
little army? Satisfied, indeed elated with the results
of the action of the 23d, Jackson determined to establish his camp right in front of the British. Leaving the
7th Infantry and a company of Dragoons at La Ronde's,
he fell back nearer the city to Rodriguez' Canal, where
the men proceeded to entrench themselves in such rude
and inartificial manner as might occur to raw soldiers.
The whole of the 24th was thus consumed. Sending to
town for all the spades and other instruments suitable

for digging, the men set to work with the greatest vivacity, widening the canal and throwing up the dirt on
the bank nearest to the city. Though the great majority
of them were unused to manual toil, there was no want of
zeal or energy in their work. A rivalry sprung up, which
could build the highest mound in front of his position or
dig the ditch deepest. Each soldier claimed the mound in
his front as his " castle," and such was the value attached
to these " castles" that the General was induced to
countermand an order he had given for the whole line
to incline to the left to make room for a small reinforcement, by the strong remonstrance of the soldiers, who
placed a higher value on their own than their neighbor's
work. The results of this zealous industry were sur-
prising. On the 24th the whole front of Jackson's line
was pretty well covered by a mound of three or more
feet high. On the extreme right the two six pounders,
which had been used on the 23d, were placed in battery,
so as to command the road.

On that very day, the 24th December, 1814, the treaty
of peace between Great Britain and the United States
was completed and duly signed at Ghent by the commissioners of the two nations. It is a painful reflection
that all the scenes of strife and bloodshed which we
shall describe occurred after the two countries had,
through their representatives, established and agreed
upon a firm and lasting peace and friendship. The
reproach and responsibility of such unnatural and unfortunate events must ever attach to that nation which,
during the discussion and negotiation of a treaty of
peace, secretly fitted out and dispatched a warlike expedition against the nation with which it was then holding
a parley.

It was in strengthening these entrenchments and in burnishing their arms, the soldiers of Jackson spent that day which they were wont to devote to social pleasures and festivities, and which was associated in their memories and hearts with the tenderest and most delightful scenes of domestic life and social peace and happiness. A stern sense of duty and an ardent patriotism sustained them under discomforts and deprivations, which were rendered more palpable from contrast with the customary festivities and light-hearted merriments which, among all Christian people, mark the recurrence of the anniversary of the great founder of Christianity.

X.

SIR EDWARD PACKENHAM.

It would be difficult to imagine a gloomier day than the Christmas of eighteen hundred and fourteen, as passed by the sons of Merrie England, in their damp, miserable, exposed and desolate camp on the plantation of Villeré. The few luxuries, which an extended predatory search of the neighboring plantations had enabled them to collect on the first day after their arrival, in the enjoyment of which they had been so disagreeably interrupted by their active enemy, were exhausted, and now officers and soldiers were reduced to the very worst kind of salt provisions and weevily biscuit. Such supplies for such troops were certainly discreditable to their commissariat. Fortunately, however, they were veterans, and could bear up against every hardship and deprivation.

Under these circumstances, it would have displayed marvelous philosophy and equanimity in the British soldiers, if even the genial associations of Christmas could have imparted a ray of cheerfulness to the gathering gloom which hung over the camp and enveloped the minds of officers and men.

The spirits of the soldiers had been greatly depressed since the action of the 23d. All that remained to sustain them was the morale and discipline for which the

British soldiers, particularly the veterans of the Peninsula, are so distinguished. Besides, they were slightly encouraged by intimations of expected reinforcements, which would render their entrance into the city certain and glorious. Amid all their disasters and difficulties, the conquerors of Napoleon's veterans could not bring their minds to regard it possible, or within the decree of Providence, that they should be foiled, prostrated, routed and disgraced by raw militia, led by an Indian fighter, who was ignorant of even the first rudiments of military science.

In all circumstances, and conditions, too, men of the Saxon and Celtic stock will divide into parties and factions and engage in feuds and controversies. The British camp was not free from these dissensions. They turned chiefly upon the wisdom of General Keane's course in his mode of landing, and in delaying to advance upon the city. Keane's friends and adherents defended him by hinting that the honor of achieving the great result was reserved for some more distinguished personage and pet of the ministry. The grade and previous service of General Keane, then quite a young officer, and the fact that he had been sent out as second to Ross, evinced very clearly that it was not the intention of the British Cabinet to entrust him with so important a command.

Some greater personage was hourly expected, and there, on the bleak and cheerless plain, the army would be detained until he arrived to lead them into the city. It would be fortunate for the military reputation of General Keane if this suggestion of his friends were founded on fact. It would relieve him of a heavy load of censure, which has always attached to his military

character, from the apparent want of decision, promptitude and military sagacity displayed in his failure to
advance, on his arrival on the banks of the Mississippi,
and in his inactivity after the battle of the twenty-third.

These blunders were felt, acknowledged and discussed
by every soldier in the British camp, and though excused
and palliated by the pretexts alluded to, they produced
a want of confidence in the General, and a desire for
some more experienced and renowned chief to lead
them.

Such a chief appeared in the British camp quite
suddenly on the morning of that gloomy Christmas, and
by his presence communicated relief, hope, and even
vivacity to the dejected spirits of the army. And well
might such a presence produce such effects upon the
veterans of Wellington, for among the commanders,
whom the brilliant campaigns of Spain had brought
into conspicuous notice, there was not one who enjoyed
more of the esteem, respect, and admiration of the British soldiers, than the Hero of Salamanca, the Hon. Sir
Edward M. Packenham, Lieutenant General and Colonel
of the 7th Foot (Royal Fusiliers). Sir Edward was a
son of the Earl of Longford, of the county of Antrim,
Ireland—whose daughter had been married to the Duke
of Wellington. The family has always been noted for
military ardor and heroism, and has contributed several
distinguished commanders to both the army and navy
of Great Britain. Quite recently the nephew and
namesake of Sir Edward, Lieut. Colonel Edward Packenham, of the Grenadier Guards, fell gallantly fighting
at the head of his regiment in the bloody battle of
Inkermann on the 5th of November, 1854. He had
previously won a brevet and the warm praise of his

commander by his gallantry at the battle of Alma, where, leading his company, he was the first to leap over the enclosure of the most formidable of the Russian batteries, and was seen quietly scratching the name of his regiment, the number of his company, with the point of his sword on the gun he had taken.

The Earldom of Longford is of modern creation, one of those which had sprung up in Ireland during the troubles, incident to the subjugation of that island, when England sought to supersede the native aristocracy, by ennobling the successful soldiers, who settled the subject province. Thus originated the Earldom from which that gallant soldier, who was sent to Louisiana, as his ancestor had been sent to Ireland, to reduce a free people into vassalage to a foreign power, derived all the consideration, which was due to rank and family. He possessed, however, a just title to a higher consideration and respect, as a gentleman, a gallant soldier, and kind-hearted man. The title was to be found, in a career of great brilliancy, of constant, severe, painful and perilous service, in the profession in which, when quite a boy, he embarked with all the ardor and ambition characteristic of Irish birth and education. He did not owe his advancement to the influence of family and friends. He fought his way up, round by round, and marked each grade with some honorable wound, so that ere he had reached the meridian of life and of military advancement, his body was scrolled over with such insignia of gallantry and good conduct. Few officers had encountered more perils and hardships, or suffered from more wounds. Entering the army as lieutenant of 23d Light Dragoons, he soon rose to the rank of Major. In the storming of the fort on the island of St. Lucie, West

Indies, in 1796, Major Packenham volunteered to lead the attacking columns. The charge was a brilliant and successful one, but the young leader was badly wounded, receiving a ball through his neck. In the same neighborhood, in the expedition to Martinique, in 1806, having been promoted to the command of that renowned regiment, the 7th Fusiliers, he was again badly wounded at the head of the Fusiliers.*

During the Peninsular war, Packenham was in constant service, by the side of Wellington, and as Brigadier of that impetuous Welshman, General Picton. Towards the close of the war he was appointed Adjutant-General, at the request of Wellington. Throughout the army of the Peninsula, he was admired and beloved by both officers and men. We have not space to describe all the brilliant actions in which he participated, but a few of the incidents of his career may not be uninteresting to those who have been accustomed to regard him with hostility and prejudice, as the leader of an expedition which was neither honorable in its design, nor glorious in its conclusion.

The brilliant courage of Sir Edward Packenham was never more conspicuously displayed than in the horrible and bloody night attack of the British, on the strongly-defended walls and fort of Badajoz. On that occasion the storming party was for sometime mowed down with merciless severity, before any one of the soldiers could reach the walls. At last, however, a few scattered men, who had escaped, succeeding in planting three ladders

---

*It is a remarkable fact, recorded by Guthrie in his work on gunshot wounds, tha the last mentioned wound repaired one of the effects of the ·revious wound received by Packenham at St. Lucie. On both occasions he was shot n the neck. The first wound when it healed, drew his head on one side, but the second restored it to its original position.

18

against the walls. As fast as the men mounted these
ladders they would be shot down by the French soldiers
on the parapet. In some cases the ladders broke, and
many of the British soldiers were precipitated below and
impaled upon the bayonets of their companions. Sir
Edward Packenham was the second man to mount one
of these ladders, being preceded by a gallant High-
lander, Lieutenant McPherson, of the 45th. Both
arrived unharmed within a few rounds of the top, when
McPherson discovered that the ladder was about three
feet too short. Still undaunted, the gallant young man
called loudly to those below, to raise the ladder more
perpendicular. Whilst he with great exertion parted it
from the wall at the top, the men with a loud cheer
brought it quickly nearer to the base. This was done
so suddenly, that McPherson was on a level with the
rampart before he could prepare for defence. He saw
a French soldier deliberately point his musket against
his body and without power to strike it aside, he had to
receive the fire. The ball struck one of the Spanish
silver buttons on his waistcoat, which it broke in half.
This changed its direction and caused it to glance off,
not however, before it had broken two ribs, the fractured
part of one being pressed in on his lungs so as almost to
stop respiration. Still he did not fall, but continued to
hold on by the upper round of the ladder, conceiving
that he was wounded, but ignorant to what extent. He
could not, however, advance. Packenham strove to pass
him, but in the effort was also badly wounded, a French
soldier firing a musket into his body, at a distance of
three or four feet. Almost at the same time, the ladder
cracked beneath them. Destruction seemed inevitable.
Before them on the ramparts stood a line of French

soldiers presenting their muskets; beneath, their own friends crowded together, formed a *Chevaux de-frise* of bayonets. Even at such a perilous and awful moment, the presence of mind of these two brave men did not desert them. Packenham grasping the hand of the wounded McPherson, said "God bless you my dear fellow, we shall meet again."

They did meet again, but not as Packenham meant, for they marvelously escaped, and recovering from their wounds, were enabled to perform many acts of conspicuous gallantry in the events which followed.

As Brigadier of the " Old Fighting Third," the division of Wellington's army so famous for its daring under the lead of Picton, the sickness of the chief devolved upon Packenham the command of the division on the eve of the battle of Salamanca When Picton heard who was to command his division, he observed, " I am glad he is to lead my brave fellows ; they will have plenty of their favorite sport." In this battle Wellington opened the fight by riding up to Packenham at the head of the Third Division ordering him to move forward, take the heights in front and drive everything before him.

"Give me one grasp of that all-conquering hand," exclaimed the enthusiastic Packenham, who entertained for his chief a most chivalric and ardent attachment, "and I WILL." How he redeemed this pledge is thus vigorously and graphically described by Alison :

"It was five o'clock when Packenham fell on Thormiere, who, so far from being prepared for such an onset, had just reached an open hill, the last of the ridge over which he had extended, from whence he expected to see the allied army in full retreat to Ciendad Rodrigo, and closely pursued by Marmont, defiling in the valley before him. To effect a change of front in such circumstances, was impossible. All that could be done was to resist instantly, as they stood. The British columns formed into line as they marched, so that the moment they came in sight of the enemy, they were ready to charge. In an instant the French gunners were at their pieces, and a cloud of light troops hastened to the front, and endeavored by a rapid fire to cover the formation of the troops behind. Vain attempt! Right onward through the storms of bullets did the British, led by the heroic Packenham, advance; the light troops are dispersed before them like chaff before the wind; the half-formed lines are broken into fragments; Durban's Portuguese Cavalry, supported by Harvey's English Dragoons, and Arentchild's German Horse, turned their right flank, scrambled up the steep sides of a bush-fringed stream, which flowed behind the ridge, yet not at first in confusion, but skillfully, like gallant veterans, seizing every successive wood and hill which offered the means of arresting the enemy. Gradually, however, the reflux and pressing together of so large a body, by enemies at once in front and in flank, threw their array into confusion; their cavalry were routed and driven among the foot. Thormiere himself was killed whilst striving to stem the torrent; the allied cavalry broke like a flood into the openings of the infantry, and his whole division was thrown back, entirely routed, on Clansel's, which was hurrying up to its aid, with the loss of three thousand prisoners."

Of this brilliant action Packenham was emphatically the hero, and for his service on this occasion was knighted.

Nor was Sir Edward Packenham less distinguished for his high honor, chivalry, and humanity, than for his courage and daring. As his name has been associated with the imputed design of sacking New Orleans, and perpetrating upon its peaceful population the most brutal and infamous excesses, which design was embodied in the alleged war-cry of the British army— "Beauty and booty"—a cry not inconsistent with the character which a portion of the army had acquired on the shores of the Chesapeake, and in the Peninsular war, we take pleasure in referring to the antecedents of Packenham, to rebut all presumption that he was cognizant of, or would have given the slightest sanction to, such disgraceful purposes. How he would have acted towards any of his command, who might have 'been implicated in such outrages, may be inferred from his conduct in Spain, when entering a town, in which certain French citizens had been outraged by some British soldiers, he caused the latter to be hung on the spot, "thereby," says Napier, "nipping the wickedness in the bud, but at his own risk, for legally he had not the power." Napier has thought proper to add, with the commendable feeling of a soldier defending a brother in arms: "This General, whose generosity, humanity and chivalric spirit excited the admiration of every honorable person who approached him, has been foully traduced by American writers. He who was preeminently distinguished for his detestation of inhumanity and outrage, has been, with astounding falsehood, represented as instigating his troops to the most infamous excesses."

Napier evidently errs in assuming for the Commander, a charge against many of his subordinates, who, as may be proved by documents now extant, freely declared the predatory purposes of the expedition. Besides, the circumstances of the enterprise—undertaken as it was, whilst the commissioners of both nations were engaged in negotiations, to establish peace between the two countries on a permanent and satisfactory basis—will ever give it a questionable character, and lead all impartial persons to believe that its main purpose was booty—the appropriation of the fifteen millions of the produce of the peaceful industry of the country, to the enrichment of rude soldiers, whose lives had been devoted to the destruction rather than to the increase of the wealth of the world. Gallant, generous and high-minded, as he personally was, Packenham's name and fame cannot be considered as entirely free from the reproach, which must attach to all those who were asso· ciated in an expedition prompted by such motives. Certainly, Sir William Napier would not deny what the pages of his own incomparable history so abundantly prove, that the British soldiers were not only capable of, but prone to the excesses which, it has so often been charged, were to follow the capture of New Orleans. Frequently, in the towns in the Peninsula, the Spaniards found better protection from their enemies, the French, than from their allies, the British soldiers. The actors in the scenes at Cumberland Island, at Hampton, Alexandria and Washington City; the incendiaries of libraries, of printing presses, of private property of every description; the mutilators of public monuments, could hardly complain, if suspected of too strong an appetite for the rich booty which was heaped up in the great depot of the Valley of the Mississippi.

This charge against the originators and projectors of the expedition to New Orleans, as one for plunder and spoils, is too well established now to be questioned. British testimony alone is sufficient to prove the truth of these allegations. This may not be an unappropriate place to quote a few authorities from that source. Major Cook of the British 43d, who was engaged in the expedition to New Orleans, and has written a lively work on this campaign, which has been well received in England, says: "Notwithstanding all these natural draw·

backs the city of New Orleans with its valuable booty of merchandise was craved by the British to grasp such a prize by a *coup de main.*" In another place he remarks, " the warehouses of the city were amply stored with cotton to a vast amount, and also sugar, molasses, tobacco and other products of this prolific soil."

The author of the campaigns of the British at Washington, Batimore, and New Orleans says: "And it appears that instead of a trifling affair, more likely to fill our pockets than to add to our renown, we had embarked in an undertaking, which presented difficulties not to be surmounted without patience and determination." A letter from Colonel Malcolm, at Cumberland Island, to his brother the Rear Admiral in the fleet, under Cochrane, which was intercepted by an American cruiser, expressing the hope that the writer would soon hear of the capture of New Orleans, adds : ' It will repay the troops for all their trouble and fatigue.' Mr. Glover, a British employee, in a letter found in the same package, to Captain Westphall, mingles prescience and avarice in the following apprehension : ' My forebodings will not allow me to anticipate either honor or profit to the expedition.' "

History, however, must acquit Sir Edward Packenham of any motives or design of plunder or brutality, in accepting this command. It was, doubtless, in the discharge of what he deemed his duty, and to gratify what he regarded an honorable ambition, that he came to assume the Governorship of Louisiana, and, with it, the Earldom, that was to reward his conquest of a Province, which Great Britain had long entertained an ardent desire to possess. We do not believe that the English Government would have allowed Sir Edward's

modesty or chivalry to prevail over the necessity of
supporting this new Earldom by some adequate moneyed
allowance; nor that they would have regarded it as at
all improper to app.y to that object, a large share of the
fifteen millions of cotton and sugar then in the warehouses of New Orleans.   If one of " the greatest soldiers,
Englishmen and Christians, that ever lived," as Sir Wil
liam Napier has styled his distinguished relative, the
conqueror of Scinde, in a funeral oration, recently delivered at the burial of that heroic soldier (no less
remarkable for its extravagance, than its terseness), did
not sully his laurels by enriching himself out of the
spoils, the treasure, the jewels and precious metals of
the subjugated Ameers, certainly his historian will not
include us in the class of American writers who have
"traduced" the memory and fame of Packenham, for
intimating that his successful entrance into the city of
New Orleans would have supplied all those deficiencies
of fortune, which too often mark the condition of meri-
torious younger sons of the nobility of Great Britain.

With Sir Edward came, as second in command, Major
General Samuel Gibbs, Colonel of the 59th Foot, a very
active and experienced officer, who had greatly distinguished himself in the East, and particularly in the
storming of Fort Cornelius, on the island of Java, and in
the Peninsular war.   There were also several distinguished staff, engineer, and artillery officers, who came
with Sir Edward Packenham.

It has quite recently—since the death of the Duke
of Wellington and the publication of his letters—come
to light, that the project was seriously discussed in the
British cabinet of placing Wellington at the head of
the expedition to New Orleans, and that he manifested

no reluctance to undertake the enterprise. In one of his
letters, recently published, he refers to the subject, saying he would cheerfully accept the duty, if it was
imposed upon him, gives some very crude views of the
manner in which the war should be conducted, and
declares his belief that the troops he had seen embark
for America at Bordeaux, in the summer of 1814, must
be very badly handled if they did not prove victors in
any contest in which they might be engaged. Fortunate
decision of the British Cabinet!* Wellington was retained at home. The ministry, however, sent some of
his ablest lieutenants—upon whose brows the laurels
of Spain were destined to be supplanted by the cypress
of Louisiana—to execute the plan of operations of their
great chief. Ross had fallen on the banks of the
Petapsco, and Packenham was sent to take his place.

Favoring winds brought him swiftly to the scenes of
his future operations. As he stepped from the barge, at
the head of Villeré's Canal, surrounded by his gallant
staff, and greeted by many of the officers of the army,
his proud heart swelled with satisfaction and hope, at
the prospect, now first opened to him, of rivaling the
fame of his great relative, by an exploit that would ring
through the world, and bring out the old Tower guns to
awaken the quiet Londoners with their thundering an-

* After the campaign, and to the day of his death, the Duke was a great admirer of
General Jackson, and whilst the latter lived, never failed when he was introduced to
an American, to inquire after the General's health. The Earl of Ellesmere, who visited
New York during the Industrial Exhibition of 1853, related to General Quitman that
being on very intimate terms with the Duke, he frequently visited him in his private
room. The Duke had a habit whenever he received any document, which afforded him
pleasure, of crumpling it in his hand and waving it over his head. On one occasion
the Earl surprised the Duke in one of these curious displays of satisfaction, which was
more than usually enthusiastic; and inquiring the cause, learned that the crumpled
document over which the great warrior was so much elated was a simple letter of introduction from General Jackson!

nouncement of another great victory won by the heroes of the Peninsula. For the first time in his life, Packenham found himself in an independent command, at the head of one of the choicest and most efficient armies that England ever sent forth. This, for a man of thirty-eight, was certainly a proud distinction. As his eye ran down the lists of the regiments of his command, Packenham could not but repeat, with his full endorsement, the remark of Wellington, as to their invincibility. Except the 93d Highlanders and the Black Regiments, they were all troops which fought through the whole war in the Peninsula, from Moore's retreat to Wellington's triumphant entry into France.

There were the Rifles, which, under Cranford and Barnard, had opened nearly every battle that Wellington fought. There were the 85, the 44th, the 21st and 14th Dragoons, all bronzed veterans, who had never known defeat, and who were as familiar with all the horrors and exigencies of war, as if they had been nursed by Bellona. Others, too, of equal renown, were hourly expected. The 43d, the 40th, and above all Packenham's own Fusiliers, the 7th, at whose head he had so often marched to victory and received so many honorable wounds. Who, under like circumstances, would not have felt the glow of pride, enthusiasm and cheerful confidence, which radiated the manly countenance of Packenham, when Keane stepped forward and, saluting him, gladly relinquished a command which had become to him a wearisome burden?

There was great rejoicing in the British camp over the arrival of Packenham. Loud cheers rent the air. Even salvos of artillery were fired in honor of the event. This joy and commotion were quite perceptible to the

American outposts, who soon ascertained the cause and communicated it to Jackson. The next day the news flew through the American lines that a famous British general—some had it the Duke of Wellington himself—had arrived in the British camp. Henceforth, it was said, the operations of the British would be conducted with much more vigor and power, and with more efficient forces and appliances than had been employed heretofore. These stories, with all their exaggerations, did not appal the spirit or weaken the energies of Jackson. Indeed, the only visible effect they produced was to communicate greater activity and resolution to all his movements and measures for the maintenance of his position. Without dismounting, for hours and hours, he paced along the line of the Rodriguez Canal, encouraging and inciting his men by every influence which he could use, to labor in the rude entrenchment which his engineers had drawn along the canal. " Here," he remarked to them, in the frontier style, " we shall plant our stakes, and not abandon them until we drive these red-coat rascals into the river, or the swamp."

Packenham, who had the eye of a soldier, was not pleased with his first glance at the position of his army. It did not take much time for him to comprehend all the perils and embarrassments that environed him. Concealing his feeling and impressions, he assembled the chief officers·at Villeré's house, where he established his headquarters.

There, in the parlor of the patriotic planter, who was then but a few miles off, aiding in the organization of the militia, who were daily dispatched to reinforce Jackson, met a score or more of the most distinguished veteran officers of the Peninsular war, to deliberate upon the means of resisting and defeating a militia general, at the head of a force of raw militia, inferior in number to their own gallant array of veteran and practiced warriors. Many of them had not seen their associates since they parted in Spain; many, like the officers of the 93d, newly arrived from the Cape of Good Hope, had not met for eight or ten years.

But there was no time for congratulations or the interchange of friendly conversation. The business before them was serious and pressing. Their consultation extended far into the night. What then and there occurred must ever be a mystery, but enough leaked out to convince the younger officers, that Sir Edward was greatly dissatisfied with the aspect of affairs, and after receiving a full report of Keane's operations, entertained but little hope of achieving the object of the expedition. He perceived and lamented the original error, in not advancing on the 23d. It was even said that he thought of withdrawing the army and attempting a landing in another quarter. But that sturdy veteran, Sir Alexander Cochrane, who attended the council, was of sterner stuff, and regarded the expedition as far from being defeated or foiled. If the army shrunk from the task, he would bring up the sailors and marines from the fleet, and storm the American lines, and march into the city. "The soldiers could then," added the bitter old Scotchman, " bring up the baggage.

The confidence of the old tar was happily illustrated by an authentic anecdote. One of the British prisoners captured on the 23d December, stated to General Jackson, that the Admiral had sworn that he would eat his Christmas dinner in the city. Jackson promptly replied, "Perhaps so, but I shall have the honor of presiding at that dinner."

It was finally determined to advance and carry the enemy's entrenchments at the point of the bayonet.

The original error in regard to the superior force of the Americans still clung to them. Even then, when they had had the opportunity for observation, which their position afforded,—and when the Americans had but two small artillery pieces, and their entrenchments were but just commenced, they neglected to advance with an army which exceeded by two or three thousand that of Jackson's command. This, for the Americans, fortunate remissness, was all due to the impression which Jackson had made on the minds of the British by his extraordinary and brilliant attack on the 23d.

Packenham, on assuming the command of the army, changed its organization, by forming two columns, or brigades, under the command of Generals Gibbs and Keane. How these brigades were composed, will appear hereafter.

Early the next day, the 26th December, Packenham rode out with his staff and Generals to reconnoitre the American lines. As far as the eye could reach along the plain, which lay before him, he could perceive no evidence of any regular force opposed to him. The only living objects he could discern were bodies of horsemen, galloping over the field in a very unmilitary fashion, apparently watching every movement in the British camp, and now and then cracking away with their long rifles at the outposts and sentinels. Then these stragglers would wheel and return leisurely to an old chateau, about long musket shot from the British sentries, which appeared to be their general rendezvous. These scouts presented more the appearance of snipe and rabbit hunters beating the bushes for their game, than of soldiers seeking opportunities to annoy their enemies. It was a novel sight to Packenham, accustomed as he was to the formal and regular mode of conducting warlike operations of the French and British armies.

Beyond these, there was no other evidence of the presence of a hostile army. This mysterious and silent aspect in front served to increase the anxiety and embarrassment of the British General. The movements of these irregular troops indicated the confidence of a powerful force strongly posted in the rear, as well as the audacity of men who had been under fire and had tasted of the horrors of war. They were no timid militiamen, like those who had offered so feeble a resistance at Washington; or, rather, in justice to the latter, many of whom were personally as brave as any who ever shouldered a musket, we should say there was unmistakable evidence of the presence among them of a chief, who inspired confidence, courage, and determination in all under his command.

This observation satisfied Packenham, that he had but one course to pursue, and that was to carry the enemies lines, wherever they were, by storm. As soon as this resolution was taken, all anxiety and care disappeared from his countenance. He immediately set to work to prepare for the advance.

But, before this could be done, a serious obstacle had to be removed. Those terrible floating batteries, the Carolina and Louisiana, still retained their position, anchored near the opposite bank of the river, and kept up a continual cannonading on the British camp. Whereever a knot of British could be seen, a shower of grape would be thrown at them with such accuracy that they would be quickly dispersed, and compelled to take shelter. Even those who took refuge in the houses were not safe. Many a social party who met stealthily in some quiet little negro hut, behind the chimneys, or in some nook of the larger houses, to enjoy a few comforts and relieve the distress and tedium of their situation by a little conviviality, would suddenly be intruded upon by a cannon-ball sent from one of Patterson's vessels, producing a very precipitate scattering of the party. It was impossible to form a column under the fire of these vessels. Orders were therefore issued to hurry up all the large cannon which could be spared from the fleet, for the purpose of bringing them to bear on the two formidable little vessels. By incredible exertions, the chief labor being performed by the sailors, under Cochrane and Malcolm, a powerful battery of twelve and eighteen-pounders was brought up on the night of the 26th, and planted on the levee, so as to command the Carolina and Louisiana.

On the morning of the 27th, the American lines were aroused by a severe and prolonged cannonading from the British camp. This was the first intimation of the presence of heavy artillery among the enemy. The Americans collected on the levee to see whence the firing proceeded. There could be no doubt of the object. It was now seen, what terrible plagues those vessels had been. All their power and skill were concentrated to destroy them. Their battery was evidently a powerful one, and was manned by officers and men who understood their business. Their fire was gallantly and briskly returned from both vessels. Never were broadsides given with more rapidity and accuracy.

The British could only escape their effects by watching the flash of the guns, and then taking refuge under the levee. Loud cheers arose from each line, at every discharge of their respective batteries, which could be distinctly heard in both camps. From the dormant window of the Macarté House, Jackson narrowly watched the combat through a telescope. Packenham stood on the levee near his battery cheering and encouraging the artillerists. The banks of the river, for some distance below, and as far above the American lines as would afford a view of the field, were lined with spectators, who regarded the scene with intense interest. A tempest of cannon balls was poured upon the devoted vessels, amid which gleamed, like flaming comets, red hot shot, whilst bursting shells and steaming rockets spread a halo of fire around them. Thus the cannonading was sustained for a half an hour before it was discovered that any effect was produced upon the vessels. At last it was quite perceptible in both armies, that the Carolina had been struck. There was a commotion upon her decks. Her firing ceased. Presently her crew were seen clambering down her sides, and taking to the boats. In good order, without alarm or confusion, the boats being all filled, pushed off for the opposite shore, not, however, without shouting a loud defiance at their foes. Then, when all had left her, a light flame was seen, rising from her deck, which the light breeze fed and kindled, until it spread through the hull of the vessel, and then tapering off with the tall masts and branching spars, involved the whole vessel in a fiery embrace. Now the British gave three loud cheers, which almost equalled the thunder of their cannon in volume, and echoed far up and down the river. Eagerly they watched the progress of the flames, as they rapidly devoured the gallant little vessel. At last the fire reached the magazine, and then, with an explosion, which shook the earth for miles around, the Carolina was blown to atoms. Her crew, however, under the indefatigable Captain Henley, gained the shore in safety, with the loss of one sailor killed and six wounded. This event drew a deep sigh from the bosoms of the several thousands of Americans who looked on. In the British camp it was hailed with unbounded delight and most enthusiastic hurras.

Well, the British might shout and rejoice. That little vessel had not given them an hour's respite since they reached the banks of the Mississippi. It had saluted them, on their arrival, with a broadside which placed a hundred of their men *hors de combat*. For the three days following, there was not an hour that it did not sweep the field in which the British lay with its terrible battery. Its destruction, therefore, might justly be celebrated as a jubilee in the British camp.

Packenham and his soldiers now breathed freer. A thorn had been removed from the side of the army, yet their flank was not entirely cleared. Absorbed in their design of getting rid of their older enemy, they had lost sight of the larger ship Louisiana, which lay higher up the stream. It was a great blunder of the British to open with their battery on the Carolina instead of the Louisiana. Whilst they were at work on the schooner, Lieutenant Thompson, on the Louisiana, was straining every nerve to get that ship beyond the reach of their batteries. Since the destruction of the

19

Carolina and the gun-boats, the Louisiana was the only
vessel left to the Americans. Jackson's last word to
Thompson was to save her at every risk. Her commander was the man to execute such an order. Thompson had displayed amazing energy in raising a crew and
equipping the Louisiana for service in a few days. He
had been driven to the necessity of scouring the streets
and impressing sailors to fill the complement of men
necessary to man his guns. With this fresh and ill-dis-
ciplined crew, he suddenly found himself in a most perplexing situation. The Carolina had been blown up, so
near that her burning fragments fell on the decks of the
Louisiana. Both wind and current were against him.
The balls of the British battery began to fall thickly
around, and the water hissed and simmered with the hot
shell that bounded towards and over her. At last
Thompson bethought him of towing, and putting all
hands to work at the boats, succeeded in moving her
slowly, until she was beyond reach of the British ; not,
however, without some damage, caused by a shell,
which fell on the decks and wounded several men. It
was indeed a narrow escape. As she moved up stream,
and gaining a position nearly abreast of the American
camp, let go her anchors, at the same time firing a defiant volley at the British, the Americans, whose hearts
and countenances had fallen under the disaster of the
Carolina, gave three loud cheers, which could be distinctly heard in the British camp.

The removal of these vessels communicated fresh
hope and confidence to the British army. Whilst the
battery was engaged with the American vessels, Gibbs
and Keane were forming their columns for the advance.
Having relieved their flank of its vigorous and active

foe, these columns could now form in the open field. Accordingly towards evening, on the 27th, a rocket was sent up from the headquarters of the General-in-Chief. At that signal the British army moved forward, abandoning ground, which had but few attractions or pleasing associations to the minds of the soldiers. Gibbs led his column under cover of the wood on the right, and Keane marched by the road near the river, keeping Bienvenu's and Chalmette's houses between him and the American lines. Thus the two columns advanced to a point within four or six hundred yards of the American lines. Night closing upon them, the soldiers were ordered to lie down in their places and refresh themselves with sleep. Promptly they obeyed the order, in the fond hope of resting and recuperating their wearied bodies. Delusive hope! There again were those untiring "land privateers" in their front, who appeared never to sleep themselves, nor willing to allow others to enjoy that blessing. There they were, hovering about the English outposts and pickets, popping away at every man who showed himself, with their terrible rifles, creeping up stealthily in squads and firing right into their pickets. There, too, the daring Hinds and his madcap troopers, dashing up to their outposts and forming with all the regularity of parade exercise, would fire volleys into the lines, and then gallop back again hurraing and shouting in savage glee and derision.

The night, instead of being devoted to sleep and rest, was made hideous to the British by these incessant annoyances. The Americans, so the indignant and disquieted Britons thought, like some of the indigenous animals of the country, appeared to prefer the night to the day for their prowling and warlike operations. The precedent of the 23d had been followed ever since. Each man among them seemed bent on some deed of individual prowess, of which he might discourse to his companions in his mess, and around the camp fires. Nor was it merely for display, or to alarm their enemies, that they engaged in these nocturnal enterprises. They looked to such practical results, as the cutting off a sentinel, the driving in an outpost, or the picking off an officer going the rounds. British writers have strongly censured this mode of warfare, as unusual between two civilized nations. One of them remarks, "While two European armies remain inactively facing each other, the outposts of neither are molested, unless a direct attack on the main body be intended: nay, so far is this tacit good understanding carried, that I, myself, have beheld French and English sentinels not more than twenty yards apart. But the Americans entertain no such chivalric notions. An enemy was to them an enemy, whether alone or in the midst of five thousand companions, and they therefore counted the death of every individual as so much taken from the strength of the whole. In point of fact, they no doubt reasoned correctly, but to us at least it appeared an ingenious return to barbarity."

This view of the subject is quite natural in a British officer, who no doubt suffered from this "barbarian mode of warfare" of the Americans. But if he had been one of the invaded, instead of the invaders; one of an army of three thousand militia contending against eight thousand veteran soldiers, who had come four thousand miles to destroy the towns, lay waste the country, and murder a peaceful people, he would, perhaps, have taken a less chivalric view of his duties and obligations. Besides, some allowance must be made for the exacerbated state of the feelings of the Americans, on account of the loss of their efficient flanking battery, the Carolina. Nor should this writer forget, in his sentimentality on the chivalry of war, the annoyances to which the Americans were subjected during the nights of the 26th and 27th, by the shell practice of the British howitzers and the rockets which kept the American camp in continual alarm. Whatever may be the opinion of ethical and historical writers, on the abstract question of duty and chivalry in this matter, there can be no doubt as to the fact, that the British soldiers had but little rest or quiet on the night of the 27th of December. They awaited the break of day with more anxiety and hope than they had hailed its decline.

XI.

A DEMONSTRATION AND A DEFEAT.

[December 28, 1814.]

THE American commander had not been idle. Established in the fine old chateau of Macarte, which then, as now, could hardly be discerned at a short distance off, through the thick evergreen trees and shrubbery in which it is embowered, within one hundred or two hundred yards of the right of the entrenchments, Jackson kept an incessant watch over every movement of the enemy, viewing their camp through a large telescope, which an ingenious old Frenchman had loaned him for the occasion, and which was established in the dormer window of the chateau, looking down the river. This chateau still stands, but little changed by the lapse of forty years. It has been the study and pride of its successive proprietors and occupants to preserve the premises, as much as possible, in the condition in which Jackson left them, after the war was over. Only such repairs as were absolutely necessary have been made. Even the cannon marks on the pavement, walls, and pillars may now be seen, and the scarred oaks, cedars and pecan trees, which surround it, still wear the signs of the strife that drenched with blood the fields around, that now smile with rural beauty and teem with agricultural wealth, and rendered the headquarters of the General-in-Chief the most ex-

posed and insecure position of the whole camp. Hundreds of the cannon balls have been dug out of the
garden, which were rained down on this favorite target
of the British artillery.

From this elevated position, Jackson perceived on the
evening of the 27th, the formidable preparations to over-
whelm him the next day. He comprehended, at glance,
the plan of Packenham, and set to work to resist and
defeat it. That was a busy night in Jackson's quarters.
Officers were seen galloping in every direction for cannon
and artillerists to strengthen the lines. When the British commenced their advance, Jackson had only the
two six pounders, which had made such a narrow escape
on the night of the 23d. These had been estalished on
the levee. On the night of the 27th, a twelve-pound
howitzer was planted so as to command the road, and
shortly after a twenty-four pounder on the left of the
twelve.

On the morning of the 28th, another twenty-four
pounder was established, under the fire of the British
battery on the levee. These, together with the battery
of the Louisiana, presented quite a formidable display
of artillery. The infantry also were strengthened. The
first regiment of Louisiana Militia was ordered to take
position on the right of the lines, and the second regiment
to reinforce the extremity of the left, which had not yet
been placed in a safe and reliable condition, though Coffee's Tennesseeans were kept incessantly at work upon
it. Other precautions had not been neglected. The
levee was cut below the lines, in order to flood the road
and drown the British, or render their advance difficult.
But fate did not favor this inglorious mode of destroying
an enemy, who was destined to be overcome with his

own weapons and by mortal valor. The river fell and the road remained undamaged. Meantime Carroll had marched his men, who were ill armed, many being supplied with fowling-pieces and discarded guns, to Canal Rodriguez, and set them to work on the entrench- ments on the extreme left.

Jackson had now a force of over four thousand men and twenty pieces of artillery. How he ever collected such a body of men and established them in so strong a position in so short a time, is far more astounding than the results which were subsequently achieved.

Packenham had at least eight thousand men of all arms,—all veteran soldiers, well armed and equipped, and supplied with all the engines of destruction known to the science of modern warfare.

The morning of the 28th was one of those beautiful, bracing, life and joy-giving days peculiar to Louisiana in the winter season. In its brightness, clearness, and temperate mildness, it was a delicious novelty to the British, accustomed to fogs, clouds, inky skies and oppressive vapors. The air was just frosty enough to give it purity, elasticity and freshness. A sparkling mist veiled the beauty of the waking morn. The evergreens which dotted and encircled the dusky plain with emer- ald, glistened with the diamond drops from heaven.

All nature seemed to be animated by these bright in- fluences. The trees were melodious with the noisy strains of the rice bird, and the bold *falsetto* of that pride of Southern ornithology, the mocking-bird, who, here alone continues the whole year round his unceas- ing notes of exultant mockery and vocal defiance. What a reproach did such a scene of natural beauty and atmospheric purity convey to those whose passions

were soon to convert it from a Paradise to a Pande-
monium !

At break of day, or as soon as the mist had melted
into the purple that spread over the horizon, to form, as
it were, a carpet on which the king of day might strut
forth upon the world, both armies stood to arms. Pic-
quets were called in. Drums were beat. The blasts of
bugles rang far along the banks of the old Father of
Waters. All the hum and buzz of some great movement were observable in both camps. Jackson occupied his old position, watching from the window of his
headquarters every movement of his enemy with the
eye of a lynx, and the heart of a lion. His countenance wore that same expression of stern determination
and dauntless courage, communicating to all around a
fearless and undoubting confidence. Often would he
cast anxious glances up the road, to the city, as if in expectation of some new reinforcement.

He was not permitted to remain long in doubt as to
the intentions of the British. Their army was soon perceived to be in motion. It advanced in two steady
columns. Gibbs with the 4th, the 21st, 44th, and one
Black corps, hugging the wood or swamp on the right,
with the 95th Rifles, extending in skirmishing order
across the plain and meeting the right of Keane's
column, which consisted of the 85th, the 95th, and one
Black corps. The artillery preceded the latter, in the
main road. Keane held his column as near the levee as
possible, and under the protection of Bienvenu's and
Chalmette's quarters. Detached from Gibbs' column
was a party of skirmishers and light infantry, under the
command of that active and energetic officer, Lieut.
Colonel Robert Rennie, whose orders were to turn the

American left and gain the rear of their camp. In this order, the British moved forward in excellent spirits and brilliant array. Packenham, with his staff and a guard composed of the 14th Dragoons, rode nearly in the centre of the line, so as to command a view of both columns. The American scouts retired leisurely before the British, firing and shouting defiance at them. The Louisiana now weighed anchor, and floated down the stream, and then anchored again in a position which commanded the road and the whole field in front of the American lines. Jackson had ordered McRea, of the artillery, to blow up Chalmette's and Bienvenu's houses. By some accident this order was only partially executed,—a fortunate circumstance, as these buildings served to mask the American lines at the strongest point, and to precipitate Keane's column with perilous suddenness upon Jackson's guns. Chalmette's, the house nearest to Jackson's lines, was blown up just as the British passed Bienvenu's. This had been ever since the 23d the headquarters of Hinds' troop, whence they were in the habit of emerging hourly in detachments to harass the enemy and reconnoitre his position. Now, for the first time, Keane beheld through his glass the mouths of several large cannon protruding from Jackson's lines, and completely covering the head of his column. These guns were manned as guns are not often manned on land.

Early in the morning Jackson's anxious glances towards the city had been changed into expressions of satisfaction and confidence by the spectacle of several straggling bands of red-shirted, bewhiskered, rough and desperate-looking men, all begrimed with smoke and mud—hurrying down the road towards the lines.

These proved to be the Baratarians under Dominique You and Bluche, who had run all the way from the Fort St. John, where they had been stationed since their release from prison. They immediately took charge of one of the twenty-four pounders. The Baratarians were followed by two other parties of sailors of the crew of the Carolina, under Lieutenants Crawley and Norris. These detachments were ordered to man the howitzer on the right, and the other twenty-four pounder, which, being on the left of Planché's battalion, had been in charge of St. Gême's dismounted dragoons.

Thus prepared, Jackson waited the approach of the British. Forward they came, in solid column, as compact and orderly as if on parade, under cover of a shower of rockets, and a continual fire from their artillery in front and their batteries on the levee. It was certainly a bold and imposing demonstration, for such, as we are told by British officers, it was intended to be. To new soldiers, like the Americans, fresh from civic and peaceful pursuits, who had never witnessed any scenes of real warfare, it was certainly a formidable display of military power and discipline. Those veterans moved as steadily and closely together as if marching in review instead of "in the cannon's mouth." Their muskets catching the rays of the morning sun, nearly blinded the beholder with their brightness, whilst their gay and various uniforms, red, grey, green and tartan, afforded a pleasing relief to the winter-clad field and the sombre objects around. On, on came the glittering array, scarcely heeding the incessant fire which that cool veteran, Humphrey, poured into their ranks from the moment they were visible. But, as they approached nearer, they were suddenly brought to a sense of their danger and audacity, by the simultaneous opening of the batteries of Norris and the Baratarians, and by a terrible broadside from the Louisiana, which swept the field obliquely to the line of march of the British column. Never was there a more effective and destructive fire. For several hours it was maintained with incessant vigor and pitiless fury. More than eight hundred shot were fired by the Louisiana alone with most deadly effect. One single discharge of this most admirably managed battery—for it hardly deserved the name of ship—killed and wounded fifteen men. A British writer has done justice to this scene.

Says the author of the Narrative of British Campaigns in America:—"That the Americans are excellent shots, as well with artillery as with rifles, we have had frequent cause to acknowledge; but perhaps on no occasion did they assert their claim to the title of good artillerymen more effectively than on this occasion. Scarcely a ball or bullet passed over or fell short of its mark, but all striking full into the midst of our ranks occasioned terrible havoc.

"The shrieks of the wounded, therefore—the crash of firelocks, and the fall of such as were killed, caused at first some little confusion, and what added to the panic was, that from the houses beside which we stood, bright flames suddenly burst forth. The Americans expecting the attack, had filled them with combustibles for the purpose, and directing one or two guns against them, loaded with hot shot, in an instant set them on fire. The scene was altogether very sublime. A tremendous cannonade mowed down our ranks and defeated us with its roar, while two large chateaux and their out-buildings almost scorched us with the flames and blinded us with the smoke which they emitted."

Under such an incessant and galling fire, there was no safety for the British except in retreat, or in a *supine* position, as it is called in military phrase; but, as it would be styled in American parlance, "taking to the ditch." For some time Keane's solid column withstood with great firmness this terrific iron storm; but it was a vain display of valor. Soon the battalions were ordered to deploy into line, and seek a cover in the ditches. Never was an order more promptly and rapidly obeyed. In a few minutes the heavy column was diluted into a thin line, and the men scrambled pell mell into every convenient ditch, or behind every elevated knoll, which presented itself. Gaining the ditches, in which they sank to their middle, the British writer, from whom we have already quoted, says "they leaned forward, concealing themselves in the rushes which grew on the banks of the canal." Truly, an ignoble position for Peninsular heroes.

The artillery could not be so easily removed or covered. The guns of the Americans were now concentrated on the British battery. The two field-pieces, which had been advanced on the road and levee, quite near to the American lines, were soon dismantled, many of the gunners were killed, and those who escaped destruction, finally abandoned their useless pieces, leaving them on the road to be knocked and tossed about, the sport of Humphrey's unerring twelve-pounders.

Thus, disastrously and ignominiously, was Keane's column broken by the American artillery. The melancholy and pensive countenance of Packenham grew dark and gloomy indeed, as he perceived his brilliant battalions melt into the earth as suddenly and magically as the clansmen of Rhoderic Dhu, in the beautifully painted scene of that noblest poem of the great Wizard of the North:

Down sunk the disappearing band,
Each warrior vanished where he stood;
In broom or bracken, heath or wood,
Sunk brand and spear and bended bow;
It seemed as if the mother earth
Had swallowed up her warlike birth.
The wind's last breath had tossed in air
Penon and plaid and plumage fair—
The next but swept a lone hill-side,
Where heath and fern were waving wide;
The sun's last glance had glistened back,
From spear and glaive, from targe and jack—
The next, all unreflected shone,
On bracken green and cold grey stone.

Never before had the British soldier, in his presence, quailed before an enemy, or sought cover from a fire.

Here was another ground of complaint for the martinette, of the ignorance and unscientific warfare of the Americans. They had mistaken a mere feint or demonstration, for a real attack—a showy display, for a practical design.

So, unlucky Keane, after sheltering himself behind the surrounding ruins of Bienvenu's, again uttered curses, both loud and deep, upon the cruel fate which had cast his lot, hitherto so brilliant, upon so dreary a field of military enterprise—a field fertile in everything but British laurels.

How fared it with Gibbs on the right? Here the prospect opened brighter, as the head of the column approached the American lines. In the view of Gibbs, who had led the storming party against Fort Cornelius, defended by over one hundred guns, and of his men, who had scaled the parapets of Badajoz, the walls of St. Sebastian, and a hundred other places of equal strength, nothing could be more contemptible than "the mere rudiments of an entrenched camp," as they were styled by a British writer. The whole work consisted of a low mound of earth, with a narrow ditch in front, not too wide to be leaped by a man of ordinary agility. So it remained through the whole campaign.

As this mound came in view, Gibbs halted his main column, whilst the skirmishers were thrown forward, and the detached party under Rennie dashed into the woods, closely pursuing the American outposts, and advancing to a position within a hundred yards of the lines, behind which Carroll was posted with his Tennesseeans. That prompt and ready officer immediately ordered Col. Henderson, with two hundred Tennesseeans, to steal through the swamp, gain the rear of Rennie's party and then oblique to the right so as to cut them off from the main body. It was a rash adventure, such as General Jackson would not have sanctioned had he been present in that part of the line. But the Tennesseeans were impatient to take part in the fight, and could with difficulty be kept within the lines. Henderson's movement might have succeeded, if he had not advanced too far to the right, and thus brought his men under the heavy fire of a strong body of the British who were posted behind a fence nearly concealed by the trees and weeds. The Colonel, a gallant and promising officer, and five men were killed by this fire, several were wounded, and the others seeing the object of the movement defeated retired behind the lines. This was the only success achieved by the British that day. Rennie, emboldened by this result, was rapidly closing on Carroll's left, which having no cannon and being defended by raw militiamen, was pretty severely pressed, when an officer came up to him with an order from Gibbs to fall back on the main column. Greatly chagrined at this order, Rennie abandoned the ground he had gained, and retired to the point from which he had advanced. Here his men were posted under the trees, idle spectators of the havoc which the American artillery was making in Keane's column on the left. And so they remained until the general retrogade movement was commenced.

On that day the Americans lost nine killed and eight wounded. That gallant officer Major Carmick, of the Marine corps, was among the wounded. Whilst delivering an order to Major Planché, near the centre of the American line, he was struck by a rocket, which tore his horse to pieces and wounded the Major in the arm and head. Of the British loss there are no precise or reliable accounts. We conjecture from general statements that it reached nearly two hundred killed and wounded. The official returns, which do not include those who were killed in the attempt to retire, admit only sixteen killed and forty-three wounded and missing. As the only weapon used by the Americans was their artillery, few of the wounded ever recovered. Among the killed were two officers, whose mode of death was remarkable, and illustrative of the precision of the American artillery. One of them was Captain Collings, of the British West India regiment, who was on duty in the 93d. When the men were ordered to hide them

selves in the ditch, and lie down on the earth, this
young officer, in a spirit of reckless bravado chose to
maintain his erect position. Major Creagh, of the 93d,
called loudly to him to lie down or he would draw the
fire of the batteries upon them. Either not hearing, or
not heeding the order, Collings walked along the edge
of the ditch for a few steps, when a cannon ball struck
his head and knocked it off his shoulders. The other
officer killed on this occasion was Ensign Sir Frederick
Eden, an English baronet, attached to the 85th. A
flanking shot from the Louisiana struck the section commanded by this officer and killed five of the men and
wounded several others. Eden himself was struck, and
horribly mutilated. He lived long enough to make his
will, and then died in a raving delirium of agony.

The Louisiana, from whose batteries the British sustained their heaviest damage, though exposed to a constant fire from the British guns on the levee, had but
one man killed.

Such was the ignominious conclusion of the imposing
demonstration or feint of the British on the 28th December, 1814. Had there been a quick eye, sagacious intellect, and a full comprehension of their position and
circumstances, to direct the movement of the army, the
result might been very different. But in this, as in many
other regular armies, the men of sagacity, enterprise,
and the requisite qualities to secure the success of such
operations, were mere subordinates, under chiefs, who
on this occasion manifested a singular destitution of
military capacity. Poor Packenham's energies were
all the while cramped and oppressed by the consciousness, which filled his mind from the first moment he
landed and perceived the situation of the army, that it

20

was involved in an inextricable strait. This fact will fully explain the apparent want of promptitude displayed in this emergency. Besides, he expected hourly the arrival of Lambert's fine brigade, which had embarked at Portsmouth at the same time with the fast clipper in which he had sailed. These fresh troops would be a great accession to his jaded and overworked force.

The partial success of Rennie on the British right shows how egregiously they had exaggerated the strength of the American lines. Rennie demonstrated the practicability of turning the American left and gaining their rear in that insecure and weakly-defended part of the line. By "weakly defended," we do not mean that the men stationed in this part of the works were not as brave and true soldiers as ever handled a gun, but that they were not in adequate force, were without artillery, the cannon being on the right, and could not be held together with sufficient compactness to resist the dash of a strong body of regular soldiers accustomed to scaling entrenchments, like the British. That the works offered no other obstacle but the strong arms and dauntless valor of the men who defended them, is sufficiently shown by the fact, that the British officers actually burst into loud laughter when they perceived the frail mound which "the ignorant Americans" chose to designate a parapet, and to which, many narrators of these events have so far burlesqued military art, as to attach a *glacis*.

They also made another discovery, which ingenious and quick-witted people would have turned to better use. They found the horrible swamp, of which they stood in such dread, that their outposts would not approach within a hundred yards of its edge, and of which such marvellous stories are related, of men who sunk into it and disappeared for ever from sight, quite practicable and passable for light troops. Why did they not avail themselves of this discovery? Why did Gibbs follow so closely the folly of Keane on a previous, and a still more notable, subsequent occasion, and let slip the opportunity of hurling his powerful column into the midst of Jackson's raw and poorly disciplined militia-men? The answer to this and many similar questions, is to be found in the impressive lesson which Jackson had taught them on the bloody night of the twenty-third.

Besides, the British had learned by this destructive reconnoissance, to appreciate the mettle and skill of the artillerists, who had so unexpectedly opened upon them from lines, behind which they expected to encounter only rifles and muskets. Jackson seemed to possess the power of Cadmus, to raise men and arms from the earth. Those two huge twenty-fours, which belched forth such torrents of iron hail, and that ceaseless twelve-pounder, appeared to have fallen from the skies into the rude embrasures from which they now peered so mysteriously and threateningly. Whence, too, came the skillful and adroit artillerists who manned them with such art and deadly power? These were themes for anxious delibera-tion and discussion among the British chiefs. The result was a conviction that their army was too weak in artil-lery. Steps must be taken to equalize the conditions of the two armies in this respect.

Though the demonstration of the twenty-eighth had thus failed, and the splendid battalions of the British had been broken into fragments, and driven to hide their shame and their persons in the ditches on Bienvenu's, they were not yet removed beyond danger. All day the American batteries swept the plain with their grape and round shot. Wherever a living object became visible, iron showers would fall with awful effect. How to draw off the army under such a fire greatly perplexed the British generals. It was at last done in a most ignoble, and, to veteran soldiers, most mortifying manner. The various regiments were ordered to break off in small squads by file to the rear, and retire as rapidly as they could beyond the reach of the American guns. This order was obeyed with alacrity, especially that part of it which required them to move by quick-step. As the squads stole off in this inglorious manner, they were plied more briskly with grape, shot and shells, and saluted with jeering, cries, and huzzas from the American lines. Nor was this retrograde movement effected without heavy loss. At least sixty men, we are assured by the author of the Narrative, which we have quoted, were killed or wounded in the retreat. Many of the men were struck in the back with cannon balls, and knocked to pieces as they hurried to the rear. Many received wounds, *a tergo*, which were deemed by the ancient Romans more calamitous than death. Finally, however, the whole army staggered beyond the range of the American batteries, and the men, exhausted by their several labors, threw themselves on the ground to rest.

To remove the dismounted guns was the next difficulty. This duty was assigned to Sir Thos. Troubridge, of the navy, who, with a party of seamen, dashed forward to the spot where the guns lay dismounted in the road. Making fast ropes to them, the sailors succeeded, by incredible exertions, in drawing the guns off and bringing them to the rear.

The day was far advanced before these difficult tasks were all accomplished, and the army drawn up in a safe position. It was now posted on the lower line of Bienvenu's, with outposts extending to the front within a few hundred yards of the American lines. Packenham resumed his headquarters at Villeré's. The hospitals, which were hourly receiving accessions, and were now quite full, were established at Jumonville's, below Villeré's.

In this position the army continued for several days suffering greatly from exhaustion, exposure, and the scarcity and bad quality of food supplied them from their commissariat. The War Department in London had never contemplated the possibility of such an army being detained eight days, within six miles of a city, which was so well provisioned. These causes produced violent dysentery among both officers and men. Having no tents, the men were driven to shelter themselves in damp huts made of cane and reeds. During the few days after the arrival of the British, the soldiers had subsisted tolerably well on the cattle of the neighboring plantations, which scouting parties were able to capture, by scattering themselves over the country. But these resources were soon exhausted; as the planters only raised such stock as they needed for their families, the quantity to be found was necessarily limited. The British were then reduced to the worst kind of army provisions, the maggoty pork and weevily biscuit. All the horses found on the plantations were appropriated by the field officers and their staffs, and by the artillery for the draught of their guns. A few of the 14th Dragoons, but poorly mounted, were assigned to guard and vidette duty.

Thus closed the first operation of Sir Edward Packenham in America. He was further than ever from his Earldom, and his several millions of "the spoils." His experience of the "ignorant Indian fighter" had been even more severe and disastrous than that of his Brigadier and countryman (Keane). The high spirits excited in the army by his arrival had descended to zero. A change of leaders had brought no relief to those devoted battalions. Defeat and disaster, difficulties and dangers, innumerable, unforeseen, and insurmountable, enveloped them at every step. A fatal web had been thrown around that army, with the skill and boldness of a master mind. Like the mysterious net weaved by the art of Vulcan, the links, though invisible, were not the less potent, tangible and irresistible.

XII.

THE BRITISH BRING UP THEIR BIG GUNS.

BITTER were the feelings of Packenham, as, accompanied by Sir John Tylden, Adjutant-General, and Captain Wylley, Military Secretary of the General-in-Chief, and other staff officers, he rode slowly back to his headquarters at Villeré's. The feint by which he expected to scare the Americans from their lines had been quite as great a failure as the attempt to frighten them with Congreve rockets, which the British had continued to throw into the American camp from the first moment the two armies came in sight of one another.

Another council of war was convoked. The chiefs quickly repaired to headquarters, and were soon engaged in earnest deliberation on the next expedient to relieve the army from its embarrassments. Packenham's depression was still quite manifest, but the obstinate and stout-hearted Scotchman, Cochrane, "knew no such word as fail." He was emphatically the soul of the enterprise, as fertile in resources as he was indomitable in energy. He showed that their failures thus far were due to the superiority of the American artillery. They must supply this deficiency by bringing more large guns from the fleet.

Certainly, out of the hundred large guns then lying idle on the decks of their three-deckers and frigates,

they could select a battery strong enough to cope with
the few old guns of the Americans. But then, it was
suggested, the Americans are entrenched. "So must
we be," was the reply of the prompt old sailor. It was
therefore determined to treat the American lines as
regular fortifications, by erecting breaching batteries
against them, and proceeding to silence their guns. The
reminder of the effectiveness of the American batteries
was received with scornful sneers. What! were the conquerors of Napoleon, the practiced veterans of a hundred
victories, the sailors and marines who, under Nelson and
Collingwood, had annihilated the navy of France, the
heroes of the Nile, of Copenhagen and of Trafalgar, to
yield in gunnery to the motley crews of American
coasters—to the privateers and pirates of the Gulf, and
the inexperienced artillerists of a young army of raw
and hastily-collected levies? Perish the base thought!
The slight successes gained by the Americans were due
to the superior metal of their guns. With guns of equal
calibre, managed by their experienced scientific artillerists, and batteries constructed according to the rules of
engineering, these advantages of their enemies would soon
disappear. Thus argued the advocates of the new plan
of breaching the American lines with heavy batteries.
There were no better artillery officers in the British
army than Colonel John Dixon and Major Munro, who
had achieved great renown in the Peninsular war—nor
than Colonel Burgoyne, son of the General whose name
figures so disastrously in our revolutionary annals, and
Major Blanchard, of the Engineers. These officers gave
their decided opinion in favor of the practicability of
silencing the American batteries and destroying their
parapet by establishing opposing batteries of large guns

brought up from the fleet.   Colonel Dixon only required
three hours to effect this result.   This plan was adopted.
The sailors and many of the soldiers were set to work to
bring up the heavy guns from the fleet, a task of immense labor and difficulty.   Three days were thus con
sumed by the British.

Jackson, in the meantime, continued with unwearied
activity to strengthen his lines and augment his artillery.
The weakness of his left, made apparent on the 28th,
was, in a measure, repaired by removing the two twelve-
pounders of Lieutenant Spotts as near as practicable to
the woods, and establishing one twelve-pounder between
that point and the centre of his line.   This piece was
confided to General Garrique, a veteran French soldier,
who volunteered for the occasion.   A six-pounder, and
afterwards an eighteen, were, under Colonel Perry, also
planted in the same section.

On the 29th, Patterson having discovered the destructive effects of a flanking fire from the other side of the
river, laid the foundation of his celebrated marine battery, by removing two twelve and one twenty-four
pounder from the decks of the Louisiana and placing
them in the battery on Jourdan's plantation, behind the
levee on the west bank of the river, so as to command
the front of the American works.   To serve this battery,
a part of the crew of the Louisiana were detached and
others were pressed in the streets of New Orleans, by
Lieutenant Thompson, who for that purpose entered
every sailor boarding-house in the city, and arrested
every nautical looking character he could find.   By
these means he soon succeeded in collecting as various
and mixed a corps of men as ever fought under the
same flag.   It embraced natives of all countries except

England, who spoke all languages except that of their commander. A perfect Babel indeed, was that famous marine battery of Patterson. It is an amazing proof of the power of discipline and of the energy and capacity of the Commodore and his able subordinate, Lieutenant Thompson, that with such discordant material they were able to render their battery one of the most efficient in the annals of modern warfare.

Early on the 30th their power had been strikingly displayed. The British had established several batteries between the river bank and the levee, for the purpose of combating and destroying the American armed vessels, which could not be reached by Jackson's guns in the lines. The marine battery was soon opened upon them, and in a few hours all the British gunners were driven from the river bank, behind the levee, and the men who were sheltered in the houses about Chalmette's and Bienvenu's were compelled to take refuge in the ditches. So constant and vigilant were Patterson's gunners that the British found it impossible to make any reconnoissance near the river.

Thus secured on his right flank, Jackson next turned his attention to the prolongation of his lines into the swamp, so as to prevent the British from gaining his rear and turning his left flank. Carroll's and Coffee's men were kept incessantly engaged in deepening the ditches on their part of the line and throwing up the dirt into a rude mound. The anxiety of Jackson about the weakness of this part of his lines was, however, quite unnecessary, for the British always kept as far as possible from the swamp. This caution was due to the terror of the Tennessee bush-fighters and dirty "shirts," as they were called by the neat and well dressed British soldiers. These wily frontiersmen, habituated to the Indian mode of warfare, never missed a chance of picking off a straggler or sentinel. Clad in their dusky brown homespun, they would glide unperceived through the woods, and taking a cool view of the enemy's lines, would cover the first Briton who came within range of their long small-bored rifles. Nor did they waste their ammunition. Whenever they drew a bead on any object, it was certain to fall. The cool indifference with which they would perform the most daring acts of this nature was amazing.

One of these bush-fighters, having obtained leave to go on a hunting-party, one night, stole along towards the British camp, over ditches and through underwood, until he got near a British sentinel, whom he immediately killed, and seizing his arms and accoutrements, laid them at some distance from the place where the sentinel had stood, and then concealing himself, waited quietly for more game. When it was time to relieve the sentinel, the corporal of the guard finding him dead, posted another in his place, which he had hardly left, before another victim fell before the unerring rifle of the Tennesseean. Having conveyed his arms and accoutrements to the place at which he left those of the first victim, the remorseless hunter took a new position, and a third sentinel, posted in the same place, shared the fate of the two others. At last the corporal of the guard, amazed to see three sentinels killed, in one night, at the same post, determined to expose no more men in so dangerous a spot. The Tennesseean, seeing this, returned to camp with the spoils of the slain, and received the congratulations of his comrades on the success of his night's hunt. Many instances of a similar character,

illustrative of the daring, the skill, and love of adventure of these hardy riflemen, are related by the survivors of that epoch. Indeed the whole army, after the
events of the 23d, 25th, and 28th, seemed to be animated by a spirit of personal daring and gallant enterprise.

The plain between the two hostile camps was alive
day and night with small parties of foot and horse,
wandering to and fro in pursuit of adventure, on the
trail of reconnoiterers, stragglers and outpost sentinels.
The natural restlessness and nomadic tendency of the
Americans were here conspicuously displayed. After
a while, there grew up a regular science in the conduct
of these modes of vexing, annoying, and weakening the
enemy. Their system, it is true, is not to be found in
Vauban's, Steuben's or Scott's military tactics, but it,
nevertheless, proved to be quite effective. It was as
follows: A small number of each corps, being permitted
to leave the lines, would start from their position and
all converge to a central point in front of the lines.
Here they would, when all collected, make quite a formidable body of men, and, electing their own commander, would proceed to attack the nearest British outpost, or advance in extended lines, so as to create alarm
in the enemy's camp, and subject them to the vexation
of being beaten to arms, in the midst of which, the
scouting party would be unusually unlucky, if it did
not succeed in "bagging" one or two of the enemy's
advanced sentinels. Prominent among the bands which
kept the British in perpetual alarm, was the command
of the indefatigable Major Hinds, whose troopers from
Mississippi and Louisiana were ever hovering about the
English outposts, charging to the very mouths of their
cannon, and driving in their pickets. Unfortunately

for the British, so at least they thought, they were unable to mount their dragoons for field or fighting service;
and Hinds, having none of his own arm to try his
mettle on, was compelled to satisfy his impatient valor,
in unequal and ineffectual, but very dangerous, and to
the British very vexatious, charges on their redoubts
and outposts.   Hinds was of great use to Jackson in
executing reconnoissances, which he always did with
brilliant daring and success.   As soon as the British
would throw up a redoubt, or commence planting a
battery in any new position, Jackson had only to say,
"Major Hinds, report to me the number and calibre of
the guns they are establishing there."   Immediately
the stalwart trooper would form his dragoons, and
advancing in an easy trot, until he had arrived within a
few hundred yards of the object of the reconnoissance,
would order a charge, and leading himself, would dash
at full speed at the enemy's position, as near as was
necessary to ascertain their strength and situation, and
then wheeling under their fire and a shower of rockets,
would gallop back to headquarters and report to Jackson all the information he possessed.   One of Hinds'
companies was composed of Felicianians, young Americans, who had settled in that beautiful portion of Louisiana lying on the east bank of the Mississippi north of
the Bayou Manchack.   This was the same company
which had aided so materially in the capture of Baton
Rouge in 1810, when a few Americans organizing at
Bayou Sara declared their independence of Spanish
dominion, and marching down to Baton Rouge, rushed
into the fort, over the big guns of the Spaniards, tore
down the flag of Spain, and supplanted it with that of
the "Lone Star," which subsequently gave place to the

"Stars and Stripes." It was on that occasion the Feliciana dragoons learned the art and acquired the habit of charging batteries. The capture by a troop of horse, of a strong fortification, well defended by cannon of the largest calibre, and strongly manned, was an achievement, which is only paralleled in the annals of warfare, by the celebrated charge of Paez with his dragoons against a hostile fleet in the Venezuelan war. There was also Captain Ogden's company, composed of young men of education and high position in society, which constituted the guard of the commander-in-chief, obeying his orders alone. It was posted in Macarte's garden. There were also the companies of Captain Chauveau and Dubuclay, the latter being chiefly Acadiens from Attakapas.

In such incessant scouting parties and volunteer operations as we have described, a majority of Jackson's command were engaged during the greater part of the night. So daring were these attacks, that on more than one occasion, the six-pounders were advanced from the lines and drawn within cannon shot of the outposts, when they would be discharged at the sentinels or any living object, generally with some effect, and always with great terror to the whole British camp, causing a general apprehension that the Americans were advancing to attack them in full force.

After midnight the skirmishers would return to their camp and resign themselves to sleep, using for their beds the brush collected from the swamp; and the Tennesseeans, who were encamped on the extreme left, lying on gunwales or logs, raised a few inches above the surface of the water or soft mire of the morass. About two hours after daybreak, a general stir would be observable in the American camp—this was for the general muster. Drums were then beaten and several bands of music—among which that of the Orleans battalion (Plauché's) was conspicuous—would animate the spirits of the men with martial strains, that could be heard in the desolate and gloomy camp of the British, where no melodious notes or other sounds of cheerfulness were allowed to mock their misery; where not even a bugle sounded, unless as a warning or a summons of the guard to the relief of some threatened outpost. A writer—who draws more freely upon his imagination than upon the authentic records of the country, and yet whose works have obtained great popularity among a people who prefer the dramatic and highly wrought to the sober, but often really more interesting facts of history—Headley, in his life of Jackson thus describes the two camps: "The two hostile camps presented a spectacle of the most striking interest. The British lay in full view of the American lines —their white tents looking amid the surrounding water like clouds of sail resting on the bosom of the river, while at intervals a random shot, or the morning and evening gun, sent their slow challenge to the foe. There was marching and counter-marching, strains of martial music and all the confused sounds of camp-life, while to them an American intrenchment, which stretched in a dark line across the plain, semed as silent as death, except when a solitary gun sent forth its sullen defiance."

This picture is the reverse of the truth. It presents a good illustration of the evil of that system of historical romancing, for which this writer has become famous. The contrast drawn by the author of " The Subaltern in America," a British officer in Packenham's army, in the following quotation, forms quite a different picture from that sketched by the imagination of Headley.

"On the summit of the centre works a lofty flag-staff was erected, from which a large American ensign constantly waved; whilst in the rear of the breast-work, a crowd of white tents showed themselves, not a few of which bore flags at the top of their poles.

"The American camp exhibited, at least, as much of the pomp and circumstance of war as modern camps are accustomed to exhibit, and the spirits of its inmates were kept continually in a state of excitement by the bands of martial music. How different was the spectacle, to which a glance towards the rear introduced the spectator, presenting exactly the same extent of front. The British army lay there without tents, without works, without show, without parade, upon the ground. Throughout the whole line not more than a dozen huts were erected, and these, which consisted only of planks torn from the houses and from fences near, furnished but an inefficient protection against the inclemency of the weather. No band played among our men nor did a bugle give its sound, except to warn the hearers of danger and put them on the alert. On the contrary, the routine of duty was conducted in as much silence as if there had been no musical instruments in the camp. It was impossible not to be struck with the contrast which the condition and apparent comforts of the invading and defending hosts presented."

After the nervousness natural to young soldiers had worn off, and the Americans had become, in a measure, hardened to their new mode of life, with characteristic self-reliance and aptitude for taking care of themselves, their camp was made to present an aspect which would have done credit to a well-appointed army. All this, too, was done without the aid of the Government. The men who defended those lines were generally gentlemen, in the social sense of the word, and provided their own equipments, arms, and all their comforts, from their own private means. Nor did the gay and high-spirited Orleanois renounce entirely their favorite amusements, pleasures and gallantries during the severe service at the lines. On the contrary, the General-in-chief was frequently compelled to administer very severe reproofs to both officers and men for sundry derelictions from duty and breaches of discipline. Sentinels would be eluded and commanders "dodged" whilst all was quiet in front, and many a gallant Creole youth would thus steal back to town, to snatch a few minutes of delightful intercourse with wife or sweetheart, and solace his spirits and his body with a few of the comforts of home and city life. But, woe to him if he were not at his post, when reveille sounded, and the signal was given for the army to get under arms!

Such was the state of affairs within the American lines during the time the British were engaged in unceasing labors, and contending against unexpected and insurmountable difficulties and obstacles, in the vain hope of rescuing themselves from the perplexing position into which they had been brought. Their movements in establishing redoubts and batteries at various points were closely watched and vigorously opposed. Crawley's thirty-two and You's twenty-four were kept busy playing upon a redoubt, which the British were throwing up on their extreme right, near the woods. Notwithstanding its great distance, many of their shot took effect, demolishing parts of the redoubts and killing

21

several men. At night the work would be repaired, and
Jackson's Artillery would be compelled with the dawn
of the day to resume the the task of demolition. It was
fine practice for the American gunners, who were thus
enabled to attain that extraordinary precision, which so
greatly amazed the British.

On the 31st, the redoubt near the woods having been
repaired and strengthened, commenced a brisk fire on
the American lines, which was warmly returned. This
cannonading was kept up on both sides, during the
whole day. Under cover of this battery several reconnoitering parties were observed, traversing the fields
and making very careful and exact observations of the
position of Jackson's batteries. These parties were not
neglected by the sleepless cannoniers of the Louisiana,
who leaving the land batteries to carry on their duel,
thought proper to keep off any intruders by throwing a
shower of grape and round shot in every direction where
any movement was observed in the British camp. Even
individuals were thus picked off, and reconnoitering
duty became equal in desperateness to that of the forlorn hope in a storming party.

Jackson soon discovered the design of the British.
The activity in their camp,—the frequent reconnoissances,—the withdrawal of the great body of the troops
to the rear,—all the signs indicated a new and more
vigorous blow than had yet been aimed at his insignificant fortifications.

On the night of the 31st the American sentinels and outposts reported that the whole British army had advanced
within five or six hundred yards of their lines, and
could be distinctly heard at work with spades, digging
the earth or hammering at certain wood-work. What

would it all mean? was the query which ran through the camp, and greatly inflamed the natural curiosity of the Americans as to what would be the next move of the red-coats? This was the inquiry of the young soldiers. There were veterans in the lines—men who had served in regular armies—old soldiers of Dumourier, Hoche, Moreau, and Napoleon, who perceived at a glance the design of the enemy, and collecting around them groups of younger soldiers, plain militiamen, explained to them, with a pruriency of military technicalities, the whole plan of the British.

They were correct in their calculations that the British were about to try what virtue there was in batteries and big guns. Packenham had consented to give the artillery and navy an opportunity of redeeming the fortunes of the army, by attempting to effect a breach in Jackson's works. Accordingly, on the night of the 31st, twenty long eighteen and ten twenty-fours having been brought into camp, with ammunition enough for six hours' continued cannonading, it was determined to throw up several redoubts within a short distance of the American lines. As soon as it was dark, half of the army was ordered out, and marched silently to the front, passing the pickets, and halting when they reached a designated spot, about four hundred yards from Jackson's camp. Here the men were ordered to stack arms and go to work with spades and picks, under the direction of the engineering officers, and the general superintendence of Colonel (now General) Sir John Burgoyne, Inspector of Fortifications in the British army, and Director of the Engineering operations before Sevastopol. The men worked with great vigor and activity The 85th and 95th hovered in front and on the flanks to

cover the working parties. The night was dark. The
utmost silence was rigidly enforced by the officers.
Each man strove to accomplish his task more promptly
and satisfactorily than his neighbor. The officers joined
in the work. Not a few hands, which were unused to
toil, were hardened by that night's labor. Every one
who had the strength wielded a spade or pickaxe,
"knowing, as we all know," remarks the Subaltern,
"that we worked for life or death." The work had to
be done with caution and silence as well as zeal and
vigor, for the "cunning Yankees" were evidently alive,
and they might thus lose the effect which the suddenness of their new movement was expected to produce.
The work in which the British were thus earnestly
employed was the erection and solidification of several
redoubts, from which it was proposed to open upon the
American entrenchments a fire which must sweep such
frail structures from the earth. In making the embankments of the redoubts, the engineers were sorely pressed
for solid material. Everything which appeared to possess
any capacity for resistance was thrown into the mounds,
so as to give them solidity and strength. Even the
hogsheads of sugar that lay around the ruins of the
sugar-houses of the plantations near, were rolled to the
front, and placed upright in the parapets, under the
belief that they would prove to be quite as useful in
resisting cannon balls as sand, which is frequently used
for this purpose. Several thousand dollars' worth of
sugar was thus wasted.

The result of these great labors was the completion,
before dawn, of three solid demilunes, placed on the
right, centre and left, at nearly equal distances apart, in
which were established thirty pieces of heavy ordnance,

with the necessary quantity of ammunition. Manned by the artillerists and the picked gunners of the fleet—the veterans of Nelson and Collinsgwood—this powerful battery was placed in the most efficient condition to open upon the enemy's lines as soon as they should become visible through the morning mist.

XIII.

BATTLE OF THE BATTERIES.

A THICK fog ushered in the first of January, 1815. To an unusual late hour of the morning, this fog hung over the fields and obscured all objects, so that neither army could see twenty yards to the front. As soon as the works were completed, the British infantry fell back about two hundred yards in the rear of their battery, where, drawn up in battle array, they awaited anxiously to observe the effect of the new plan of operations, and prepared to take advantage of the expected breach which was to be made in the American works. The artillerists and sailors stood with lighted matches behind the compact redoubts, which were so constructed as to be defended, as well against the flanking fire of the Louisiana and of Paterson's batteries, as against the batteries in front. Thus they stood, impatiently waiting for the sun to dissipate the heavy vapors which concealed its face long after it had risen above the horizon.

The Americans not being disturbed at break of day, as their veterans had predicted, by the apprehended bombardment, had resumed their equability and careless demeanor. Indeed, they had turned out, to honor and salute the New Year, by various joyful demonstrations. A grand parade was ordered. At an early hour all the troops were out in clean clothes, with bright arms, and cheerful countenances. The different military bands pealed forth their most animating strains. The various regimental and company standards were unfurled, and fluttered gaily in the morning breeze. Officers rode to and fro through the camp, full of pride and enthusiasm. Many citizens who had been permitted to come into camp, to see their relations and friends, were walking carelessly over the field in which the tents were pitched. All was animation, confidence, security and joviality in the American camp. This condition of affairs in the American lines was perceived by the British, who chafed with impatience to convert the scene into one of a very different character. The day was far advanced before the heavy fog which obstructed the view from the British batteries rolled up, like a stage-curtain, and the bright sun came forth to reveal and expose the animated spectacle of the American camp. But the British did not pause to contemplate this scene. At a signal from the central redoubt, thirty large cannon belched forth their fiery missiles upon the American lines at point blank distance. At the same time, to render the fire more impressive and startling, myriads of Congreve rockets were thrown up from the redoubts, which filled the firmament with flaming orbits and rained meteoric showers upon the fields around and upon the American camp. It would be vain to deny that the Americans were startled by the suddenness and violence of this cannonade Their parade was quickly ended. The men broke ranks and dispersed, not as some British writers have represented, in terror and alarm, but to proceed to their respective posts in the lines. The post of duty on this occasion was not the post of danger, for it was only when standing immediately behind their

parapet that the Americans were safe from the shot and
shells of the enemy. No one in their camp was in
greater danger than the General-in-Chief. The headquarters at Macarte's was the favorite target of the
British battery near the road. Here Jackson, surrounded
by his staff, was taking a hurried breakfast, when, as
the first intimation of the opening of the British batteries,
there came a terrific crash of balls, rockets and shells,
which, piercing the frail walls of the old chateau, passed
through every part of it, scattering bricks, splinters of
wood, and furniture, and plaster in every direction, so
that several of the General's aids were thickly covered
with the rubbish. It was a miracle that no one was
hurt, though for ten minutes after the batteries opened,
not less than a hundred balls, rockets and shells struck
the house. It became too warm a place, for even the
fearless General. Calling his aids around him he walked
towards the lines. Here he found the men all at their
posts, regarding with breathless anxiety and some
degree of nervousness, the shock which the tremendous
cannonade of the enemy communicated to their embankment, and to the very ground upon which they stood.
It was indeed a scene calculated to awe and alarm raw
soldiers and civilians. The incessant roar and blaze of
thirty large cannons, the tremor of the earth under the
heavy weight of the missiles, the awful hissing and
crashing of shells, the "red glare" of streaming, circling
rockets, and the thick smoke, which the dampness of the
atmosphere gathered over the scene, formed a picture
of the awfully sublime, such as new soldiers are not
often required to face, nor ever expected to view, without some degree of anxiety, not to say alarm. But
nobly did Jackson's men face these terrific demonstra-

tions. The artillerists stood ready with their guns pointed and matches lighted, waiting until the smoke of the British guns should disappear and expose the position of their batteries. Jackson's first glance, when he reached the line, was in the direction of Humphrey's battery. There stood this "right arm" of the artillery, dressed in his usual plain attire, smoking that eternal cigar, coolly levelling his guns, and directing his men. "Ah!" exclaimed the General, "all is right; Humphrey is at his post, and will return their compliments presently." Then, accompanied by his aids, he walked down the line to the left, stopping at each battery to inspect its condition, and waving his cap to the men as they gave him three cheers, and observing to the soldiers, "Don't mind these rockets, they are mere toys to amuse children."

Presently the American lines broke their ominous silence. Humphrey led off on the right with his twelves, firing several volleys before the other guns began, thereby creating the false hope in the breasts of the enemy that their terrific cannonade would be gently returned. But soon Dominique, and Norris, and Spotts dissipated this delusion, and with their larger guns joined the chorus. Next, the veteran Garrique with his twelve pounder, directed his particular attention to the redoubt on the British right and in his front, whilst Crawley made the earth tremble under the reverberations of his huge piece. And now once fairly opened, the batteries of the Americans poured forth, without pause or cessation, a constant stream of fiery missiles, which soon destroyed the hope of the British that it was to be a one-sided affair. There is nothing in this brilliant campaign more remarkable than the vigor, destructiveness, and complete success of this cannonade on the part of the Americans. The coolness of the commanders of the batteries, the precision of their fire, and the regularity of their discharges, amazed the veterans in both armies. The phlegmatic Humphreys, with his eternal cigar, his keen eye cocked carelessly over the embrasure, his quiet manner, and those inspiring words of command, "Let her off," which preceded the discharge of his pieces; the prompt energetic bearing of Lieut. Spotts, a small man of indomitable courage, commanding a hardy band of those besmoked tars, who from the decks of the Carolina had hurled such a terrible tornado into the British camp on the night of the 23d of December; the agile, wiry, quick-eyed and ferocious Dominique; You, standing on the very edge of the embankment, exposed to the storms of British shot, and in loud and defiant terms in French, exciting his grim, scarred, and desperate warriors, to fire more briskly, to cram their pieces to the mouth, with those terrible chain-shot, and ponderous ship cannister, and every description of destructive missile; Norris, calm, and officer-like, handling his piece and directing his men as if merely exercising them; Crawley with equal phlegm and ease, leveling his monster with fatal precision; and the enthusiastic Garrique, stirring up the warm blood of his old Napoleon artillerists, who, before their ancient foe, felt the vengeance, the hostility of long years welling up in their bosoms, and banishing all fear or pity. These were some of the main features in that memorable scene, which greeted the proud and dauntless gaze of the heroic Jackson, as he passed slowly down the lines, infusing spirit, courage, and vigor into all, who beheld his erect bearing, his flashing eye, and determined countenance. And so, for an hour the fire raged and the batteries belched forth their iron lava,—and, to the lookers on, it appeared as if those guns were as inexhaustible as Vesuvius. In that combat, it was quite obvious that the British had several advantages. Their batteries presented a very narrow front and slight elevation on a spacious plain, the surface of which was from four to six feet below the level of the American platforms. The American works offered a fair target, in a line about one thousand yards long, the top of the parapet being higher than the platforms of the British. Nor were their guns badly handled. It could not be otherwise, manned as they were by veteran artillerists and the famous naval gunners,—who had fought at Trafalgar, the Nile, and Copenhagen. Their shot rarely missed their object. Several of their balls struck the American guns.. Dominique's twenty-four had its carriage broken; Crawley's thirty-two was also damaged, the foretrain of Garrique's twelve was broken, and two caissons, in one of which there were a hundred pounds of powder, were blown up.

But what were all these proofs of skill and good practice, compared with the extraordinary achievements of the American gunners? The British, it will be remembered, had at least thirty guns of the largest calibre; the Americans only ten of various calibres, several being six-pounders. Yet, in an hour and a quarter after the batteries opened, the British fire began to slacken. It was evident they were hurt, damaged, crippled. With intense interest and eagerness the Americans strove to pierce the smoke which enveloped the British redoubts, in order to ascertain the extent of the damage. Soon, it was quite perceptible on both sides, that the embankments of the batteries were all beaten in, the guns exposed, and some of the artillerists killed. The infantry, which had been ordered to be ready for an advance, when a breach was made in the American works, grew impatient, and became so exposed that it was deemed prudent to retire them again into the ditches. As the fire of the British slackened, that of the Americans increased in power and accuracy. There was a slight flickering of hope in their bosoms, and a feeble cheer, when an American caisson blew up. It was a brief exultation. The Americans shouted back their defiance, and redoubled their fire. With a terrible crash, the heavy round and chain shot tore through the thick and compact mound of the redoubts, and scattered into fragments. Then it was discovered, that a great error had been committed, in using hogsheads of sugar in the construction of their parapets. The balls penetrated these hogsheads as if they were so many empty casks, dismounting the guns, and killing the men in the very centre of the works. It was thus shown that sugar is a very different material from sand.

. On the other side, the Americans were equally unsuccessful in attempting to employ one of the great staples of the country for warlike purposes. A flatboat, which lay near the American camp, had in it some fifty bales of cotton, the property of that since famous cotton speculator, Vincent Nolté, who had purchased them from Major Planché, commandant of the Orleans battalion. In the hurried construction of the embankment, these bales had been rolled out and thrown into the pile of earth to increase its bulk. On this day, the enemy's balls striking one of these bales knocked it out of the mound, set fire to the cotton, and sent it flying about to the great danger of the ammunition. The bales were consequently removed, and some of them falling on the outside of the breastwork into the ditch, there issued from them a heavy smoke, which blinded the artillerists, and seriously obstructed their operations. Some of the men of Planché's battalion volunteered to extinguish the burning cotton, and, slipping over the breastwork, succeeded in doing so, not, however, without injury, one of the parties being seriously wounded. After this no cotton bales were ever used in the breastwork. Yet, a vulgar error has long prevailed that Jackson's defences were composed chiefly of this great staple, which, though modern science has discovered to possess certain inflammable qualities, suited for some of the operations of war, is, perhaps, one of the most insecure and dangerous materials out of which a breastwork to resist cannon balls, shells and rockets could be constructed. The imaginations of the British, excited by avarice, by the prospect of sharing the immense quantity of this valuable product, reported to be accumulated in the city of New Orleans, might be excused, for seeing such a vast heap of it, lying, like the apple of Tantalus, within their grasp, and alluring them to death and disgrace. But American writers are scarcely pardonable for a repetition of this absurdity, that Jackson's lines were composed, in whole, or in part, of cotton bales. The experience of this campaign demonstrated, that sugar and cotton were intended for peaceful uses, for the nurture, conservation and protection of humanity, and not as aids and appliances in promoting man's destruction and encouraging his passions. It demonstrated this other valuable truth, that the soil of

Louisiana is the best material out of which to construct
its own defence. It was the sole material of Jackson's
slight breastwork. The British balls were embedded in
the soft elastic earth, where they remained without
shaking or weakening the embankment. Indeed, they
contributed to render it more solid. The only inlets
through which they had access into the lines, were
through the embrasures for the cannon, and nearly all
these were penetrated several times. But the British
were not able to pursue these advantages. Their works
were rapidly melting before the fire of the Americans.
Soon their redoubt was completely silenced, and the
parapets levelled with the plain. Then the Americans
raised the most stentorian huzzas, as the British artillerists were seen stealing out of their demolished works,
and running as fast as they could for the nearest ditch.
The American batteries waxed warmer, and continued
their fire at the other redoubts, until they, too, were
soon in a condition similar to that which had been the
first object of their fury.

And now the sun had nearly reached the meridian,
and a momentary respite being ordered in the American lines, to allow the pieces to cool off, the smoke
ascended from the stricken plain. Lo! what a scene
was presented to the exulting army of Jackson. As if
by magic the terrible works, so scientifically and labo-
riously constructed, from which the iron death was to
be poured upon the patriotic defenders of their own
soil, whose formidable aspect had excited such alarm
and anxiety, but a few hours before, had vanished like
the "baseless fabric of a vision, and left not a wreck
behind." The big guns which had won so many victories for England on the sea, lay all crippled, broken,

dismantled, and heaped up with rubbish, while those who had so often hurled destruction and defiance from their mouths, were retiring with a speed worthy of English "blood and bottom," to the rear. Never was work more completely done—more perfectly finished and rounded off. Earth and heaven fairly shook with the prolonged shouts of the Americans over this spectacle. Still the remorseless artillerists would not cease their fire. The British infantry would now and then raise their heads and peep forth from the ditches in which they were so ingloriously ensconced. The level plain presented but a few knolls or elevations to shelter them, and the American artillerists were as skillful as riflemen in picking off those who exposed ever so small a portion of their bodies.*   Several extraordinary exam-

* Colonel John Burgoyne, the engineer who constructed these works, which were so effectually demolished by Jackson's artillery on the 1st of January, 1815, has experienced other disasters of a like character during his long service. The failure of the bombardment of Sevastopol during the present campaign, where he (John Burgoyne) directed the English works, has provoked from some military critic in the London *Times*, the following severe review of his military career, which will be found interesting from the similarity of the error charged upon Sir John in his operations before Sevastopol with that committed by him at New Orleans, and as a remarkable example of an officer who has learned nothing from the most impressive and striking experience, and memorable disasters :

"It is a curious coincidence in the history of one's life, that Sir John Burgoyne should, in the prime and at the end of his military career, have commanded the engineers in two great sieges, and twice have been foiled from the very same circumstances. In 1812, when the Duke of Wellington advanced against Burgos, the town was unfortified, an old castle had been modernized, and the French had thrown up three lines of earthworks around the hill on which it stood. These had been executed in haste, and in defiance of all rule, but against those we fired, sapped, and mined in vain ; two thousand French soldiers held the place against an English army commanded by a general, undefeated up to that time, but who was then forced to retreat, to abandon his siege train, and the campaign of that year was a failure. After forty-two years, Sir John again commands before Sevastopol, and again the same thing occurs. A few earthworks are thrown up in haste before our very eyes, and the career of a victorious army is arrested. And why is this? Had Sir John been able to read the signs of the times, the lesson so rudely taught him at Burgos would not have been thrown away. Our Engineers would have known what earthworks were, and been prepared with means to destroy them, if such be possible ; or we should never have sat d' at

ples of this skill were communicated to the writer by a
British officer who was attached to Packenham's army.
A number of the officers of the 93d, having taken
refuge in a shallow hollow behind a slight elevation, it
it was proposed that the only married officer of the party
should lie at the bottom, it being deemed the safest
place. Lieutenant Phaups was the officer indicated,
and laughingly assumed the position assigned him.
This mound had attracted the attention of the American
gunners, and a great quantity of shot was thrown at it.
Lieutenant Phaups could not resist the anxiety to see
what was going on in front; and peeping forth, with not
more than half of his head exposed, was struck by a

---

before them as we have done, to run the risk of failure. We are reduced to our present straits simply and solely because Sir John, at the head of a large party of veterans, has, during the forty years of peace, resisted every improvement in military
science as a personal insult to their superior knowledge and experience, and they
have, in consequence of their position, been able to keep things pretty much as they
were at the end of the last war. Sir J. Burgoyne is preëminently what in official parlance is termed 'a safe man;' he never troubled the ministry for money to make scientific experiments, or to improve the education of engineers or artillerymen. For
every inventor he had a bucket of cold water administered in the blandest manner
possible. He possessed above all men, the art of keeping things smooth and quiet in
Pallmall, and rose in favor and in fortune accordingly. He hoped, of course, that
these things would last his time, and so they would have done but for this ugly Russian
war, which has destroyed all these visions of quiet; and we now find ourselves
engaged in a struggle with the most barbarous nation of Europe, whose soldiers are
serfs, whose officers are half educated, and whose military system is corrupt to the
core, yet in every scientific point they have shown themselves as superior to us in military, as we are to them and the rest of Europe in military engineering. Their artillery
silences ours without difficulty. The shells are larger, and thrown with greater precision than ours, and their skill in fortification amazes our officers, who can make no
head against it. Their science, in short, has made up for all their other deficiencies,
and neutralized all the intelligence and bravery of our noble soldiers; and for all this
we have to thank Sir John Burgoyne and his band of co-obstructives, who have
reduced the skill of the most scientific and enterprising people of Europe below the
level of the most barbarous. Will even the people of England and Parliament, though
generally so ignorant and careless on such matters, submit to this much longer? It
has required a war as dreadful as this one is, to open our eyes to the absurdities of
our military system; but if it does so effectually, those who have fallen because of
their superiors, will not all, at least, have fallen in vain."

twelve-pound shot, and instantly killed. His companions buried him on the spot on which he fell, in full
uniform. Several officers and men were picked off in a
similar manner.

During the cannonading, the British had sent a
detachment of light troops through the woods on the
left of the Americans, to see what impression could be
made on that quarter. But Jackson, warned by the
experience of the 28th, had given special attention to
this part of his lines. As soon as the British showed
themselves in this quarter, Coffee ordered his men to
drive them into the swamp, and drown them. The agile
Tennesseans, leaping like cats from log to log, and
utterly indifferent to mire and water, satisfied the
heavy, beef-eating, bog-fearing Britons, that they could
beat them at swamp fighting, and soon drove off the
intruders. On the Levee the British battery had been
quite active and efficient in holding the Louisiana at
bay, and exchanging shots with Patterson's marine battery on the right bank of the river. They fired with
great precision, and several of their shot struck Patterson's works, but produced no serious injury. The main
object of this battery was to destroy the Louisiana.
For this purpose, shot were kept constantly heated.
But the Louisiana remained beyond the reach of this
battery. Humphrey, after completing the demolition of
the redoubts in front, now turned his attention to that
on the Levee, and, uniting his fire with Patterson's,
soon demolished the work.

The British had abandoned all their redoubts. But
still they were not out of the reach of the American
guns. Impatiently they waited for the cover of night
to escape from the fierce clutch of their indefatigable

22

foe, and gain once more that desolate, but now desired camping ground, from which they had advanced with such high hopes the night before. Even this movement was attended with difficulty and danger; for when night drew her sable curtain over the scene, the American scouts resumed their old predatory practices, and crept near enough to throw their whizzing bullets at every visible living object. Never were brave men more dispirited and cast down than Packenham's soldiers, as they wended their slow and dreary way back to their old camp. They had been without food or sleep for sixty hours. They were worn down with fatigue, suffering, exhaustion and exposure to the damp night air. What was worse than all, they were prostrated in hope and spirits. No wonder they murmured audibly against such labors, trials and deprivations. Military glory had ceased to occupy their minds and imaginations. Avarice was extinct in their hearts. They thought only of the present, the dark, gloomy, desolate present; of their unavailing advances, their unaccountable failures, their severe losses, their incessant fatigues. If men ever were driven to the verge of despair, if an army ever reached a condition, which would have palliated, if not justified mutiny and rebellion, certainly the soldiers of Packenham were in that state on the night of the 1st of January, 1815. Nor did their labors end with the retirement of the army. Again the men were ordered out to drag the dismounted guns into camp. It was a terrible task. The soil was soft, and the guns were very heavy. It was not until morning that all the guns which were considered of any value could be removed. Five of them were left behind, and subsequently became the property of the

Americans. This labor being accomplished, the troops were all called into camp. The officers and men eagerly threw themselves on the damp ground, and were soon wrapped in deep slumber. That whilom busy and active camp, was now as still and quiet as a grave-yard.

Different feelings and desires agitated the American army. The infantry had regarded with unbounded joy and pride, the brilliant performances of the artillery, which monopolized the labor and glory of the day. Indifferent to the shower of balls, shells and rockets, which were thrown into every part of the line, the men who were not on duty, would crowd around the guns, to witness the wonderful precision and coolness with which they were directed and managed. Many of the infantry were employed in aiding the artillerists, bringing the ammunition, and performing other useful tasks about the batteries.

Among those who were thus engaged, was one, whose memory is cherished with pious devotion by thousands in the community, which he so long blessed with his inexhaustible benevolence. The 1st of January, 1815, witnessed the only scene of contention and bloodshed, in the long, peaceful and virtuous life of that pure-minded philanthropist, Judah Touro, whose fame is coequal with the boundaries of this Republic, and has extended to distant and foreign lands, which he has brightened and comforted by his beneficence.

After performing other severe labors as a common soldier in the ranks, Mr. Touro, on the 1st of January, volunteered his services to aid in carrying shot and shell from the magazine to Humphrey's battery. In this humble but perilous duty, he was seen actively engaged during the terrible cannonade with which the British opened the day, regardless of the cloud of iron missiles which flew around him, when many of the stoutest-hearted clung closely to the embankment or sought some shelter.   But in the discharge of duty, this good man knew no fear, and perceived no danger.   It was whilst thus engaged, that he was struck on the thigh by a twelve-pound shot, which produced a ghastly and dangerous wound, tearing off a large mass of flesh.   Mr. Touro long survived this event, leading a life of unostentatious piety and charity, and setting an example of active philanthropy, which justly merited the fervent gratitude and warm affection in which he was held by the community of which he was justly regarded as the Patriarch—the "Israelite without guile."

No charitable appeal was ever made to him in vain. His contributions to philanthropic and pious enterprises exceed those of any other citizen.   The same patriotism which prompted him to expose his life on the plains of Chalmette, dictated that handsome donation of ten thousand dollars for the completion of the Bunker Hill Monument, and has characterized a thousand other deeds of like liberality, performed " by stealth," which were no less commendable for their generosity than their entire freedom from sectarian feeling or selfish aim.

An incident, illustrative of the beauty of friendship and gratitude, of the noble and gentle traits of humanity, may serve as an agreeable relief in this narrative of strife and bloodshed.

Judah Touro and Rezin D. Shepherd, two enterprising merchants, the one from Boston and the other from Virginia, had settled in New Orleans at the commencement of the present century. They were intimate, devoted friends, who lived under the same roof, and were scarcely ever separated. When the State was invaded, both volunteered their services, and were enrolled among its defenders. Mr. Touro was attached to the Regiment of Louisiana Militia, and Mr. Shepherd to Captain Ogden's Horse Troop.

Commodore Patterson, who was an intimate friend of Mr. Shepherd, solicited Gen. Jackson to detach him, as his Aid, to assist the Commodore in the erection of his battery on the right bank of the river, and in the defence of that position. It was whilst acting as Patterson's Aid, that Mr. Shepherd came across the river, on the 1st of January, with orders to procure two masons to execute some work on the Commodore's battery. The first person Mr. Shepherd saw, on reaching the left bank, was Reuben Kemper, who informed him that his old friend Touro was dead. Forgetting his urgent and important mission, Mr. Shepherd eagerly inquired whither they had taken his friend. He was directed to a wall of an old building, which had been demolished by the British battery in the rear of Jackson's headquarters, and on reaching it, found Mr. Touro in an apparently dying condition. He was in charge of Dr. Kerr, who had dressed his wound, but who, shaking his head, declared that there was no hope for him. Mr. Shepherd, with the devotion of true friendship, determined to make every effort to save his old companion. He procured a cart, and lifting the wounded man into it, drove to the city. He administered brandy very freely to his fainting and prostrate friend, and thus in a great degree kept him alive.* On reaching the city, Mr. Shepherd

* The good old man used to say this was the only time he ever drank to excess

carried Touro into his house, and there obtaining the services, as nurses, of some of those noble ladies of the city, who devoted themselves with so much ardor to the care and attendance of the sick and wounded of Jackson's army, and seeing that he was supported with every comfort and need, he hastened to discharge the important duty which had been confided to him, and which he had nearly pretermitted, in responding to the still more sacred calls of friendship and affection.

It was late in the day before Shepherd, having performed his mission, returned to Patterson's battery. The cloud of anger was gathering on the brow of the Commodore, when he met his delinquent or dilatory aid, but it soon dispersed, when the latter frankly and promptly exclaimed,

"Commodore, you can hang or shoot me, and it will be all right; but my best friend needed my assistance, and nothing on earth could have induced me to neglect him." He then stated the circumstances of Mr. Touro's misfortune, and the causes of his dilatory execution of the duty assigned to him. Commodore Patterson was a man—he appreciated the feelings of his aid, and thought more of him after this incident than before. They continued warm friends throughout the campaign, and ever afterwards.

Shepherd and Touro, with a friendship thus tested and cemented, were ever afterwards inseparable in this world. Death alone could sever them, and then only in a material sense. Such fidelity deserved the rich reward which fortune showered on them. They became millionaires, and as the most valuable of their possessions retained the esteem and regard of the community of which they were the patriarchs.

On the 18th of January, 1854, the venerable philanthropist, Judah Touro, was "gathered unto his fathers," amid the lamentations of the whole population of New Orleans. Public journals in their columns, and divines in their pulpits, offered eloquent and just tributes to his virtues. No man ever died in the city, who was more universally regretted, or whose memory will be more gratefully preserved. A few days before his death—to wit, on 6th January, 1854—Mr. Touro made a will, disposing of his immense property. That will is an eternal monument of his goodness and philanthropy. It is not less remarkable for its liberal and discriminating charity, than for the earnest affection and gratitude which the good old man cherished for all who had been kind to him in life. After distributing one-half of his estate among various charitable and religious institutions, including a splendid legacy of $80,000 to that much-needed institution, an Alms-House in New Orleans, and handsome endowments to all the Hebrew congregations in the country, as well as a large legacy in favor of the project of restoring the scattered tribes of Israel to Jerusalem, with numerous private legacies to individual friends, Mr. Touro thus nobly embodies and expresses the gratitude and friendship, which, for nearly forty years, had warmed his heart towards his old friend and constant associate for half a century:

"And as regards my other designated executor, say my dear, old and devoted friend, Rezin Davis Shepherd, to whom, under Divine Providence, I was greatly indebted for the preservation of my life, when I was wounded on the 1st of January, 1815, I hereby appoint and institute him, the said Rezin Davis Shepherd, after the payment of my particular legacies, and the debts of my succession, the uni versal legatee of the rest and residue of my estate, movable and immovable."

As residuary legatee, Mr. Shepherd inherits a property sufficient to make him wealthy, if he were not already so; but the worthy legatee, regarding this handsome donation as a testimonial of gratitude and friendship, has determined to apply it to such uses as he knows would have gratified his old friend, if he were alive. He has therefore offered to expend the greater part of it in the improvement of a street in New Orleans upon which they had both passed their lives--the scene of their old and long friendship, and which Mr. Shepherd desires to consecrate to the memory of his old friend, by improving it conformably to a darling plan of Mr. Touro, and by bestowing the name of the deceased philanthropist upon it.

Such are the incidents of a friendship, even in this age of commerce and mammon-worship, as true, as noble, as constant, as pure and unselfish as that which the poets have immortalized in the beautiful episodes of Orestes and Pylades, of Nisus and Euryalus, of David and Jonathan.

Jackson's loss on the 1st of January was marvelously small, considering the immense number of shot and shell that fell in his camp. Thirty-four killed and wounded were the reported loss. Nearly all the killed were of persons, many of them spectators, who gathered on the roads and in the rear of the camp, to see or hear what was going on. Such results were quite as wonderful as the other incidents of this wonderful campaign.

XIV.

TWO NOTABLE WARRIORS AND REVOLUTIONISTS.

THE retirement of the British, after the disastrous repulse of the first of January, restored quiet and confidence to the American camp, and afforded the " Hunters " an opportunity of resuming their favorite occupation and amusement, of annoying the outposts of the enemy, night and day, by sudden attacks of detached parties, and often by penetrating their camp, or creeping near to their lines of communication and picking off sentinels, decoying deserters, and driving in pickets. These scouting parties, composed of volunteers from the various corps, would organize, select their officers on the spot, and embracing the first leave of absence from duty in their lines, would suddenly dash upon some exposed point of the British camp, and regard it very poor luck, if they did not pick off a " redcoat " or two. General Jackson frequently needed the services of these scouting parties to ascertain the movements of the enemy, and perform other services, requiring courage, caution, skill and fortitude. That sagacious man never failed to perceive and select the proper agents he required for any trust. Indeed, his quick and correct observation of character was the real secret of much of his success, and of his great command over men. It is one of the highest attributes of genius.

In this crowd of chivalric warriors, assembled in

Jackson's camp, who were ever ready for any duty, how onerous or perilous soever, there were two chiefs, to whom the General's attention was frequently called by their gallant bearing and soldierly virtues. Their previous histories were familiar to him. They were men who had figured conspicuously in important events. It will no doubt be regarded an excusable digression, from the regular course of this narrative, to snatch from the perishing records, in which their deeds are chronicled, some memorials of men, who were representatives and embodiments of prevailing ideas of their age. They were of that class of adventurers who have achieved so much for the Southwest, the Valley of the Mississippi, and the State of Louisiana, by giving practical effect to the principle, that every people have the right to possess and control the country which they occupy and cultivate, free from foreign domination. In that age they were called Liberators and Patriots; now they might be denounced as "Pirates and Fillibusteros." One of them lived to see his design consummated, and those who were instrumental in effecting it, lauded as heroes and patriots. The other died too soon, and had he lived to a much greater age, would still have been far from a realization of the dream, which, in his youth, he prosecuted with so much enthusiasm and earnestness. The field of the ambition and labors of the one was the Valley of the Mississippi; that of the other was, unfortunate, ever struggling, ever enslaved Ireland.

Reuben Kemper, the indomitable enemy of Spanish dominion in America, lived to see the last remnant of that once splendid power extinguished on this continent.

General Humbert, the hero and chief of the French expedition which aimed at the establishment of Irish Independence in 1798, was disappointed in his early hopes and struggles, but lived long enough to see his old enemy and Ireland's oppressor, subjected to the bitterest defeats and most mortifying disasters that ever fell upon that proud and haughty power. •

These two remarkable men met for the first time on the Plains of Chalmette. Jackson did not regard them as " Pirates and Robbers," because they had left their own countries to aid an oppressed people to throw off the yoke of foreign despots. He viewed them in their true light, as brave, sincere, reliable men, lovers of liberty, and foes of despotism. He gave them his confidence, and entrusted them with " enterprises of great pith and moment." They never failed to justify this confidence.

Reuben Kemper was one of several brothers who were born in Virginia, and early emigrated to the West. Their father was a venerable and remarkable character. He was a Baptist preacher, no less distinguished for his piety, natural eloquence, and all the patriarchal virtues, than for his imposing figure, his great simplicity of conduct and manners, and love of frontier life. This venerable man lived to a great old age, in the neighborhood of Cincinnati, Ohio, of which State he was an early settler. He had seven sons, all youths of mark--of extraordinary strength, courage and daring. Three of them, Nathan, Reuben and Samuel, settled in the Mississippi Territory, near Pinckeyville, adjacent to the present Louisiana line, which then divided the territory of the United States and Spain. Their strong sense, pleasing address, manly carriage and intense *Americanism* soon rendered the Kempers very popular and influential among the frontiersmen, as well those settled in the Spanish colony of Florida, as those residing in the Mississippi Territory. They were the leaders, in agitating the scheme of driving the Spaniards out of the country, and claiming Florida as belonging to the Americans under the cession of 1803. Henry Clay, in his first speech in the United States Senate, maintained the American title to that country, and urged the Administration of Mr. Madison to occupy it. With the newly acquired territories of Louisiana and Mississippi, surrounding three sides of it, the isolated colony of Spain certainly presented a very tempting bait to American ambition, and seemed to be held by his Catholic Majesty out of sheer obstinacy or pride. Several plots were concocted by the Kempers and others, to revolutionize this colony, and forays were made by them into the Spanish territory. In 1805 they marched with forty mounted men, armed with long rifles, to the vicinity of Baton Rouge; but their approach being announced, the Spanish Governor prepared to receive them in such force, as rendered the attempt too serious an affair; they therefore returned to Mississippi, to " bide their time."

At last the Spanish Governor determined to nip the conspiracy in the bud, by seizing the chiefs, and making terrible examples of them. Accordingly he induced a number of Americans, by promise of large grants of land, to proceed in a body into the Mississippi Territory, for the purpose of kidnapping the Kempers and bringing them to Baton Rouge, to be dealt with according to Spanish law. The party were armed with guns and clubs, and consisted of a dozen white persons and several negroes. They entered the house of Nathan Kemper, and dragging Reuben from his bed where he was sleeping, beat him with clubs until he was insensible, and then tied him. They also dragged Nathan from the side of his wife, who received some blows from their clubs in the scuffle, and after beating him severely, secured him in the same manner in which Reuben had been treated. The brothers asked, "What was the meaning of this outrage; what have we done?" A voice answered, "You have ruined the Spanish country." They were then gagged with sassafras roots, and ropes tied around their necks. In this condition they were compelled to run before the horses of the kidnappers, who held the ropes, all the way to the Spanish line. Samuel Kemper was soon seized and treated in a similar manner, being beaten with clubs and dragged for a hundred yards by a rope around his neck. The three brothers, on their arrival at Tunica, on the Mississippi river, were delivered to Colonel Samuel Alston, on behalf of the Spanish Government, who placed them in a boat to be sent to Baton Rouge. They were tied on their backs to the bottom of the boat. Dr. Towles, long a respected citizen of Feliciana, Louisiana, hearing of the outrage, crossed the Mississippi, and hastened to the American fort at Pointe Coupée, on the Louisiana side, and informed Lieutenant Wilson, the commander, of the circumstances. But as there were many boats descending the river at this time, there would be some difficulty in discovering which contained the captives. This difficulty, however, was removed by Reuben, who, as the boat neared the fort, which he discovered from a glance at the opposite bank, cried out, in a stentorian voice, "It is Reuben Kemper the Spaniards are taking to the mines." The words could be distinctly heard by the garrison, and Wilson immediately ordered out a boat with an armed party, by whom the kidnappers were arrested, the Kempers released, and the Spanish agents delivered over to the authorities of the United States to be tried. For sometime, so great was the excitement against them, that they had to be guarded by a strong military force.

The subject of this outrageous kidnapping was brought before Congress, and the celebrated John Randolph, from the Committee on Foreign Affairs, reported a bill to raise a military force to guard the American territory and repel and punish Spanish aggressions. It was not, however, acted upon.

This outrage upon the Kempers hastened the revolution which, in 1810, resulted in the capture of Baton Rouge and the entire extinction of Spanish power on the Mississippi river. The Kempers enjoyed the satisfaction of making a triumphal entry into the town from which they so narrowly escaped being sent in chains to the mines of Cuba.

But this did not satisfy their revenge, nor obliterate the recollection of the insults to which they had been subjected. With great perseverance and vigilance they hunted, one by one, the individuals who had been engaged in the kidnapping outrage, and inflicted upon them the severest punishments. Certainly, if men were ever justified in manifesting the passion of revenge, the Kempers were, towards those cowardly ruffians. If their mode of obtaining such satisfaction appear cruel and brutal, some allowances must be made for the stern and rough habits and notions of frontier life. Reuben and Samuel Kemper captured Kneeland, one of the kidnappers, and inflicted upon his naked back one hundred lashes, then one hundred more for their brother Nathan who was absent, cut off his ears with a dull knife, and then let him loose. These gory trophies of their revenge were long preserved in a bottle of spirits and hung up in one of the Kemper's parlors. Reuben caught another of the kidnappers, named Horton, and chastised him as long as his strength would permit. Barker, another, was seized by the Kempers at the Court-house, at Fort Adams in Mississippi, under the eyes of the Judge, and nearly flayed alive. Col. Alston, who commanded the Spanish guard, placed over the Kempers, died of a disease contracted by lying in an open boat, to avoid the attacks of the injured brother.

Such was the revenge of the Kempers. They were not yet content. Passing from individuals, they next directed their ire and vengeance against the Spanish Government which had authorized and directed the outrage against them. Reuben proclaimed at Baton Rouge, that the work was not finished; that whilst he lived the Spaniards should not occupy an inch of the North American continent in peace. He accordingly got up an expedition against the Spanish Fort of Mobile in conjunction with Major Kennedy, Dr. Holmes, and other adventurous spirits. This enterprise failed by the treachery of one of the parties, and the interference of the United States authorities. Reuben narrowly escaped capture on that occasion.

It was not long before another opportunity was afforded to Kemper of gratifying his insatiate hostility to the Spanish race.

In 1812, there arrived in the United States an astute Spaniard, by the name of Jose Alvarez de Toledo, who, in coöperation with Barnardo Gutierrez, a Mexican, who had been connected with the revolution in that country in 1808, fled to the United States, and resided some years in New Orleans, devised a plan for reviving the revolution, and invading and detaching that portion of Mexico, which is now included in the State of Texas. Reuben Kemper was sought as the most efficient person to organize an American party to execute this plan. He eagerly accepted the commission, and aided by Colonel Magee, succeeded in assembling at Washington, in the State of Mississippi, a force of four hundred and fifty Americans. Col. Magee was the real commander, Gutierrez was the ostensible chief, and Toledo acted as political adviser and director. Kemper was second in command under Magee. This expedition entered Texas in October, 1812, and after capturing Nacogdoches pushed on to La Bahia del Espirito, now called Goliad, which has since become so mournfully famous as the scene of the brutal massacre and desperate courage of some of the noblest martyrs in the cause of Texan independence. Here the expedition was surrounded and besieged by a strong Spanish force under Salcedo and Herrera. This siege, which was continued for several months, was enlivened by many skirmishes between the hostile armies, in all of which the stalwart form of Kemper was conspicuous. Many a swarthy Spaniard fell before his unerring rifle, or sunk to the earth under the crushing blows of his sabre. His love of these rencontres was insatiable. He led in person twenty-seven sallies against the besiegers, and always with dreadful effect. In the last of these skirmishes, there were two hundred Spaniards killed. Finding all their efforts to reduce the garrison vain, the Spanish Generals

suddenly retreated, whereupon Kemper, who had succeeded to the command of the expedition by the death
of Magee, marched out, and following rapidly upon the
retiring Spaniards, fell suddenly upon them, with such
vigor and fury as nearly to annihilate the united armies
of Salcedo and Herrera, strewing the field far and wide
with the victims of the American rifle and hunting-
knife. On this occasion Kemper slew several of the
Spaniards with his own hand. Four hundred Spaniards
were killed in this affair, and a great many prisoners
taken. The Americans lost but five killed and fourteen
wounded.

The Spanish Generals now fled in terror with the
remnant of their force to San Antonio, which they
fortified. Gutierrez and Kemper followed them with
their little band of warriors, and occupied a position
near the town. So intense was the terror of the Spaniards, who were greatly superior in numbers, of the
invincible valor and ferocity of the enemy, led by the
" giant warrior," that they surrendered on the first
demand sent to them by Gutierrez. Accordingly, on
the 31st March, 1812, the Spanish Generals walked
out of the town, into the camp of Gutierrez, bearing a
white flag, and offered to surrender on the single condition that their lives were spared. Gutierrez, who was
full of revenge towards the Spaniards, for their cruelty
to Morelos and other Mexican patriots, made an evasive
reply, conveying an intimation that their request would
be granted. The Spaniards then surrendered at discretion. Having delivered up their swords, they were
secured between files of soldiers, and marching in front
of Gutierrez's army, crossed the river, and were safely
lodged in the Alamo, which, in 1836, became the cradle
23

of Texan liberty, and the scene of prodigies of American valor. Gutierrez then entered the town of San Antonio and established a Provincial Government there, which he called a Junta. The first act of the Junta was to try the Spanish prisoners. They were condemned to be banished from the country. But whilst they were in charge of a guard, a party of sixty Mexicans, in command of Capt. Antonio Delgado, suddenly seized them, and dragging the unfortunate prisoners to the bank of the Salcdo, carried them over in boats. Arriving on the east side of the river, near the spot where Kemper had achieved his brilliant victory, Delgado's party hastily dismounted from their horses, and with no other weapons but their blunt knives, which these monsters carried in their girdles for camp use, they cut the throats of their prisoners, accompanying the cruel deed with every species of insult and indignity. "Some of these assassins, with brutal irony," says a writer who lived near the scene of the occurrence, "whetted their knives on the soles of their shoes in the presence of their bound victims." This same writer saw this band of murderers the following day, led by the chief, halt in front of the quarters of Gutierrez, and announce to the latter what they had done. At the same time, Delgado placed in Gutierrez's hand a list of the fourteen victims, which included two Governors, and Generals Salcedo and Hererra, one Colonel, six Captains, and five other officers. Delgado's men, in the meantime, suspended from their saddles pieces of bloody garments and jewelry —trophies of their cowardly brutality. That Gutierrez was privy to this outrageous deed, was proved, not only by the facts stated, but by a subsequent confession, in which, after denying any direct agency in the murder of the prisoners, he added, "God thus permitted their death as a signal punishment of the barbarities which these unfortunate victims had previously perpetrated." Thus the Mexican chief, who shared none of the laurels of the brilliant victories achieved over the Spaniards, satisfied himself by monopolizing all the infamy with which this expedition must ever be associated. We are thus minute in recording these facts because the incident is an interesting one, which is barely glanced at in the histories of the country ; and because it furnishes an illustration of the character of Reuben Kemper. Though fierce and unsparing in battle, Kemper abhorred all cruelty and cowardly brutality. The murder of the Spaniards, in cold blood, produced in the mind of that gallant chief the most profound disgust for the race, and after denouncing the conduct of Gutierrez, he resigned, and with several other Americans returned to the United States.

When New Orleans was threatened, and the call sent forth for soldiers to defend the city, Kemper joined the Feliciana Dragoons, and was among the first volunteers who arrived in the city. His experience and cool courage recommended him to General Jackson, as the leader in many important and dangerous scouting enterprises and reconnoissances, which he invariably executed with consummate address and courage. On several occasions he penetrated the British lines with a select party of bush-fighters, and reported to Jackson the condition and movements of the enemy. The General was constantly apprehensive that the British would steal up the Bayou Bienvenu, through its northern branch, and gaining his rear, enter the city by the Gentilly Ridge. There were continual rumors and alarms of such a design. To ascertain the truth, Kemper was sent with twenty men to reconnoitre their position at the junction of Bayous Mazant and Bienvenu, the most important point along the line of the British communications. It was here the British had stepped ashore from their boats. The enterprise was one of the greatest peril, as it compelled Kemper to separate his party a great distance from the American outposts, and carried him into the very centre of the British lines. It was, however, performed with no less success than daring, under perils and fatigues which would have appalled any other man. The results were of immense advantage to Jackson, in quieting all apprehensions of the approach of the enemy in that direction, who, in truth, were equally fearful of being cut off from the fleet and depot, by a sudden assault of their indefatigable antagonists. To guard against this, they burned the prairies in front of a redoubt which they had thrown up at the head of the Bayou, where their principal magazine was established and a strong guard posted. Sentinels stationed in the tops of the trees, were scattered along the Bayou, to observe the approach of any parties across the prairie. Many similar enterprises were performed by this gallant man. No individual in Jackson's whole army, performed more efficient service.

Kemper survived these events many years, pursuing a life of peaceful industry in one of the parishes of Louisiana. After the defeat of the Spaniards, and the extinction of their power on this continent, and the repulse of the British, his military ambition subsided into a quiet love of rural life, and a faithful devotion to all the duties of a good citizen. He died at Natchez about the year 1826, and was buried with military honors by that gallant corps, the Natchez Fencibles, then commanded by John A. Quitman, one of the most distinguished of the Generals of the Mexican war of 1848, and who shares many of those chivalric ideas, which led Reuben Kemper to abandon peaceful pursuits and incur the most serious perils and sacrifices in the execution of the cherished sentiment, that this continent was the rightful heritage of the great race which alone has succeeded in establishing here durable and enlightened institutions, and improving the civilization of the Old in the New World. We are not sure that the last-mentioned chieftain is altogether free from the bitter prejudice which marked the life of Kemper against the Power that now concentrates upon Cuba the despotism that once lorded over half of the American continent.

Kemper died, respected by all who knew him. Indeed, he was a man to be respected anywhere. Of gigantic frame, noble, open countenance, frank and gallant bearing, kind and courteous, but firm, and, when aroused by a sense of injury, fierce and vindictive, ardently patriotic and uncompromising in his Americanism, a practical devotee to the doctrine of the duty of all freemen to aid in expanding the area of liberty, and a firm believer in " the manifest destiny " of the American race, to possess and rule this continent, Reuben Kemper will long be remembered as the type and model of that class of men, who have rescued the vast and teeming valley of the Mississippi from the roaming savages, and from the weak hands of a declining and foreign dynasty, and made it the scene of a great confederacy and empire which is destined to outshine old Rome in wealth, greatness, and power.

There was another prominent volunteer chief and leader in many perilous enterprises, who, having no regular command, rendered himself conspicuous for his conduct and gallantry, in detached scouting and reconnoitering service, as well as highly useful to Jackson, in many of the more important arrangements, that required a knowledge of military service and art. This was Gen. Humbert, the victor of Castlebar, and leader of that desperate and chivalric expedition from France to Ireland in 1798. The life of Humbert possessed one prominent point of similarity with that of Kemper, in the fact that both had been engaged in the most daring efforts to revolutionize foreign States, which had signalized their era. They were alike, too, in the qualities of unflinching courage, dauntless resolution and fearless love of adventure. But here the similitude ends. Their military ideas were quite antagonistic, their habits and tastes dissimilar. Humbert was a stern soldier, familiar with the routine, as practised in the best disciplined armies, a firm believer in the potency of science, as applied to the conduct of war, an exacting martinet in all the rules and punctilios of the profession. Kemper was a natural warrior, trained in the rough scenes of border life, accustomed to rely on individual courage and skill. Humbert confided in the touch of the elbow of disciplined troops. Kemper in the rifle and hunting-knife of the backwoodsman, fighting on his own hook. Their appearance indicated their dissimilar tastes and ideas. Kemper was tall and rawboned, of long limbs, slouching carriage, swinging his arms about with that air of independence and indifference, peculiar to the backwoodsman. His apparel was coarse, badly fitting and badly worn. There was in his whole bea×

ing, an almost studied contempt for effect and military display and fashion. Humbert was a stout, squarely and compactly built man, of the most rectangular uprightness of carriage and rigid exactitude of movement. His air was thoroughly military, and his dress neat and well fitting. To the day of his last sickness, he never abandoned the old uniform of the General of the French Republic. It is within the recollection of many, now in the bloom of life, what a great sensation the veteran General was wont to excite among the residents of the old Square of the city, as every day at noon, clad in the same old, well preserved, military frock, with the chapeau of the French Revolution on his head, and the sword of a General under his arm, he would march with all the port and precision of an officer on duty, to an ancient café kept by an old comrade in arms, on the levee, near the French Market. On arriving at the café he would salute his old comrade with a grand *air mili taire*, and then laying his sword on the table, would proceed leisurely to arrange the dominoes for a game at that very quiet, favorite diversion of elderly Frenchmen, with any lounger who might happen to be present. A glass of cogniac, frequently replenished by his faithful friend and host, would serve to give spirit to the game.

Thus would the veteran spend the greater part of the day, now and then relieving its tedium by vivacious conversation and exciting reminiscences exchanged with his admiring comrade, until his prolonged potations, producing their usual effect, would arouse him to more active but less dignified demonstrations of his natural ardor and military enthusiasm. Then he would appear in the character which attracted the admiration and curiosity of the little Creole boys, who, fired with mili tary pride and ambition, would regard with intense interest "le grand Général de la République Française" as, flourishing his sword, he walked down the streets, shouting at the top of a powerful voice, snatches of the Marseillaise and of the *Chant du Départ*, and other revolutionary airs.

Alas! the poor old Gaul had outlived his generation. He had descended from times of military emprisé and ambition to an era of trade and money-scrambling. Mammon had long since displaced Mars in the world around him. If, thus isolated from the bustling crowd, he was driven to the use of that oblivious antidote, by which the gloomy present could be momentarily banished, and the glorious past, with all its exciting scenes and noble associations, brought vividly to mind, due allowance must be made for the weakness which circumstances forced upon a gallant and sturdy old soldier who in his day had played a conspicuous part in events of great moment. Yes, that old soldier, who died twenty years ago in poverty and destitution, who was indebted to an old quadroon woman for his only attendance in sickness, and was buried at the public expense, had once been a proud General of the French Republic in its palmy days. To him was entrusted the command of the expedition to emancipate Ireland from English rule, in 1798. A more desperate enterprise was never conceived. Its character, events and results have found a parallel in the expedition of Narcisco Lopez to Cuba, in 1851. For a long time this design had occupied the most anxious deliberations of the French Republic. The presence in Paris of several prominent Irish patriots served to keep alive this feeling and encourage the plan of striking "*perfide Albion*" in this her weakest point.

The French never doubted the assurance that the Irish
were united and harmonious in their devotion to republican liberty; that they were as hostile to the British
dynasty as the French were to the Bourbon rule.   Various plans of invasion were proposed, and great preparations were made to carry them out.   Failure upon failure, disaster after disaster followed, and frustrated all
the efforts of the Irish patriots to organize an efficient
expedition to proceed from France.   One great difficulty
was to obtain a leader in the French army of sufficient
experience and prestige to take charge of such an expedition.   They were all willing to go with a large army,
but none would venture with a mere experimental force.
It was in vain the Irish patriots Tone and Sullivan
represented that the Irish people were united in the
cause; that they only needed a small disciplined force
and arms to give direction to their unconquerable ardor;
that a large army might either create that jealousy which
all people are prone to feel towards foreigners, even when
acting as allies, or might induce an entire dependence
upon a force which they regarded as sufficient to accomplish the object without their aid; that a people, to
appreciate their independence, must achieve it themselves.   These are precisely the arguments which encouraged and emboldened the companions of Narcisco Lopez
in his expedition to Cuba, in 1851.

France was then (in 1798) crippled in power and
means, with the Old World arrayed in arms against her,
and constantly threatened with internal revolution,
changes and discord.   About this time, too, the Direc-
tory, composed as it then was of a more philosophic and
conservative class of republicans than had wielded the
destinies of the nation for some years before, began **to**

adopt a more pacific and prudent policy. Still it could
not hazard its popularity by discouraging, even if it did
not afford material aid, to the enterprise of liberating
" oppressed Ireland." Officers and soldiers of the army
were, therefore, allowed to volunteer for the expedition,
and arms and munitions were furnished to them. At
this moment, Humbert stepped forward to volunteer to
lead this forlorn hope. He had served with distinction
on the Rhine, under Pichegru, Moreau, and Dumourier,
and was an officer of acknowledged courage and energy.
Repairing to Rochelle, he immediately set to work, in
conjunction with the Irish patriots, Tone, Teeling, and
Sullivan, to organize an army out of a heterogeneous mass
of adventurers, who had assembled there, composed of
straggling French soldiers, Irish volunteers, British
deserters, and a few earnest enthusiasts in the cause of
universal freedom and republicanism. To obtain money
and supplies for the expedition, Humbert was driven to
the expedient of a military requisition on the merchants
of Rochelle, who were glad enough to pay an illegal tax
to be rid of so discordant and adventurous a force.
After a thousand annoyances, difficulties, and troubles,
being compelled to shoot several of his men to enforce
discipline, Humbert succeeded in sailing out of the port
of Rochelle with his motley band of liberators. The
Irish triumvirate, as they were called—Tone, Teeling,
and Sullivan—accompanied him. They were in the
highest spirits, and almost certain of victory and success. They were assured that the people of Ireland
were ripe for a revolution, which was to rid the green
isle of the Saxon. So confident were they of this result,
that the future government of the island, the whole
organization of its civil administration, had been discus-

sed and carefully digested and prepared. They looked
even beyond this. When they had gained their independence, and extorted security for the future, they
would next demand indemnity for the past. They would
require the West India islands as compensation for
the woe and poverty which English misrule had brought
on the island. Humbert was impulsive, enthusiastic, and credulous. He could not doubt such earnest
assurances of his Irish confederates. He hated England
with intense earnestness. Treachery, falsehood, pride,
avarice, grasping covetousness, and reckless brutality,
were the characteristics he assigned to the English.
Despite these feelings, however, doubts would frequently
cloud the bright prospects of the expedition, so glowingly
painted by the voluble and enthusiastic Irish. His impressions of the character of his allies were not elevated
by an observation of the conduct of those engaged in
the expedition. Still, he was embarked in the enterprise, and determined to prosecute it with courage and
energy.

Humbert effected a landing at Killala, on the southern
coast of Ireland, in August, 1798. His force consisted
of less than a thousand men, including a battalion of
good French soldiers well officered. At Killala, he
arrested the Protestant Bishop, and detained him as a
prisoner, treating him with a respect and courtesy which
did not please the excited and wild mob of peasants that
soon began to pour into the town, greatly perplexing
and embarrassing his arrangements, rather than adding
to his strength and resources. Ignorant of their language, their peculiarities and customs, Humbert was
almost driven mad by the turbulent and unruly character of his confederates—the oppressed race which he had

come to liberate. They set at defiance all military sub-
ordination and discipline, and even ridiculed the stiff
carriage and neat appearance of the French regulars.
When the officers assumed any control over them, they
rolled their eyes, pouted their lips, and cracked many a
joke at the impudence of the " interloping foreigners."

At last, however, having by dint of superhuman
efforts, reduced his command to something like order,
Humbert commenced his march into the country. His
battalion of regulars advanced in military order, but it
was flanked, followed and surrounded by the disorderly
host of wild-looking, ragged peasants, with their long
uncombed hair hanging down their necks and shoulders, barefooted, with signs of starvation, of poverty,
misery, and oppression, in their countenance, carriage,
and habiliments. And yet, they were full of enthusiasm
and patriotism, and marched gaily along, swearing, hurraing, singing in the exuberance of their joy and hope
of the rescue of " Sweet Ireland" from the vile Saxon.
Nor was patriotism their only inspiration on this occasion. Whisky, the inseparable concomitant of all such
enterprises, was an important element and agent of the
revolution. Its importance in this respect is appreciated
even in this enlightened age. The patriots of Killala
celebrated their imaginary independence, as too many
Americans do that real independence which was declared
on the 4th July, 1776, by getting drunk and falling by
the road-side, so that Humbert's advance was marked by
the bodies of the victims of alcohol, rather than by
those of the perfidious Saxons whom he had come to
annihilate. Ammunition carts were loaded with whisky barrels, and at every halt there was a general biba-
tion. Mingled with the men, who thus encumbered

Humbert's march, were many women and children. The small, regular, compact body of disciplined soldiers, looked even smaller from being enveloped by such a rabble. They were perplexed and astounded at the conduct of their allies—of patriots, who would bear no restraint, submit to no discipline, who all wanted to be officers, chiefs, and leaders, who sneered at the generous devotion of their allies, and frowned on any assumption of authority by them. Humbert saw at a glance the folly and hopelessness of the enterprise.

"We shall all be taken, and probably shot," he remarked to his aid; "but then France will be committed to the enterprise, and will be bound to avenge us. So *Vive la République! Vive la République! En avant! En avant!*"

And thus the enthusiastic and heroic Frenchman advanced rapidly towards Castlebar. Here he encountered a considerable force of royalists, strongly posted with artillery. The French battalion steadily advanced on the royalists, but a few discharges of the English guns scattered in every direction Humbert's auxiliaries. Charging gallantly with his Frenchmen, Humbert succeeded in putting the royalists to flight with considerable loss, and achieved a brilliant and decided victory. He then made a triumphal entry into the town of Castlebar. Here he was joined in greatly augmented numbers by the peasantry of the country, who with scythes, pikes, and every rude weapon imaginable, crowded into the town and made it hideous with their wild revelry. They imagined that the last blow had been struck, and that Ireland was now free. Humbert was compelled to tarry here for the reinforcements daily and hourly expected from France. These reinforcements were rapidly proceeding to Killala, but unfortunately the fleet under Bompard, which was conveying them, was attacked in the Bay of Killala by the squadron of Sir John Warren, and entirely destroyed. Thus was Humbert's last hope annihilated.

Meantime, Lord Cornwallis, with a powerful army, was gradually surrounding Humbert, as he himself had been surrounded by the French and Americans at York-town, Virginia, some fifteen years before. As the rumors of the approach of the British began to thicken upon him, Humbert observed his allies rapidly falling off, and slinking out of the town, until at last he was left in the village of Boyle with his French veterans, and a few of the Irish leaders who were too far committed to retreat. Humbert called a council of his officers, and proposed to fight it out, offering themselves a sacrifice on the altar of Irish independence. His officers, who had been disgusted with the enterprise from their landing and first acquaintance with their allies, were not so enthusiastic and devoted. Under their advice he determined to surrender. Accordingly, Lord Cornwallis had the satisfaction of receiving the sword of the French general, an event well calculated to remind that distinguished Briton of a memorable scene in his own military history. Humbert was released on parole, and finding no prospect for promotion in France, came with many other soldiers of the old French Republican school, whose republicanism was of too earnest and uncompromising a character for Napoleon's views, to New Orleans.

When Jackson arrived, in 1814, to assume the defence of the city, Humbert was one of the first to tender his services as a volunteer. He proved eminently serviceable during the campaign. Having no regular command, he was always ready for any detached service, how perilous and difficult soever it might be. Mounted on a large black charger, it was his custom every day to emerge from the American lines, and trotting down the road to a point within musket-shot of the British outposts, to take a deliberate observation of their camp through a field glass; after completing which, he would wheel his horse and leisurely return to the American encampment, disregarding the balls, which frequently rained around him from the British batteries, and report to Jackson the exact condition of the enemy's camp. For these and other services, Humbert was highly complimented in Jackson's dispatches. The old Frenchman, in return, declared that Jackson was worthy to have commanded in the army of the Rhine—which distinction was alone necessary to complete his military greatness and renown. But though thus eulogistic of Jackson, the veteran did not include in his good opinion the mass of the soldiers whom Jackson had the "misfortune to command." He could never be persuaded that the rude, dusky, awkward, slouching, bush-fighters from Tennessee, with their careless, unmilitary carriage, their reckless, undisciplined, barbarian style of fighting, could be converted into soldiers. What particularly annoyed him, was the habit these "*sauvages*" had of thinking for themselves—discussing the merits of their officers and the expediency of orders from their commanders, and assuming to reason and judge when their only duty was to act and obey. A disagreeable illustration of this habit was brought home to the general on a certain occasion, when, being ordered out for a reconnoissance with a detachment of Coffee's men, he brought them under the severe fire of a British redoubt—whereupon these independent, self-thinking soldiers, not relishing or appreciating the necessity of losing their lives in so unprofitable an undertaking, quietly wheeled their horses and returned to the lines, leaving the veteran cursing and swearing in the field, amid a shower of British shot.   When Humbert reported this " infamous conduct" to General Jackson, the General could not refrain from a smile—but seeing one of the men of the detachment near his quarters, he called him, and frowningly asked, " Why did you run away?"   " Wall, general," replied the bush-fighter, " not understanding French, and believing our commander was a man of sense, we *con*-strued his orders to retire out of the reach of the cannon balls, and so we just kinder countermarched."   The General had much difficulty in interpreting this excuse to Humbert, who shook his head, and continued to the day of his death profoundly skeptical of the soldierly qualities of the Tennesseans.

XV.

PREPARATION FOR THE FINAL CONFLICT.

COMPLETELY and disastriously foiled in his attempt on the 1st of January, to create a breach in the American lines with his powerful batteries, Packenham, with mortification visible in every feature and action, withdrew his army to its old position in the rear, leaving his carefully and scientifically made redoubts, his dismantled guns and broken carriages a confused mass of ruins. Gibbs' brigade encamped at Bienvenu's, and Keane's at Lacoste's. The General-in-Chief resumed his old headquarters at Villeré's, which he had abandoned in the morning, with a confident expectation of shifting them before night, permanently, to the Government buildings in New Orleans.

The army murmured audibly. Such incessant labors and repeated failures were enough to try the patience of the most hardy veterans. These trials were the more severe to victors, like the Peninsular heroes, who had scarcely ever before experienced a reverse—whose previous campaigns presented an unbroken series of victories and successes. Sickness and hunger added to their distress and disgust. The dysentery prevailed to a frightful extent, and the men were reduced to half rations of the most repulsive and unsavory food. That necessary nourishment of the soldiers, coffee, had entirely dis-

24

appeared, and a vain effort was made to substitute for it a decoction of burnt biscuit. Sugar, of which an abundance lay about them, in the broken hogsheads of the planters, whose estates they occupied, became an important article in their commissariat. By mixing it with broken biscuit, the soldiers succeeded in making cakes, which were more palatable than any of the food furnished to them by the army purveyors.

Another council of the chiefs was held, which was a brief one, as it had but one proposition to consider and adopt. It was Sir Edward's own plan. It was worthy of his bold character, and has never been justly censured or criticised. The plan was to storm the American lines, on both sides the river, commencing with those on the right bank, which, being carried, would enable the British to enfilade Jackson's lines, and drive him from his position, or cut off his communications with the city. Such a plan gave Packenham the great advantage, that, having the larger force, he could afford to divide his army, whereas Jackson's men were hardly sufficient to defend his own lines. If he had known Jackson's real condition, Packenham could not have adopted a plan better calculated to embarrass and defeat his enemy. With a sufficient force, say fifteen hundred or two thousand men, and several batteries to defend the lines on the right bank, Jackson would have felt quite safe in that quarter, but as it was, he had not half that force. Indeed, he was perilously weak on that side.

Packenham determined to pass a detachment of fifteen hundred muskets, with some artillery, to the right bank, and pushing forward under cover of the night, to reach the American lines before day, to storm them as soon as it was light, and after they were carried, and the battories turned upon Jackson's position, the lines on the left bank were to be stormed by the main army. The duty of conveying the troops across the river was assigned to Vice-Admiral Cochrane, who adopted a novel, bungling, and exceedingly laborious mode of bringing the barges from the bayou, the head of which, or its junction with Villeré's canal, lay two miles from the river bank. He set the sailors and soldiers to work to excavate the old plantation canal and prolong it to the river. It was an herculean labor for an army already exhausted with fatigue and sickness. Vainly the officers and men suggested that it would be far easier to drag the barges on rollers, as they had previously dragged cannon that were heavier than the boats. The obstinate old Scotchman persisted in his plan, which was finally, by the incessant labor of the whole army, completed on the 7th of January. Packenham was reconciled to this delay by the hope of receiving some important reinforcements, which had embarked from England on the 26th October. These at last arrived on the 6th January, and consisted of two fine regiments, the 7th (Fusileers) Packenham's " own," Lieut. Col. Blakeney, and the 43d Light Infantry, Lieut. Col. Patrickson, the whole under Major-General John Lambert, Colonel of one of the Household Regiments (the Foot Guards.)

There were no two regiments in the British army which stood higher—had been engaged in more battles, and had won more laurels than the 7th and 43d. "The Hero of Salamanca" felt his heart throb with pride and soldierly enthusiasm, as he cast his eyes along the ranks of his old regiment, and recognized the familiar faces of such a number of his old comrades in so many bloody and perilous scenes. General Lambert, though a young officer, like the other chiefs of the expedition, had fleshed his sword under Wellington. He enjoyed the confidence of that distinguished commander as an officer of approved courage and discretion. His services had been conspicuous towards the close of the Peninsular war, when he led a brigade in the advance into France, and particularly in the battle of Toulouse. General Lambert was an Englishman by birth, and had been sent out to America, like other young Generals, to win distinction and fortune.

Packenham's army consisted now of ten thousand of the best soldiers in the world, which he divided into three brigades, under Generals Lambert, Gibbs, and Keane. Besides these, there was a strong force of marines and sailors, which not only relieved the army proper of a great deal of labor and camp duty, and other service, but was also ever ready to take a part in the fighting.

For several days before the 8th, the troops were kept continually in motion—either at work on the canal, or in reviews and parades. Their spirits revived as the evidences thickened around them of the approach of some decisive movement, and as they observed the confidence and activity of their officers. They anticipated the preparations justly, and looked forward with vivacity to the storming of the contemptible lines of the enemy, paltry indeed, compared with those more formidable works in Spain, which they had stormed when defended by French veterans, instead of the "broad-brimmed shepherds" who now held them at bay.

The plan of execution of Packenham's new and decisive movement was as follows: Colonel Thornton, with the 85th, one of the West India regiments, and the marines and sailors, making a detachment of 1,400 muskets, with a corps of rocketers and three carronades in barges, to protect his flank, was directed to pass across the river on the night of the 7th, and steal upon the Americans before day.

On the left bank Gibbs, with the 44th, 21st, and 4th, at a signal to be given, would storm the American left, where it was deemed weakest: whilst Keane, with the 93d, 95th, and the light companies of the 7th, 43d, and some of the West India troops, would threaten the American right—drawing his fire, and taking advantage of any opportunity that might occur for a blow at him. On the left, the two British batteries destroyed on the 1st were to be restored and armed with six or eight eighteen-pounders, were to engage and keep employed the American batteries on their right, and thereby prevent them from opening on the storming column. The advance of the latter were to carry fascines or bundles of cane with which to fill up the ditch, and ladders, on which to mount the parapet. The order entered on the regimental books, and dated the 7th January, 1815, is given by one of the survivors of these events as follows: "The troops will be under arms two hours before daylight to-morrow morning, when the army will form in two columns in the following order: The right column, consisting of the 4th, 21st, 44th, will take post near the wood, the 44th leading and bearing the gabions and fascines; the left column, composed of one company from the 43d regiment, one from the 7th—the 93d, and the fifth West India regiments, shall station itself on the left, and on the road, and with the 95th extended, shall keep up communications between the heads of the two columns; a general assault will then be made on the enemy's lines, and the commander of the forces places the fullest reliance on the gallantry of the troops and the skill of their officers; that arrangements were made to assure success; and that he confidently expected that to-morrow would add an additional laurel to the many which already adorned the brows of his brave followers."

Such was Packenham's plan of attack, and the general order directing the mode of executing it.

And how did Jackson prepare to meet and repel these formidable arrangements, the nature and object of which were soon known to him? First, he dispatched messengers to hasten the advance of the reinforcements of his frightfully meagre force. Gen. Philemon Thomas arrived in the city on the 1st January, with 500 militia from Baton Rouge. On the 4th January the long-expected drafted militia of Kentucky relieved Jackson by their presence, but in such plight as to make it quite questionable whether they were any addition to his effective strength. These gallant men had hurried from their homes, travelling fifteen hundred miles, without supplies and clothing, under the infatuation that they would find an abundance of arms and clothes provided by the government, at New Orleans. They little knew that long before their arrival, Jackson had exhausted all the Government's, the State's, and the City's supplies of arms and munitions to furnish his little army. Under this delusive hope, General John Thomas brought his two thousand two hundred and fifty Kentuckians to the city. About one-third of these were armed with fowling pieces and old muskets. Nearly all of them were in want of clothing, having left home with but one shirt apiece. The poor fellows had to hold their tattered garments together, to hide their nakedness, as they marched through the streets. If this fact reflects seriously upon the Federal Government of that day, it speaks volumes for the ardent patriotism of the gallant Kentuckians, who are ever foremost in encountering any danger and sacrifice in the defence of the honor and integrity of their country. Such a spectacle produced a lively sensation among the grateful and patriotic citizens of New Orleans. Immediate steps were taken to relieve the wants and distress of the gallant men of the West, who had left comfortable homes to fight for so distant a section of the Union. The Legislature appropriated $6,000, and the people, including the volunteers and militia of New Orleans, the inhabitants of Attakapas, and of the river parishes, augmented this sum to $16,000, which was laid out in the purchase of blankets and woolens, and these being distributed among the ladies of the city, were made into comfortable clothes within a few days after the money was raised. Thus were provided for the suffering militia one thousand two hundred blanket-coats; two hundred and sixty-five waistcoats; one thousand one hundred and twenty-seven pair of pants; eight hundred sheets; four hundred and ten pair of shoes, and a great number of other articles of clothing. Here was a striking example of the public spirit of the citizens, of the ardent patriotism of the ladies of New Orleans, and likewise of the economy which was observed in those days in the expenditure of money. The sum which was thus made to contribute so largely to the health and comfort of a whole brigade, would barely serve, in these days of contractors and of governmental extravagance, to supply a single company with the necessaries of a campaign. All honor to the ladies of New Orleans for this noble display of gratitude and generosity; all honor to the veterans De Buys, Soulie, and Loncaillier, for their energetic efforts in behalf of the destitute soldiers.

Jackson had received an actual reinforcement of not over 2500 men since the 23d. With these he had to guard the approaches to the city by the northern branches of the Bienvenu, where he maintained outposts, and to defend the lines in front of the enemy, on both sides of the river. Such a force, compared with that of the British, of which he had a clear and distinct view from the window of Macarte's, would have dispirited and unnerved any other man. To Jackson it gave new vigor, heroism and intensity of purpose. His eyes grew more bright and his lips set firmer together, as every day and hour added to his perils, without increasing his means of resistance. His wasted frame seemed to take new life, galvanized by the heroic soul which tenanted it. He was everywhere. His aids found it difficult to keep up with him. His noble bay charger, foamed and smoked with the continual exercise of galloping from post to post. Nor was he oppressed only with the cares of his army—of maintaining his post. There were the annoyances of timid counsels, of the fears, the doubts, the intrigues of civilians and politicians, who had no confidence in his ability to defend the city, and who dwelt upon the horrors of a sack as a consequence of a vigorous resistance.

"Was not this, in a good part, the same British army which had perpetrated the atrocities of San Salvador and of Washington city?" was gloomily whispered by some timid citizens. These were certainly serious and appalling apprehensions to fathers, husbands, and civilians generally. But to the immortal renown of New Orleans be it said, that few, very few, indeed, there

were who gave way to these fears. Jackson had communicated his spirit to the great mass of the population.
And though historians, politicians, and others have
thought it due to the reputation and glory of Jackson,
to exaggerate the discontent and apprehensions of a few
timid persons in New Orleans into a deep-laid scheme
of treason ; and though we are aware that partisans and
intriguants succeeded in instilling into the mind of the
General himself this suspicion, yet it is due to truth, to
history, and the reputation of this gallant city, to say
that, with abundant means and facilities for procuring
the evidence of such inglorious purposes and feelings,
their existence has never yet been established.

It is no longer necessary, if it ever was, to the fame
of Jackson, that the libel should be perpetuated. That
the reported resolution of Jackson, in case his lines were
forced, to fall back on the city, to fire it, and fight the
enemy in the blazing streets and in the tumult of a con-
flagration, should excite great alarm, was quite natural.
But we feel confident in the assertion, that in no community in the world would such a desperate step have been
more generally acquiesced in and excited less terror and
distress than in New Orleans. As the best evidence of
the justice of this opinion, we need only state the fact
that the people remained in the city after this report
'ecame rife, and after it was known that the General
.ad replied to certain inquiries as to his purpose, in case
his lines were carried, that "if the hair of his head knew
what his determination was, he would cut it off," with
an intimation provoked by rumors of the disloyalty of
the Legislature, that if his lines were carried their ses
sion would be a warm one !

We have little doubt that Jackson's determination

was as reported, and still less that he would have executed it.

On the 6th January, sailing-master Johnson—the same who was so vigorously defended Pass Christian against Lockyer's barges—slipping out of the Chef-Menteur with three boats, succeeded in capturing a British brig loaded with rum and biscuit, on her way to the Bayou Bienvenu. Ten prisoners were taken on the brig, who were conducted to Jackson's head-quarters. From them Jackson received confirmation of his suspicion that the enemy were digging a canal to aid in transporting troops to the other side of the river. He determined, therefore, to strengthen that part of the defences.

After the 23d December General David Morgan, commanding the quota of Louisiana militia who occupied the English Turn when the British arrived at Villeré's, was ordered to pass across the river and take position opposite Jackson's lines. But Morgan preferred a position somewhat in advance of Jackson's, and accordingly established himself on Raquet's Canal, about three hundred yards in front of Patterson's Marine Battery. His command consisted of 260 effective militia men. Here he was soon joined by the 2d Regiment of Louisiana Militia, Col. Z. Cavellier, 160 men; and on the 6th January by Colonel Dejean's regiment, which completed his line to the river. With this weak force Morgan commenced to throw up an entrenchment for two hundred yards; the remainder of the line, two thousand yards, was left with no other defence but the ditch. Colonel Latour, whose able history is the text book of this campaign, had directed General Morgan's attention to a much more practicable line some distance in his rear, where the space to be defended between the river and the swamp, was only nine hundred yards. This line could have been defended with one thousand muskets, or with five hundred muskets and one or two batteries.

On the left, Jackson's lines had been daily strengthened, the men working incessantly on them, widening and deepening the ditch, and increasing the height and bulk of the parapet. On the 6th, some of the more scientific officers suggested to Jackson to strengthen the right by throwing up a redoubt, or horn-work, in which some cannon could be planted to enfilade the front of his lines, and defend the extreme right of his position. When Jackson saw a plan of the work he condemned it, but was persuaded to allow it to be built. It was accordingly thrown up, with three embrasures, which commanded the road, the river-bank, and flanked the · front of the lines. A shallow ditch, that had run dry by the falling of the river, surrounded the redoubt, which had not been completed on the night of the 7th. Jackson, when he saw this work, shook his head, and remarked to one of his aids, "That will give us trouble."

Let us survey these famous lines of Jackson's. Time has spared many memorials of the great achievements we relate. The scene of these events has experienced slighter changes in the last forty years than the arena of any similar occurrences in this land of change and progress. As if to rebuke the deficiencies of our historical records, nature has preserved, in almost their original state, the physical characteristics of the scenery associated with the most glorious triumphs of the American arms. The reader need only acquaint himself with the leading facts of the campaign, and then proceeding six yards below the city, he may take his position in the gallery of Macarte where Jackson himself stood on the afternoon of the 7th January, 1815, closely observing through a telescope the movements in the British camp, situated two miles down the river. Here he will command a splendid view of the whole scene of this campaign. He will perceive the embankment, somewhat worn by time and the elements, behind which Jackson's men stationed themselves. He can trace it clearly and distinctly from the river to the swamp, in which it is lost to view. It becomes more distinct as it approaches the swamp, the ground near the river having been more exposed to the action of the plow and the tramp of men and cattle. The river having caved some hundred or two feet, the line of the levee has been slightly changed, and the road has worn away the mound and the vestiges of the redoubt on the extreme right. There is a handsome villa, quite ancient too in its aspect, standing near the road in the centre of the lines and about a hundred yards from the ditch. This, however, has been built since the war. Chalmette's buildings, which were destroyed by the Americans to give full play to their artillery, were at least two hundred yards in rear of this edifice. All else is as it was in 1815. Jackson's head-quarters are nearly concealed by a luxuriant growth of the graceful cedars and cypress,—which here assume the most symmetrical proportions, tapering off into perfect cones and pyramids. A thick orange hedge almost excludes a glimpse into the handsome garden, where bloom all the flowers and shrubs of this rich soil and benignant clime. But the buildings stand as they did then, but slightly changed by the lapse of time. They are scarred in many places with marks of the severe cannonade to which they were exposed. The view stretches far down the river; and is quite monotonous. The same broad, open field, divided by numerous ditches, and relieved at intervals of miles, by groves wherein nestle the homesteads of the planters and the neat little cottages of the negroes, complete the panorama. The noble Mississippi moves along with the same sublime grandeur, in the same course and at the same height as when, by its calm power and majesty, it inspired Jackson with that sublime courage and resolution, of which it is so mighty a symbol.

Those fields are the same, too. The plain of Chalmette, thus named after the owner of the ground in front of Jackson's lines, has the same dimensions now that it had then. It is an unbroken level, usually when not in cane, covered with a luxuriant growth of stubble or weeds, and cut into numerous small ditches. Solitary live oaks, reverently spared by the plowman, loom out grandly at long distances apart from the grey or brown plain. The swamp, too, has preserved its line of separation from the fields. It presents the same contour as in 1815—with that identical bulge or projection within two or three hundred yards of Jackson's lines, which served as a cover for the British in their advance. Near the swamp, and within it for some distance, the mound erected by the Tennesseeans is almost as prominent and clearly defined as it was, when the gallant bush-fighters rested their long rifles on its summit.

So much for the present aspect of these classic plains. What was their appearance in the memorable month of January, 1815 ?

Jackson's lines were drawn along an old mill race which separated the plantations of Rodriguez (Macarte's)

and Chalmette. In the early days of the State, mills
were located at the heads of canals, which were dug
from the river towards the swamp, and through them a
large body of water was projected from the river, the surface of which is several feet higher than the land in the
rear. Rodriguez's canal had long been abandoned, and
was nearly filled up with dirt and grass, so that it presented the appearance of a simple draining ditch. This
position recommended itself to Jackson by the fact, that
it left him the smallest space between the river and the
swamp to defend. It gave him the narrowest front he
could find near the position of the enemy. This was its
only peculiarity, which would have attracted the notice
of amost every man, who was driven with a small force,
to the necessity of entrenching, to defend himself against
a larger. It was Jackson's own selection. To this point
he marched his army on the 24th, and ordered his men
to widen the canal in front, throwing up the dirt into a
parapet. The story that General Moreau had previously
perceived the advantages of this position, and recommended it in case the city was approached in that
quarter, is an absurd fiction, obvious to all who have
ever observed the character of the country.

Owing to the irregular, independent and hurried manner in which the parapet was thrown up, the men being
continuously at work on it from the 24th December to
7th January, it presented, when completed, quite an
irregular appearance. In some places being twenty
feet thick and in others of scarcely sufficient solidity to
resist the enemy's balls; in some places having a height
sufficient to conceal the tallest men and in others hardly
reaching the belt of an ordinary sized person. The
mound was composed entirely of earth dug from the

canal and the field in the rear. The experiment of using cotton bales and other articles in raising the embankment had been discarded, and the elastic, tenacious soil of the alluvion preferred to all other materials, being superior for such uses even to brick or granite.

On the first of January, there was but a small part of the line, which could not be penetrated by the balls of the enemy, but on the 6th it was rendered cannon-proof nearly the whole length. This was the work of men who were unaccustomed to physical labor. The vigor and alacrity with which merchants, lawyers, young clerks, and others, who had hardly ever performed a day's work of manual labour in their lives, prosecuted this task for ten or twelve days, showed the earnest purpose and ardent resolution of Jackson's patriotic comrades.

The lines extended a mile and a half from the river to the woods, and then penetrated the swamp, as far as it was deemed possible to turn them, resting on the extreme left on an impassable swamp. That part of the lines, which passed through the woods was frail and rude, not being made to resist artillery. The average height of the parapet was five feet. In many places the men had to stoop to sight their guns from the mound. Nothing could have been ruder or simpler than this whole work, which is made to figure in history, as one of the most formidable fortifications that an invading army ever encountered. It is just such a parapet as the whole Delta of the Mississippi would present to an enemy, who might attempt to advance up the river. With embrasures cut in the levee, filled with cannon of sufficient calibre, well manned, the hostile navies of the world would find it nearly as difficult to reach **New**

Orleans by the Mississippi river, as for the Allied Squadrons of France and Great Britain to pass the frowning and lofty granite batteries of Cronstadt and reach the famous stronghold of Russian power, St. Petersburg. Cannon balls will break, crush and dislodge granite, coral and even iron walls, but from the soil of the Mississippi bottoms they will rebound as if made of India-rubber.

The artillery of Jackson was thus distributed. On the road within and near the levee was the battery of Colonel Humphrey of the regular artillery. It consisted of two brass twelves and a six-inch howitzer. These pieces enfiladed the road and grazed the flank of the redoubt. This battery was located about seventy yards from the river. The two twelves were served by U. S. artillerists, and the howitzer by the dragoons of Major St. Gême.

Battery No. 2, distant ninety yards from No. 1, consisted of one twenty-four-pounder under Lieutenant Norris of the navy, and was served by sailors from the Carolina.

Battery No. 3, fifty yards from No. 2, consisted of two twenty-fours, manned by the Baratarians and French privateers, under their famous chiefs, Dominique You and Bluche, who had been released from prison, to which they had been committed under indictments for piracy, for the purpose of aiding Jackson to defend the city.

Battery No. 4, distant twenty yards from No. 3, consisted of one thirty-two-pounder, and was served by part of the crew of the Carolina, under Lieutenant Crawley.

Battery No. 5, distant one hundred and ninety yards from No. 4, commanded by Colonel Perry and Lieutenant Kerr of the artillery had two six-pounders and one eighteen.

Battery No. 6, commanded by General Garrique Fleaujeac, a veteran of Napoleon's wars, who had served in Egypt and Italy, was manned by a detachment of the Francs of the battalion D'Orleans, under the immediate command of Lieutenant Berbel, had a brass twelve. It was situate thirty-six yards from No. 5.

Battery No. 7 had a long brass eighteen pound culverin and a six-pounder, under Lieutenant Spotts and Chameau, and was served by gunners of the U. S. artillery. It was one hundred and ninety yards from No. 6.

Battery No. 8 had a small brass carronade, which could not be expected to render much service, as it was badly mounted. It was placed in charge of a corporal of artillery, and was served by some of Carroll's men, and was distant sixty yards from No. 7. This completed Jackson's batteries. His artillery force may be summed up as follows: Four sixes, (including those in the redoubt), three twelves, two eighteens, three twenty-fours, one thirty-two, one six-inch howitzer, and one small brass carronade. There was also a mortar, which remained for some time in the camp, of no use, because no person could be found in the army who knew how to plant it. This task was at last performed by a French veteran of the name of Lefebvre, but it did not prove a very effective weapon. Jackson's artillery consisted of sixteen pieces, of various calibre. The heaviest of the artillery were placed on the right, to resist the British batteries and repel the attack in that quarter. As a part of his defence, the marine battery on the right bank, under Patterson, consisting of three twenty-fours and six twelves, which that active officer had placed in

25

battery between the 30th December and 6th **January,**
and which flanked the enemy on the left bank, must
not be forgotten. This would swell Jackson's artillery
force to twenty-five pieces—quite a formidable proportion of artillery to so small a force of infantry.

The latter were distributed as follows: The redoubt
on the extreme right was occupied by a company of the
7th infantry, under Lieutenant Ross. The two sixes
were served by a detachment of the 44th, under Lieutenant Marant. Tents were pitched in this redoubt.
On the extreme right, between Humphrey's battery and
the river, were stationed Beale's rifles, thirty in number.
From their left the 7th infantry extended to Battery No.
3, covering Humphrey's and Norris' guns, taking in the
powder magazine, built since 1st January.

This regiment was 430 strong, under that active young
Creole, Major Peire. Between the two guns of Battery
No. 3 (You's and Bluche's), the company of the car-
bineers were stationed, and the remainder of Plauché's
battalion of Orleans, and Lacoste's battalion of free men
of color—the former numbering 289, the latter 280—
filled up the interval from No. 3 to No. 4 (Crawley's
thirty-two), covering the latter gun. Daquin's battalion
of free men of color, 150, and the 44th under Captain
Baker, 240, extended to Perry's battery, No. 5.

Two-thirds of the remaining length of the line was
guarded by Carroll's command, who was reinforced on
the 7th by one thousand Kentuckians under General
Adair, consisting of 600 men under Colonel Slaughter
and 400 under Major Harrison, who were all of Major-
General Thomas's Kentucky Division of 2,250 for whom
arms could be obtained.

On the right of Battery No. 7 (Spotts') fifty marines

were stationed, under Lieutenant Bellevue. The extreme left was held by Coffee, whose men were compelled to stand constantly in the water, and had no other beds but the floating logs which they could make fast to the trees. Coffee's command was 500. Ogden's horse troop, fifty strong, was stationed near headquarters; Cauveau's, thirty, near them; and Hind's squadron, 150 strong, was encamped in the rear, on Delery's plantation. Detachments of Colonel Young's regiment of Louisiana militia were stationed in the rear, near Pierna's canal, to prevent the enemy coming into the camp in that direction, and also to prevent any persons from leaving the lines. Outposts were thrown out five hundred yards to the front. Jackson's whole force on the left bank of the river amounted to 4,000 men, but his lines were occupied by only 3,200, of which less than 800 were regular troops, and those mostly fresh recruits, commanded by young officers. The consolidated report, in the Adjutant-General's office, gives Jackson, on the 8th January, 1815, on the left bank of the river, a force of 5,045—in which, however, Major Harrison's Kentucky battalion is not included.

Jackson's army was divided into two divisions. The troops from the right to the left of the 44th, were under the command of Colonel Ross, acting Brigadier General, and the left of the line under Carroll and Coffee, the former as Major-General, and the latter as Brigadier-General.

How grossly and shamefully untrue is the statement of nearly all the British historians, that Jackson had an army of twelve thousand. Alison, in his fourth volume of his History of Europe, says: "Including seamen and marines, about six thousand combatants on the

British side were in the field; a slender force to attack double their number, entrenched to their teeth in works bristling with bayonets and loaded with heavy artillery. .... General Jackson, an officer since become celebrated both in the military and political history of the country, commanded a military force destined for the defence of the city, which amounted to about twelve thousand men." It will be seen that this great standard historian quadruples Jackson's force, and by the vagueness of his terms, conveys the idea that the British were but six thousand, which was the number of their storming columns, exclusive of their reserves, of Thornton's detachment, and the sailors and marines.

So Bissett, in his History of the reign of George III., states that the American force collected for the defence of New Orleans, consisted of 30,000 men. The author of the Narrative of the British army at Washington, Baltimore, and New Orleans, an actor in the events he describes, after mentioning the conflicting estimates of the American force, varying from 23,000 to 30,000, chooses a middle course, and supposes the whole force to be about twenty-five thousand. Baines, in his History of the French Revolution, approaches the truth, and sets down the force on each side at about ten thousand men.

Besides the arrangements for defence mentioned, there was another characteristic precaution of Jackson. He had directed another entrenchment to be thrown up a mile and a half in the rear of that which he occupied with his army, in which were posted all those of his army who were not well armed or regarded as ablebodied. With rare exceptions, the men in charge of this line were armed only with spades and pick-axes.

Should the enemy succeed in carrying his main works by escalade, Jackson intended to throw forward his mounted force, and under their protection fall back to and rally upon his second line. A third line had also been drawn still nearer the city, upon which the men had commenced working quite vigorously.

On the 6th, it was well understood by Jackson that the British intended to cross the river, but whether for the purpose of concentrating their force on the weak defences on the right bank, or for a simultaneous and concerted advance on both banks, could only be conjectured by the American commander. To obtain some information on this point, Jackson sent his intelligent and sagacious aid, Col. John R. Grimes, across the river, to observe the movements of the enemy at Villeré's, and report upon the condition of Morgan's defences. Colonel Grimes executed this order in a prompt and efficient manner. He saw at a glance, that the enemy were preparing to throw a detachment across the river, and he advised General Morgan to march his whole force down, under cover of the levee, take post opposite Villeré's, and when the enemy approached in their boats, to open fire upon them. Completely protected by the levee, a better entrenchment than that which Jackson had thrown up on the left, there is little doubt that if this advice had been adopted, Morgan would have destroyed the British detachment, which might attempt to cross the river, or at least driven it back. But, instead of pursuing this sensible and practicable plan, Morgan stationed his advance, consisting of 120 militia of Major Arnaud's battalion, under Major Tessier, armed with fowling-pieces and musket cartridges, on Mayhew's canal, in front of his own position, and several hundred yards from the place where the British would probably land. Of course this small force could cover but a small portion of a position so illy chosen.

On the night of the 7th, Commodore Patterson and his volunteer aid, R. D. Shepherd, proceeded down the right bank of the river, and arriving at a point opposite the scene of the British preparations, where they appeared to be most actively engaged, observed closely their proceedings. They could hear a considerable commotion in the enemy's camp—the sounds of men pulling and dragging boats, as if in great haste—the splash of boats, as they fell into the river—the orders of officers, and expressions of relief and satisfaction of the laborers, as some work appeared to be finished. They could even discover, by the camp fires, a long line of soldiers drawn up on the levee. They hastened back to Patterson's battery. On their return, Patterson observed the very weak and insecure position of Morgan, and after consulting with that officer, directed Mr. Shepherd to cross the river and inform General Jackson of the state of affairs, and beg him to reinforce Morgan, who had not men enough to occupy his lines. Shepherd crossed the river, and arrived at Jackson's headquarters about one o'clock on the morning of the 8th. He informed the sentinel on guard that he had important intelligence to communicate to the General, and was accordingly ushered into the room, where Jackson lay on a sofa, snatching a few moments of rest from the great fatigues of the day. Around the General lay his aids, on the floor, all asleep. On Shepherd's entering, Jackson raised his head and asked,

"Who's there?"

Mr. Shepherd gave his name, and added that he had

been sent over by Commodore Patterson and General Morgan, to inform him, General Jackson, that the appearances in the British camp, indicated that the main attack was to be made on the right bank, and that Morgan required more troops to maintain his position. " Hurry back," replied the General, rising from his recumbent position, "and tell General Morgan that he is mistaken. The main attack will be on this side, and I have no men to spare. He must maintain his position at all hazards." Then looking at his watch, and observing that it was past one o'clock, he exclaimed aloud, addressing his sleeping aids: "Gentlemen, we have slept enough. Arise. The enemy will be upon us in a few minutes ; I must go and see Coffee." The aids arose hastily and commenced buckling on their swords, when Mr. Shepherd departed, and recrossing the river, delivered the reply of Jackson to Morgan.

Jackson did not, however, neglect Morgan ; but ordered General Adair to send a detachment of 500 Kentuckians to the lines on the right bank. This detach ment was placed under the command of Colonel Davis. It was very badly armed and was greatly delayed in crossing the river. At the naval arsenal, on the right bank, the Kentuckians received some old muskets, but when they commenced their march to join Morgan, there were but 260 of them armed, and some of these had common pebbles instead of flints in their locks. They were, however, hurried forward without rest or food, and after a fatiguing march of five or six miles arrived at Morgan's lines ; thence they were ordered forward to the advance position already occupied by Tessier. They arrived here greatly fatigued, and formed on Tessier's left but a few moments before the enemy appeared in sight.

Morgan's whole force consisted of 812 men, all militia, and but poorly armed. On his left he had two six-pounders, which were placed in charge of Adjutant John Nixon of the Louisiana militia, and a twelve-pounder under Lieutenant Philibert of the navy.

Patterson's battery being in the rear of and masked by Morgan's lines, could not be used in defence of the same. The guns were turned so as to flank the front of Jackson's lines on the left bank.

Such were the arrangements of the two armies for the expected final combat.

There was little sleeping in the American lines on the night of the 7th. The men were all engaged in cleaning their pieces, preparing cartridges and performing various duties of preparation for the conflict. The outposts and scouting parties were all alive as usual, watching every movement in the British camp with characteristic American curiosity. They could hear very distinctly corresponding notes of preparation on the enemy's side, among which were the noises of the workmen engaged in reconstructing the redoubts, near the Chalmette buildings, which had been destroyed on the 1st of January.

There was intense anxiety, but no fear in Jackson's little army. The citizen soldiers had now grown to be veterans. They had learned to confide in their General, and in themselves, and if these were not sufficient to nerve their arms for the struggle, the recollection of those dear ones, who then reposed in the city behind them, with so much confidence in their devotion and heroism, inspired every heart with heroic courage and determination.

XVI.

THE BATTLE OF NEW ORLEANS.

THE VICTORY.

[The Eighth of January, 1815.]

By the same conveyance which brought the reinforcements of Lambert, the British soldiers received a most
acceptable addition to their comforts, in the shape of a
supply of fresh provisions. A refreshing supper on the
evening of the 7th produced no little vivacity in the
camp, and after packing their knapsacks, burnishing their
arms, filling their cartridge-boxes, and arranging their
neatest toggery, that they might appear before the
famous beauties of New Orleans to the greatest advantage, the soldiers destined to storm Jackson's lines lay
down to refresh their bodies for the coming struggle.
At the same time, Thornton with his command, moved
to the bank of the river, where the men were drawn up
and kept waiting for the boats which were to transport
them to the opposite side. The patience of Thornton
was sorely tried by the delay in the arrival of the boats.
After the British had excavated a canal of sufficient
depth, the banks began to cave in just as they were
dragging the boats through the water, and thus their
progress was greatly impeded. The providential and
quite unexpected falling of the river was the cause of

this obstacle.   The sailors were at last compelled to drag the boats through the mud, and were thus enabled to launch upon the river about one-fourth of the boats needed, by three o'clock in the morning.   Dismissing one-half of his force, Thornton ordered his own regiment, a division of sailors and a company of marines, to crowd into the boats, making about seven hundred men, and then the flotilla under Captain Roberts pushed off from the left bank of the river.   This was not Thornton's only unexpected obstacle.   Deceived as all strangers are by the quiet, smooth current of the Mississippi, Captain Roberts imagined that the oars of his sailors could keep the boats right ahead and enable him to disembark at a point opposite that of his departure.   He was grievously mistaken.   The Mississippi current at this point runs at the rate of five miles an hour.   The barges of the British, instead of holding up against the current, were swept by it a mile and a half down the stream.   Thus it happened that before Thornton's detachments could step ashore, the eastern sky began to be streaked with the light of the coming day.

Long after the men in the British camp had fallen asleep, full of hope, confidence, of bright dreams of wealth, luxury, and spoils of "booty and beauty," the officers kept awake in their little circles, discussing the chances of the morrow's combat.   The older and more experienced commanders, to whom the delay in bringing up the boats was known, were gloomy and desponding. Some of them openly expressed their belief that the *ensemble* of the plan was lost, and it would have to be gone over again.   Col. Dale, of the 93d Highlanders, a brave and thoughtful officer, being asked his opinion, turned to Dr. Dempster of his regiment, and giving him

his watch and a letter, said : "Deliver these to my wife
—I shall die at the head of my regiment." The conduct
of Col. Mullens, of the 44th, was even more desponding,
and far less heroic. His wife, an elegant lady, was then
in the fleet, and had come over to grace the fashionable
circles of New Orleans. She had been the life of the
squadron, contributing, by her fascinating manners and
vivacity, to brighten many of the dull and gloomy hours
of the long voyage. But her husband was far from
being the soul of the army. Son of a lord, he had
obtained his promotion more by influence than merit.
Among the officers who have carved out their names
and commissions, by their own good swords, the designation of Mullens to lead the advance of the storming
party was ascribed to the natural *esprit de corps* of their
aristocratic commander, himself the son of an earl.
Perhaps they were correct, but Packenham and Mullens
took very different views of the privileges of the sons
of peers. Packenham regarded that an honor and distinction, which he frequently enjoyed, never without
glory, and never without grievous wounds, which
Mullens looked upon as a death sentence. He had
received one honorable wound at Albuera, and that
sufficed to fill the measure of his ambition. Besides,
Colonel Mullens, whether prompted by his regard for
his own safety, or his good sense, had the sagacity to
perceive the hopelessness of the enterprise; and to
declare that conviction in the hearing of both officers
and men. He stated that his regiment had been ordered
to execution—that their dead bodies were to be used as
a bridge for the remainder of the army to march over
to a like fate.

The young officers were in better spirits. They had

no doubt of their success, and in a gay and jovial manner discussed their individual chances in the battle, speculated on the ulterior results of the campaign—on the prospect of accumulating fortunes—where they would be quartered in the city—what frolics they would have—what distinction they would enjoy in the gay society of New Orleans—what "jolly letters" they would write home, and what handsome presents they would "send to the girls they left behind them," not forgetting mothers, wives, sisters and cousins.

About the hour when Jackson aroused his aids, Packenham having refreshed himself with a short slumber, repaired from his head-quarters at Villeré's mansion, to the mouth of the canal, and there discovered the mortifying delay in the transportation of Thornton's detachment across the river. A cooler headed commander would have perceived the serious interruption which this accident made in his plan of operations, and conformed his other movements to it. In other words, he would have countermanded the advance on the left bank, which it was now certain must follow that on the right, but which, if executed under the orders that had been issued, should precede it. But Packenham was a self-willed, gallant and somewhat reckless man, who believed that courage and daring were the chief reliance in all military operations, who never, like Lysander, eked out the lion's skin with the fox's. The orders of the 7th were, therefore, adhered to.

Before day, Gibbs' and Keane's men were aroused from their lairs, and forming, advanced in line some distance in front of the pickets, about 400 or 500 yards from the American lines. Here they remained, listening in anxious suspense for the firing on the other side

of the river. Not a sound could be heard across the
calm surface of the great, silent Mississippi. A thick
fog involved the army, and shut out all in front and
rear from their view. The minutes, the hours flew
rapidly by, and not a sound of Thornton could be heard.
The truth was, that gallant officer had not even landed
his men, when Gibbs began to form his column for the
advance. The mist was now breaking. The American
flag, on its lofty staff in the centre of Jackson's lines,
began to wave its striped and starry folds above the
vapory exhalations from the earth, within full view of
the British lines, and the dark mound, behind which the
guardians of that standard stood with arms at rest, became faintly visible. On the mound stood many a sharp-
eyed soldier, painfully stretching his vision to catch the
first glance of the enemy, that he might announce his
approach, or have the first fire at him. This honor was
reserved for Lieutenant Spotts, who, perceiving a faint
red line several hundred yards in front, discharged his
heavy gun at it. Slowly the fog rolled up and thinned
off, revealing the whole British line stretching across
two-thirds of the plain. At the same moment a rocket
shot up near the river; another on the right, near the
swamp; and then the long line seemed to melt away
suddenly, puzzling the American gunners, who were
just bringing their pieces to bear upon it. But the
British had only changed their position and then
deployed into column of companies.

Forming his column of attack in admirable order,
Gibbs now advanced towards the wood, so as to have
its cover, the 44th in front, followed by the 21st and
4th. The column passed the redoubt on the extreme
right of the British, near the swamp, where the men of

the 44th were directed to pack the ladders and fascines, at the same time stacking their muskets. The batteries of Spotts' No. 6, and Garrique's No. 7, and the Howitzer No. 8, now began to play upon the column with some effect. There was no time to spare. The 44th, with the rest of the column, rushed past the redoubt, some of the men picking up a few fascines and ladders as they marched, and, fronting towards the American lines, advanced steadily in compact column, bearing their muskets at a shoulder. In his advance Gibbs obliqued towards the wood, so as to be covered by the projection of the swamp. But he could not elude the fire of the batteries, which began to pour round and grapeshot into his lines with destructive effect. It was at this moment whispered through the column that the 44th had not brought the ladders and fascines. Packenham hearing it, rode to the front, and discovered that it was but too true. He immediately called out to Colonel Mullens, who was at the head of his regiment, "To file to the rear and proceed to the redoubt, execute the order, and return as soon as possible with his regiment." The execution of this order produced some confusion in the column, and some delay in its advance. Gibbs, indignant at' this disturbance and the disobedience of Mullens, and perceiving his men falling around him, exclaimed in a loud voice, "Let me live till to-morrow and I'll hang him to the highest tree in that swamp." But the column could not stand there exposed to the terrible fire of the American batteries, waiting for the 44th, and so Gibbs ordered them forward. On they went, the 21st and 4th, in solid, compact column, the men hurraing, and the rocketers covering their front with a blaze of their combustibles. The American batteries we have named were

now playing upon them with awful effect, cutting great
lanes through the column from front to rear, and huge
gaps in their flanks. These intervals were, however,
quickly filled up by the gallant Redcoats. The column
advanced without pause or recoil steadily towards
Spotts' long eighteen, and Chauveau's six (No. 9).
Carroll's men were all in their places, with guns sighted
on the summit of the parapet, whilst the Kentuckians,
in two lines, stood behind, ready to take the places of
the Tennesseeans as soon as their pieces were discharged,
thus making four lines in this part of the entrenchment.
There they stood all as firm as veterans, as cool and cal-
culating as American frontiersmen. All the batteries in
the American line, including Patterson's marine battery
on the right bank, began now to join those on the left
in hurling a tornado of iron missiles into that serried,
scarlet column, which shook and oscillated like a huge
painted ship tossed on an angry sea.

"Stand to your guns," cried Jackson, as he glanced
along the lines, "don't waste your ammunition—see that
every shot tells."

Again he exclaimed, "Give it to them, boys; let us
finish the business to-day."

The confused and reeling army of Redcoats had
approached within two hundred yards of the ditch, when
the loud command of Carroll, "Fire! fire!" rang
through the lines. The order was obeyed, not hurriedly,
excitedly, and confused, but calmly and deliberately, by
the whole of Carroll's command, commencing on the
left of the 44th. The men had previously calculated the
range of their guns, and not a shot was thrown away.
Their bullets swept through the British column, cutting
down the men by scores, and causing its head and flanks

to melt away, like snow before a torrent. Nor was it one, or several discharges followed by pauses and intervals ; but the fire was kept up without interruption—the front men firing and falling back to load. Thus the four lines, two Tennesseeans and two Kentuckians, sharing the labor and glory of the most rapid and destructive fusilade ever poured into a column of soldiers.

For several minutes did that terrible, incessant fire blaze along Carroll's front, and that rolling, deafening, prolonged thunder fill the ears and confuse the sense of the astounded Britons. Those sounds will never cease to reverberate in the ears of all who survived that merciless fire.

The roar of the cannon, the hissing of the shells, the low, rumbling growl of the musketry, the wild scream of the rockets, the whizzing of round shot, the sweeping blast of chain-shot and the crash of grape, formed a horrid concert.

Then was seen the great advantage which the Ameri cans possess in the skill with which they handle fire· arms—the rapidity with which they load, the accuracy of their calculation, and the coolness of their aim—qualities developed by their frontier life, and their habit of using arms from boyhood.

There were scarcely more than fifteen hundred pieces brought to bear on the British column, but in the hands of Tennesseeans and Kentuckians they were made as effective as ten times that number, fired by regulars of the best armies of Europe. Against this terrible fire, Gibbs boldly led his column. It is no reflection upon even those veterans, to say that they halted, wavered, and shrunk at times, when the crash of bullets became most terrible, when they were thus shot down by a foe whom they could not see. But the gallant Peninsular officers threw themselves in front, inciting and arousing their men by every appeal, and by the most brilliant examples of courage. The men cried out, "Where are the 44th? If we get to the ditch we have no means of scaling the lines!" "Here come the 44th! here come the 44th!" shouted Gibbs. This assurance restored order and confidence in the ranks. There came at least a detachment of the 44th, with Packenham himself at their head, rallying and inspiring them by appeals to their ancient fame—reminding them of the glory they had acquired in Egypt and elsewhere, and addressing them as his "countrymen" (the 44th were mostly Irish). The men came up gallantly enough, bearing their ladders and fascines, but their colonel was far in the rear, being unable, even with the assistance of a servant, to reach his post over the rough field. Packenham led them forward, and they were soon breasting the storm of bullets with the rest of the column. At this moment Packenham's bridle arm was struck by a ball, and his horse killed by another. He then mounted the small black creole pony of his Aid, Captain McDougall, and pressed forward. But the column had advanced now as far as it could get. Most of the regimental officers were cut down. Patterson, of the 21st; Brookes, of the 4th; and Debbiegs, of the 44th, were all disabled at the heads of their regiments. There were not officers enough to command, and the column began now to break into detachments, some pushing forward to the ditch, but the greater part falling back to the rear and to the swamp, until the whole front was cleared. They were soon rallied at the ditch, were re-formed, and throwing off their knapsacks, advanced again.

26

Keane, judging very rashly, that the moment had arrived for him to act, now wheeled his line into column (it had been, as we have seen, intended as a reserve to threaten, without advancing upon the American lines), and with the 93d in front, pushed forward to act his part in the bloody tragedy. The gallant and stalwart Highlanders, nine hundred strong, strode across the ensanguined field, with their heavy, solid, massive front, of a hundred men, and their bright muskets glittering in the morning sun, which began now to scatter a few rays over the field of strife. Onward pressed the Tartan warriors, regardless of the concentrated fire of the batteries, which now poured their iron hail into their ranks. At a more rapid pace than the other column, the 93d rushed forward into the very mælstroom of Carroll's musketry, which swept the field as if with a huge scythe. The gallant Dale fulfilled his prophecy, and fell at the head of his regiment, a grapeshot passing through his body. Major Creagh then took the command. Incited by the example of the 93d, the remnant of Gibb's brigade again came up with Packenham on their left and Gibbs on the right. They had approached within a hundred yards of the lines.

At this moment the standard-bearer of the 93d feeling something rubbing against his epaulette, turned, and perceived through the smoke the small black horse which Packenham now rode. It was led by his Aid, as he seemed to have no use of his right arm. In his left hand he held his cap, which he waved in the air, crying out, "Hurra! brave Highlanders." At this instant there was a terrible crash, as if the contents of one of the big guns of the Americans had fallen on the spot, killing and wounding nearly all who were near. It was then the Ensign of the 93d saw the horse of Pakenham fall, and the General roll from the saddle into the arms of Captain McDougall, who sprang forward to receive him. A grape-shot had struck the General on the thigh, and passed through his horse, killing the latter immediately. As Captain McDougall and some of the men were raising the General, another ball struck him in the groin, which produced an immediate paralysis. It is an interesting coincidence that Captain McDougall was the same officer into whose arms General Ross had fallen from his horse in the advance on Baltimore. The wounded and dying General was borne to the rear, and laid down in the shade of a venerable live oak, standing in the centre of the field, beyond the reach of the American guns. A surgeon was called, who pronounced his wound mortal. In a few minutes the gallant young officer breathed his last, and his faithful Aid had to lament the death of another heroic chief, who, after winning laurels that entitled him to repose and glory enough for life, perished thus ingloriously in a war of unjust invasion against his own race and kindred. The old oak under which Packenham yielded up his soul still stands, bent and twisted by time and many tempests —a melancholy monument of that great disaster of the British arms!

Gibbs fared even worse than Packenham, for desperately wounded shortly after the fall of the General-in-Chief, he, too, was borne to the rear, and lingered many, many hours, in horrible agony, until the day after, when death came to his relief. Keane also fell badly wounded, being shot through the neck, and was carried off the field. There were now no field officers to command or rally the broken column. Major Wilkinson, Brigade

Major, shouted to the men to follow, and pushed forward.

Followed and aided by Lieutenant Lavack and twenty men, he succeeded in passing the ditch, and had clambered up the breastwork, when, just as he raised his head and shoulders over its summit, a dozen guns were brought to bear against him, and the exposed portions of his body were riddled with bullets. He had, however, strength to raise himself, and fell upon the parapet, whence his mutilated body was borne, with every expression of pity and sympathy, by the generous Kentuckians and Tennesseeans, to a place of shelter in the rear of the camp. Here the gallant Briton received every attention which could be rendered to him. Major Smiley, of the Kentuckians, a kind-hearted gentleman, endeavored to cheer the spirits of the dying soldier, saying, "Bear up, my dear fellow, you are too brave a man to die." "I thank you from my heart," faintly murmured the young officer. "It is all over with me. You can render me a favor; it is to communicate to my commander that I fell on your parapet, and died like a soldier and a true Englishman." In two hours the gallant Wilkinson was a corpse, and his body was respectfully covered with one of the colors of the volunteers.

After the fall of Wilkinson, the men who followed him threw themselves into the ditch. Some made feeble efforts to climb up the parapet, but it was too slippery, and they rolled into the fosse. The majority, however, were satisfied to cower under the protection of the entrenchment, where they were allowed a momentary respite and shelter from the American fire. The remainder of the column broken, disorganized, and panic-stricken, retired in confusion and terror, each regiment leaving two-thirds of its men dead or wounded on the field. The 93d, which had advanced with nine hundred men and twenty-five officers, could muster but one hundred and thirty men and nine officers, who now stole rapidly from the bloody field, their bold courage all changed into wild dismay. The other regiments suffered in like manner, especially the 21st, which had lost five hundred men. The fragments of the two gallant brigades fell back precipitately towards the rear.

At this moment Lambert, hearing of the death of Packenham and the severe wounds of Gibbs and Keane, advanced slowly and cautiously forward with the reserve. Just before he received his last wound, Packenham had ordered Sir John Tyndell, one of his Staff, to order up the reserve. As the bugler was about to sound the "advance," by order of Sir John, his right arm was struck with a ball, and his bugle fell to the ground. The order was accordingly never given, and the reserve only marched up to cover the retreat of the broken columns of the two other brigades.

Thus, in less than twenty-five minutes was the main attack of the British most disastrously repelled, and the two brigades nearly destroyed. On their left they had achieved a slight success, which threatened serious consequences to the American lines. . Here the advance of Keane's brigade, consisting of the 95th rifles, the light infantry companies of the 7th, 93d, and 43d, and several companies of the West India regiments—in all, nearly a thousand men, under the gallant and active officer, Colonel Rennie, of the 21st—had crept up so suddenly on the Americans, as to surprise their outpost and reach the redoubt about as soon as the advance

guard of the Americans, which was threatened by
Gibbs's advance, had fallen back from their left, and
was now hurrying into their lines. The British were so
close upon the retiring guard, that the Americans were
unable to open their batteries upon them, fearing that
they would kill some of their own men. It was with
difficulty that Humphrey could keep his gunners from
applying the match to his pieces that completely commanded the road, down which the Americans mingled
with the pursuing British, were retiring. At last,
reaching the redoubt, the Americans clambered over
the embankment and the leading files of the British
following, succeeded in also gaining the interior, where,
being supported by others, they engaged in a hand-to-
hand fight with the soldiers of the 7th infantry, whom
they drove out into the lines, which were reached by a
plank across the ditch separating the redoubt from the
main lines. But they did not hold the redoubt long, for
now the 7th infantry began to direct its whole fire upon
the interior of the redoubt, which very soon made it too
hot for the British. In the meantime, the mainbody of
the detachment advanced in two columns, one on the
road, and the other filing along the river under cover of
the Levee. The 7th infantry and Humphrey's batteries
poured into the column on the road a most destructive
fire. Those on the river bank were protected by the
Levee from the fire of the batteries, and troops in the
lines, but attracted the attention of the hawk-eyed Patterson, on the right bank of the river, who gave them
scattering volleys of grape, which strewed the river
bank with the dead and wounded. It was here, Rennie
advanced at the head of his command. He had been
struck on the calf of the leg by a grape shot, which

tore a ghastly wound. He still pressed on, huzzaing and encouraging his men. The heroic bearing of this gallant officer rushing so impetuously into the very jaws of death, excited a thrill of admiration in those Americans who observed his conduct. Perhaps this feeling obtained for Rennie a brief respite, and reserved for him the only glory which was achieved by the British on that field. Advancing with several other officers and men, he reached the ditch on the extreme right, within a few yards of the river's edge, and climbing up the parapet, gained the summit of the breastwork. The Orleans Rifles, who defended this part of the line, fell back a few yards, in order to have better aim. Rennie, with two others—Captain Henry, of the 7th infantry, a tall and stalwart Irishman, and Major King, of the same regiment—gained the breastwork, and waving his sword, shouted in a loud voice, " Hurra, boys, the day is ours !" The words had barely passed his lips (and they were distinctly heard within the American lines) when the sharp cracking report of the Rifles gave awful warning of the fate of the adventurous Britons. They had made themselves the targets for the famous marksmen of New Orleans. Their dead bodies, rolling heavily from the parapet into the ditch, justified the reputation of the Rifles as sharp-shooters. Thereupon, the remainder of Rennie's column fell back, hurrying to the rear as rapidly as they could under cover of the Levee. That portion of the detachment which had advanced on the road, suffered greatly from the fire of Humphrey's, Norris, You's, and Bluche's batteries, and from the well-directed musketry of the 7th infantry, and was soon compelled to retire in disorder. This attack on the extreme right of the American lines occurred at the same time with the first advance of Gibbs's column on the left.

There is some force in the suggestion of a British officer, writing of these events, that it would have been wiser for Keane, with his main column, to have followed up his advance and thrown his whole force upon the American right, where Rennie succeeded in scaling the parapet.

As the detachments on the road advanced, their bugler, a boy of fourteen or fifteen climbing a small tree within two hundred yards of the American lines, straddled a limb and continued to blow the " charge " with all his power. There he remained during the whole action, whilst the cannon balls and bullets ploughed the ground around him, killed scores of men, and tore even the branches of the tree in which he sat. Above the thunder of the artillery, the rattling of fire the musketry, and all the din and uproar of the strife, the shrill blast of the little bugler could be heard, and even when his companions had fallen back and retreated from the field, he continued true to his duty, and blew the charge with undiminished vigor. At last, when the British had entirely abandoned the ground, an American soldier, passing from the lines, captured the little bugler and brought him into camp, where he was greatly astounded, when some of the enthusiastic Creoles, 'who had observed his gallantry, actually embraced him, and officers and men vied with each other in acts of kindness to so gallant a little soldier.

A more melancholy spectacle was presented, when some of the Americans brought within the lines the bodies of Colonel Rennie and the two other officers who had fallen in the ditch. There arose a warm discussion among the Rifles for the honor of having "brought down" the Colonel. Withers, the crack shot of the company then, and for a long time after a highly respectable merchant of New Orleans, exclaimed :

"If he isn't hit above the eyebrows, it wasn't my shot!" On examination it was discovered that the bullet had entered the head of the gallant Briton just over the eyebrows. Withers was, therefore, recognized as his slayer, and the mournful duty was devolved upon him of preserving the valuables, including the watch, purse, and epaulette of the unfortunate officer, and transmitting them to his widow, who was then in the fleet lying off the coast. The two other officers killed with Rennie, Captain Henry, of the 7th, and Major King, of the same regiment, were fairly riddled with rifle balls; the first named having received no less than five balls in various parts of his body. Henry and King were in full uniform, Rennie wore his grey overcoat.

Whilst this terrible slaughter was being enacted on the extreme right and left of the American lines, the centre remained inactive. A few men on the right of Planché's battalion fired without orders, when the 7th infantry commenced their fire, but they were quickly silenced by their officers as the enemy were too far off, and they only wasted their ammunition. From Planché's battalion to the left of the 44th, including Planché's, Daquin's, and Lacoste's battalions, and the 44th, at least eight hundred men, not a gun was fired, save a few, which were discharged at an angle of forty-five degrees, in order that the bullets might fall into the ranks of the enemy, and a few scattering shots by the left company of the 44th, which, however, were instantly suppressed. The gallant volunteers chafed with impatience at the restraints to which they were thus subjected in being compelled to look on, idle spectators, of so glorious a conflict. They could with difficulty be prevented from stealing from their posts to the right or left, to have a shot at the *capotes rouges.* If, however, they did not contribute to the predominant music of the conflict, the roar of the cannon and the rattling of musketry, they served to enliven and vary the monotony of those sounds, and offered an additional stimulant to the courage and ardor of the men, by the inspiriting melody of their fine band.

It is a rare circumstance in a battle, that martial music can be sustained throughout the action. In the American army, such an occurrence was a phenomenon never before observed in any battle. The moment the British came into view and their signal rocket pierced the sky with its fiery train, the band of the Battalion D'Orleans struck up "Yankee Doodle"—and thenceforth, throughout the action, it did not cease to discourse all the national and military airs in which it had been instructed. The British had not this incentive. Their musical instruments had never been taken from the box in which they were afterwards found by the Americans. They advanced with no blasts of trumpet, with no stirring roll of drums and lively notes of the piercing fife—with not even the monotonous martial scream of the bagpipe, arousing the pride and heroism of the Highlanders. A few buglers in the light infantry regiments contributed the only musical sounds, to relieve, on their side, the awful din and tumult of the battle.

Subtracting the centre of Jackson's lines already

enumerated, at least one-half of Coffee's men, who
never fired a gun, and a large number of Kentuckians,
whose pieces were so defective as according to the testimony of some persons, to place the Tennesseeans in
more danger from their friends and supporters in the
rear than from their enemies in front, there were
actually less than half of Jackson's whole force engaged
in the battle. There is no instance in history where so
small a force achieved such destructive results. It is
true, the batteries contributed largely to these results,
but not to the extent that is generally estimated, as the
heaviest of Jackson's guns were kept quite busy returning the fire of the two batteries, which the British had
thrown up on the night of the 7th, in the centre of the
field and near the road, on the ruins of Chalmette's establishment, from which they maintained a continuous fire
during and after the advance of the storming parties.
Norris', Crawley's, You's and Bluche's batteries gave
their particular attention to these batteries, and succeeded in silencing them shortly after the general retrograde movement of the British lines. In the swamp,
on the extreme right, the British had thrown out a
detachment of skirmishers under Lieut. Colonel Jones
of the 4th. These succeeded in getting quite near
Coffee's men, but becoming mired, were either killed or
captured by the Tennesseeans, who astonished the
Britons by the squirrel-like agility with which they
jumped from log to log, and their alligator-like facility
of moving through the water, bushes and mud. Some
of the prisoners taken in the swamp were of the West
India Regiment, who were greatly comforted in their
forlorn position by the idea that they were captives of
men of their own color and blood, deceived by the

appearance of the Tennesseeans, who, from their constant exposure, their familiarity with gunpowder, and
their long unacquaintance with the razor, or any other
implement of the toilette, were certainly not fair representatives of the pure Caucasian race. The unfortunate
red-coated Africans soon discovered their error, when
they were required by their facetious captors to "dance
juba" in mud a foot deep.

It was eight o'clock—two hours since the action commenced—before the musketry ceased firing. As long
as there was a British soldier visible, though at a distance which rendered it quite futile to endeavor to
reach him with musket or rifle, a cartridge would be
wasted in the vain attempt. At last the order was
passed down the lines to "cease firing," and the men,
panting with fatigue and excitement, rested on their
arms. At this moment Jackson, who during the whole
action, had occupied a prominent position near the right
of Planché's battalion, where he could command a view
of the whole entrenchment, now passed slowly down
the lines, accompanied by his staff, halting about the
centre of each command, and addressing to its commander and the men, words of praise and grateful com-
mendation. His feeble body now stood erect, and his
face, relaxing its usual sternness, glowed with the fire
of a proud victor in the noblest of all causes, the
defence of his country's flag, the protection of the lives,
the property, and honor of a free people. And as he
passed, the band struck up "Hail Columbia," and the
whole line, now for the first time facing to the rear,
burst forth into loud and prolonged hurras to the Chief,
by whose indomitable heroism and energy they had
been enabled to inflict so awful a punishment upon the

enemy, who had invaded their homes and sought to dishonor their flag. But these notes of exultation died
away into sighs of pity, and exclamations of horror and
commiseration, as soon as the artillery, which had kept
up the fire at intervals after the musketry ceased, being
silenced, the smoke, ascending from the field, revealed
a spectacle which sent a thrill of horror along that
whole line of exultant victors. The bright column and
long red lines of a splendid army, which occupied the
field where it was last visible to the Americans, had
disappeared as if by some supernatural agency. Save
the hundreds of miserable creatures who rolled over the
field in agony, or crawled and dragged their shattered
limbs over the muddy plain, not a living foe could be
seen by the naked eye. The commanders, with their
telescopes, succeeded, with some difficulty, in discovering, far in the rear, a faint red line, which indicated the
position of General Lambert, with his reserve, stationed
in a ditch, in what that officer designated in his dispatch, a *supine* position, meaning that the men, after
getting into the ditch, which covered them to the waist,
leaned over flat on their faces, and thus escaped the
cannon-balls of the Americans. These were the only
live objects visible in the field, but with the dead it was
so thickly strewn, that from the American ditch you
could have walked a quarter of a mile to the front on
the bodies of the killed and disabled. The space in
front of Carroll's position, for an extent of two hundred
yards, was literally covered with the slain. The course
of the column could be distinctly traced in the broad,
red line of the victims of the terrible batteries and
unerring guns of the Americans. They fell in their
tracks : in some places, whole platoons lay together, as

if killed by the same discharge. Dressed in their gay uniforms, cleanly shaved and attired for the promised victory and triumphal entry into the city, these stalwart men lay on the gory field, frightful examples of the horrors of war. Strangely, indeed, did they contrast with those ragged, unshorn, begrimed, and untidy, strange-looking, long-haired men, who, crowding the American parapet, coolly surveyed and commented upon the terrible destruction they had caused. There was not a private among the slain, whose aspect did not present more of the pomp and circumstance of war, than any of the commanders of the victors. In the ditch there were no less than forty dead, and at least a hundred who were wounded, or who had thrown themselves into it for shelter. On the edge of the woods there were many, who, being slightly wounded, or unable to reach the rear, had concealed themselves under the brush and in the trees. It was pitiable, indeed, to see the writhings of the disabled and mutilated, and to hear their terrible cries for help and water, which arose from every quarter of the plain. As this scene of death, desolation, bloodshed and suffering, came into full view of the American lines, a profound and melancholy silence pervaded the victorious army. No sounds of exultation or rejoicing were now heard. Pity and sympathy had succeeded to the boisterous and savage feelings which a few minutes before had possessed their souls. They saw no longer the presumptuous, daring, and insolent invader, who had come four thousand miles to lay waste a peaceful country; they forgot their own suffering and losses, and the barbarian threats of the enemy, and now only perceived humanity, fellow-creatures in their own form, reduced to the most helpless, miserable, and pitiable of all conditions of suffering, desolation and distress. Prompted by this motive, many of the Americans stole without leave from their positions, and with their canteens proceeded to assuage the thirst and render other assistance to the wounded. The latter, and those who were captured in the ditch, were led into the lines, where the wounded received prompt attention from Jackson's medical staff. Many of the Americans carried their disabled enemies into the camp on their backs, as the pious Eneas bore his feeble parent from burning Troy. Some of the British soldiers in the ditch, not understanding the language of the free men of color who went to their assistance, and thinking that their only object was to murder or rob, fired upon them. This at least is their only apology for conduct, which was regarded as very atrocious, and produced considerable excitement in the American lines. The Americans thus killed and wounded were unarmed, and were engaged in the duty of the good Samaritan, attending the wounded and relieving the distressed. It has been charged that they were fired upon by order of the British officers, out of chagrin and mortification for their defeat. If this be true, it is a pity that the names of such officers could not be known, that they might be separated from those whose conduct throughout the campaign proved them to be honorable and gallant soldiers, and high-toned gentlemen. In this manner several Americans were killed and wounded. Indeed more casualties occurred to the Americans after the battle than in the principal action. The British evidently mistook the humane purposes of the Americans, and even when there was no other alternative, manifested a disposition to resist capture. One officer who was slightly wounded, declined surrendering to one of the Tennesseeans, whose appearance was not very impressive, and disregarding his call, was walking off, when the Tennesseean, drawing bead on him, cried out, " Halt, Mr. Red Coat: one more step and I'll drill a hole through your leather;" whereupon the officer surrendered—exclaiming at the same time, " What a disgrace for a British officer to have to surrender to a chimney-sweep !"

Of course there was a general desire among the Americans to procure some lawful trophy—some memento of their great victory ; and many of the men wandered over the field in pursuit thereof. They were quite successful in securing many such mementoes, among which were the field glass of Packenham, and an elegant sword, believed to be Packenham's, but which was afterwards claimed by General Keane, and delivered to him by order of Jackson. Packenham's glass was identified, and remained in the possession of Colonel, afterwards General, Garrique Fleaujac, who commanded one of the batteries on the left. The trumpets of Gibbs and Keane were also picked up on the field, and became the property of Coffee's brigade. At least a thousand stand of arms were gathered by the Americans from the scene of the slaughter. The prisoners and wounded being now collected within the lines, were placed in carts or formed into detachments to be sent up to the city. Every attention was given to their relief and comfort. Many of the prisoners seemed not at all disheartened by their capture, but indeed gave manifestations of joy and satisfaction, especially the

Irish, who declared that they did not know whither they were bound when they left the old country—that they never wanted to fight the Americans.

"Why, then," asked some of the American guard, "did you march up so boldly to our lines, in face of such a fire?" "And 'faith were we not obliged, with the officers behind, sticking and stabbing us with their swords." There were unmistakable proofs of the truth of this remark on the bodies of many of the men, whose clothes and flesh were cut evidently with sharp instruments.

Some distance in the rear of Jackson's lines, the greater part of the adult population of New Orleans, not connected with the army, were gathered in anxious suspense, observing the progress of the battle, and receiving with the most greedy zest and intense anxiety, every fact or rumor, which passed from the front to the rear sentinels. Far towards the swamp a number of boys, eager to see what was going on, climbed the trees, and thus commanded a distant, but rather confused view of the battle. When the guns ceased firing, and after the terrific tumult of the battle, which could be distinctly heard far to the rear, and even in the city, had settled into silence and quiet, only broken by the loud hurras of the Americans, the anxious spectators and listeners in the rear, quickly comprehending the glorious result, caught up the sounds of exultation and echoed them along the banks of the river, until the glad tidings reached the city, sent a thrill of joy throughout its limits, and brought the whole population into the streets to give full vent to their extravagant joy. The streets resounded with hurras. The only military force in the city, the veterans, under their indefatigable commander, the noble old patriot soldier, Captain De

27

Buys, hastily assembled, and with a drum and fife paraded the streets amid the salutes and hurras of the people, the waving of the snowy handkerchiefs of the ladies, and the boundless exultation and noisy joy of the juveniles. Every minute brought forth some new proof of the great and glorious victory. First, there came a messenger, whose horse had been severely taxed, who inquired for the residences of the physicians of the city, and dashed madly through the streets in pursuit of surgeons and apothecaries. All of the profession, whether in practice or not, were required to proceed to the lines, as their services were needed immediately. "For whom?" was the question which agitated the bosom of many an anxious parent and devoted wife, and for a moment clouded and checked the general hilarity. Soon it was known, however, that this demand for surgeons was on account of the enemy. All who possessed any knowledge of the curative art, who could amputate or set a limb, or take up an artery, hurried to the camp. Next there came up a message from the camp to dispatch all the carts and other vehicles to the lines. This order, too, was fully discussed and commented on by the crowd, which gathered in the streets and in all public resorts. But like all Jackson's orders, it was also quickly executed.

It was late in the day before the purpose of this order was clearly perceived, as a long and melancholy procession of these carts, followed by a crowd of men, was seen slowly and silently wending their way along the levee from the field of battle. They contained the British wounded; and those who followed in the rear were the prisoners in charge of a detachment of Carroll's men. Emulating the magnanimity of the army, the citizens pressed forward to tender their aid to their wounded enemies. The hospitals being all crowded with their own sick and wounded, these unfortunate victims of English ambition were taken in charge by the citizens, and by private contributions were supplied with mattresses and pillows, with a large quantity of lint and old linen for dressing their wounds, all of which articles were then exceedingly scarce in the city. Those far-famed nurses, the quadroon women of New Orleans, whose services are so conspicuously useful when New Orleans is visited by pestilence, freely gave their kind attentions to the wounded British, and watched at their bedsides night and day. Several of the officers, who were grievously wounded, were taken to private residences of citizens, and there provided with every comfort. Such acts as these ennoble humanity, and obscure even the horrors and excesses of war.

From the city the news of Jackson's triumph flew rapidly through the neighboring country. It soon reached a gloomy detachment which, under Jackson's orders, had been condemned to a mortifying and disgusting inactivity at the little fort of St. John. Here on the shores of the placid Pontchartrain the roar of Jackson's batteries, on the morning of the 8th, could be distinctly heard. It was known that this was the great attack— the last effort of the British. Their absence from the scene of such a great crisis, was humiliating beyond all expression to the gallant men of this detachment. One of them, an officer, the late venerable Nicholas Sinnott, a stalwart and determined veteran, who had wielded a pike at Vinegar Hill, bore this disappointment with ill grace and little philosophy. In the excitement of the moment, he could with difficulty be restrained from heading a detachment to proceed to the lines, and expressed his disgust in words which were not forgotten to the day of his death by his intimate friends and associates. " Oh! there are the bloody villains, murthering my countrymen, and myself stuck down in this infernal mud-hole!"

XVII.

BATTLE OF NEW ORLEANS.

THE DISASTER.

[Eighth of January, 1815.]

THE general rejoicing and exultation in the American camp, and in the city, which had been interrupted by the calls of humanity and the pity excited by the disasters of the enemy, were destined to receive another serious shock, and to be suddenly changed into intense anxiety, as the news which had been in the possession of the Commander-in-chief from an early hour, leaked out, that all had not gone well on the other bank of the river, and that the British actually commanded their lines, and had advanced to their rear. It may be better imagined than described, how profoundly the camp was agitated by this alarming intelligence. It was but too true. The British attack had been as successful on the right, as it had been disastrous on the left bank. Jackson might safely say, as Napoleon, with far less truth, remarked, when he heard of the defeat of his fleet at Trafalgar—"I cannot be everywhere." There can be little doubt that if he had commanded on the right bank, the only disgrace which sullied the glory of the campaign would have been avoided.

We have seen how Morgan sent forward his advance, consisting of less than three hundred ill-armed and fatigued men, to occupy a line a mile in front of his own—a line stretching from the levee to the swamp—which could not have been manned by less than a thousand men, with several pieces of artillery. Had even these three hundred men been sent to the point where the British landed, and stationed behind the landing, Thornton's crowded boats could not have reached the river's bank.* They would have enjoyed the advantage of daylight, for it was half-past four when Thornton stepped ashore—a mile further down stream than he had calculated. His men were formed in columns, just as the rockets, ascending on the other bank, announced the commencement of the attack in that quarter. This landing had been effected without the slightest interruption. Covering his flank by three gun-boats, each bearing a carronade in the bows, under the command of Captain Roberts, Thornton pushed rapidly forward up the road, until he reached Morgan's advance position. Here, dividing his force, he moved a detachment of the 85th against Tessier's position, while, with the remainder of his regiment, he held the road against Davis. As Thornton advanced, Roberts opened his carronades on Davis's command. The detachment of the 85th rushed on Tes-

---

* In support of this opinion, we need only refer to the fact that the British always believed that the success on the right bank was due to their taking the Americans by surprise. The author of the Campaigns of the British army at Washington and New Orleans, says: " Had they (Morgan's men) stood firm, indeed, it is hardly conceivable that so small a force could have wrested an entrenched position from numbers so superior; at least it could not have been done without much bloodshed. But they were completely surprised. An attack on this side was a circumstance of which they had not dreamed; and when men are assaulted in a point which they deem beyond the reach of danger, it is well known that they defend themselves with less vigor than when such an event was anticipated."

sier's party with great vigor, and put them to flight, after firing a few scattering shots. Tessier and his men being on the extreme right, and unable to reach the road before the British had occupied it, were compelled to fly into the swamp, where many of them suffered great distress, and were unable to reach the camp, in the rear, for many hours. Meantime, Thornton, pushing forward with his main body, consisting of the 85th, the sailors and marines, soon put Davis's weak detachment to flight, closely following on their heels. The Kentuckians being raw troops, did not, of course, retreat in very good order. As they fell back in great confusion upon Morgan's lines, the general rode out, and meeting Colonel Davis, directed him to form his men within his lines, on the right of the Louisiana militia. Davis obeyed the order, but instead of the five hundred men Jackson had ordered across the river, there were but one hundred and seventy to cover lines of three or four hundred yards. These were stationed some distance apart, so as to present to the enemy rather the appearance of a line of sentinels, than of a continuous body of troops, to defend a small ditch and rude parapet. Insignificant as these works were, if Morgan had received the intended reinforcement, he would have been able to maintain his position. Instead of six hundred, his real force, he would then have had nearly a thousand men and three pieces of artillery.

There was no lack of courage and determination on the part of Morgan and his command. They stood firmly at their posts, and prepared to repel the enemy with nerve and resolution.

Thornton, as he gained the open field in front of Morgan's works, extended the files of the 85th so as to cover the whole field, and with the sailors formed in column on the road and the marines in reserve, advanced steadily on Morgan's lines. Lieutenant-Colonel Gubbins commanded the 85th, Major Adair the marines, and Captain Money the seamen. The bugler sounded a shrill and animating charge, and amid a shower of rockets under the direction of Major Mitchell of the artillery, the British tars rushed forward. They were received by a crashing discharge of grape from Philli-bert's twelve-pounder and two sixes under adjutant John Nixon, of the First Louisiana militia, and gunner, James Hosmer and Mr. Batique. The seamen recoiled from this fire. There was another and another volley from the batteries, which killed and wounded several of the seamen. Among the wounded was their gallant commander, Captain Money, who had been distinguish-ed in the operation in the Chesapeake, and in the attack on Washington City. He fell at the head of his men. At this the Americans began to hurrah and ply their pieces more briskly. But Thornton, seeing the hesita-tion and recoil of the seamen, rushed forward with the 85th, under a fire of musketry from Morgan's lines, and, despite a severe wound received by him in the advance, succeeding in obliquing the storming party towards the centre of Morgan's line, and strengthening it by a division of the 85th under Captain Schaw, whilst two other divisions of the 85th advanced briskly against the centre and extreme right of Davis's position. Thus Thornton, showing a skill and judgment superior to that which had been displayed on the left bank, occu-pied the whole front of the American lines, while Roberts opened upon the batteries of Morgan's extreme left, with his carronades. As Thornton closed upon Davis's command, the Kentuckians perceiving that they were about to be hemmed in between two divisions of the enemy, one penetrating the centre, and the other the extreme right, fired one volley, and then abandoning their position, began to fall back in great confusion towards the road in the rear.

General Morgan rode to the right, and called out to Colonel Davis to halt his men. Davis replied that it was impossible. " Sir," exclaimed Morgan, in an angry tone, " I have not seen you try." And then, turning to the fleeing Kentuckians, he shouted to them—"Halt, halt! men, and resume your position." At the same moment Adjutant Stephens, a brave Kentuckian, who had been badly wounded, cried out, " Shame, shame! Boys, stand by your general." But the men were already panic-stricken and unnerved, and moved rapidly and disorderly from the right towards the roads, Morgan following them on horseback, and endeavoring in every way he could to rally them. He succeeded in bringing back some of the fugitives, but a shower of rockets falling in their midst revived their alarm, and now they scattered, running as fast as they could towards Morgan's left. Meantime the Louisiana militia kept up a brisk fire on the advancing British, discharging eight volleys with considerable effect. But their right being now uncovered, the British hastened to rush over the ditch, and, scaling the parapet, gained the inside of Morgan's lines. The Louisiana troops being now in danger of being intercepted—their batteries having discharged their last cartridge, of which they had but twelve, they were compelled also to abandon their position, which they did in tolerable order, and under fire of the enemy, after spiking their guns and tumbling them into the river. Patterson's battery on the Levee, some three hundred yards in Morgan's rear, had been constructed to operate on the other bank of the river, and had been engaged since daylight in an incessant fire at the British in front of Jackson's position. Seeing that Morgan's lines were forced, Patterson had wheeled his guns round so as to command the road, when, perceiving Davis's men running in wild disorder, right upon his battery so as to cover the advance of the British, and General Morgan so vainly striving to rally them, the gallant commodore, greatly incensed at his countrymen, cried out to the commander of a twelve-pounder, which had been brought to bear in that direction, to fire his piece into the " d——d cowards." The midshipman, a half-grown youth, raised the match to apply it to the piece, when the order was countermanded ; and the commodore, perceiving that his battery was unmasked and exposed, having recovered his calmness, directed the guns to be spiked, and the powder to be thrown into the river. He then abandoned his position, and retired by the road, walking with Mr. R. D. Shepherd, his volunteer aid, in the rear of his men, only thirty in number, and alternately denouncing the British and the Kentuckians. Patterson was followed by the Louisiana militia, who fell back in good order until they reached the Louisiana, which had been moored about three hundred yards behind Patterson's battery. The sailors being unable to get her off, the militia halted, and by fastening a hawser and foreline, succeeded in having her towed out into the stream beyond the reach of the enemy, who would have been too happy to destroy this great plague, which had so continually harassed their camp. Finally, the Louisiana militia rallied at Casselard's, and forming on Boisgereau's canal, prepared to make a stand there. But the British never reached this position. After advancing in excellent spirits with a full belief that all had gone well on the other side of the river, they had barely reached Patterson's battery when Colonel Dickson, of the artillery, arrived direct from General Lambert, with the crushing intelligence of the terrible disasters which had crowned their efforts on the left bank. Previous to Dickson's arrival, Thornton had been reinforced by several companies of sailors and marines, and he felt quite strong in his position; but Dickson now declared that it could not be maintained; and, hurrying back to Lambert, so reported; whereupon orders were transmitted to Thornton to retire from his position, recross the river and join the main body. The execution of these various orders consumed a great part of the day. Meantime, Jackson, greatly concerned at the state of affairs produced by the events on the right bank, busied himself in organizing a strong force to throw across the river to Morgan's relief. That force was placed under the command of General Humbert, who, but for the unworthy jealousy of some of the militia officers towards a distinguished military hero of foreign origin, would, no doubt, have recovered the lost ground, and wiped off the disgrace of Morgan's defeat. But the disinclination of the American militia to serve under Humbert, and their lack of zeal in preparing to execute his orders, produced a delay, which was no less mortifying to the gallant Frenchman, than unworthy of the Americans, who displayed these petty feelings.

After the wounded in front of Jackson's line had all been brought into his camp, and provided with proper attendance, the men in Jackson's lines were ordered to resume their position, stand to their arms, and be ready to repel another attack. Jackson was not the man to be carried away by exultation and joy, so as to neglect the necessary precautions to secure his victory. Indeed, he was as prudent as heroic.

About noon on the 8th, several Americans, who had advanced some distance in front of the lines, announced the approach of a party from the British camp. It consisted of an officer in full uniform, a trumpeter, and a soldier bearing a white flag. The three advanced on the levee to a position within three hundred yards of Jackson's lines, when the trumpeter blew a loud blast, and the standard-bearer waved the white flag. The whole army now gathered on the summit of the parapet, and looked on in anxious suspense and curiosity. Jackson ordered Major Butler, with two other officers, to proceed to the British party, and receive any message it might bear. The officer courteously received Major B., and delivered him a written communication, which that officer hastened to present to General Jackson at his head-quarters at Macarté's. The message contained a proposition for an armistice, to bury the dead. It was signed "Lambert," without any title or designation of rank. General Jackson directed Major Butler to state to the officer bearing the message that he would be happy to treat with the commander-in-chief of the British army, but that the signer of the letter had forgotten to designate his authority and rank, which was necessary before any negotiations could be entered upon. General Lambert had erred in thinking that a militia general and Indian fighter might be imposed upon by so shallow a device, employed to conceal the fact of the death of the commander-in-chief. The delegation with the flag of truce returned to the British head-quarters, and in half an hour appeared again before the American lines, with propositions now signed by " John Lambert, Commander-in-Chief of the British forces."

The first proposition, as a basis for the armistice, offered by Jackson, embodied an admirably sagacious stroke of policy. It was on these terms: that although hostilities should cease on the left bank, where the dead lay unburied until twelve o'clock on the 9th, yet it was not to be understood that they should cease on the right bank; but that no reinforcement should be sent across by either army until the expiration of that day. Such condition produced the expected result; Lambert asked until ten o'clock on the 9th to consider the proposition: meantime he sent orders to Thornton to retire. That officer, covering the movement by an advance towards the American position, set fire to the several saw-mills in his rear, and after destroying the ammunition and stores which he had captured, retired in good order, his rear-guard being, however, pressed by an advance party of Americans, upon which they kept up a running fire. It was dark before Thornton succeeded in crossing the river. That night the Americans regained their lines on the right bank, and by early morn Patterson had restored his battery, in a more advantageous position than it had previously occupied, announcing the gratifying fact to Jackson at daybreak by a discharge of several large pieces against the British outposts.

Disgraceful as the defeat on the right bank was, it is due to the Kentuckians, who were the chief actors in the affair, to remind the reader of the hard usage to which they had been subjected in their long and fatiguing march

during the day, and to their ill-armed condition.
Whether these facts will be sufficient to acquit them of
all blame, or to mitigate the censure which has been so
often and freely bestowed on them for their conduct,
are questions we feel no desire to discuss.   It should not
be forgotten, however, with what promptitude and self-
sacrificing patriotism these men had abandoned their distant homes, and hurried at an inclement season of the
year, to the defence of this remote settlement.   It is
hardly conceivable that such men should be faithless to
duty and honor, and the conclusion that their retreat was
an unavoidable necessity, is more reasonable as well as
more consonant to the pride and feelings of Americans.

The Americans achieved glory enough that day, to
bear with equanimity the slight mortification inflicted
by this event.

To complete our narrative—not to aggravate the shame
of this disaster—it is necessary to state that Morgan lost
but one man killed and five wounded.   The British loss
was much more serious.   The 85th had two killed and
thirty-nine wounded, including their colonel ; and the
sailors and marines had four killed and forty-nine
wounded, including Captain Money.   Several of the
wounded died before the detachment re-crossed the
river.   The dead were buried in the plain in front of
Morgan's lines.

It was in this action that the British acquired the
trophy which is their sole record of their achievements
on this day.   It is a small flag which now hangs amid
the trophies of the Peninsular war in Whitehall, London, with this description : "Taken at the battle of New
Orleans, January 8, 1815."   There is as much appro-

priateness in such a record, as there would be in the French arraying in public a British regimental standard captured at Waterloo !

General Lambert having consented to Jackson's propositions, early in the morning of the 9th a line was staked off, about three hundred yards from the American intrenchment, and detachments of soldiers marched from both camps, who were stationed near this line, but a few feet apart, to carry out the object of the armistice, to wit, the burial of the dead. The dead bodies, which were strewn so thickly over the field, were then brought by the Americans to the lines, where they were received by the British and borne to a designated spot on Bienvenu's, which had been marked off as the cemetery of " the Army of Louisiana." In carrying the dead the Americans used the clumsy and unwieldy ladders intended by the British to be employed in scaling the American parapet. Many British officers assembled to witness the ceremony. It was to them one of deep mortification and sorrow. These feelings were increased by the presence of several American officers, whose natural *sang froid* was misinterpreted into untimely exultation. This misconception led the British officer, from whom we have already derived so much information relative to this campaign, into the following burst of feeling :

" An American officer stood by, smoking a cigar, and apparently counting the slain, with a look of savage exultation, and repeating, over and over, to each individual that approached him, that their loss amounted to eight men killed and fourteen wounded. I confess that when I beheld the scene I hung down my head, half in sorrow and half in anger. With my offi cious informant I had every inclination to pick a quarrel; but he was on duty, and an armistice existed, both of which forbade the measure. I could not, however, stand by and repress my choler; and since to give it vent would have subjected me to a more serious inconvenience than a mere duel, I turned my horse's head and galloped back to the camp." The bearing of General Lambert's secretary, Major H. C. Smith, of the 95th rifles, who met a soldier's death at Waterloo, was more manly and philosophic, if less honest and sincere. Entering into a conversation with Captain Maunsel White, who now survives, a respected and honored planter and patriot, living on his magnificent estate (Deerange), in the parish of Plaquemines, Major Smith coolly remarked, looking very calmly upon the acres of dead around him: "O! it is a mere skirmish—a mere skirmish!" "One more such skirmish," replied Captain White, "and devilish few of you will ever get back home to tell the story."

The bodies of the officers were first-delivered to the British. Those of Colonel Rennie, Major Whittaker, Captain Henry, and Majors Wilkinson and King, being familiar to both officers and men, were received with sorrowful and tearful silence. They were chiefs and heroes in the army, who left behind no superiors in that band of veterans, who had signalized their valor in many combats, and were ever amongst the foremost in all perilous enterprises. Rennie was particularly lamented, for throughout the operations on the Chesapeake and in Louisiana, he had proved to be the most efficient light infantry officer next to Thornton in the army. The dead officers were carried to headquarters, and such as had friends to attend to the sacred duties of securing them a Christian burial were interred at night, in Villeré's garden, by the light of torches, with appropriate religious ceremonies. Others were disembeweled, and their bodies deposited in casks of rum, to be carried to England. Such was the disposition of the bodies of Packenham and Gibbs, and, we believe, of Colonels Dale and Rennie.* But the remainder of the dead, including hundreds of officers and men, were hastily and imperfectly buried in the rear of Bienvenu's plantation. The spot thus consecrated has never been invaded by the plough or the spade, but is regarded to this day with awe and respect by the superstitious Africans, and is now occupied by a grove of stunted cypress, strikingly commemorative of the disasters of this ill-fated expedition.

In estimating the loss of the British in this disastrous affair, we are met by several conflicting statements. Between these various estimates it is not, however, difficult to form an approximate calculation, which will not fall far short of the reality. That estimate will show that the loss sustained in the attack on the left bank of the Mississippi was the severest ever sustained in any battle by the British army. Deducting the reserve, Lambert's, which was not under fire, the 14th dragoons, who guarded the camp and hospital, and Thornton's command, there could not have been more than six thousand men engaged in the attack on Jackson's lines. Of these, according to the estimate of Colonel Hayne, who was designated by Jackson for this duty, there were at least 2,600 placed *hors de combat*, to wit:

* The tree, a noble Pecan, under which the viscera of Packenham were buried, still stands in the yard of Villeré's, the subject of a superstition much cherished by the Creoles, that ever since that occurrence it has ceased to bear fruit.

28

Killed 700
Wounded 1400
Prisoners 500

The British reports do not vary essentially from this report, except in the statement of the killed, which, in the regular (British) returns, only embrace those who were killed on the field, and not those who died shortly after being carried off.

Their report is as follows:

STAFF.	Killed.	Wounded.	Missing.	Total
Generals..................	2	1	0	3
Brigadier Major,..........	1	1	0	2
Deputy Ass. Qr. M. G.	0	1	0	1
FOURTH FOOT.				
Commissioned Officers, ...	2	24	1	27
Men.....................	40	234	53	327
SEVENTH FOOT.				
Officers..................	2	4	0	6
Men.....................	39	49	0	88
TWENTY-FIRST FOOT.				
Officers..................	3	4	9	16
Men.....................	67	153	227	449
FORTY-THIRD FOOT.				
Officers..................	2	2	1	5
Men.....................	11	40	5	56
FORTY-FOURTH FOOT.				
Officers	2	9	1	12
Men.....................	33	154	79	266
NINETY-THIRD FOOT (Highlanders).				
Officers..................	3	9	3	15
Men	60	368	102	530
Carry over, ...267		1053	481	1803

	Killed.	Wounded.	Missing.	Total.
Brought forward, ...267	1053	481	1803
NINETY-FIFTH FOOT (Rifles).				
Officers................ 0	7	0	7
Men.................... 11	94	0	105
FIRST AND FIFTH WEST INDIA REGIMENTS.				
Officers................ 0	5	0	5
Men.................... 5	19	1	25
Total casualties of British on left bank 283	1178	482	1845

On the right bank the loss was as follows:

	Killed.	Wounded.	Missing.	Total.
THIRTY-FIFTH FOOT.				
Officers................ 0	2	0	2
Men.................... 2	39	1	42
ROYAL MARINES.				
Officers................ 0	3	0	3
Men................... 2	13	0	15
ROYAL NAVY.				
Officers................ 0	2	0	2
Men.................... 2	18	0	20
Total casualties on right bank, 8	77	1	84

Grand total of the British loss on the 8th of January, 1815:

	Killed.	Wounded.	Missing.	Total.
On the left bank........... 283	1178	482	1845
On the right bank 8	77	1	84
Grand Total.............. 291	1255	483	1929

Of the officers killed, there were two Generals—
Packenham, Lieutenant General, and Gibbs, Major

General; three Colonels and Lieutenant Colonels—Dale, T. Jones, and Rennie; three Majors—Wilkinson, Brigade Major, King, and J. A. Whittaker; three Captains—Henry, Hichins, and Muirhead; four Lieutenants and Ensigns—Crowe, Donald McDonald, Davies, and McLorkey. Of the wounded, there was one Major General—Keane; one Deputy Quarter-master General—Delacy Evans; five Colonels and Lieutenant Colonels—Brooke, Faunce, Patterson, Thornton, and Debbieg: all but the first and last being severely wounded; three Majors—Brigade Major Shaw, slightly; Williamson and Ross, severely. Captains Fletcher, Erskine, Page, Ryan, Boulger, McKenzie, Ellis, Travers, Isles, Money (Navy), severely; and Craig, Elliot, and Mullens slightly, thirteen. Lieutenants and Ensigns—Brooke, Martin, Richardson, Squire, Farrington, Marshall, Andrews, Benwell, Higgins, Waters, Geddes, Meyricke, D. Campbell, Smith, Brush, Philan, W. Jones, White, Hayden, Donaldson, Urquhart, Gordon, Hay, Reynolds, Sir J. Ribton, Gosset, Blackhouse, Barker, McDonald, Morgan, Pelkington, and Wilson, severely, thirty-two; Ellis, Parnal, Hopkins, Salvin, Boully, Hearn, Gerard, Fernandez, Newton, Richardson, Lorentz, McLean, Spark, McPherson, Elliott and Morgan (Marines), Millar, slightly, seventeen; Total lieutenants and ensigns wounded, forty-nine. Of the missing, there was—Major McAfie, one; Captains Kidd, Simpson (severely wounded, and taken prisoner), and Brady, Lieutenants Lavack, Carr, Quinn, Munro, McDonald, and Graves, seven—all severely wounded and taken prisoners; and Stewart, Armstrong, Fonblanque, Knight, and B. Johnson, five—captured without being wounded.

Grand total of officers killed and wounded:

KILLED.

Generals...............................	2
Colonels and Lieutenant Colonels,..........	3
Majors	3
Captains.................................	3
Lieutenants and Ensigns	5

WOUNDED.

	Severely.	Slightly.
Major General......................	1	0
Deputy Quarter-master General.......	1	0
Colonels and Lieutenant Colonels	3	2
Majors.............................	2	1
Captains...........................	10	8
Lieutenants and Ensigns	32	17
Midshipman.........................	1	0

	Severely Wounded.	Missing.
Captains	2	0
Major	0	1
Lieutenants	6	5

Considering the number of the wounded who after-wards died, the total of mortality in this battle has been estimated, by competent judges, at one thousand men. Colonel Maunsel White, now a survivor of the war, with another officer, counted the British dead on the field: they were 356; and he thinks there must have been others in the swamp. The Adjutant of the 93d, Mr. Graves, who was found on the field, badly wounded, was taken charge of by Colonel (then captain) White, and attended by him during his confinement in the city, now resides in Brooklyn, N. Y. He states that the 93d mustered, on the morning of the 8th, one thousand men and twenty-four officers, and that after they had retreated from the attack, and were collected in the rear, there were ten or twelve officers and one hundred and thirty men!

The Americans lost in their lines but two men killed; they were shot on the left—one through the neck and the other through the head. There were two others killed in the redoubt on the right. The others, making in all eight killed, lost their lives in the swamp by unnecessarily exposing themselves; or were shot after the action by the British soldiers who were concealed in the ditch, or in the bushes near the swamp. The aggregate loss was eight killed and thirteen wounded, which number, compared with that of the British, exhibits a disparity without a parallel in ancient or modern warfare.

XVIII.

CLOSING INCIDENTS.

OUR task is nearly finished. The great battle has been fought. The dead have been buried, and gloom and silence have settled over that field, now for ever classic in American history. In sorrow, misery, shame, and dejection, the British have withdrawn further off from the scene of the most dismal disaster their arms ever encountered. Every house for miles along the river is occupied with their wounded, and the labors of their surgeons are incessant and herculean. But worse even than wounds, physical agony and sickness, is that torment of "the mind diseased," for which there is no minister—the consciousness of defeat and disgrace, that has entered the soul of those hitherto victorious veterans. These feelings alternately prostrate their victims into a deep silent gloom, or break out in fierce and fiery denunciation of those, whom their passions selected as the scape-goats of their disgrace. The poor 44th came in for the chief share of the maledictions. It had failed in its duty—it had not brought up the ladders and fascines. And even when the heroic Packenham at last took the regiment out of the hands of its imbecile colonel, it had flinched. So great was this indignation, that the other regiments would not associate with any officer or private, wearing the uniform of the 44th. Was this just or honorable? That Colonel Mullens should have obeyed, at all sacrifices, the order given to him, there can be no question; but his disobedience was not even a cause, much less a prominent one, of their defeat. The order was neither a just, nor a wise one. To require a whole regiment to stack its arms and bear ladders for the rest of the command, was unusual and inequitable. This duty ought to have been imposed upon detachments from the various corps, as the forlorn hope is organized. But, of what avail would have been the prompt execution of this order? The ladders and fascines were not necessary to pass the paltry ditch, and scale the insignificant parapet of the Americans. A robust man could nearly have leaped from the field to the mound, behind which the Americans stood. The British must have imagined that they had high walls to mount, like those of Badajoz and St. Sebastian. Their great difficulty was to reach the ditch; they could never have used their ladders and fascines, if, instead of the 44th, every private in their army had borne them. They were shot down before reaching the ditch. The fascines and ladders only impeded and harassed them. With their heavy knapsacks, these unwieldy articles only made them "surer game" for the Tennessee marksmen. Colonel Mullens and the 44th were not, therefore, the cause of their repulse. The true cause was the skillfulness and steadiness of the American militia, in the use of firearms. Such was the sagacious conclusion of an eminent French soldier, who visited this field many years after. It was the Marshal Count Bertrand Clausel, the same who had commanded the French division at Salamanca.

which Packenham had routed. Settling in Mobile, Alabama, this distinguished soldier, who had figured so conspicuously on so prominent an arena—who had commanded at Bordeaux during the Hundred Days, and to whom the Duchess of Angoulême surrendered as a prisoner—now, with the characteristic philosophy of Frenchmen, became an humble gardener, who furnished the market of Mobile with vegetables, driving his cart himself. Conceiving a desire to behold the field of the defeat and death of his old and victorious foe, he visited New Orleans in 1820, in company with the celebrated Count Desnoettes, Napoleon's faithful companion in the retreat from Moscow—the same whom the Emperor selected, on his affecting parting at Fontainebleau, as the dearest of all his friends. These gallant and distinguished Frenchmen being escorted to the battle-field of the 8th of January, 1815, by some of their countrymen, who had participated in that affair, were greatly puzzled to know how such good soldiers as the English could be repulsed by so weak a force from such trifling fortifications. "Ah!" exclaimed Marshal Clausel,* after some moments of reflection, "I see how it all happened. When these Americans go into battle, they forget that they are not hunting deer or shooting turkeys and try never to throw away a shot." And there was the whole secret of the defeat, which the British have ascribed to so many different causes. It is the agility with which the Americans wield every species of firearm, and the habit of cool, steady aim, which renders them so

---

* Marshal Clausel was restored to his position in the army by Louis Philippe and became Governor of Algeria, and was the commander and military instructor of General Canrobert, the French commander in the operations before Sebastopol.

destructive in battles, where they are not restrained or confused by any military manœuvre or exigency.

It is no part of our design to give all the details of the events which followed the battle of the 8th; nor shall we turn aside to engage in those unprofitable discussions, growing out of subsequent events, to which some writers and politicians have assigned prominent places in this drama. They will be barely glanced at.

The British were not left long to their gloomy reflections and bad passions. The American batteries again resumed their tasks of incessantly annoying the hostile camp, firing at every knot of men that could be discerned in the British camp, and keeping their sentinels and outposts constantly on the guard, dodging and ducking as the balls flew around them. Prominent among those who were most active and earnest in this annoyance to the British, was Commodore Patterson, who relieved himself of the disgust and indignation, which had been created in his bosom, by an uninterrupted fire at the British camp from a new battery he had thrown up in advance of Morgan's position.

Save these regular and customary salutes of the British camp by the various batteries on both sides of the river, nothing of great interest occurred until the 11th, when the curiosity of the Americans was excited by the distant rumbling of artillery far down the river. It was soon understood that this was the expected attack on Fort St. Philip, a fortification on the left bank of the Mississippi, about eighty miles below the city, and some thirty from the mouth of the river. The fort, which was a rude, irregular work, stood in a bend of the river, so as to have a long sweep above and below it. It was surrounded by an impenetrable morass, and on the lower side by the Bayou Mardi Gras. There were twenty-nine guns mounted in the fort, of which there were two thirty-twos, established in the curtain of the fort on a level with the river. The others were twenty-fours, one thirteen inch mortar, and several howitzers. The fort had been in preparation some months before. Jackson visited it in December, perceived its vast importance and great strength, and gave orders to have certain additions made to it. Several detachments of troops were sent down to reinforce the garrison. A number of negroes were employed to bring in timbers and perform other work necessary to the solidity and strength of the fort.

Among other sagacious preparations, the magazine was completely disguised, and several smaller ones established in various places. The garrison consisted of two companies of United States artillery, 117, under Captains Wolstoncraft, Murray, and Walsh; two companies of the 7th infantry, 163, under Captains Brontin and Waide; Lagan's Louisiana Volunteers, 54; and Listeau's free men of color, 30; in all 366. To these are to be added the crew of gun-boat No. 8, which had been hauled into the Bayou. The whole force made 406 effective men under that staunch and able officer, Major Overton, of the rifle corps. Below, a guard was established to watch and announce the approach of the enemy.

It manifests a palpable want of combination and military skill in the British generals, that their plan of advance upon the city was not so arranged as to secure possession of the river before their land troops occupied its banks. It ought to have occurred to them that their flank would be exposed in case the Americans had com-

mand of the river, as they must necessarily have vessels
which could be easily converted into floating batteries,
to harass and impede, if not to arrest, their advance.
This error was brought home to them very painfully by
the sudden and destructive volley fired into their camp
on the night of the 23d by the Carolina. Whether
orders had been issued to the vessels, which undertook
to ascend the river to coöperate with the army, or they
were proceeding on their own account, we are unable to
say. But it is certainly true that these vessels did
not appear off the Balize, where the British had previously established themselves, until the 8th, and did
not come within sight of the obstacle to their progress
up the stream, until noon of the 9th. Overton's guard-
boat hastened to announce their arrival to the Fort.
The vessels consisted of two bomb-ships, the Herald
sloop-of-war, the Sophia, a brig, and a tender. Small
as this squadron was, had it arrived at Packenham's
camp and in time to coöperate in the attack on Jackson's
line, or even if it had arrived after that event, and
before the evacuation by the British, the consequences
might have been very serious to the American arms.
But they were not destined to surmount so easily the
obstacle in their path. Overton prepared to give them
a warm reception. Cunningham, of the gun-boat, with
his sailors, took command of the 32's; Walsh commanded the right bastion; Wolstoncraft the centre, and
Murray the left; the infantry under Brontin stood in
the rear of the curtain to support the batteries, and act
as occasion might require. At three P. M. the bomb-
vessels, approaching within a mile and a half of the
Fort, as if to sound the left battery, opened on them;
they then retired beyond the range of the Fort's guns,

and anchoring behind a point of land 3760 yards from the Fort, turned broadsides towards it, and running up their flags, commenced the action. Their first shell fell short, the next burst over theFort, and the others which followed fell into the soft earth, bursting, so deep in the ground as to create only a tremulous motion. The vessels remained some distance below the bombs. The bomb-ships threw their shells all night—one shell every two minutes—at the fort, but without effect. At night they reconnoitered in small boats, and came so near that their men could be heard talking. The wind was then blowing up the river. The garrison were too intent upon the vessels to notice these boats. During the 10th and 11th the bombardment was continued, the fort firing a few shots to keep up the spirits of the men, but without effect. On the 11th, the flag-staff was struck by several fragments of shell, and the flag was nailed to the halyards; another shell severed them, and down it came. An hour was consumed in restoring the flag, which was gallantly done by a sailor, over whose head several shells burst while sitting on the crosstree, making fast the flag. The contractor's house was mistaken for the magazine, and struck, killing one man, and wounding another. On the 12th, 13th, and 14th, the firing was kept up incessantly, many shells bursting over the fort, killing one man, and wounding several others, and damaging one of the 32's. The men in the fort were busily employed, and much exposed in repairing these damages and strengthening the fort. In the meantime, heavy rains fell daily, and the interior of the fort was a sheet of water, and the men were constantly wet and almost frozen. On the 13th, having received shells and ammunition from New Orleans, the fort opened its fire, and threw several shells over the bomb-ship. One of these took effect, and created much confusion on board. But on the 17th, they began to fire at the fort with more accuracy, and lodged several shells in the parapet, one of which burst in passing through the ditch into the angle of the centre of the bastion. This was their farewell shot. The next day at early dawn their ships were observed descending the river with all sails set. The garrison gave three cheers, and fired a volley as a salute to their foiled and mortified foe. This bombardment had been incessant from the 9th to the 18th of January, during which they fired 1,000 shells, being seventy tons of iron; and twenty thousand pounds of gunpowder, besides small shells. The casualties were only two killed and three wounded. At least a hundred shells fell within the fort, damaging and battering the shops and stores, and tearing up the earth within, and for many yards around.

Here was another able and decisive repulse of the British, which constituted an important link in the defence of the city, and reflected the highest credit upon the garrison and its gallant commander, who, as General Overton, long resided in the northwestern part of Louisiana, one of its most esteemed and honored citizens. There were other detached operations, which were attended by a like success.

Purser Shields, of the Navy, a well-known citizen of New Orleans, and Dr. Morrel, an esteemed physician, headed a brilliant little affair against the British lines of communication on the Lake. It will be remembered, that these gentlemen had been sent, after the battle of the gun-boats, to the succor of the American wounded, who were captured on the occasion. Arriving at the time the British were preparing to land their troops, the Vice-Admiral Cochrane thought proper to detain them until the army had executed the design in which it was then engaged. These gentlemen protested that they had come under a flag of truce, and that their detention was a breach of the rules of war. But it was in vain. Finally, when the British had been repulsed, they were released on the 12th January, and arrived in the American camp. During their detention by the British, these gentlemen were very badly treated; their flag was not respected; they were robbed of their clothes and other property; they were not permitted to see their wounded countrymen; and the sailors of the boat that brought them to the fleet, were compelled to work on the British boats. Such conduct was characteristic of Vice-Admiral Cochrane, who was a rough, brutal, and overbearing officer. It may be well conceived that high-spirited gentlemen like Mr. Shields and Dr. Morrel, did not bear very patiently the remembrance of the indignities to which they had been subjected in the British fleet. Hence, on their arrival in Jackson's camp, they busied themselves in getting up an expedition, by which they might obtain some little satisfaction for their injuries, and some compensation for their exclusion from the honors and glories of the defence of the city. Organizing a little band of volunteers, they proceeded with four boats, one having a carronade in its bows, out of the Bayou St. John into the Lake, and thence to the fort and encampment at Petites Coquilles. Here, being reinforced by two other boats, they glided stealthily along the shores of Lake Borgne, towards the Rigolets, in pursuit of any stray boats of the enemy. On the 20th, they perceived a large barge, full of soldiers, on its way from the Bayou Bienvenu, and immediately the boats commenced pur- suit. The carronade being brought to bear on the barge, she quickly surrendered, the men on board throwing their arms into the Lake. It proved to be a British barge, having on board thirty-seven British soldiers of the 14th dragoons, under Lieutenant Brydges' and Cornet Hammond, who were on their way to the British squadron. These prisoners were placed in charge of five armed men, and were conducted to the American camp at Chef Menteur. Shields and Morrel then made another sortie and captured several boats, a schooner and sixty-three prisoners, but owing to the wind and high currents, their boats became separated, and the schooner unmanageable, and their prisoners refractory. So they concluded to set fire to the schooner. The fire having attracted the notice of the British boats, several of them approached her. Shields and Morrel landed near the mouth of the Rigolets. The British attempted to cut them off by landing a party above them, but Morrel, with a party of twenty men, having approached, suddenly opened upon them from the high reeds, and after three volleys, caused them to leave in haste. Finally, the party being in great danger of capture from the British boats, which several times attacked them, but were beaten off, Dr. Morrel was sent over to Petites Coquilles for reinforcements. Shields, left alone with the prisoners and a small guard, seeing a gun-boat in the distance, bearing up towards him, concluded that he would retire, and so discharging his prisoners on parole, hurried to meet Morrel and Newman, who were preparing to join him with a reinforcement at Petites

Coquilles, where he arrived safely with twenty-two prisoners. The result of this brilliant little enterprise shows how much the British could have been annoyed if our gun-boats could have got under the fort of Petites Coquilles and escaped capture on the 14th December. There were other exploits performed by detached parties, which we are prevented from describing, by the apprehension of rendering these sketches too voluminous. Their glory and splendor, which, in any less brilliant campaign, would have secured high renown to those participating in them, are lost in the superior radiance of those greater events, that have rendered the Defence of New Orleans, in 1814, the most complete and brilliant campaign in modern history.

On the 17th January, a cartel for the exchange of prisoners having been agreed upon, the 18th was fixed for the pleasing ceremony of receiving some of the best citizens of New Orleans, whose long detention in the British fleet had produced much anxiety among their friends. The ceremony was a joyous and exciting one. A detachment of Plauché's battalion and the whole of Beale's rifles were formed in column, and, preceded by the splendid brass band of the volunteers, marched, under Captain Roche, to the line indicated near the British outposts; there they were formed as if for a review. Presently the American prisoners were escorted by detachment of the British 95th rifles, and the officers in command saluting Captain Roche, delivered to him a roll of the prisoners, which, being called out, all answered to their names. Roche then called out, "Forward, Americans!" and the whole band advanced down the line of the battalion under a salute. Open column was then formed, and the ex-prisoners being placed in

29

front, the procession marched towards the American lines, the band playing a lively air. As they approached the lines, there was a simultaneous shout of joy from the whole American army, and when they had got within the entrenchment, there were hundreds of personal friends who rushed forward to embrace and welcome them. Most of these ex-prisoners were leading gentlemen of the city, who had been captured on the night of the 23d. Jackson sent for them, and on their arrival at his headquarters, congratulated and complimented them in very warm terms. Though it had been a source of great mortification to these gallant men, to be absent from the army during its great trial, their detention in the fleet had been rendered quite tolerable, if not pleasant, by the kindly and courteous conduct of the British naval commander of the Royal Oak, on which ship most of the prisoners had been detained, and by other naval officers.

We pass over many minor incidents of the campaign, in order to approach the great event which relieved Louisiana of the presence of the foe that had so long desecrated her soil, and threatened her honor and safety.

After the battle of the eighth, Lambert was not long in arriving at the conclusion, that the expedition had signally failed, and all that was left to him was to collect the fragments of the army and retire as speedily as possible, from the scene of so many sad disasters and painful associations. With this view, he proceeded with great prudence and caution, in making the necessary arrangements for the withdrawal of the army. As scores of his men were daily deserting, he had reason to apprehend that his watchful foe would harass his retreat, and omit no opportunity to inflict further injury upon him. To retire as they had come, in boats, was impracticable. There were not boats enough, and it would not be safe to divide the army in the presence of an enemy emboldened by recent victories. To meet this exigency, he directed the engineers to extend the road, which ran for some distance along the bayou, through the swamp to the lake shore, keeping as near as possible to the bank of the bayou.

This was a very severe and difficult task, which occupied the engineers and strong working parties for nine days. It was finally completed, and an apparently tolerable good road was made along the bayou, crossing it by bridges of boats from the right to the left bank, until it reached an elbow of the bayou, when the road took a direct course through the prairie until it terminated on the lake shore, near the Fishermen's Village. This road was made of reeds, made up into bundles, and stamped down. But for the continued rains it would have been a very good way. At the confluence of the Bienvenu and Jumonville, and of the former with the Mazant, small works were thrown up to cover the retirement of the army. Having completed this road, the whole of the wounded, except those which could not be removed, were placed in boats; then all the civil officers, the contractors, surveyors, &c., together with all the field artillery, stores, &c., followed, and were dispatched to the fleet. The large ship-guns were. spiked, their carriages broken, and then left on the field.

And, now, all that were left were the infantry. Having relieved himself of all incumbrances, Lambert prepared, on the night of the 18th, to steal off with his army.

Accordingly, the whole army was silently and stealthily formed in column, the engineers, sappers and miners in front. The camp fires were lighted anew. The piquets were all stationed as usual. Each sentinel was prepared with a stuffed paddy to place in his stead. The piquets were directed to form, as the column reached the bayou, into a rear-guard, and follow the army. Thus, while darkness covered the field, the army took up its line of march, in silence and dread. Not a cough or sneeze could be heard in the whole column, and even their steps were so planted as to create no sound. Thus they proceeded for some distance along the bayou in a pretty good road ; but when they began to diverge from its banks into the swamp, the continual tramping made the road very bad, and the rear of the column had to march up to their knees in mud. With no other light but the faint twinkle of the stars, this fine army which, but a few weeks ago, had advanced along the same road so full of pride and hope, now stealthily slunk through the dark, damp swamp, full of alarm, shivering with cold, and depressed by defeats, hunger and exposure. They marched all night, and just as the break of day began to relieve the surrounding darkness by a faint glimmer of light, they reached the desolate shores of Lake Borgne, and drew up on its banks exposed to a keen western wind that came across the broad surface of the lake. Nor did their arrival here improve the spirits or prospects of the men ; they were now sixty miles from the fleet. Suppose, from high winds or other causes, the boats should not arrive, they might starve there for want of provisions, or from cold—for there was no fuel but the dry weed, that burnt up like tinder.

Here the army remained in this desolate situation

until the 27th, when the whole reëmbarked and finally reached the fleet, with a few casualties, and after much suffering and distress.

This retreat was the ablest feature of the campaign, and reflects high credit upon the commander of the British and the discipline of the army.

During the campaign, which was thus terminated on the part of the British, the *Jamaica Gazette* contained the following article, which was extensively copied throughout the States:

" The British are, no doubt, before this time in possession of New Orleans. .They have eight thousand regular troops and two thousand sailors and marines. The enemy's force are the 7th and 44th regiments, and 10 or 12,000 militia, who are compelled to serve. It is said that General Jackson sent a message to Sir Edward Packenham, saying that he felt for the awkward predicament into which the British army had been brought, and not being desirous to take advantage of it, he would allow Sir Edward ten days to reëmbark with the whole of his force. If this offer had been rejected, he could not be answerable for the consequences. Sir Edward answered in a laconic style, that in ten days he would give him an answer."

" There is many a truth, that is said in jest." If not in the exact terms of this British journal, a message of that import, conveying the idea here expressed, was delivered by Jackson, from his lines, on the 8th of January 1815. Precisely in ten days thereafter, the successor of Packenham gave a very different answer from that ascribed to Sir Edward, by withdrawing the army from its position, and acting on the sensible hint, which proved to be no idle bravado, of the American general.

Early on the morning of the 19th, rumors of the **retreat** of the British began to circulate through the

American camp. Officers and men collected in groups on the parapet to survey the enemy's camp, and much discussion arose as to whether they had really gone, or were only "playing possum"—to use a common American phrase—laying in wait to entice them from their entrenchment. Their camp presented pretty much the same appearance; their huts were standing, flags were flying, and sentinels were posted. General Jackson and his staff surveyed the camp through the powerful telescope stationed in the window of Macarté's. The general was not satisfied that they had gone. His aids were of the same opinion. At last the veteran Humbert, was called on for his opinion. He took a view through the telescope, and immediately exclaimed "they are gone!" When asked his reason for this belief, he called the attention of the general to a crow flying very near to one of their sentinels. This showed that they were images, stuffed paddies. The whole plot was now understood. Jackson ordered a reconnoitering party to proceed to the front. Whilst it was forming, a flag of truce was seen approaching the lines. It was borne by a medical officer of the British army, who announced that he had a letter from General Lambert to General Jackson. Eagerly the general broke the seal and perused the letter, which was a courteous one, announcing that the British army had departed, and their commander-in-chief solicited the kind attentions of General Jackson to the sick and wounded, whom, to the number of eighty, he was compelled to leave behind. Soon the intelligence flew through the camp, and loud hurrahs were heard in every direction. But Jackson's vigilance was not to be lulled by even this gratifying incident. He ordered Colonel Laronde, who understood the coun try, to proceed with Colonel Kemper and a detachment of Hind's dragoons, and harass the enemy's rear, and directed Major Villeré, with a small party, to scour the woods about his father's house. Owing to the precautions of the British to protect their rear with redoubts, these attempts were not productive of any advantage, except to warn the too impetuous of the Americans from undertaking what so many recommended—the pursuit of the enemy by the whole army. Never were the sagacity and wisdom of Jackson more conspicuously displayed than in checking this impulse of the army. The counsel of Themistocles, in the assembly of the Grecian chiefs, against destroying the bridge across the Hellespont, so as to cut off the retreat of the discomfited army of Xerxes, did not display a profounder wisdom than the refusal of Jackson to pursue, with his raw troops, a desperate and powerful army like Lambert's. It was a sharp reproval of an impetuous young officer, who, advocating the pursuit, declared that " if he had ten thousand Tennesseeans or Kentuckians, he could march into London," " And when you make the attempt," said Jackson, " I should like to be there to command you."

Dispatching Dr. Kerr, surgeon-general of the army, with the British surgeon, to the hospital at Jumonville's, Jackson rode forth, accompanied by his aids, to inspect the British camp. He found fourteen pieces of large cannon left behind, many implements of war, and a great quantity of private as well as public property of the British army. Visiting the British officers at their hospital, he assured them of his sympathy and of every attention, which their condition needed. One of these wounded officers was Lieutenant D'Arcy, of the 43d, whose legs were carried away by a cannon ball, some days after the 8th. The circumstances of these wounded men being made known in the city, a number of ladies rode down in their carriages with such articles as were deemed essential to the comfort of the unfortunates. One of these ladies was a belle of the city, famed for her charms of person and mind. Seeing her noble philanthropy and devotion to his countrymen, one of the British surgeons conceived a warm regard and admiration which subsequent acquaintance ripened into love. This surgeon settled in New Orleans after the war, espoused the Creole lady, whose acquaintance he had made under such interesting circumstances, and became an esteemed citizen, and the father of a large family. This was the late Dr. J. C. Kerr, recently deceased, whose gallant son, Victor Kerr, was murdered by the Spanish authorities at Havana, in the party of Colonel Crittenden, in 1851, uttering as his last words, "I die like a Louisianian and a freeman!"

Jackson now turned his attention to the distribution of his troops, so as to command all the approaches of the city and guard against the return of the enemy. He then prepared to re-enter the city, which in so brief a campaign, and by such brilliant courage and wise prudence, he had rescued from dishonor and disgrace, to receive the homage of a grateful and devoted people.

XIX.

)

THE FINALE.

On the 20th of January Jackson entered the city for the first time since the 23d of December, when he marched forth to meet the enemy. He was received with boundless demonstrations of joy. The people attended him in crowds to his quarters in the Faubourg Marigny, in the fine old Spanish edifice which now stands a conspicuous monument of the past. The first display of popular feeling was too wild to be controlled by any regular method or system. At Jackson's request the Abbé Dubourg, Apostolic Prefect of the State of Louisiana, appointed the 23d as a day of public thanksgiving to the Almighty, for his signal interposition in behalf of the safety and honor of the country. That day was ushered in by a discharge of artillery, which caused many a citizen and soldier to leap from his pleasant couch, under the delusion that it was all a dream, that his toil was over and the enemy had really departed. New Orleans, never before or since, exhibited so gay and happy a scene, as on that bright 23d of January, 1815. All the contentions, horrors, sufferings, and troubles of the war were forgotten, and a spirit of unrestrained happiness, of cordial harmony and goodwill, pervaded the whole population.

Fully to appreciate the animation and enthusiasm of

that memorable day, it is necessary to listen to the glow
ing details of the surviving veterans who participated
in those joyous scenes, and whose declining days are
constantly made happy by those proud reminiscences.

The old cathedral was burnished up for the occasion.
Evergreens decorated the entrance and the interior. The
Public Square, or Plaza, blazed with beauty, splendor
and elegance. In its centre stood a graceful triumphal
arch, supported by six Corinthian columns and festooned
with evergreens and flowers. Beneath the arch stood two
young children on pedestals, holding a laurel wreath,
whilst near them, as if their guardian angels, was a
bright damsel, representing Liberty, and a more sedate
one personifying Justice. From the arch to the entrance of the cathedral the loveliest girls of the city
had been ranged in two rows, to represent the various
States and Territories. They were dressed in pure
white, with blue veils and silver stars on their brows.
Each bore a small flag, inscribed with the name of the
State she represented, and a small basket trimmed with
blue ribands and full of flowers. Behind each a shield
and lance were stuck in the ground, with the name,
motto and seal of each of the States. The shields were
linked together with verdant festoons, which extended
from the arch to the door of the cathedral.

Precisely at the appointed time, Gen. Jackson appeared with his staff at the gate of the plaza fronting
the river. He was received with salvos of artillery.
Entering the square, he was conducted to the arch,
where the two little girls, reaching forward with blushing, smiling faces, placed the laurel wreath on his brow.
What a benign smile relieved the sternness of that heroic
countenance, when the innocent faces of the pretty little

ones arose to his view, as with so much pride and delight they performed the high task assigned to them. Who would not be stern and heroic in defence of those dear ones? Who would not incur every peril, as well against the jealousy and discontent of friends, as against the open hostilities of foes, in such a cause?

Such were, no doubt, the reflections that passed through a mind, which combined in an extraordinary degree the strong and tender traits of humanity. And now, with the laurel on his brow, amid the enthusiastic shouts of the people, he descends the stairs of the arch, and is met by a lovely young lady, radiant with all the charms of Creole beauty—with face, form, manners and expression, such as the most aspiring artist might have dreamed of as the model for his Venus. Fit representative of Louisiana, this beautiful damsel addresses the laureled chief in a speech glowing with gratitude and eloquence. All the rigor has faded from that stern countenance, and the victorious General humbles himself at the shrine of female beauty and innocence, and replies in words that thrill with emotion, that his merits have been exalted far, far above their real worth. But the modest confession is drowned by a shower of flowers, amid which, the Hero, supported by his staff, is led to the entrance of the Cathedral. Here he is met by the patriotic and revered Abbé Dubourg, clad in pontifical robes and supported by a college of priests. The reverend gentleman addresses him in a speech of more than ordinary eloquence, in which, whilst due praise is accorded to the Hero, the ascription of the higher glory is given to that Divine Source of all wisdom and goodness, by whose inspiration and influence those signal services were directed to the salvation of the

country and the confusion and defeat of her enemies.
Jackson replies briefly, tastefully and modestly. He is
then conducted into the Cathedral and escorted to a
conspicuous seat near the altar. *Te Deum* is then
chanted in the grand and impressive manner in which
that melodious outburst of gratitude is usually rendered
by the choirs of the Roman Catholic church. The
people join in the noble hymn. The gallant battalion
d'Orléans guards the entrance of the Cathedral and fills
the aisles. The war-worn countenances of the young
Creoles next to the person of the General, are objects of
warmest regard to the hundreds of mothers, wives,
sisters and lovers, who crowd the interior of the Cathedral on this joyful occasion.

The ceremony being concluded, Jackson retired to
his quarters. That night the whole city was illuminated.
At last, the people, wearied by the wild enthusiasm and
inexhaustible joyfulness of the great event, sunk into
slumbers that were no longer disturbed by dreams of
sack, ruin, bloodshed and devastation. And so concluded the triumphal festivity of New Orleans, which
had been so miraculously saved from dishonor and
destruction.

The next day Jackson resumed his severe cares and
toils. The enemy had not yet abandoned the shores of
Louisiana. Even whilst the city resounded with the
notes of rejoicing and triumph, the powerful remnant of
his army lay shivering on the banks of Lake Borgne.
Jackson's force was still weak. It is true, troops were
daily pouring into the city, and the long expected arms,
sent by the Federal authorities, had arrived. But the
British, too, had been reinforced. They might attempt
the attack in another quarter. They had their honor

to redeem, and would be desperate in the attempt. This was no time to relax his vigilance and discipline. Martial law, which had been so effectual in the preservation of the city, must be continued. As an evidence of the presence of the enemy in their neighborhood, the fact was made known that a detachment, under Hinds, Humbert and Latrobe, having gone to reconnoitre the British rear, was fired upon, and one man killed. It was not, in truth, until the 27th, that all the British army had reëmbarked; and then they did not leave the bays adjacent to New Orleans, but proceeded to Dauphin Island, near the mouth of Mobile Bay, where their ships came to anchor, and the troops being landed on the island, formed the first regular camp.

Now ensued the most vexatious and disagreeable task of the General, to reconcile the militia to longer detention from their homes and families. Flushed with victory and pride of their exploits, impatient to rejoin their friends and participate in the public rejoicings, many of Jackson's army, assigned to the most important trusts, manifested a restlessness and disregard of wholesome restraint, which it was necessary to check. Martial law had been declared on the 15th December. It had been the shield and buckler of the city—its proclamation the clarion which had hushed all discord, and called all classes to the common defence. Jackson could never have educed such order, energy, harmony —such complete and glorious results, from the chaos in which he found affairs when he arrived in the city, except by taking the control entirely in his own hands, and thereby quieting the conflicts and divisions between the various parties and authorities that had previously claimed to administer the government and police. This

declaration of martial. law, we have said, had received
the approbation of the leading official and prominent
characters of the State. Its necessity and utility need not
be based, as has erroneously been done, on a suspicion
of infidelity and treachery among the population and
officials. Such a suspicion was groundless; it was the
offspring of the gross misrepresentation of zealous
partisans, and of a too easy credulity. No such feelings had ever entered the hearts of any Louisianians,
nor of the foreign population then identified with the
State. But for other reasons and objects this declaration
of martial law was necessary, in order to produce
harmony and efficiency in a great emergency, for which
the ordinary processes and institutions of the constitu
tion and laws were inadequate. We need no better
illustration of its necessity than when, after the repulse
of the British, some of Jackson's men began to falter,
and shrink from duties, the importance of which was
so clearly perceived, and so deeply felt by him, who
bore the great responsibility of preserving the laurels
already gained. In extenuation of this impatience, it
should be remembered that sickness prevailed among
the militia, and their stations were exceedingly exposed
and uncomfortable. Murmurs loud and open were
uttered by them, which were caught up by their over
anxious friends in the city, and echoed through its
public resorts; and several of Jackson's most efficient
soldiers, Frenchmen who had not become naturalized,
were induced to claim the protection of their consul;
and were thus enabled to abandon their posts. They
were willing and eager to fight, but not to incur the
more trying duties of the camp. Disgusted and irritated
by these desertions, Jackson ordered all French citizens

who claimed this exemption, out of the city. This order excited some indignation.

Jackson, who, under the representations of Governor Claiborne and others, had been led to suspect the fidelity of the Legislature, had incurred the hostility of some of its members, who were eager to embrace any opportunity of impairing his hold on the popular esteem. His apparently harsh measure against the French citizens was made the pretext for publications which were calculated to produce disaffection and ill-feeling in the army. Jackson traced one of these publications to Mr. Louaillier, a member of the Legislature, and ordered him to be arrested, and tried under martial law, for this act of mutiny. Louaillier had been a very active and useful citizen during the defence of the city, and his arrest on that account excited considerable sympathy. Application was made for a habeas corpus to Judge Hall, of the United States Court, and the application being granted, Jackson deemed it a violation of his jurisdiction under martial law, and ordered the arrest of the Judge. He was accordingly arrested, and conducted beyond the limits of the city. We content ourselves with stating the main facts of these unhappy conflicts, without entering into the details, or the discussion of the questions of law which have grown out of them.

On the 4th February, Jackson dispatched a commission composed of his Aid, Edward Livingston, Captain Maunsel White, of the Louisiana Blues, and R. D. Shepherd, Esq., Aid of Commodore Patterson, to the British fleet. This mission had several objects. Livingston's duties referred to the negotiations of a cartel for a further exchange of prisoners, and the return of the slaves of the planters which had been taken away by the British army. Captain White being a relative of the planters who had lost the largest number of their slaves, was authorized to receive them in case they were delivered. These gentlemen arrived in the British fleet at an inoportune juncture. It was on the 7th February, just after General Lambert and Admiral Cochrane had commenced their preparations to take Fort Bowyer. Admiral Cochrane stated that their visit was an untimely one, but received them courteously on the flag ship, the Tonnant, where they remained for several days. Quite an agreeable intimacy sprung up between these gentlemen and the chiefs of the British army and navy, which was marked by many incidents of a highly gratifying character to the Americans. One of these was the presentation of a sword, which had been found on the battle-field, and was claimed by General Keane, as the gift of a very dear friend. It was generally believed that this was Packenham's sword. The British prisoners declared that it was the commander-in-chief's, and the officers on the occasion of the presentation manifested great surprise that it should be claimed by Keane. It is well known that Packenham was struck in the sword arm some minutes before he received his mortal wound, and that when he was advancing near the American lines he had no sword, but waved his cap in his left hand. Jackson, however, could not resist the claim so warmly urged by Keane, and Mr. Livingston was instructed to deliver the sword, which he did on board of the Tonnant, accompanying the act with some appropriate and eloquent allusions to the value which a gallant soldier must attach to the weapon he had worn so honorably in so many perils and con-

flicts. General Keane responded in handsome terms.
The hilarity which followed the scene, prompted some
.of the younger officers, who had not been in the action
of the 8th, to twit, in a familiar manner, the gallant
General for the very equivocal circumstance, of losing
his sword in battle. The General, who was as quick-
witted as brave, promptly replied, "My young friends,
if you had been where I was on the 8th of January
last, you would have lost your heads as well as your
swords."

In the unrestricted intercourse and conversation,
which arose between the Americans and the British
officers, the former ascertained that both the British
officers and soldiers were exceedingly disgusted with
the expedition which had terminated so ingloriously—
that the war was one that did not from the first engage
their feelings or satisfy their consciences, and that they
looked to the conclusion of peace between the two
countries, as an event that would give them unalloyed
delight and satisfaction. The younger officers consoled
themselves by dwelling on the sad disappointment of
the civilians who had come over to administer the civil
offices of the new colony of Louisiana, and particularly
the indescribable distress of the unfortunate gentleman
who had resigned the profitable appointment of Collector of Barbadoes, and with bag and baggage, including five marriageable daughters, had come over ·
to assume the Controllership of the finances of the
expected territorial acquisition. The young ladies,
being well educated and quite fashionable, were to take
the lead in the gay assemblies in New Orleans. Oh!
how keen must have been the chagrin of these gentle

30

maidens, to be compelled thus to return to the dull circles of Barbadoes!

It was whilst these Americans were detained on the Tonnant, that the British landed a large force on the tongue of land at the extremity of which stands Fort Bowyer, and surrounded it on the sea-side by their squadron, and by gradual approaches, by cutting off all reinforcements, and bringing a powerful force of riflemen to bear on the fort, from trenches, which were extended within fifty yards of the guns, and by establishing several redoubts, with heavy eighteen and twenty-four pounders, during all of which operations the fort kept up a brisk fire, succeeded in compelling Colonel Lawrence to capitulate on honorable terms. Lawrence had less than four hundred men, his provisions were greatly reduced, and the rude and ill-made fort was entirely indefensible against an attack by land. Lawrence had gained glory enough in his brilliant defence on the 15th September, 1814, to save his capitulation from the slightest suspicion or censure. A whole British brigade, composed of the 4th, 21st, and 44th regiments, and the 95th rifles, cutting off communications with Mobile, whence a reinforcement had been sent to his relief, under Major Blue, and the presence of the powerful squadron in their front, would have rendered further resistance rash and vain. The capture of Fort Bowyer was a preparatory measure to an expedition against Mobile, with the possession of which, the British hoped to obliterate the shame of their failure before New Orleans. Lawrence marched the garrison out of Fort Bowyer with all the honors of war. The capitulation was so arranged as to enable some of the naval commanders to get up a drama which might add to the importance of the achievement. A great dinner was given on the occasion, on board the Tonnant, at which Admiral Codrington took the head of the table, and the Americans were seated on his right. After a sumptuous repast, and as the dessert and wines were brought on the table, the curtains of the cabin were drawn aside, and a full view of Fort Bowyer presented to the company at the very moment when the American flag descended the staff, and that of Great Britain, ascending under a salute of artillery, waved in its place. "Well, Colonel Livingston, you perceive," remarked Admiral Codrington, "that our day has commenced," pointing to the British flag.

"Your good health," replied Mr. Livingston, touching glasses with the exultant Briton. "We do not begrudge you that small consolation."

Small it proved, indeed, as the opening fortunes of the British were suddenly closed by an event which occurred on the 13th, just two days after the surrender of Fort Bowyer. On that day Mr. R. D. Shepherd was standing on the deck of the Tonnant conversing with Admiral Malcolm, a gentleman of the most amiable and genial manners, when a gig approached with an officer, who coming aboard the Tonnant, presented to the Admiral a package. On opening and reading the contents, Admiral Malcolm took off his cap and gave a loud hurrah. Then turning to Mr. Shepherd, he seized his hand and grasping it warmly, exclaimed, "Good news! good news! We are friends. The Brazen has just arrived outside, with the news of peace. I am delighted!" adding, in an under tone, "I have hated this war from the beginning."

Thus, was the design against Mobile happily nipped in the bud.   Mr. Livingston and his companions returned to General Jackson, with the news of the peace, on the 19th February.   Jackson announced the news to his army, but warned them that the treaty had not been officially announced, and they must not be thrown off their guard by the mere report.   The ratification of the treaty, by our Government, was essential to its validity.

Another incident which marked the intercourse of the Americans and British, during the sojourn of the latter on Dauphin island, is worthy to be here inserted. It is related in an address, delivered by a surviving veteran of Plauché's battalion. who now commands the brigade of which that battalion was the origin and nucleus, Brigadier-General H. W. Palfrey.   Whilst the British were on Dauphin island, a young corporal who belonged to one of the most respectable Creole families, attached to the Carabiniers, was sent with a flag of truce to the British camp, to endeavor to persuade the slaves, who had been taken off by the British, to return to their owners.

The young corporal, then in his citizen's dress, carried strong letters of recommendation from General Jackson to the Commander-in-chief, General Lambert, and to the Admiral of the fleet, and from Edward Livingston, Esq., to Admiral Cochrane.   The answer of the British General was, that he could not compel any of the slaves to return; that they had followed the army against his will; but that any of them who would voluntarily return, might do so, and for that purpose he would facilitate an interview with them, both on the island and on board of the fleet lying in and off the Mobile Bay, which was done.   Many of those slaves had sailed a day or two before, for some of the West India Islands; and of those remaining, forty or fifty consented to return, and did return.

On the night of the 23d December, the late Landry Lacoste was taken by surprise, at his brother's planta tion, below town, by General Keane's Division, when the General gave him his word of honor that all pro- perty of Louisianians would be respected, and that all cattle used by the army would be paid for. After the retreat of the army, Mr. Lacoste having ascertained his loss of cattle, prepared a statement of the same, amount- ing to about $350, and placed it in the hands of the young corporal, with a request that he would demand payment of the same from General Keane. The corpo- ral accordingly called upon the General, at his quarters, and found him leaning on a large pine tree—he not having recovered from a wound received in the thigh, in the battle of the 8th January. On being presented with the account, the General colored and immediately said—

"Sir, this is a most extraordinary demand. When the promise was made to pay such claims, it was under the belief that the Creoles would have sided with us, or at least remained neutral; and they have, on the con- trary, shown themselves our bitterest enemies; for such of them as have been our prisoners, have deceived us in every information given by them."

To which the corporal answered:

"Thank you, General, for this declaration, that among the Creoles you have not been able to find a traitor, for I am one of them. The message I have brought is from a friend who merely requested me to remind a British officer of his word of honor.   I have fulfilled my promise to him, and have nothing more to say."

With this remark, the corporal retired, and was about one hundred yards from the pine tree when stopped by one of the General's aids, with a polite request to return to him; to which the corporal answered—

"Say to your General, if he has any message to send to me, that I will receive it under that flag," pointing to the vessel which had brought him to the island.

An hour after, a small bag of money, containing three hundred and fifty dollars, in English money, was placed in the hands of the corporal.   About twenty-five years afterwards, Mr. Landry Lacoste having died, the very same bag was brought by his executor to the corporal, then a merchant, to ascertain the value of that money in New Orleans.

While on the island, the Commander-in-chief gave a splendid dinner to the young corporal in the cabin of the old Dauphin island pilot Lamour.   He was seated between General Lambert and Admiral Cochrane, in full uniform, with their brilliant staff.   Among the guests was Colonel Burgoyne, of the corps of engineers, Major Smith, who fell in the field of Waterloo, Captain D'Este, son of the late Duke of Sussex, and a young American officer of the Navy, sent out by the Commodore of the New Orleans station to arrange an exchange of prisoners.   This was the dinner party at which the young corporal had found himself; nor had he ever drunk wines or liquors of any sort before.   Challenged by every one of the company to a glass of wine, he thought that good breeding required that he should drink bumpers, and it was not long before he felt as if the number of guests around the table was doubling, and the cabin dancing. His blood was aroused by some indiscreet remarks made by Captain D'Este, who, perceiving from his dress that he was not an officer of high grade, rather abruptly asked him his rank in the army.

"Corporal!" was the prompt response.

After a short pause, to see the effect upon the company, the corporal continued—

"I have told you, sir, my rank in the army, and I will now tell you the rank in society of an American volunteer corporal. Whenever our country is attacked, every citizen becomes a soldier. The moment it was known you intended invading Louisiana, the whole country prepared to meet you; we knew that we would do so with a bold heart, but we also knew that we were ignorant of the art of war; so that in organizing we elected for our leaders, not the exalted in social position, or worldly wealth, but such as were known to have military experience. And so it is that most of the volunteers who met you on the 23d of December and 8th of January, were commanded by mechanics and tradesmen, emigrant veterans of the French army, whilst the ranks numbered the *élite* of the city. Sir, what do you think of our citizen soldiers?"

General Lambert at once replied,

"I know all this; and had Captain D'Este inquired, I could have enlightened him on that subject?"

After this, the gallant young corporal was much *fêted* among the officers of the British army and navy.

At length, on the 13th of March, General Jackson received official confirmation of the ratification of the treaty, which he communicated to General Lambert, and announced to the army, in a general order, revoking the general order relative to martial law, ordering a final cessation of hostilities against Great Britain, and proclaiming a general pardon for all military offences, and the enlargement of all persons confined for the same. The following day Jackson discharged his militia, after a warm tribute to their gallantry and devotion. These patriotic men, after passing through the campaign with little loss, began to suffer greatly, in their camps, from dysentery. At least five hundred fell victims to it in the course of one month. The British suffered from the same cause, in their encampment on Dauphin Island. There were as many as two thousand on the sick list at one time.

After the revocation of martial law, occurred the affair which has been so much discussed in political circles, the imposition of a fine of one thousand dollars, by Judge Dominick Hall, upon General Jackson, for a contempt of Court in imprisoning the Judge. An exceedingly angry discussion grew out of the matter, which was handed down to the succeeding generation, and only terminated a short time before the death of the General. Suffice it to say, respecting a controversy, which is now ended, that the Judge regarded his arrest as an unjustifiable outrage upon the dignity of his court, and required Jackson to show cause why he should not be punished. Jackson responded, and besides many legal exceptions, contended that martial law had been rendered necessary by the emergencies of the State, that he had been advised to declare it by the leading dignitaries of the country, including Judge Hall; that it had proved to be a most beneficial measure; that under this law he had arrested and imprisoned Louallier for creating mutiny and disaffection in the camp; that Judge Hall had disregarded the martial law and undertaken to take cognizance of a military offence, and restore the arrested party to his liberty and to the power of producing further difficulty. For this he had directed his arrest. The reasons were deemed insufficient, and the General was condemned to a fine of one thousand dollars. The court, when this order was entered up, was crowded with the friends and admirers of Jackson. They were disposed to manifest their dissatisfaction in a turbulent manner. But they were soon silenced by the noble demeanor of Jackson. He immediately drew a check for $1000, handed it to the Marshal, and retiring from the court-room, was greeted by loud cheers from the crowd in the streets. Conducted to Maspero's coffee-house (at present the St. Louis Exchange), he addressed his friends, urging upon them to manifest their appreciation of the liberty for which they had so gallantly fought, by imitating that prompt submission which it was the duty of a good citizen to render to the authorities of his country. Immediately a subscription was started to refund the thousand dollars paid under the orders of Judge Hall. The amount was raised in a few minutes, a generous struggle and rivalry arising among the citizens to subscribe the requisite sum. It was deposited in the Bank upon which Jackson had drawn his check, but the stern soldier refused to receive the amount, and desired that it should be placed at the disposal of the ladies, to be expended in providing for the widows and orphans of those who had died in the defence of the city. Thirty-seven years after these occurrences, when Jackson had approached the limits of human life, and was tottering to the grave, the remembrance of this incident embittered his thoughts and clouded the declining sun of his life. He had outlived all the reproaches, censures, hostilities and jealousies which his eventful life had provoked. A grateful people had manifested their affection and gratitude by elevating him to the highest honors of the Republic; his political and civil battles had been crowned with as great and brilliant victories as that which closed his military career; and now this spot alone lingered on his escutcheon, and blurred the bright pages of his history! Softened by religion and age, the old hero responded to the solicitations of his friends, that it would add to the calm dignity and quiet of his passage from this to another and better world, if this single reproach upon his character could be obliterated. The Congress of the Nation honored itself and gratified the people by refunding this fine, and thus enabled the Hero of New Orleans to sink into the long-yawning grave, beneath the oaks of the Hermitage, with a placid dignity worthy of his great career.

But we anticipate. The chagrin of this judicial fine was more than compensated by the tokens of public gratitude, which were showered upon Jackson from every part of the country. Congress, taking the lead, passed resolutions full of eloquent gratitude to Jackson and his comrades in arms. The legislatures of the various States followed with equally earnest and eloquent expressions. There was but one Legislature which withheld from Jackson this tribute, and that was the Legislature of the State which he had rescued from invasion and dishonor. A sense of dignity more than a want of gratitude prompted this omission. The Legislature had been harshly dealt with, not by Jackson, but by those who, having the command of Jackson's ear, sought to enlist his power and influence against their political

foes. Hence the stories about the treachery and infidelity of the legislators, which, though recorded in all
the histories, have no other source but party malice or
idle gossip. The calumny has obtained a place in all
the volumes written in reference to this affair, that the
Legislature had really discussed and considered the expediency of surrendering the State to the British. There
is not a tittle of proof to sustain this charge. The Legislature, reflecting the state of parties among the people,
was divided into various personal and partisan factions.
There was a French, or Creole, and an American party;
there was a party for, and a party against, Governor
Claiborne. There were representatives of the old Federal and Republican parties. But there was no party
that was friendly to the British, or indisposed to a
vigorous resistance. Governor Claiborne imparted to
Jackson's mind some anxiety about the fidelity of the
Creoles. The want of confidence which they had manifested in the Governor was ascribed by him to disloyalty
to the Republic, of which they had become citizens.
Others of "the American party" confirmed this apprehension. But it was founded on error, misconception, or
blind jealousy. The whole population of New Orleans
was true and loyal. None were more ardent and bitter
in their opposition to the British than the descendants
of their hereditary foe—the gallant sons of La Belle
France.

It is not necessary to the greatness or fame of Jackson that the population of New Orleans should be
calumniated and falsely accused. It is time, indeed,
that those who have committed this error of logic, of
truth and justice, should acknowledge and retract a slan
der and suspicion so peculiarly unjust and inapplicable

to the city which gave the most brilliant proof of loyalty and devotion to the Union and Republic that can be found in history.

It has been said that there were spies who communicated to the British the state of affairs in the city. We have shown in one of our early chapters who they were. A few poor miserable fishermen, of no nationalty, who lived in the swamps and bayous, were moved by their necessities and the glitter of what, to them, seemed untold wealth, to act this base part.

The circumstance of the Legislature being excluded by an armed force from their halls has been grossly misrepresented. That occurrence sprung from a grave misconception. The Speaker of the House of Representatives, a French refugee, from St. Domingo, who had lost a large property by the English invasion of that island, including one of the militia colonels, spoke with great concern and alarm of the reported threat of Jackson, in case his lines were carried, to fall back upon the city, fire it, and fight the enemy amid the flames. The militia colonel reported the conversation to one of Jackson's aids, with the expression of his belief or suspicion, that the Legislature was about to discuss the policy of surrendering the city. The aid mixed the facts and his suspicions together, and communicated them to Jackson, whilst he was riding along the lines in the midst of the cares, perils and excitements of the camp. Jackson sent his aid to Governor Claiborne, and directed him to inquire and ascertain the truths of the statements, and if they were correct, to blow up the Legislature. The Governor, on receiving this message, adopted a middle course. He could find no facts to justify the charge, but deemed it prudent to occupy the

Hall of the Legislature with troops, and set a guard over the representatives. It was a harsh, unjust, un-called-for measure. After one day's suspension, the Legislature met, and its first action was to vindicate its honor, which it did, with dignity and manliness. For this reason the Legislature, not so much for the indignity offered to it, but because it looked to Jackson for defence and reparation against the calumnies of which it had been the object, omitted in its resolution of thanks, and in the letter of congratulation addressed to the several chiefs, the tribute to him who was the great hero and chief over all. The modest and noble Coffee, in responding to the letter of thanks addressed to him, by order of the Legislature, reproved, with exquisite delicacy, this unworthy omission: " While," he said, " we indulge the pleasing emotions that are thus pro-duced, we should be guilty of great injustice, as well to merit as to our own feelings, if we withheld from the Commander-in-chief, to whose wisdom and exertions we are so much indebted for our success, the expression of our highest admiration and applause. To his firm-ness, his skill, his gallantry—to that confidence and· unanimity among all ranks, produced by those quali-ties, we must chiefly ascribe the splendid victories, in which we esteem it a happiness and an honor to have been a part." Praise from such a source—the tribute of one hero to another—will amply compensate for the silence, or even the censure of the legislators of that epoch, or of those who sought to perpetuate their ani-mosities.

The gratitude which Jackson had so profoundly ex-cited in the bosom of the great popular masses, recon-ciled him to all the mortifications which the necessities

of his position had elicited.   With his soldiers, the gallant militia and regulars, who had shared his toils, this
feeling warmed into the wildest enthusiasm, like tinder
touched by the spark, at the indication of ingratitude,
by their political representatives.   A glorious demonstration of this feeling was afforded on the plains of
Macarté, on the old camp ground, where all the troops
then in the city assembled on the 16th March, little
over two months since the battle, to fight over that
glorious fight—realize the brilliancy of their achievement, and for the last time survey the arena of their
glory and gallantry.   General Edmund P. Gaines, the
hero of Fort Erie, appeared on the field, at the head of
the 3d, 7th, and 44th regulars and the uniformed volunteers of the city.   The army was reviewed by Jackson.
An address was then presented to him, signed by the
commanders of the volunteer companies, which glowed
with affection, devotion and gratitude.

And thus Jackson parted from his comrades in arms,
leaving in the hearts of them all, feelings, which still
animate the souls of the few remaining veterans of that
epoch, who linger among their descendants, as beacons
to guide and excite the patriotism of the present generation.

After transacting other duties of an unimportant character, Jackson handed over the command to General
Gaines, and left the city for his residence at Nashville.
The honors he there received—the further transactions
of his life—his political and civil career, surpassing in
grandeur his brief military service, do not fall within
the scope of these sketches.   We cheerfully resign these
themes to abler hands.   Our ambition will be satisfied
if we have succeeded in bringing more distinctly before

the minds of our readers, the events of the campaign, which has indissolubly blended, in undying glory, the names of JACKSON AND NEW ORLEANS.

SUPPLEMENTARY CHAPTER.

THE war with the Seminole Indians on the southern frontiers of Georgia again called him from his retirement, in the winter of 1818. Shortly after the breaking out of hostilities, he was ordered to assume the command of the forces operating in that quarter. On the ninth of March, 1818, he joined General Gaines at Fort Scott, with nine hundred Georgia militia. Early in April, he was reinforced by one thousand volunteers from West Tennessee, and fifteen hundred friendly Creek Warriors, under their chief, McIntosh.

General Jackson now found himself at the head of four thousand five hundred men, with whom he marched to the Indian town of Mickasauky, which he laid waste. The hostile savages fled into Florida, whither he followed them, and took refuge in the neighborhood of St. Marks, the Spanish authorities of which endeavored to protect and shelter them. Accordingly, the American commander took possession of the town, and sent the garrison to Pensacola. On the sixteenth of April, he destroyed the Suwanee villages, and then returned to St. Marks, where two of the principal instigators of the Indian outrages, whom he had captured, a Scotchman and an Englishman, whose names were

Arbuthnot and Ambrister, were tried by a court martial, sentenced to death, and executed. Not long after, intelligence was received that the governor of West Florida, at Pensacola, in violation of the treaty with Spain, was affording countenance and protection to the fugitive Seminoles. General Jackson proceeded thither without delay, seized Pensacola, on the twenty-fourth of May, and on the twenty-seventh Fort Barrancas surrendered to his authority. St. Augustine was also captured by a detachment under General Gaines. The seizure and occupation, by the American troops, of these places of refuge for the hostile Indians put an end to the outbreak, and in the month of June, General Jackson, whose health had become seriously impaired by the unfriendliness of the climate, returned home, and subsequently resigned his commission.

The Spanish posts in Florida seized by General Jackson were afterwards ordered to be restored, but his conduct was approved by President Monroe, and a resolution of censure, offered in the House of Representatives, was voted down by a large majority. Any difficulty with Spain that might have grown out of his proceedings was obviated, by the cession of Florida to the United States, in the winter of 1819. General Jackson was very appropriately selected by the American Executive, as the commissioner to receive the territory, and on the first of July, 1821, he issued a proclamation at Pensacola, officially announcing its annexation to the United States. His administration of the executive affairs of the new territory, owing to the bad state of his health, was quite brief; during it, however, he came in collision with the Spanish ex-governor, in an effort

31

which proved successful, to protect the rights of several orphan females. His firm and unyielding will, and his determined purpose, were never exhibited in a more characteristic, or more creditable manner. His health continuing to grow worse, he transferred the authority with which he had been clothed, to his secretaries, on the seventh of October, 1821, and immediately set out for Nashville.

The gallant soldier was not forgotten. In August, 1822, he was nominated for the presidency as the successor of Mr. Monroe, by the legislature of Tennessee. In 1823 he declined the appointment of minister to Mexico, tendered to him by the President, and, in the same year, he was elected to the Senate of the United States. On becoming a prominent candidate for the presidential office, he resigned his seat. At the election in 1824, he received a plurality of the electoral votes, but as there was no choice by the colleges, the question was referred to the House of Representatives, by whom his principal competitor, John Quincy Adams, was elected to the office. In 1828, he was again a candidate, and received one hundred and seventy-eight of the two hundred and sixty-one electoral votes. In 1832 he was elected for a second term, by a still larger majority.

It is not within the scope of this work, to notice in detail the political services of General Jackson. A brief recapitulation of some of the most important acts of his administration must suffice. On the twentieth of May, 1830, he vetoed the Maysville road bill, and on the tenth of July, 1832, the bill to recharter the United States Bank. On the sixteenth of January,

1833, his celebrated nullification message, recapitu-
lating the facts, and many of the arguments, contained
in his proclamation of December previous, was issued.
In October, 1833, the public deposits were removed
from the United States Bank. On the fifteenth of
April, 1834, he protested against the resolutions of censure adopted by the Senate, which were afterwards, in
January, 1837, expunged from their journal; and on the
fifteenth of January, 1835, his warlike, but patriotic message, in regard to the refusal of the French government
to pay the stipulated indemnity, made its appearance.

His long public career finally terminated on the third
of March, 1837, when he issued a farewell address to
the people of the United States, and retired forever
from the harassing cares and responsibilities of an official position, to the peaceful shades of his own quiet
Hermitage. The wife whom he had so ardently loved,
no longer lived to bless him with her affection, and
cheer him with her smiles; she had been taken from his
side, by death, in December, 1828, yet her memory was
ever a sweet solace throughout the closing hours of his
earthly pilgrimage.

General Jackson had gained a world-wide reputation
by the bravery and skill displayed in his Indian campaigns, and in the war with Great Britain. Lafayette
was a guest at the Hermitage, on his visit to this country in 1825, and, twenty years later, the portrait of the
general was painted, when almost in a dying condition,
to adorn the gallery of Louis Philippe, the King of the
French. He was known and honored by the great and
good in every land. Whatever may be said of the
domestic policy of his administration, in his intercourse

with foreign nations he inspired or enforced respect, and few, perhaps none, of our presidents, Washington alone excepted, ever commanded greater consideration abroad.

A peaceful close was vouchsafed to the stormy and eventful life, the prominent incidents of which have been briefly portrayed in this sketch. The Imperial prisoner of St. Helena died amid a raging storm, shouting, in imagination, to his marshalled legions, while the winds howled and shrieked above his head ; the words, *Tête d'armée !* were the last to leave his lips, as his eye glazed in death, and his frame was convulsed with the last agony.   At the close of a Sabbath afternoon, in the bright summer time, when Nature had spread her richest garniture over her wide domains, and grove and forest were vocal with sweetest melody ; in the presence of his family and friends, by his own fireside, on the eighth of June, 1845, Andrew Jackson calmly yielded up his spirit.   For weeks and months he had suffered under a painful disease, yet not a murmur escaped him.   His heart was stayed on a noble hope— a hope sure, steadfast, and unfading—the priceless hope of the Christian !

> " Serene, serene,
> He pressed the crumbling verge of this terrestrial scene,
> Breathed soft, in childlike trust,
> The parting groan ;
> *Gave back to dust its dust—*
> *To Heaven its own !"*

In person General Jackson was tall and thin.   His frame was well knit, but gaunt.   He had an iron visage and a commanding look. His eyes were a deep blue, bright and penetrating. He was frank and easy in his manners, courteous and affable in his address.

His character was decidedly pronounced. It was full of salient points, remarkable for their strength, and the fitness and harmony of their combination. He was kind and affectionate, benevolent and humane; pure and earnest of purpose; inflexibly honest; physically and morally brave; ardent and sincere in his patriotism; direct in his professions; and resolute and unflinching in determination. He possessed a firm will, was clear in judgment, and rapid in his decisions. His temperament was restless, though not mercurial. He had an abundance of what the French call *fortes emotions.* His passions were intense, and what he did, he did with all his might. Like Cicero, he was a *new man;* and, by his own unaided exertions, raised himself from comparative obscurity, to the highest distinction. He was a good hater, but he never forgot his friends; and there are many who still prize his friendship, bestowed while in life, as a favor from heaven.

All these traits and characteristics were strikingly exhibited, both in his civil, and military career. His style as a writer partook of his mental peculiarities; it was rugged and uneven as the mountain torrent; yet it had a nervous eloquence, that never failed to produce a deep impression, and indicated a powerful grasp of thought. As a soldier, he was fruitful in expedients; he had the genius, perseverance and skill, of Hannibal —the indomitable will and energy, without the selfishness, of Napoleon. He was persevering, cool, and intrepid—hardy in endurance, and gifted with rare courage. In a word, as the historian Alison remarks of the French soldier of fortune—"He was not a great man because he was a great general : he was a great general because he was a great man !"

www.ingramcontent.com/pod-product-compliance
Lightning Source LLC
Chambersburg PA
CBHW032021110726
47901CB00004B/1165